Sports and Riches

The Sequel to SportsFan Chronicles™

KURT WEICHERT

Sports and Riches: The Sequel to SportsFan Chronicles™
Copyright © 2013 Kurt Weichert
Published by SportsFan Chronicles, Inc.

For more information please visit www.sportsfanchonicles.com
Follow the author on Twitter: @kurtweichert

Book design by:
Arbor Books, Inc.
www.arborbooks.com

Printed in the United States of America.

Sports and Riches: The Sequel to SportsFan Chronicles™
Kurt Weichert

1. Title   2. Author   3. Fiction/Humor

Library of Congress Control Number: 2013905668
ISBN 13: 978-0-9892138-0-6

ACKNOWLEDGMENTS

During the preparation of this manuscript, I received encouragement from Darci Weichert and Brandon Weichert. I received help from Dianne Morris. I am grateful to them all.

A NOTE TO THE READER

Sports and Riches is the sequel to *SportsFan Chronicles*™, a series of fictional comedies. Kurt and Brian are best friends with a shared dream: NFL ownership. In the first book Kurt and Brian won the largest lottery in history—half of it, anyway. The windfall allowed them to quit their jobs. It also put them one step closer to realizing their once-impossible dream of becoming owners in the greatest league in the world. They were filthy rich, but realized they needed a lot more money to purchase a franchise. So they did the unthinkable and persuaded the other lottery ticket holder to combine his fortune with theirs. The catch? He happened to be their hated ex-boss, Frank.

For readers who didn't get a chance to read the last book, the main character is a fictional version of me. As for my real-life friends, I left them out so as not to embarrass them. Instead each character is a composite of people I've encountered through the years, and the situations are much the same—combined events.

The basis for *SportsFan Chronicles*™ and *Sports and Riches* is a body of scripts I wrote for television in the 1990s called *The Sportsfan*. Despite positive response to the project, I decided to take a hiatus and found myself taking a long break from writing.

It was inevitable that the characters would not be still until they could continue their journey, and that they would not be silent until their tale was told. And so it was, over a decade later, I was ready to return to writing. I have decided go back to my roots: sports and comedy.

Don't forget to follow me on Twitter, @kurtweichert, and visit my website: www.sportsfanchronicles.com.

CHAPTER 1

That's What the Sign Says

Kurt parked his car and started across the parking lot toward the building. He stopped in his tracks at the sound of a loud voice that could only be coming from a megaphone. "A megaphone? What the hell is that?"

"It needs to be raised another two feet and more to the left," yelled Frank, megaphone in hand, as a large crane lifted the new company logo onto the building. He was a pudgy man in his midforties and was sweating profusely even though the weather was mild. Despite his eight-figure portfolio, he always came to work in ill-fitting, run-of-the-mill polyester suits that had him mistaken for a vagrant on more than one occasion.

Kurt's daily must-have Starbuck's was still steaming as he took a small sip and looked around, wondering not what but why Frank was commanding a job better left to the experts. A few college interns who worked directly under Frank turned toward Kurt to say good morning then returned their gaze to Frank, who continued yelling at the sign company workers.

"I said the left, you idiot. You do know the difference between left and right, right?" All the interns started laughing at Frank's brash way of handling the sign installers. They saw what Frank failed to see. His left was their right and until he got that, he would have to continue his barrage of searing comments and epithets. They weren't going to tell him.

Kurt waved at the interns and shook his head as he walked past the angry crane operators. The sign was massive…something you would see in Las Vegas, not in Chicago. The new company logo was the reason for the new sign displaying a giant SFC with the words Sportsfan Chronicles underneath the logo letters. While Kurt, Brian, and Frank had agreed to name their young company the Sportsfan Chronicles, they more often referred to it as SFC.

Upon entering his new corporate headquarters, Kurt was greeted by Kalia who took his arm and virtually moved him along at a fast clip. "Kurt, Chuck needs you in his office right away. Pronto. His word."

Kurt looked at his watch and then smiled at Kalia. "It's too early in the morning to see Chuck. I have a new rule. No speaking to Chuck first thing in the morning, whether it's morning or afternoon. 'First thing' being the operative phrase." That merited a laugh from Kalia, who continued to gently but firmly guide him from the reception area and toward Chuck's office.

Kalia, a slim and petite woman, surprised Kurt with the strength of her grip on his arm. It was easy to believe that she had at one time been a dancer. She came to SFC from Pointy Foods where she had been given a temporary job in the aftermath of one of Chuck's more obnoxious stunts.

She excelled there. It was a natural progression of events that she would leave Pointy Foods and join the guys at SFC, where she grew into her position and was now as essential as any one of the partners. Perhaps more so since she managed the daily affairs of all departments and, more importantly, managed Frank.

"I think it is important. As a matter of fact, I know it's important." As they walked from the reception area toward the back of the building, Kurt couldn't ignore that this was arguably the coolest office in America. Staffed with lots of young people, where every day was casual Friday, job performance was anything but casual. They clearly liked their work in the Pit.

The Pit occupied the ground-floor space in the atrium-style center of the building. It was a large open area with an abundance of workstations, lots of open space, and more than a few employees wearing Rollerblades. Also in abundance were skateboards and bikes resting in every available nook, because half the employees didn't even own a car.

"Okay, Kalia, what's this morning's drama?" asked Kurt, knowing full well he could rely on Kalia's opinion.

"It's Vanessa Roberts. She's thinking about leaving SFC and moving back to Northern California." That definitely got Kurt's attention. "Brian is talking with her in the conference room right now." Kurt stopped to look at Kalia. "So, tell me, why I'm going to Chuck's office instead of the conference room?"

"I don't know why, but Chuck was very clear in telling me to take you to his office instead of the conference room."

As Kurt entered the office, Chuck greeted them by his door. "Thanks, Kalia." Kalia left the room, and Chuck closed the door behind her, giving Kurt more than enough time to see what Chuck was wearing.

"What the hell is going on, Chuck, and why the hell are you dressed like that again?" Chuck's new thing was to dress like Facebook's Mark Zuckerberg, who was famous for wearing hoodies and jeans around the office. Not that anyone would ever confuse the two. True, if Zuckerberg dyed his curly hair blond, it might be a match. And though Chuck was ten years older than the Facebook founder, he'd maintained a trim, youthful appearance. No, the two would never be confused, at least not in Chicago, because Chuck's face was the one stenciled onto the Chuckles' Deli sign, and you couldn't walk a half-dozen blocks in the city without seeing one of those. "I thought Alice made you quit dressing like that."

"Aw, come on, Kurt, she's my girlfriend, but make no mistake, I wear the pants in our relationship," responded Chuck, by now looking quite smug and disproportionately pleased with himself.

"Oh, that's right. Your pain-in-the-ass girlfriend is out of town with Darci right now, so I guess you do wear the pants or, in this case, jeans, in your relationship…when she's not around, that is." Kurt turned his head sideways to better take in Chuck's version of Zuckerberg's style and said, "I don't think Zuckerberg wears skinny jeans and you look ridiculous, Chuck." Chuck was used to catching flack from Kurt and Brian and his expression didn't change upon hearing Kurt's unsolicited fashion review.

Kurt was quietly waxing contemplative over the state-of-the-art surveillance system when Chuck walked over to a newly added video monitor and turned up the volume. "Listen up. I recently added the conference room to my surveillance system. Already paying off. Vanessa Roberts is thinking about quitting SFC, and Brian is in there with her trying to find out why. We absolutely cannot lose her. She is way too smart and talented to leave. Plus she's working on some lucrative projects right now."

Kurt nodded in agreement. "She probably wants more money. That employment contract Frank tricked her into signing is embarrassing. Crank it up a bit more, I wanna hear what Brian is saying to her."

When they turned up the volume, they heard Brian clearly. "Vanessa, you said that your boyfriend is pressuring you to move back to California and I understand that, believe me, I do. I also agree you are being paid way below what you should be paid. So I'm prepared to offer you ten thousand dollars more per year."

"Thanks, Brian, the money would help, but I don't think my boyfriend will be happy. It's not just about money. He's really jealous right now."

"He needs to get over being jealous of your success, Vanessa. He needs to sit back and smell the roses."

"It's not that simple. He's not jealous of my success. He's jealous of my boss. He thinks I have a thing for my boss."

"Now that I don't understand. Yeah, you work in Frank's department, but you have a thing for Frank?" said Brian in his most incredulous tone. "Frank? Your boyfriend thinks you're attracted to a loud, drunk, smelly man who likes to wear the same wrinkled polyester suit every day?"

"No, silly, I got mad at my boyfriend because he's always taking me for granted, and I wanted to make him jealous, soooo I might have told him that you have a thing for me."

"Wow, I wasn't expecting that." Brian paused and then leaned over and smiled at Vanessa. "You know, if you really want to make him jealous, you could sleep with me...no strings attached, of course. You know, a little..."

Not waiting to hear the rest, Kurt jumped out of his seat, propelled by every legal ramification imaginable. "Chuck, erase this video now." He charged into the conference room. "Hello, Vanessa, so sorry I'm late for this meeting. Unavoidably detained, but better late than never...right, Brian?"

Brian wasn't much older than Chuck, and there was already some white creeping into his brown hair, but he kept up on his gym membership. It wasn't difficult to imagine Vanessa honestly considering the clumsy proposition. "Bad timing, bro. I've got it handled," interjected Brian, almost whining. "Let me finish my meeting with her alone."

"Sorry, Brian, no can do. Vanessa is one of our brightest young stars. I need to give her our new offer." Turning his head toward her, "Vanessa, I reviewed your current pay. Not up to par. I've decided to sign a twenty-thousand-dollar annual salary increase for you. That, of course, includes the added benefits for that level. Standard operating procedure. That level requires only a signed confidentiality agreement. Everything else in your file is fine. This is effective immediately." Kurt was careful to sandwich the "confidentiality" reference between the more positive incentives.

"Wow. Thanks, Kurt. I'll take it," said Vanessa without a moment of hesitation.

"Great. Good to hear. You'll continue to work for Frank. Keep up the good work."

Brian, not to be outdone or outwitted, said that he had been about to offer her a position in his office. "I am sure you were," said Kurt, carefully enunciating every word. "Yeah, I'm sure you were, but she needs to continue to work on the website for our new sports magazine."

Not needing to hear anything else, Vanessa left the conference room happy, with Kurt relieved and Brian clearly annoyed. At the sound of the door closing, Kurt turned to Brian. "Are you crazy

or what? Are you trying to get us sued for sexual harassment...
again? If that's the case, you're doing a damn good job of it. I guess
practice makes perfect, eh, Brian? Did you not learn a thing the
last time?"

"What are you talking about, Kurt? I haven't a clue," answered
Brian at his disingenuous best.

"Do you think I came in by accident, apologizing for being
late for a meeting I knew nothing about? We were watching you
the whole time on Chuck's video surveillance camera!"

"Crap, you heard all that? Well, you can't blame me. She is
pretty good looking."

"I thought you would have learned after the last settlement
you had to pay. That was fifty thousand dollars to get that one to
walk away without suing our ass, and your answer is that she's
'pretty good looking'? Where's your head, bro?"

"Come on, what are you complaining about? I forked out the
money. Fifty thousand dollars, and I didn't even get to first base
with her."

"That you 'didn't even get to first base' is your considered
response? It's the comments, Brian. You gotta tone it down, bro.
Larger companies than ours have been brought down by less, and
all you're thinking about is first base? I don't get it!"

"Come on, Kurt, I never had to worry about that at Pointy
Foods."

"That's because you never had any money when you worked
at Pointy Foods. You also had no employees working for you. You
didn't worry then, but you'd better worry about it now. We just
worked at that company. Now we are the company. Just neutralize
your comments to our female employees, so we don't get sued
again. No sexual innuendo, no double entendres, no anything.
Business, just business! Oh, one more thing, it's less about the
money and more about reputation bringing us down."

"We didn't get sued. That other chick threatened to sue us, but
I settled with her before she sued us."

"Oh, well, that's very reassuring Brian. And, by the way, drop the word *chick* when you are referring to employees. Even that has liabilities."

Brian looked up, not quite sure whether or not Kurt was serious. It appeared he was. Knowing when to push back in protest and when to be satisfied with saying okay, Brian opted for the last word, knowing full well that all-business Kurt would have something else to add. "Is there any other lecture you want to give me before our big company meeting?"

"Now that you mention it, yeah, there is. Why are you still dressing like Steve Jobs all the time? Come on, Brian, you wear black shirts with the black jeans at work every day. I don't know who's worse, you and your Steve Jobs attire or Chuck and his Mark Zuckerberg hoodies."

"Hey, there's a big difference between Chuck and me. Admit it, Chuck looks like the Unabomber, while I on the other hand look good."

"If you say so. At least you're not wearing skinny jeans. Come on, we've got to go downstairs to get ready for our staff meeting in the Pit."

"Sorry, Kurt, you can't say that. It sounded like you said a meeting about our staff's tits."

"Good one, Brian, good one. I said, staff. Meeting. In. The. Pit," replied Kurt, again carefully enunciating every word. "Just don't get us sued!"

"All this money and power have made you too politically correct. Boring."

CHAPTER 2

What's in a Name?

Kurt and Brian went down to the stage at the back of the large room known as the Pit. The space was massive enough that the large open area buffered the stage from all the workstations. Kalia's voice could be heard over the intercom, asking all the employees and interns to make their way forward. Having arrived first, Brian and Kurt were sitting by themselves.

"Where's pie-eyed Frank the Tank? Isn't he usually the first one up here?" asked Brian as he looked around for Frank.

"He was outside with all the interns, verbally abusing the sign company workers. My guess is he's trying to teach our interns a business lesson."

"Right, Kurt, a lesson on how to be a big asshole… You know, complain enough, and you'll always get a discount. At least that's his theory."

"I can't believe he's our partner…equal partner. It was only a couple of years ago that I wanted to kill him, and now he's a big part of our team."

"I hate to admit it, oh God, how I hate to admit it, but he has done a good job. I mean, he has really kept our operational costs down, and he's on top of our sales team."

"Yeah, remember what it was like when we worked for him? When we were that sales team? I do. All those stupid Napoleon Bonaparte speeches and all his lies and broken promises. And of course who could ever forget his motivational insults?"

"Yeah, but didn't we always get him back ten times over? Made it worthwhile!" said Brian. "The funny thing is, this younger group of employees really think Frank is funny. And he's a lot easier on them than he ever was on us."

"Brian, of course he's a lot easier on them. They're making us an insane amount of money!"

"He also loves being an owner. He actually believes they're his disciples. Kurt, no doubt in my mind, if we had been making that amount of money, he would have used a whip, thinking we'd make that much more. Admit it, it was somewhat personal and here it's not. These kids are his disciples. Forget his being our boss, we were equals, and he didn't like that one bit. Twisted."

"Way too analytical for me. Napoleon's happy, we're all happy, and I don't want to be around when the little Corsican resurfaces." Kurt banished the thought and took the microphone as Kalia walked them on stage.

"Come on, everybody, take a break from whatever you're working on. Gather round." Kalia leaned over and quietly said, "Almost everybody is here except Chuck. He just disappeared, and I can't find him. Neither can I find six members of his team."

Ignoring Chuck's absence, Brian asked Kalia if Frank was done screwing around with the sign outside. "Yes, I told him we're getting ready to start. He keeps telling the installers that the sign is crooked, but honestly, it's not. In fact, it's perfect."

Kurt turned to see Frank and an imminent disaster. "Uh oh, here he comes, and it looks like that's the owner of the sign company with him. Oh no, now it looks like our marketing director is standing between the two them. I better get over there."

Kurt walked over to Frank to ask what was going on, praying that nothing was going on and knowing that something most definitely was going on or, at the very least, brewing. Brewing he could handle; going on was another matter whenever Frank was involved. "Okay, Frank, what's up?"

Frank, his long-sleeve polyester shirt untucked and askew,

was still drenched with sweat that was dripping onto the megaphone still clutched in his right hand. "What's going on here is we are not paying these morons until the sign is perfect."

The angry sign company owner, equally determined to be paid and to be heard, outshouted the megaphone. "The sign is perfect! I just got here and double-checked my guys' work. I can show you the measurements. It is perfect!"

"It's not perfect, and I want a ten-percent discount, so I can find another company to adjust it…now!"

"You got it. The sign is perfect, but I'll give you ten percent off if you pay me now, so I don't have to see your ugly mug again."

"Deal!" The sign was perfect, and everybody knew it.

Frank scribbled a note on a piece of paper and handed it to the marketing director, authorizing accounting to cut a check. The sign guy left before Frank could change his mind, vowing to never again do business with anyone named Frank.

Kurt walked close to Frank and whispered, "Really Frank? What did you save us, two thousand dollars? Now who's going to change the lightbulbs when they go out on that giant sign of yours? Was it really worth it?"

Expecting no answer, nor wanting one, Kurt turned to walk away. Frank placed the megaphone to the back of Kurt's head, making him jump when he yelled, "Yes, it was worth it!"

Frank's interns appeared to be amused by his management style. "Take notes, kids… always try to squeeze more from our vendors!"

Kurt, whose ears were still ringing, and Frank finally joined Brian on stage, where he was pacing stage left to stage right and back again, waving at the staff as if he was the celebrity he thought he was.

Kurt now addressed the issue at hand. "Brian, where is Chuck?"

"Who knows? Let's get this meeting started on time for once. We don't need him," answered Frank as he walked up to the microphone and addressed the staff while conveniently forgetting that he himself had already delayed the meeting.

"Listen up, everybody. We have some announcements to make. We hit our eighteenth-month goals, we now have our new large corporate headquarters, we've grown our staff to over one hundred, and I can say that we have become one hell of a successful conglomerate. What have we become? We have become the Sportsfan Chronicles, also known as SFC. You saw that big, beautiful sign on our new building. Look at it with pride because this is our brand. We are venture capitalists. We are Internet entrepreneurs. We have great food products licensed and distributed to restaurants and supermarkets all over the country, and this is only the beginning. We still have a long way to go to reach our ultimate goal, and what is our ultimate goal?"

The entire room yelled in unison: "To buy a professional football team!"

"Exactly! Eighteen months ago, Kurt, Brian, and I invested most of our lottery winnings into this company. That's over two hundred million dollars toward the goal of purchasing a football team. Kurt, come on up to the microphone and say a few words."

"Thanks, Coach Frank."

Frank made Kurt jump once again when he yelled in the megaphone right behind Kurt's head, "You're welcome."

"Give me that thing, Frank. Go stand over there by Steve Jobs." Kurt grabbed the megaphone and asked Kalia to take it away and hide it.

Everyone was laughing as Brian said, "You bet I am the next Steve Jobs," except Kurt, who was not laughing as he caught Brian smiling and waving at Vanessa Roberts.

"Sure you are, Brian. Anyway, you guys have been great, and we're going to continue investing into as many more companies that can help us reach our goal as we can. The main reason for this meeting was to thank you for your hard work."

Kurt let the applause die down. "Now it's time for a little history lesson. The Chicago Bears is owned by the McCaskey family. The McCaskeys are descendents of the great George 'Papa Bear' Halas. I'm going to bottom line this… We have accepted the fact that the Chicago Bears will probably never be for sale in our lifetime. So, with that in mind, we are now going to pursue every opportunity to purchase another team or try to get the league to let us bring another team to Southern California."

Cheers erupted at hearing the words *Southern California.* "We now have decided what we will name the team… It came down to the Terminators or the Warriors, and our final decision is the Warriors."

With perfect timing, the Olympic theme blared through the speakers. Totally taken by surprise, Kurt asked, "What the hell is that?"

Chuck's voice then drowned out the music. "Not so fast, everybody!" Six of the interns were already strolling down the aisles dressed like Olympians. "Hey, Zeus and Poseidon, start passing around the fliers."

And with that, Chuck stepped forward and joined Kurt, Brian, and Frank on stage.

Chuck, smiling at the crowd and acknowledging the enthusiastic response, stepped forward once again, raised his hand, and waited a moment before speaking.

"I hear ya, I hear ya, but slow down a minute here. Before that decision is made final, I think we should give a little more time to consider going with 'Olympians.' The marketing value? Infinite possibilities. Just for one minute, think of the marketing we can get out of this with the right name. That name, the right name, is Olympians."

Kurt slowly shook his head as he listened to Chuck in his best revival style stir up the already deafening crowd. This was a typical Chuck moment, which he had seen many times before. Chuck could rally up crowds like no one else.

"Nice try, Chuck. We're going with 'Warriors'! If we weren't going with 'Warriors,' we would go with 'Terminators,' but that's not the case so 'Warriors' it is. Final! Brian, do you have anything to say to our staff?"

"Yeah, actually I do. I say we end this meeting. You guys have to finish your work. Why? Because our staff is invited to my house tomorrow for a company barbeque!"

At the mention of a barbeque, the crowd erupted in cheers. They had heard of past barbeques even before joining the company. *Legend* was the only word that came to mind. To actually be a part of that was beyond their hopes and work was far from their collective mind.

Also legend was Frank's genetic imprint for work. "You heard the man, now hear me: get back to work...now!"

Not doubting for one minute that the spell was broken and that they would disperse as commanded and return to work, Frank turned to Kurt, Brian, and Chuck. "Let's get back to the conference room. We have another matter we need to discuss with Chuck."

All eyes briefly glanced at Chuck before the foursome headed back to the conference room. A sense of foreboding hit Chuck; he couldn't recall doing anything specific to rile Frank. On the other hand, almost anything Chuck did riled him.

CHAPTER 3

Another Meeting

As soon as the conference room door was closed, Frank started. "Listen up, Chuck, I am, eh…Kurt, Brian, and I are the owners, and as owners, We get to pick the name of the team. Get it?"

"Well, not exactly. I'm also an owner."

"A minority owner, Chuck, min-or-it-y owner of two percent."

"I'm working on that." In order to buy more shares of the Sportsfan Chronicles' stock, Chuck had been systematically selling off his large chain of delis. Kurt knew he had sold only twenty of his fifty-eight delis to date. Chuck's ex-wife, Camilla, and their son, Prince Charles, were working toward litigation as she sought to share in the SFC profits. So far, Chuck had avoided court only by participating in mediation. While mediation was better than court, it still had the effect of keeping Chuck at a standstill.

Kurt wanted to keep the meeting civil, but he couldn't help asking, "Chuck, what's up with your delis? I thought you'd sold half of them already. Surely that would be enough to buy more stock now."

"You know it's never that simple, Kurt. Yeah, I sold a third of them, but I can't access the damn money."

"What are you saying? You sold but haven't been paid? Uncollected funds or something like that?"

"You know Camilla. You know how she is. She got the courts to tie up most of the funds because she wants more child support for Prince Charles. The funds are as frozen as she is! That's it! I'm not selling the rest of the delis until Uncle Walter gets her to stop coming after me for more funds. You know she's scared of him. If anyone can handle her, it's my uncle Walter. Mediation was his idea because it stalls her, too."

In a conflict between Chuck's ex-wife and Chuck's uncle, Walter was just barely the lesser of two evils. Chuck had been warned repeatedly to keep his uncle Walter's involvement to a minimum. He'd served several years in prison for masterminding a Ponzi scheme, and his reputation was such that just a passing association with even a minority owner of SFC could potentially tarnish their image.

A momentarily forgotten Frank wanted to get back on course. Despite hopes that Frank would soften his edges, it was evident that he had not changed at all. For him, one plus one equals two, and two times nothing is nothing. "Until you come up with a lot more money, you will have only two percent, and that, sonny boy, isn't squat. And if we raise all the additional capital without you, then that is all you'll ever have: two percent."

Brian was rapidly losing interest in Chuck's business affairs but was interested in Chuck's preoccupation with technology. "Hey, Chuckie, what's with the hidden cameras? Don't deny it, I know they're all over the place, but I wanna know where they are from now on. I don't want you spying on me."

"Cameras? Oh, yeah… Be glad they're there and don't complain. I might well have saved you from another sexual-harassment claim!"

Well-chosen words at ill-chosen times were oxygen to Frank. "Sexual harassment claim? What sexual harassment claim?"

Brian broke in before Chuck could say one more word on the matter. "Forget it, Frank. He's exaggerating as usual. Nothing like that happened."

Kurt saw that a discussion over a name was degenerating into something else. "Don't worry. I already talked to him about his comments…"

"Yeah, yeah, yeah. I don't need another lecture!"

"Listen up, just keep it in your pants when it pertains to our staff, lover boy," Frank said in typical Frank fashion, which Kurt generally ignored.

Kurt tried again to reroute the conversation. "As I was saying, I already discussed this. Listen, Brian, you do realize you might have a couple of hundred people at your house tomorrow? You've invited the staff. You know they're going to invite their friends. Did you give this any thought at all before spouting off...again?"

"Yeah, so? I invited the staff. So what?"

"This is the core of your problem, Brian, you never think ahead...no matter what it is. Women. Barbeque. Whatever. What about our neighbors? You should expect over two hundred people to show up with that blanket invitation of yours. Think about it, the neighbors are going to be royally pissed, especially with the parking!"

After Kurt and Brian won the lottery, they both built luxury houses in a nice suburb—one across the street from the other. It had been great so far, but Brian's lack of forethought on this one hinted at unrest in the neighborhood.

"Hey, Kurt, you do me an injustice. I thought this one out very carefully. I invited the neighbors this time. I told them it was a block party. I even chartered some buses; most of those are going to meet at the staff apartments, pick 'em up there, and cart 'em here. Problem solved."

Frank had convinced the guys to have a company-owned apartment complex in Lincoln Park for the purpose of renting the units to the majority of the staff members. Of course Frank occupied the penthouse to better keep an eye on the employees and spy on his loser nephew, Meathead.

Frank hired Meathead because he promised his sister that he would teach her kid to be a responsible worker. Meathead's only job so far had been to be Frank's driver and to keep Frank's apartment clean and his refrigerator stocked with food and beverage. Emphasis on beverage.

It was just as well that Meathead wasn't present at company

headquarters. He and Frank were polar opposites, constantly arguing about business and government policies. Frank started calling him *Meathead* after learning of his attendance at the Occupy Wall Street protests.

Kurt broke in, "Great idea. What about you, Frank, are you riding in the bus or is your nephew going to drive you?"

"Meathead's driving me."

"And you, Chuck? Are you still planning on picking Alice up at the airport tomorrow? If you are, could you pick up Darci and drop her off at our house tomorrow morning?"

"Got it covered. Consider it done, buddy."

Darci had been promoted to head clothing buyer for a major upscale department store. Shortly after her promotion, she hired Alice and since then, Darci and Alice had been spending a lot of time in New York City, because her corporate headquarters were in Manhattan's famed Garment District. Despite the demands of his own job, Kurt noticed that he would start to get agitated when Darci was away for more than a week. They'd both acknowledged that they enjoyed their respective freedoms and that there were fears (from both of them) that getting married might somehow "ruin" what was already a closer relationship than that of most of the married couples they knew. But he still missed her on the mornings they didn't share a breakfast.

It was small compensation to Kurt that, whenever Darci was away, Chuck's obnoxious girlfriend, Alice, would also be gone. While Kurt would grudgingly admit that she had some surface attractiveness, he couldn't imagine how any man could tolerate her toxic, man-hating personality for any length of time. Yet Chuck seemed to miss his girlfriend as much as he missed Darci.

Kurt adjourned the meeting before any further conflict could arise, already dreading what tomorrow's barbecue would bring.

CHAPTER 4

Victor Pays a Visit

The next morning, Kurt awoke to the smell of eggs and coffee. He had fallen asleep the night before while still on the couch in the man cave. Brian and Kurt had been shooting pool and watching the ball game on the high-def TV. Brian had let himself out, leaving Kurt to wake up next to the bar piled with empty pizza boxes and two pyramids of empty beer bottles. "Shit, I must have overslept."

He rolled off the couch, raced upstairs toward the kitchen, and started yelling at the doorway, "I'm sorry I wasn't awake when you got home, but thanks for making me one of your awesome breakfasts. I guess you still love me, huh."

As Kurt crossed the kitchen threshold, the newspaper was lowered, revealing the face of the person sitting at the kitchen table. It wasn't Darci.

It was Chuck, sitting there reading Kurt's newspaper and eating the breakfast that Darci made, and that was only one step above seeing Alice, had she been there.

"Of course I still love you sweetie."

"Very funny, Chuck… Where's Darci? And quit eating all my breakfast."

"Darci and Alice are upstairs in the hen room."

"Come on, Chuck, speak English. What's a hen room?"

"Well, my man, you have the man cave and she has the hen room…or hen house."

"Hen room? What room would that be, and more to the point, what are you and Alice still doing here? You said you'd bring Darci home, but you never mentioned anything about hanging around my house."

"We thought we'd stick around here and just walk across the street together later when Brian's barbeque starts. Makes more sense than driving back home and then driving back here when we're already here."

"Geez, Chuck, it starts at two. It doesn't start for another four hours!"

"Actually it starts in less than two hours. It's almost noon now."

"Shit, I really did oversleep."

"Whaaaat? Were you, Brian, and Victor hanging out in the man cave late last night?"

"No, just Brian. We were watching the ball game, shooting pool and playing some video games. No Victor. Just us."

"Really? Well, why was Victor's Ferrari parked at Brian's house at seven in the morning if he wasn't here last night?"

"What are you talking about? And why the hell were you driving past our house at seven in the morning? Picking up Alice's stalking habits, are you? Or are you back to your old peeping Tom habits? Even my neighbors are not safe from your stalking, Chuck."

"No, compadre, nowhere near... I left early for the airport and figured I'd swing by and see if you wanted to come with me, but obviously you were in no condition to hear the doorbell."

"You know, I thought I heard the annoying doorbell in my sleep," Kurt said, as he poured coffee into his mug. Trying to brighten his own mood, he conceded, "At least you left me some coffee... What the hell, two drops of creamer? Dude... Who puts an empty container back in the refrigerator? Who does that, Chuck?"

Chuck was still laughing, pleased with his comedic genius. "This is too funny. If you could've seen the look on your face when you poured the cream. I couldn't wait to see that. It's all I could think about when I put it back in your refrigerator."

"Really, Chuck? You planned that? You really are a pain in the ass. Now, where's the creamer?"

Chuck continued laughing. "Don't worry. I saved you some breakfast."

"That was awfully nice of you. Now get out of my chair."

"Sit in that one."

"Whatever."

Kurt ate breakfast while Chuck checked his voice mail. Kurt then got up and walked to his front porch with Chuck. As he'd said, Victor's Ferrari was parked in Brian's driveway. A half-dozen other cars were parked on the street, no doubt help hired for the party.

"What the hell is Victor's car doing at Brian's house?"

"Surprised? I already told you it was there. Maybe Victor went over there at six in the morning to help set up."

"No to that, Chuck. It doesn't add up. It doesn't bode well, either. I feel a disaster in the wind."

Kurt yelled across the street to Brian, who was directing the many people he had hired to set up and to especially work the barbeque. Chuck's grilling at one of the bigger outdoor parties they had many years ago was still a bad memory. "Hey, Brian, get your ass over here."

Brian waved at them as he jogged over. "Hey, bro, it looks like things are shaping up for the barbeque. Dude, I took the rest of the pizza last night. I figured you weren't going to eat when you crashed on the couch."

"Did you even sleep last night?"

"Yeah, I got a few hours in at my house."

"Question, Brian: why did Victor come over to your house last night when we were over here?"

"Victor? He didn't come to my house. He's screwing one of our neighbors."

"Oh yeah? And who would that be?"

"I probably shouldn't say. That way you can deny knowing. You know, plausible deniability."

"Who, Brian? Please tell me it's not your new next-door neighbor. Not her, please no."

A first-round draft pick for the Chicago Bears recently rented the luxury house next to Brian's for one of his girlfriends, Mary Lee Sanders from Gainesville, Florida. Gorgeous was one word that would describe her. Very strong and intimidating would describe her defensive linebacker boyfriend, Bulldog Williams. Most significant was that Bulldog was much more than a nickname.

Brian said nothing, but his eyes tilted in the direction of Mary Lee's house.

"Noooo, not Bulldog's girlfriend."

"I'm not saying who it is, but let me ask you this: do you really think that Victor would risk sleeping with one of Bulldog's girlfriends?"

"Was that a question?" Before Brian could answer, a huge SUV pulled into Mary Lee's driveway. Kurt, Brian, and Chuck watched her greet Bulldog by the front door as they saw Victor sneaking out a side window and then running over to Brian's back door. The six-foot-eight linebacker wrapped one arm around the slim blonde, lifting her off the ground for a kiss. He was apparently so glad to see her that he didn't seem to notice that she was dressed only in a pink bathrobe. Still, she was wearing more than Victor. Dressed only in his silk boxers, the remainder of his clothes in his hands, Victor kept in shape and his wiry muscles were apparent, even from a distance. But there was no doubt in Kurt's mind who would win if Bulldog should ever confront Victor about his visits. Just as there was no doubt that, should he find out, there would be a very short and very brutal confrontation.

"I guess that answers that question, Brian." Chuck was laughing hysterically at seeing Victor climbing out the window. "I can't believe my lying eyes. Victor's sleeping with Bulldog Williams' girlfriend!"

Brian joined in the laughter when he saw the look of horror

on Kurt's face. "Are you guys crazy? You think this is funny? That means collateral damage. I want no part of any collateral damage."

"Aw, come on, Kurt, take it easy. Even Chuck here thinks it's funny."

"Even Chuck? Chuck thinks everything is funny. This is trouble on our doorstep, and on top of that, Bulldog has to stay out of trouble. Has to! The Bears don't need him in this kind of trouble. And if the Bears don't need that, we don't need it."

Brian didn't seem to understand the ramifications, the potential fallout of this situation. With a shrug, he offered, "First of all, I have nothing to do with her. Second, Victor doesn't feel guilty because Bulldog's longtime girlfriend, Stacy Biggs from Tampa, doesn't know about Mary Lee from Gainesville and that's why he rented this luxury house in the suburbs. He and Stacy live in a condo in the city. Get it? One here and one there."

Kurt just shook his head. "What that has to do with anything is beyond me. I'm heading inside."

Brian waved them off. "I'll see you guys in a little bit." He jogged back across the street to his house while Kurt and Chuck went back inside.

"Can you believe that? Victor is sleeping with Bulldog's girlfriend. He must have a death wish, I swear."

"This is too much, Chuck. I'm going upstairs to see Darci. I still haven't seen her yet."

Kurt and Chuck walked upstairs toward the amazingly elegant master suite designed by Darci. She had designed most of the house, with the exception of Kurt's man cave.

His man cave consisted of an incredible game room, a top-of-the-line wet bar, and a large, state-of-the-art home movie theater. No feature was overlooked and everything was of the highest quality, causing Chuck to remark, "Wow, Darci knows how to decorate."

"Yeah, true, but come on, Chuck, I had a part in designing this house."

"Yeah, you think I don't know that. You're good at man cave stuff, but she's good at all of this," said Chuck, pointing to beautiful mural on the wall, "That's a nice mural of angels. I'm sure you had nothing to do with that."

"I like the mural in my man cave better—the one of Michael Jordan. It was designed specifically for that space. My kind of art!"

"That's a funny one, you passing the ball to Michael Jordan. I like the one of you holding the Super Bowl trophy standing between Walter Payton and Mike Ditka."

"So, Chuck, when you think about it, to a lot of sports fans, I might have a better eye for art."

"Well, let's not go that far. Painting the number seventy-two on your refrigerator was a little too much."

"No way is it too much. Hey, that was Refrigerator Perry's jersey number. I thought it was awesome. Still do."

As Kurt and Chuck approached the kitchen and dining areas, they could hear Darci talking to Alice. "Yeah, I had to draw the line on that issue. Our kitchen's granite countertops and stainless appliances just don't look the same with a giant seventy-two adorning a sleek, stainless refrigerator. Kurt did that, you know. He painted on it."

"Hey, at least you let me move that refrigerator into the man cave." Kurt made it to Darci's side, where they greeted each other with a kiss and a long hug. They'd been dating for over ten years, and Kurt still couldn't see that she'd aged a day. Looking back at old photographs, she seemed locked in the body of the woman he'd met, even keeping all the energy of her midtwenties. If anything, the joy and confidence that accompanied her success and elegance made her look more beautiful. Even when dressed in utilitarian denim.

Kurt shut his eyes during the hug and wished he'd kept them closed afterwards. Alice and Chuck were sticking their faces close to his during his embrace with Darci. "Wow, get out of my face. Are you guys sick in the head? Who does that?"

For some reason Chuck and Alice thought this was funny.

Chuck's occasional boisterousness and his almost constant and always inappropriate laughing was bad enough, but Alice doing so in tandem lent a nightmarish quality to it. Dark brown hair that fell across her broad shoulders, blue eyes that sparkled like the expensive contact lenses they were, full lips, flawless skin tanned to a healthy shade... All the parts were there for a beautiful woman. But to Kurt those parts just crashed together into a sort of harpy clown.

Even her voice grated on him like nails on a chalkboard. "Don't worry. If you're feeling good, you'll get over it. Did you miss me, too?'

"Alice, how can I miss you if you won't go away." An inward shudder nearly took over as he contemplated the impossible— that he would ever miss Alice. Never would happen. Rejoice in her absence he had been known to do, but miss her? Never, perish the thought.

"Wow, you look like shit. Is that in style now?" said like the Alice he knew her to be and never, never to be missed.

"Alice is right, honey, you do look a little messy today."

"Not surprised. A long, late night and a too-early morning. Brian and I hung out in the man cave, and I fell asleep on the couch pretty late last night."

"How late did this long night of yours last?"

"Don't know exactly. I recall ordering pizza at one in the morning, and it didn't arrive until almost two."

"Typical. You're not surprised, are you, Darci? This is SOP."

Ignoring Alice as only Kurt could, he went on, "That's why I slept in so late this morning, and Alice, I don't need your attitude. No one does."

"Why, Kurt, I don't have an attitude; I have a personality you can't handle."

"It's called being a bitch. Yeah, you got me, can't deny it."

"You say I'm a bitch like that's a bad thing."

"Tell me, Alice, do they ever, ever shut up on your planet?"

Darci finally let go of Kurt, with only a little annoyance

showing on her otherwise lovely face. "Oh my God, you two will never change." Even through the scowl, Kurt saw a bit of a smile. The bickering was a routine, a familiar pattern, and her exasperation was just part of the act.

"Well, Darci, it's like this. I wasn't expecting to wake up and see Chuck and Alice in our house. Then there's the kissing thing. How normal is it to stare and breathe on people like that? Really. Your friend here has no boundaries, no filters, and until that changes, I won't be changing."

"Would this be a good time to tell you that they may be staying over?"

"Whhaaaat? Here? Why?"

"You know, Kurt, if the barbeque turns into a late-night party, Darci already said Chuck and I could spend the night."

"Oh yeah, great! Let us all pray for an early end to the night's festivities. By the way, if you have guest manners, this might be a good time to dust them off. If you have a problem with that, go stay with Brian."

Either unaware of or studiously ignoring the usual Kurt and Alice byplay, Chuck segued into matters at hand, "Hey, Kurtis, can you help me out with Alice's suitcases?"

"I'd like to help you out; which way did you come in?'

"Very funny, Kurt. Chuck, put our bags in the bedroom right next to the master suite," Alice said.

"No, no, no. Chuck put them in the bedroom down the hallway."

Alice shook her head. "Forget that, Kurt, I can't sleep in there because that bedroom is facing east. Chuck, put them in the bedroom right next to the master suite as I requested."

"Alice, who gives a shit if it's facing east? Certainly not I. Take that bedroom or go somewhere else. This is not a hotel, and I'm not a concierge."

"The sun rises in the east, and you have inadequate window treatments in that room; they're useless in keeping the sun out."

"My girl here likes her beauty sleep."

"From the looks of it, she needs a lot more…and she won't get it here. It's down the hall or sleep elsewhere. She clearly has no friends, because she doesn't know how to behave, do you, Alice?"

"Oh, you are such a comedian. Isn't he, Chuckie? A real comedian."

"Yeah, well, as the Bard said, many a truth is said in jest. There is absolutely no way you two are going to be in the room next to us, more specifically, next to me. No way!"

The silence prompted Kurt to continue his justifiable rant. "Final word, you can stay in the room at the end of the hallway. If not, there is no room at the inn. Being the nice guy that I am…" Kurt grabbed a blanket off the bed and walked down the hallway, stopping along the way to grab a hammer, nails, and stepladder.

He then nailed the blanket to the window frame, covered the offending window then walked back to Alice and Chuck. "There you go. Problem solved."

Uninterested in a reply or a response, Kurt continued in mock formality, dripping with sarcasm, "And now, if you'll be kind enough to excuse me, I am going to enjoy a warm, uninter- rupted shower. Should you need anything, I trust you'll let me know later. Adieu."

"You should. You need to!" Alice's infamous last words were expected, and Kurt would have secretly been disappointed if this had been an exception.

CHAPTER 5

A Quick Shower

Kurt walked into the bathroom and shut the door, enjoying the prospect of warm water and soap washing away the ills of the morning. He knuckled his head ten minutes later at being caught by surprise when the flow of water stopped just prior to rinsing off shampoo and soap. Of course Chuck would think it was funny to turn off the water. What else would Chuck think? That was how his mind worked. Kurt wondered if he was more annoyed at not being able to rinse off or at being caught by surprise once again.

"Chuuuuuck, turn the water back on! Now!"

The water flow resumed and lasted for about thirty seconds before ceasing as abruptly as it began.

"Chuck, turn it back on. This is not funny!"

The water was turned back on and Kurt rushed through the remainder of his shower, not trusting the water would continue to flow. And therein lay Chuck's fine and unique talent of keeping Kurt off-balance. Would he stop at two interruptions or was a third about to occur?

He was finally able to finish getting ready for the barbeque but not without wondering, "What next?" as he headed downstairs to join Darci, Alice, and Chuck in the living room.

"Chuck, do you really think it's funny to shut off the water while I shower? I mean, what exactly is humorous about that?"

"Yes, I think it's funny. And everything. Everything was funny about that, especially my mind's-eye vision of you in there all soaped up and nowhere to go."

"Kurt, I really did try to stop him."

"Don't worry about it, Darci. I know how hard it is to stop Chuck. He's unstoppable…a virtue of his empty mind!"

Alice was standing by the front window, uncharacteristically silent on the subject and seriously focused instead on the house across the street. "I can't believe Victor is sleeping with the big football player's girlfriend."

"Chuck, you told them? Really? You broke the man code? Disgusting. Busy gossiping like an old hen. No wonder there wasn't a third water shutoff."

Chuck, feeling no shame and apparently feeling no "brotherhood of man," laughed. "Of course I told them. You would've done the same."

"No, I would not have 'done the same.' Really, this could be serious. You see how big that guy is? What if he has a temper to match? Ever think of that, Chuckie? Here's a little food for thought: how about he comes after the messenger, too?"

Kurt, Darci, and Chuck joined Alice in staring out of the window. Kurt remarked on the substantial number of people arriving when Darci asked, "What's with the buses? Yeah, there's a lot of people, but not enough to have buses, surely?"

Kurt recalled that Darci had still been out of town when the barbeque was announced and had no idea this was more than a small barbeque. "Brian decided to invite all of our employees. I reminded him that the neighbors would be none too happy with that many cars blocking everything, so he chartered buses to eliminate that problem. He arranged to have the buses pick them up at the apartment complex. Brilliant on his part."

"That's still a lot of people. Neighbors are going to be annoyed… noise, activity, more noise, and if memory serves, much more than one would expect at a barbeque."

"Possibly not. He invited all the neighbors, too. Apparently all but a few accepted, so there's not much they can say. All that's left is to invite the cops… The best way to avoid having them on your ass."

"Still. A lot of people. More than I expected there to be."

"I know, and it's not supposed to start for another hour."

"Well," added Chuck with his usual keen sense of the obvious, "it looks like it started early."

"Come on, Darci, let's head on over there. Chuck can wait on Alice." Kurt added under his breath, "With luck, she'll find something else to do."

It was Darci, not Chuck or Alice, who snapped in response. "Heard that, Kurt. Alice is my friend, so drop it…at least for the afternoon. And don't forget they are most likely staying over."

As Kurt locked the front door, muttering, "Thanks for reminding me," Frank's nephew Meathead pulled into Kurt's driveway. Frank had hired his nephew as a driver and, family or no family, Frank was sitting in the back seat. Kurt and Brian suspected there was more to it than that and believed Frank sat in the back seat more out of habit than anything else. There had been many a drunken night and as many taxis taking him home.

Frank's nephew was a good twenty years younger than him, with longer hair, but there was no mistaking the two were related. He was just as out of shape and just as shabbily dressed as Frank, although Meathead preferred oversize T-shirts and jeans to Frank's cheap polyester suits. The shirt he was wearing today bore the name of a band Kurt had never heard of. Stepping out of the car, he didn't look directly at Kurt when he spoke to him. "My uncle said that we should park in your driveway."

"That's fine, Mea…eh…" Kurt was at a loss for what to call the guy. *Meathead* didn't seem quite right. "Yeah, that's fine. Just move it to the other side, in case I need to get my car out."

Meathead jumped back into the car and started backing up as Frank, thinking they were parked, was getting out of the back seat, thereby falling back in the car through the still-open car door.

It was shades of the past, seeing Frank half in and half out the backseat of a moving car. Kurt remembered many a similar situation.

"What the hell are you doing, Meathead? Are you trying to kill me?"

"No, Kurt told me to move the car over to the other side, so I'm moving it to the other side."

"Perhaps next time you could make sure my door is not open before moving the car. That is part of the job, Meathead!"

"Okay, sorry."

Darci leaned over and quietly asked Kurt what Meathead's real name was. Kurt whispered back, "I'm not sure. Muncie? I think it's Muncie? Maybe not. I really don't know. Never thought to ask. I just know him as Meathead."

"Muncie? What made you think it's Muncie, of all things?"

"Frank was always joking that his nephew was conceived in Muncie. He called him Muncie Duncie until his sister threatened him, so he changed it to Meathead."

"That's awful. *Meathead* doesn't sound so bad now."

So Meathead (aka Muncie, maybe) and Frank joined Kurt, Darci, Alice, and Chuck, then walked over to Brian's house together.

Never fully able to abandon his former supervisory role, Frank looked around, assessing the state of affairs and started barking orders, even though he was not hosting this event. "Listen up, Kurt, we need to make sure that Brian doesn't lose control over this barbeque. I don't want our young employees and interns losing control and leaving a stain on my company."

"I know that, Frank. *Our* company doesn't need bad press with some stupid video being posted on YouTube. Making us look bad to the National Football League is the very last thing we need. And Frank? Let me remind you, it is *our* company."

"Exactly" was Frank's stock answer for everything. In this case, Frank conceded that others shared in the company's ownership and liability. The likelihood and ramifications of Frank being Frank were uncomfortably numerous.

"And Frank, the drinking? Go easy with your drinking."

"I can handle my liquor."

"Sure you can, Frank. History says otherwise. I mean it, Frank. Easy on the booze."

"Okay, Kurt, as long as you're on this protocol kick, you need to remind your friend Brian that we are the owners of this large company and most of his guests are our employees. I have no intention of bailing him out of jail, either."

As they crossed the street, heading to the barbeque, Kurt pulled Meathead aside, slipped him fifty dollars and whispered, "Make sure you don't leave your uncle alone today. It's more important than you know."

"You shouldn't have to pay someone to babysit my uncle."

"Fine then… Gimme back the fifty bucks, and you can do it for free."

"Aw, come on, Kurt. I'm just saying, it's pretty sad that I have to babysit my uncle all the time, but never mind, I can use the extra cash. It's funny, he thinks he's keeping an eye on me, but I'm the one keeping an eye on him."

"Well, don't tell your mother that, and just keep Frank under control. That's all you have to do. Just keep him under control or out of the way and out of sight."

"I'll try my best, but it's not always easy, Kurt."

"And that's why I'm paying you the big bucks. Look, if things get out of hand, you can always come and get me. Puleeeeze, just keep an eye on him."

As they made their way to the packed barbeque, Kurt, Chuck, and Frank were repeatedly stopped and greeted by various employees, causing Darci to remark, "Your employees sure do love you guys. They look like puppy dogs getting doggie treats."

"Hmmm, good description. You know more than anyone that we don't have the usual work environment. Most of our employees are still in their twenties and eager to work their creative minds off. "

"I get that, but it's like they know this is different."

"We're not going to stifle them with protocols dreamed up by some dried-up human resources officer. These kids are super smart. Frank's not the problem he was to us. We didn't worship him; these kids hang on his every word...and Chuck's. Listen to them. They keep asking him why he isn't wearing one of his ridiculous hoodies."

Alice heard it, too. "Don't get any ideas, Chuck. You're not going back to wearing them. You promised to quit dressing like that at work."

"I know, but come on, Alice, that's my look at the office. It's me. This is a new era, and the staff is into all that. My hoodies inspire confidence."

"That's Zuckerberg's look, not yours. You need to be original."

"What you have in mind is anything but original. Anyway, I am original, Alice, I wear different pants... You know, the pants you like on me."

"The skinny jeans? Well, that's something, anyway, but I want you to dress in nicer clothes when you go to work. Those hoodies make you look like a gangster."

Kurt remarked to Darci on Chuck's conversation with Alice. "Chuck can be such a dork. A gangster in skinny jeans...only in Chuck's world."

"That's just Chuck; he's trying to fit in."

"Fit in, Darci? Fit in? Fit in to what? The jeans?"

"Fit in with the really young crowd."

"He's such a geek. Hey, Chuckie, pull up your pants. We're tired of seeing your coin slot."

"Very funny, Kurt, I'll take that as a compliment. I'll have you know it's chic to be geek."

Alice shook her head. "Okay, sheik, those pants are extra tight on you. As much as I hate to agree, he's right; pull 'em up."

"I'll try."

"Hey, where's Brian?" asked Kurt, realizing he hadn't seen him. He had someone watching Frank, but Brian needed watching, too.

Frank shrugged. "I don't know. I'm heading over there to get a drink, but did I not tell you we had to keep an eye on him?" He ambled off toward the booze before Kurt could respond.

Kurt was thinking that this was going to get complicated as he pointed to Frank and told Meathead to stick with him as he walked to the other side of the yard where a bartender was making drinks.

Before Kurt could start looking for Brian, Darci pointed into a crowd. "Hey look, there's Bernie."

They made their way through the crowd to Bernie, who was stuffing something in his mouth. In lieu of a greeting, Kurt asked, "Bernie, what the hell are you eating?"

Bernie was in better shape, physically, than Frank, which was about the best one could say about him. He was wearing one of his usual casual-day Bears jerseys, in a size large enough to hide his beer-gut. It was one of the older jerseys, with several small holes in the neckline and shoulders. He almost finished chewing before answering, "And hello to you, too, Kurt. It's a veggie burger."

"A what? Brian never said he wasn't going to have any Angus burgers today."

"He does have 'em, but I wanted one of these instead...low fat."

"Since when did you ever care about eating healthy?"

Chuck was grinning as he added, "Yeah, Bernie, just two weeks ago, we watched you eat fifty wings and drink ten thick lagers at your sports bar. Right, Kurt?"

"Yeah, well, that was then. I want to get back in shape again."

"What do you mean back in shape? Again? You've never been in shape before," said Chuck, remembering the one and only time he had seen Bernie attempt exercise. Not that strapping himself into a machine that did all the work could be considered exercise. That had been a halfhearted attempt to get into shape before the infamous Pointy Foods basketball game.

"Yeah, I was. Back in college, I played sports." Bernie, too, apparently forgot his efforts to make the team.

"I went to college with you and the only sports you ever played were beer pong, quarters, and coed slow pitch softball."

Alice asked, "They had beer pong back then?" in a clear dig at both Kurt and Bernie's ages.

Both of them ignored her. "Listen, I just need to get in shape."

"Why? What's with the sudden lifestyle change?"

"I just need to get in shape. Okay?"

"You were winded a few days ago at Wrigley Field. When you were walking up the steps, I heard you huffing and puffing. I thought you were going to pass out on the dude selling lemon ice. In fact you almost did knock him over."

Chuck was laughing hysterically. "I wish I could have seen that."

"Well, you couldn't because you are banned from Wrigley Field, Chuck. You still are, aren't you? Your new nickname should be Steve Bartman the Second. But that's not fair to Steve because he actually was a Cubs fan."

Kurt was none too subtly reminding Chuck that his ban from Wrigley Field was for interfering with a Cubs outfielder. It was the event that had led to the arrest Frank had mentioned earlier, which was probably why it was fresh in his mind. Still, old habits die hard, and Chuck would never learn.

As if to confirm his own unchanging obnoxiousness, Chuck cried out, "Gooooo White Sox!"

"Isn't it funny that you always become a White Sox fan when they're in first place and the Cubs aren't doing that well?"

"I run with the winners, baby. No shame in that. Anyway, why would I run with a loser?"

"You are a fair weather fan."

"Yeah, and I can't remember the last time the Cubs have had fair weather. I gave up on them."

"And you'll be back on their band wagon once they start winning again."

Ignoring the bickering, Bernie was insisting Chuck had it all wrong, "It has nothing to do with getting winded at the Cubs game. Holy shit, look, Bulldog Williams is here. I'm going over to talk to him." Bernie bolted over to join the ever-increasing number of people surrounding Bulldog, but Chuck wasn't going to drop the subject.

"Kurt, the reason Bernie is trying to lose weight is because he feels inadequate. Remember earlier in the week when the bachelors were chosen for the Chicago charity bachelor auction?"

"Oh, that thing that you guys signed up for? I had forgotten."

"Yeah, well, Bernie signed up for it, too, but they didn't pick him. Why didn't you sign up for it, Kurt?"

"Gee, Chuck, I wonder why. You know as well as I do that I didn't sign up for it because I'm not a bachelor."

Chuck started laughing again.

Darci was clearly not amused. "That's not funny, Chuck. Kurt and I will get married when the time is right."

"Yeah, like the Super Bowl in Dallas last year."

"Knock it off, Chuck. That was a bad couple of weeks. Darci doesn't need this…neither do I. I think Alice is rubbing off on you!"

Chuck had no intention of letting this go. "You were fine until the Bears got beat by the Packers, and then you cancelled the trip to the Super Bowl."

"That's only part of it, but yes, I didn't want to get married at that Super Bowl unless the Bears were playing in it."

"Kurt and I are planning on getting married this year."

"And I'll believe that when I see it." With little hope of deflecting Chuck, Kurt returned to the subject at hand, "So why is Bernie on the health kick?"

"Bernie's on a health kick because they chose Brian and me to be part of this year's group of bachelors. They passed on Bernie."

"Aw, poor Bernie," said ever-sympathetic Darci, thinking discussing this in her presence might have been awkward for Bernie.

"He was with me when I received the invitation with the list of bachelors on it. I had a hard time stopping laughing when I saw that Brian and I made it and Bernie didn't."

"When are you not laughing?"

"I did try to stop when I saw what looked like a tear in his eye. I really did. Kurt, you know how it is when you try to stop laughing, and it just makes you laugh harder."

"Speak for yourself, Chuck. I've seen you like that, and to tell you the truth, it's really annoying."

True to form, Chuck again started laughing uncontrollably. "Every time I tried to say I was sorry that he didn't make the list, it just made me laugh even more. I must have said I was sorry at least a couple of dozen times."

Kurt started laughing himself, "I imagine you did...laughing harder every time you did. The truth is, Chuck, you can be such an ass, and I don't know why I'm even laughing right now. Each apology, according to you, included you being chosen while he wasn't. Every apology. Did you think of just saying sorry and being done with it? No, you just hammered away."

"See what I mean? It's funny!"

Alice finally weighed in with a stern, "No, it's not funny, and you are not going to be in that celebrity auction next week."

"Aw, come on, Alice. Why not?"

"The same reason Kurt's not: because you are with me. Do you even have to ask that?"

Kurt threw up his hands. "Whoa, Alice, I'm not with you. I would have to be blind to be with you."

Chuck stopped laughing just long enough to say, "Now that's not funny, either. Kurt, you know that Alice is beautiful."

"Yeah? Beautiful is as beautiful does...and therein lies her problem."

Darci, letting her opinion be known, added, "It really isn't funny, Kurt, and no need to be rude. Half the guys at the barbeque can't keep their eyes off Alice."

"And the other half have their glasses on."

Three voices in unison: "Funny, Kurt, really funny."

"Chuckie, Chuckie, no appreciation or gratitude for me taking the heat off you," replied Kurt, shaking his head in mock disappointment.

"Yeah, baby," replied Chuck, still hearing that half the men at the barbeque were ogling Alice. Strangely, it never bothered Chuck that Alice consistently received admiring stares from other men. He actually seemed to revel in the attention she unfailingly received.

"I think I'm going to puke." Kurt just didn't get it. How could anyone be attracted to the witch? "No accounting for taste, I guess."

Returning to the topic of the bachelor auction, Chuck began to whine, "Come on, Alice, it's just for fun. I wanna do it."

"No, I don't want you doing the auction and that's the way it is. Besides, those women at the auction are not interested in bidding on unavailable men. They're on the prowl. What's wrong with you?"

CHAPTER 6

Meeting Bulldog

Brian returned, walking up from behind and surprising the four of them. "Are you looking for me?"

"Yes, look at all these people, Brian."

"It's okay, Kurt. No one's going to complain. Most of our neighbors are here at the barbeque."

"Including Bulldog Williams."

"I know. And so is Bulldog's girlfriend and Victor. I know, because I was just over there."

"Geez, Brian, a recipe for disaster." The wheels in Kurt's mind were turning as he wondered how to preempt the inevitable.

"This should be fun," said Chuck, who seemed to relish conflict as long as it was someone else's. And he made sure it usually was.

"I was over there, but I haven't talked to him yet. I don't think he has a clue that the Italian Stallion and his girlfriend are screwing around."

"Let's hope it stays that way. We need to talk some sense into Victor before he gets himself hurt." Kurt glanced away, imagining murder and mayhem. Then he saw, from across the yard, Vanessa Roberts waving at Brian in full view of her boyfriend. Then he saw Brian wave back to her with a smile and a wink, causing her angry boyfriend to give Brian a dirty look.

Could this get any worse? wondered Kurt. "Brian, what are you doing? I saw the smile and I saw the wink. Are you kidding?

You're going to make that boyfriend of hers go crazy if you play this little game."

Unaware of the previous day's incident, Darci asked, "Kurt, what's this all about?"

The last thing Kurt wanted was Darci being caught up in this drama. But before he could think of a tactful response, Brian guilelessly replied, "Our employee's boyfriend has been hanging out a lot with another girl at his work. Now she wants to make him jealous with me."

"And just how, exactly, did you get all those details?" Kurt was thinking this was getting worse by the minute.

"She called my cell phone about an hour ago. So I told her I would be happy to make him jealous."

"Brian, *no*! Don't even start that game with one of our employees."

"I'm just trying keep up our employees' moral."

"Will you ever get it? Speaking of which, is that Mickey Twain, the comedian?"

"Yeah, I asked Berrie who was performing at his comedy clubs this week. And when I heard it was Mickey Twain, I said he has to do a gig at my barbeque. You love it when Mickey comes to town."

"Yeah, I do, but don't you think he is way too raw for this barbeque? And Brian? *Moral* and *morale*…they're not the same."

"Hey, we're all adults here."

No sooner had the words left Brian's mouth when one child chasing another crossed the lawn and ran through the yard.

"You were saying? Brian, look around you. There are kids here."

"It must be one of the neighbor's kids. I'll make a warning before he goes on."

"Not good enough, Brian. And too late. Mickey is funny, but every word he says is sandwiched with fuck…fuck this…fuck that...fuck you...fucking asshole...motherfucker. After I'm done listening to him, I start dropping the f-bombs myself."

"That is so true. Can't argue with that. But, come on, admit it, it's funny when that fucking happens."

"Yes, it is, I suppose, but I'm not sure it's the right choice for our entire staff and neighbors."

"Okay, just relax. Let's go over and talk to Mickey and see if he can tone it down."

"Brian, define 'tone it down.' Even if he agrees, we've got to be on the same page, and knowing Mickey, I doubt we will be."

As the group made its way to the stage area, Bulldog caught sight of Brian and stopped signing autographs to catch up to him.

"Hey, Brian you sure know how to throw one hell of a sporty barbeque. I feel like I'm back at home in Everglades City."

"Sporty? What's that mean?" Alice was getting a little suspicious that things were not as they appeared, but then again Alice was always suspicious.

"Well, butter my butt and call me a biscuit. Who is this pretty lady?"

"This is Alice, and she's all mine, Bulldog." Chuck seemed to be amused by this behemoth of a man and his appreciation of Alice.

"Well, lucky you, she's hotter than a two-dollar pistol. How'd you get one like this?"

Kurt was spreading himself thin trying to keep on top of everything and be present everywhere, but talking to Bulldog was no chore. "Hey, Bulldog."

"Well, cut my legs off and call me Shorty. I didn't know my new neighbor Kurt had such an attractive wife. Hello, I'm Bulldog, and I now play for the Chicago Bears."

"Hello, Bulldog, nice to meet you," said Darci.

Chuck, feeling the need to clarify relationships, corrected Bulldog. "They aren't married."

"Not married? What's wrong with you, Kurt?"

"I don't know, Bulldog. I'm going to have to work on that, for sure."

No one was going to escape Bulldog's scrutiny and his efforts to get it all sorted out. "Hey, Brian, where's your date?"

"I don't have one today."

"What? Did you and Vicky get in a fight?"

"Vicky? Who's Vicky?"

"You know, your boyfriend Vicky…Victor."

Chuck was laughing again, enjoying the fact that there was no shortage of laughable matters today.

"He's not my boyfriend."

"Aw, what? Did you guys break up?"

"I don't know how you got that idea, but I'm not gay and neither is Victor."

"Really? Now why would Mary Lee tell me that you two were gay?"

Simultaneously, they all looked across the lawn to Victor, who, with his arm around her, was laughing with Mary Lee. Another runaway train occurred to all of them.

"Well, now, I surely hope those two just didn't pee down my back and tell me it was raining."

"Oh shit," Kurt muttered, breaking the spell.

"No, Bulldog, she was probably confused. It's easy enough to do. There's so many of us and just one of her…," said Brian, making it worse by making no sense at all.

Chuck was laughing, still laughing, never stopped laughing.

"I have a feeling I might have just let a rooster in the hen house," he said, sending Chuck into even more gales of laughter.

If indeed it was possible, Chuck was laughing even louder.

"What the hell are you laughing at? You sound like a damned rooster after a cackling hen."

"I'm sorry, Bulldog… It's just that… I don't know… Maybe it's the funny things you say or how you say 'em."

"I gotta say you're just about as useless as a boar with tits."

And that started Chuck laughing even more. If he didn't stop, someone was going to make him stop and no one was taking a bet on who that would be.

"Stop your damn laughin'. I'm going over there to find out what the hell is going on."

As Bulldog marched toward Victor and Mary Lee, Kurt and Brian signaled that Bulldog was catching on to them. Mary Lee, taking the hint, walked up to Bulldog. "Hey, baby what's the matter?"

"You know, Mary Lee, I didn't just fall off the turnip truck yesterday."

"What are you trying to tell me, darlin'?"

"Why did you tell me Victor is gay? You two have been spending a lot of time together."

"He's not gay? Oh, baby, I must've just imagined that he was. You know, *gay*. Don't worry, I'm sure he's as limp as a dishrag around me, being gay and all."

"But he isn't!"

"You know everybody is scared of you. Come on, let's go over there and get you something to eat. You know how you get when you're hungry."

You couldn't exactly call it a truce, but the two of them headed off to get some food.

"Victor, get over here." At the tone of Kurt's voice, Victor thought it better to not delay in joining Kurt. "Victor, have you lost your mind?"

"Oh, Kurt, *amico mio*, why do I have to explain? *Che bellissima.*"

A third (and always unwelcome) voice asked, "What's that mean?"

Kurt didn't even turn to look at her as he answered, "Geez, Alice, you're everywhere! It's Italian, and it means the most beautiful girl. I've heard Victor use it more times than I can count."

"Yes, how you say… She is from the country."

"What country? What is he talking about?"

Knowing how contrary, relentless, and deliberately obtuse

Alice could and would be, Kurt figured it would be easier to keep answering her. She wasn't going away until she was good and ready, no matter what. "I think Victor means she's from the South and he's relating that to country music."

"That's a what I said, she's from a country."

"No, you didn't say that. You said she is from a country. What is this, Kurt, some sort of man code?" Alice was being Alice, and Kurt decided to ignore the question, wishing he could ignore her.

"I figured it out. Victor met her, and he probably never met a true Southern girl, and he can't control himself."

"She's a beautiful!"

"They're all beautiful, Victor. More to the point, you did see her boyfriend, the big man that gets paid a lot of money to beat up other big men on the football field? You did see him, didn't you?"

"Yes, he talk a funny. This big man, he talk funny."

"You talk funny." Alice was like a dog with a bone.

Still ignoring her, Kurt tried to make Victor grasp the enormity of the situation. "Victor, he does talk different than people from Chicago and Italy, but talk has nothing to do with this. People in the South, people familiar with him, like to say that he can be meaner than a sack full of rattlesnakes."

"That I don't understand."

"Okay, how about this one? His papa said he gets wild as a hog. When he's on the football field, he's like a bull in a china shop. Get it?

"I still don't understand. Rattlesnakes, hogs, and bulls in china shops?"

Chuck couldn't contain his laughter...again. "Hey, Kurtis, how do you know all those Southern sayings? Do you know any more?"

"Sure, he's tougher than a one-eared alley cat. And if you don't get the hell out of here, you might be deader than a doornail."

"Ah, yes, that a I understand. It's okay. He doesn't know."

"Well, Victor, don't count on that too long. I think he's catching on."

"I got one, last week Bulldog said his cousin was so buck-toothed that she can eat corn on the cob through a keyhole."

Brian, too, was not getting the point, and his non sequitur response caused Chuck to laugh even louder. "You guys... I got to write this stuff down."

Thinking it best to just change the subject entirely, Kurt suggested, "Come on, guys, let's grab some drinks and go talk to Mickey Twain."

The group stopped at the bar area where all the drinks were being served. Kurt noticed that Frank had a group of employees listening to his stories and, figuring it was as good a time as any to check on things, waved Meathead over to him. "How's your uncle holding up?"

"I think he's starting to get drunk. He's been talking about Napoleon Bonaparte for the last twenty minutes."

Kurt walked over to the group to listen to Frank and size things up for himself.

"Napoleon once said, 'Ability is nothing without opportunity,' and we here at Pointy Foods—"

Frank was interrupted by Thomas, one of his employees. "We don't work for Pointy Foods."

Without pause, Frank amended, "I mean we here at Sportsfan Chronicles have given you the opportunity to do something great."

Kurt interrupted Frank and tried to get him to take a break from drinking. "Sounds like a great speech, Frank, but why don't you guys go eat some food. Remember, Napoleon also said, 'An army marches on its stomach.'" Knowing his suggestion would go unheeded, Kurt turned to his backup. "Make sure your uncle eats a lot of food and try to keep him away from the booze for a while."

"I'll try my best, Kurt," Meathead said, then cleared his throat and extended his hand.

"Okay, here's another twenty, but keep Frank under control."

"Thanks, Kurt. I wouldn't take that, but I really need the money."

With drinks in hand, Brian led the group to the stage where Mickey Twain was getting ready to perform. "Hey, Mickey. Thanks, buddy, for coming!"

"You're welcome, just make sure you remember to pay me well you rich fucking bastard."

Brian reminded him that he was getting paid very well for this gig when Mickey turned to Kurt, "Well, if it isn't my old Chicago drinking buddy, Kurt fucking Weichert."

"Hey, Mickey, it's been a while." Kurt was silently wondering if this was a big mistake. Mickey wasn't on stage yet and already the f-bombs were virtually raining down on them, despite the very obvious presence of families with children in tow.

"Not long enough, you piece of shit. Hey, I'm glad to see Darci is here. How are you, darlin', and when are you going to leave this dickhead and marry me? Kurt, did you ever tell her about the time we got shit faced and you woke up with—"

Kurt grabbed Mickey in a bear hug, managing at the same time to put his hand over Mickey's mouth. "Mickey, quit bullshit-ting. One of these days she might actually believe you."

Mickey started laughing as he broke away from the massive hug. "You know I love it when my comedy tour comes to Chicago. You bastards are always fun to hang out with after the show."

"Yeah, about the show." Brian, more comfortable in avoiding serious issues, uncharacteristically addressed the content of the monologue or, more precisely, the presentation. "Hey, listen, Mickey, you need to tone it down, way down. This is not your usual crowd. I invited my neighbors, completely forgetting about their children. I didn't know they were going to bring their kids. Even without the kids, we still have our employees. Most of them are here, too. So I need a clean version of Mickey Twain today. Would you do that, buddy?"

"Yeah, yeah, I understand. Of course, no problem. I'll give you the G-rated version of the show."

"Aw, thanks Mickey; you know, you can even give us the PG version of your show, that'll work." *In for a penny, in for a pound,* thought Brian, knowing even a PG-rated monologue would be too raw for this crowd. PG was the only way to go, but Brian had a nanosecond of doubt when he heard the quick response.

"Gee, swell, guys. Golly gee, I'll give you a nice, clean, entertaining show. So, Brian, grab the microphone and let's get this thing started. The rest of you stand right here and give me some good cheers."

Kurt sensed something bad was about to happen. This was too easy, too out of character, too, too…too everything! Nothing fit, yet he could hardly act on imagination and one out-of-character "golly gee." He wondered if the mike had a remotely controlled "cough" switch? Was there even such a thing? Studios had "bleep" switches, but this was a cookout with a RadioShack mike and speaker. No, this was going to be bad, no two ways about it.

On the other hand, he could be wrong. Yeah, maybe Mickey was okay with this. Or not. He always had the feeling that Mickey was a bit off center, a bit twisted, and always unpredictable.

CHAPTER 7

Twain's Act

Kurt's mental argument continued as Brian took the mike. "Hey, everybody, gather round. It's time for some comedy. Not just comedy but arguably the best in comedy, and the show is about to start."

It didn't take long for the guests to gather around the stage in Brian's backyard. "I am honored to have one of my favorite comedians perform in my backyard today."

One the neighbors moved closer to the stage so that the children could see and hear everything. The neighbor leaned into Kurt, saying how much his kids had enjoyed the comedian who had performed on a Disney cruise he and his family took last year in Florida. "Oh, brother," Kurt muttered, his mind churning.

Brian, without a wayward thought of concern, was now ready to start the show. "It is my pleasure to introduce the inimitable, one and only, Mickey Twain."

The applause was immediate, the cheering was loud, and all the guests were smiling expectantly; children, if not in hand, were playing nearby within clear view and earshot.

"Oh gee, golly, thank you, Brian. Here, Brian, I brought you a chair. Why don't you sit over there, but stay on the stage so everybody can see you."

"Oh, dear God." Kurt now knew for sure this was going to be worse than anything he could imagine: "gee," "swell," and "oh gee, golly"? Those words were undoubtedly the last of anything PG.

A grinning Brian sat down. "Oh no, it sounds like you are going to roast me."

"Hello, everybody, I'm Mickey Twain. I just wanted to let everybody know that Brian has asked me to keep it clean today. He wants me to keep it rated G."

"I said PG! Come on, Mickey, give me a break."

Kurt then overheard a little girl, "Daddy, this is rated PG… just like the movies," which was enough for him to lean over and warn Darci, "This is going to be really bad. Really, really bad."

And then Mickey began his show. "Let's get this started and Brian, why don't you take your PG-rated bullshit and shove it up your fucking ass."

Mickey looked over at Brian, smiled and winked at him. What followed was an hour of vulgar, degenerate, abusive comedy directed at the audience. Anyone daring to leave was singled out and torn to pieces. He showed mercy to no one, not to children, not to the elderly, not to the handicapped. Anyone seen attempting to leave was targeted, and Mickey deliberately crossed the line with every opportunity to do so.

He had probably been calculating this since hearing the PG request and was no doubt gratified, though not surprised, to see Kurt and his friends standing there, visibly squirming as he made it happen. Despite being virtually immobilized by shock, they realized they, too, would feel the sting of Mickey Twain's barbs if they tried to leave.

Besides, leaving had other problems, not the least of which was the association of "leaving the sinking ship" in the eyes of employees and guests alike. *Guests? More like hostages*, Kurt thought.

They were all together in this, except for one lone person heard laughing hard at every word, one lone person who was laughing so hysterically that he was literally holding his sides while tears ran down, cheeks contorted by facial muscles held too long in one position. Chuck. And true to form, he didn't try to contain himself. He had a hard time even standing up. When asked later why he didn't try to contain himself, he started laughing all over again saying, "I did contain myself, but I escaped."

Darci and Alice wanted to leave as soon as they realized this was beyond an X-rated, hate-filled rant. They stayed, trying not to listen. "Darci, why don't we leave? It will only last until we're out of sight."

"Leave? One, I am too scared and, two, the children. Some of the parents have three or four and they need—" Darci cut herself off when she picked up a crying child and tried to cover the child's ears and run at the same time. She took the hand of another and the parents followed, each with a child in hand.

"Fuck, Kurt, if I had a piece of ass like that waiting for me at home, I wouldn't be coming to some shitty-ass barbeque. Hell, just put some—" Darci was mercifully out of earshot before she could hear anymore of the offensive "compliments" about her anatomy.

Reading the disgust on Alice's face, Mickey next turned his verbal bile in her direction. "Not that Jugs here has anything to be ashamed of. So you're with this jackass." He nodded toward Chuck, who didn't stop laughing even when the attacks were directed toward the woman he loved. "So... Is this guy always laughing? I mean, honestly, when you're doing him, is he like..." What followed was a crude impression of a man laughing during a moment of passion. It was accompanied by pelvic movements that brought fresh gasps from the audience.

Alice's face flushed in what was either rage or embarrassment. She, too, picked up one child and took the hand of another. Between the two of them, they had four children with the parents still following behind. The foul vocal barrage of profanity and pornographic references relentlessly followed them until they were far enough away to no longer hear or be seen by Mickey Twain, comedian of shame.

Contrary to Mickey's plan, Darci's move in picking up the first child and Alice immediately following suit emboldened the rest of the guests and a virtual exodus occurred, leaving Mickey Twain on stage with Brian still frozen in his chair. Chuck laughed even harder. A speechless Kurt was still in front of the stage, staring ahead, knowing and wondering at the same time what had just happened…what was still happening.

The bar area, slightly removed from the stage, was surrounded by most of those employees who came alone. They enjoyed their own show with a slightly drunk Frank waxing eloquent on the virtues of Napoleonic warfare. Meathead nudged Frank upon sighting the empty yard, and Frank, momentarily nonplussed, thought the party was over.

"What the hell? Get me one for the road, bartender." The bartender, who had figured there would be no more tips, had closed shop and left. Seeing no bartender, Frank yelled, "Someone get me a cab!"

With Meathead running after him, Frank climbed into one of the empty buses. "Take me to Pointy Foods."

Kurt, the blood drained from his face, eventually regained movement and his power of speech. "It looks like Mickey ended Brian's barbeque early. Everyone's leaving. All the banquet workers Brian hired are cleaning up and shutting down. Oh my God, Bernie, looks like some are already gone…just when a drink would be in order."

"Yeah, well… I've got to get Mickey back to my nightclub; he's got to perform at eight tonight."

Brian finally unfroze himself enough to get off the stage. "Hey, Bernie! Mickey hijacked my barbeque and offended just about everybody in the audience."

"Except for Chuck," Kurt corrected.

"Yeah, Kurt, except for Chuck. No surprise there!" Brian, angry beyond reason, blamed Bernie.

The three of them looked up to see that the foul-mouthed comedian had shifted his focus to the lone remaining person standing by the stage. Mickey had no problem playing to a party of one, and he verbally abused Chuck about everything from the way he dressed down to his skinny frame. Instead of getting angry, Chuck just kept laughing.

"Kurt, I better get Mickey out of here before Chuck wets or sharts his pants."

"Yeah, you do that. At least your boy here won't need a sound check before he goes on. He's already projecting to the back row, not that we have a back row left. Man, is your crowd in for a treat tonight!"

Even adults-only crowds had limits, and Bernie was a little concerned. Mickey had never been this wound up before, and he was clearly still on a roll. But seeing Kurt indicate that the show was over, he offered a seemingly sincere, "Sorry, pal, see you later."

Brian made it clear that he didn't want to pay Mickey after he ruined the barbeque.

Bernie shook his head. "Not pay Mickey? You really don't want to piss him off. Trust me. I know Mickey. He'll target you and never stop. You'll be made fun of at every show he does across the country, and he'll take gigs at other clubs here in town just because this is your turf. He never gives up. He never gives in. Just pay him. Consider it money well spent just to have him go away. Don't even think about it. Call it hush money."

Although Chuck was still laughing loudly, it was no surprise that Mickey overheard every word. He left Chuck on autopilot and warned Brian to resist any idea of not paying. "Okay, Brian, we're out of here. Don't you dare try to get out of paying me, you little piece of shit."

"It's okay, Mickey, I talked to Brian. There's no question about it. You'll be paid. Come on, let's get to the club. Your audience awaits you."

"Gee, Bernie, thanks... You have a big heart and a stomach to match."

Kurt was grateful the focus had shifted once again but felt Mickey was still out of line. After all, he wasn't on stage anymore. "Mickey, give Bernie a break. He's trying to get into shape. He's not that overweight. Just big-boned."

"Then his big bones are definitely fat." Of course Chuck was the only one laughing.

"What are you laughing at, Chuck? You're so ugly, you have

to put a bag on your head to get your dog to hump your leg. You are so ugly, you stuck your head out the window and got arrested for mooning."

Despite Chuck's continued laughing, Kurt was sure he heard a collective sigh of relief from the remaining guests when Mickey Twain finally left.

CHAPTER 8

Made in the Shade

After Bernie and Mickey left, Kurt, Darci, Chuck, and Alice walked back home, went straight to the couch and sat down, staring ahead with expressions of relief.

"Well, since the barbeque ended early, you two can head back to your place after all."

Still smiling, Chuck shook his head. "Nope, we're spending the night anyway. It'll be fun."

Darci took hold of his arm, no doubt in an effort to keep him calm. "Alice and I thought it would be fun if they hung out with us tonight and stayed over."

"I knew they weren't planning on leaving today. Just giving it a try."

Alice, her earlier flush gone and apparently bearing no ill will toward her boyfriend for the horrible things he'd not only allowed but encouraged Mickey Twain to say to her, cooed, "Chuck, sweetie, drive me to the grocery store so we can grab some stuff for tonight."

"Really?" Kurt was thinking that this was a first, and then Darci put an end to that.

"Come Kurt, let's go."

And so they all left, with Chuck driving them to the local grocery store. Kurt was getting pissed at Chuck, because he kept driving past the front parking spots.

"What the hell are you doing? You're driving past the front parking spots."

"We have to park back here by the tree so we can get some shade. Alice doesn't like the car to get too hot."

"No way! We're not going to park at the back of this enormous parking lot when there are plenty of front spots available, just because Alice wants you to park by a tree."

Again in that soothing tone, Darci added, "It's not a big deal, Kurt. I do it all the time."

"Not with me, you don't. Ridiculous! This is ridiculous."

"You don't have to wear makeup, Kurt."

"And you, Alice, don't wear enough makeup. Besides, I don't get it. You were just outside at a barbeque all afternoon."

"But this is different. The sun will make the car feel like a hundred degrees by the time we get back, so I want the car sitting in the shade."

"Park in the front and just crack the windows."

"No, we're fine back here. Come on, we're wasting time, let's go inside and get what we need."

"I repeat, this is ridiculous. Has anyone noticed that Alice always calls the shots regardless of what anyone else thinks?"

"Yes, Kurt, I call the shots and am proud of it!"

They got what they needed and started toward the checkout counter, with Kurt grumbling all the way there. Chuck interrupted the process when he left to grab a couple more items, holding up the line even more. Kurt was no longer grumbling alone as the irate customers behind them joined in.

Darci whispered, "Kurt, you need to pay for this one because Alice and Chuck picked up the tab the last time we went out."

"Pay? Pay what? We have to check out and get a total first, and we're not moving and neither is anyone else in the line."

With that, Kurt got an idea. He took his credit card and swiped it, hoping to beat Chuck, but he caught up to them in time and told the cashier to add his items. And those items were a copy of GQ magazine on top of a box of Night Light Condoms.

Kurt was already annoyed when he finished paying but became angrier when he saw the clerk bagging the box of condoms.

"What the hell is that?"

Chuck smirked. "Gee, Kurt, what do you think it is?"

"Chuck, shouldn't you be buying those in private? And Night Lights? It figures. You are so rude."

"What's the big deal? Nothing in a supermarket is private anyway!" He started laughing. Again. "Everything goes down the conveyer belt, no privacy here, buddy."

"Just 'cause they sell 'em here doesn't mean you have to buy them here. Go to a drug store!" Kurt's sensibilities were often a source of humor for Chuck, who knew Kurt wasn't finished with the subject. "Ugh, I just paid for your condoms, and so I guess you're planning on having sex with Alice in my house tonight."

Another blush, lighter than the one she'd had at the barbeque colored Alice's cheeks. "Oh, Chuck, how embarrassing. I should be mad at you for buying those in public, but seeing Kurt so uncomfortable makes it okay…this time."

Chuck just smiled and raised his eyebrows.

Darci, too, was a little uncomfortable, but decided that it was more important to smooth things over. "Kurt, sweetie, look at it this way, we survived a bad afternoon and we have our friends with us and your glass is not half empty; it's half full."

"It's half full and cracked and leaking, Darci. As for you, Chuck, the only good news is at least you won't be getting Alice pregnant. You guys would produce one very obnoxious kid. Chuck, you have one obnoxious kid already. Let's pray nothing tears. You'd have an obnoxious dayglow kid." Kurt couldn't resist laughing. "A dayglow kid. Too much!"

"Kurt, please. Be nice."

"Hard to do with the prospect of walking a mile across the hot asphalt of this massive parking lot just to get to the car. These spaces are for the employees, not the customers. Do you see cart corrals here? No, you don't. The cart corrals are back there where we were meant to park; so not only do we have to walk the distance, but one of us has to walk the food buggy back to the cart corral!"

"Kurt, you're ranting. Enough with the cart corral. Who says that anyway?"

Alice wasn't about to let this go without adding her two cents. "Kurt, what's with the cart? Nobody takes them back. They expect you to leave them. That's why they hire baggers."

"Last word, Alice, first and foremost, my car is what's up. You and others like you are the cause of damage to my nice Escalade! Do you ever do the right thing just because it is the right thing to do, Alice?"

"Yeah, but not where you're concerned, Kurt. Let's go."

———

They got back to the house and hung out together in the man cave. Upon seeing they had returned, Brian walked over and joined them. They avoided talk of the disastrous barbeque and ended up instead talking about their game plan for raising enough capital to purchase a professional football team.

Darci took the turn in conversation as a convenient point to leave the room. "Kurt, Alice and I are going upstairs to start on dinner." Chuck got up and started walking upstairs with Darci and Alice.

"Chuck, just where exactly do you think you're going?"

"Upstairs with them."

"No, you are not. What's wrong with you? You would rather go upstairs in the hen house versus being down in the man cave?"

"Alice, I'm going to hang downstairs with the guys." Chuck's tone suggested that he was asking for permission rather than stating an intention.

Kurt shook his head. "Alice, do me a favor, will you? Open your purse and give Chuck his balls back."

Alice's reply was a simple, "No."

The girls went upstairs and while Kurt and Brian were shooting pool, Chuck played pinball with the volume on mute.

CHAPTER 9
The Workout

Kurt started the conversation with what was first and foremost on his mind: the football franchise. "Our company has done a great job so far, but we still haven't gotten half the money needed to purchase a football team."

Brian nodded in agreement. "The Jacksonville Jaguars sold for around seven hundred fifty million dollars. We're going to need at least that amount. How much do you think we have now?"

"Not quite enough, we're right around three hundred fifty million dollars."

"Wouldn't we would have more if Chuck kicked in the money he promised?"

"Uncle Walter sent me an e-mail this morning, saying his lawyers were able to shut down my ex-wife's lawyers yesterday. I think I'll be able to access my money now."

"Good, it's about time you started contributing more."

Kurt was a little annoyed. "And you were going to tell us this when?"

Stung by Brian's comment, Chuck ignored Kurt. "That's not true, Brian, I've done a great job recruiting those talented college students from Harvard, MIT, and Stanford. They've created a lot of our new, profitable Internet-related start-ups. That's money."

"Right. But you're forgetting that was my idea, Chuck, not yours."

"Yeah, your idea, but I'm the one who got them to sign with

us instead of those other venture capitalists on their tails. Even Frank is impressed with my persistence. I worked the idea. If I hadn't, it would still just be an idea."

"Chuck, you stalked them…all of them. You flew to their colleges wearing that hoodie of yours. You hounded them until they signed."

"What can I say? It worked. My persistence worked, dogged persistence! Uncle Walter taught me early… The one thing in common with all the business greats is persistence, and I exercised that, so don't tell me I haven't contributed enough!"

"Okay, Chuckles, so you're saying your contribution is the stalking portion. And that equates money."

"Yes. Exactly." Chuck wasn't being deliberately obtuse; he believed his every word.

"Okay, guys, we've got everything hinging on the Sportsfan Chronicles' new brand of products and…"

Still heated, Brian wanted to point out what he thought was one little, important salient fact. "But they are all still being developed."

"What about all the new offers we've received for side businesses and quick deals? Are you ignoring those?"

"Well, no, we have the inventor… We haven't backed him yet."

"Good point, I guess we should check him out. What else do we have?"

"How about the video for that reality-TV, Internet guy. You know, Darci's childhood friend."

"Skippy? I don't like him."

"Geez, Kurt, why? Because he dated Darci when he was a teenager? When they were teenagers? Come on. This is business, not high sc—"

"No, stop right there! Because the dude has been obsessed with her his entire adult life, that's why. He still is obsessed with her. Arrested development is what it is."

"Why? Because he sends her flowers on Valentine's Day?"

"Yes! And her birthday."

"Okay, he's willing to make us a ton of money with the Sportsfan Workout. He'll do it to impress her. He's an exhibitionist."

While Chuck was gratified the focus had shifted, he was also annoyed at being out of the loop. "How come I don't know about this?"

"Because I don't want to do it. Why would I waste time discussing something I don't want to do, Chuck?"

"Okay, I get that, but why is it called the *Sportsfan Workout?*

Brian wasn't willing to let it go. "This is a workout video for sports fans, and I think it has possibilities. It's a video for the everyday guy that sits more on the couch watching sports than being outside playing them. This guy is a monster at marketing himself, and that means extra, free-of-charge marketing for us. Check him out on YouTube. You'll see."

"Yeah, but this guy, Skip, wants us to be in the video. I'm against it."

"But he made a good point. We're starting to get known around the country for being those guys who won the lottery and are trying to buy a professional football team. A lot of people from around the country are pulling for us."

"So, what you're saying, Brian, is that this guy wants to tap into our so-called new celebrity status and use it to get his name out there."

"His name is already out there. What he's trying to do is get his own reality network. He's developed a bunch of extreme reality shows, and he wants to sell infomercials in addition to that. He wants us to do this video and promised us an insane amount of money to do it. Too much to ignore!"

"Well, let me remind you, it's not all money."

"Okay, so he's going to pay us in part with his new company stock, a lot of it."

Chuck was almost jumping as he yelled, "Oh my God, guys, this is awesome! Let's do it. I'm in; I want to do this."

Kurt rolled his eyes. "You mean, you literally want to do this, don't you, Chuck? You! That's why you're on board. You see yourself jumping around on camera. Skip's not the only exhibitionist. That exercise session before the old Pointy Foods game a couple of years ago does not qualify you for participating in a televised show under our name."

"Come on, Kurt, leave him alone. What do we have to lose?"

"Our dignity. That's what. Do you have to ask after hearing my little reminder?"

"Brian's right, and anyway, who cares about that?

"Let's do it."

"Okay, Brian, I will agree to us talking to him, but I'm not making any promises. And Chuck? Get your imagination in check. You are not going to be prancing around to techno wearing a T-shirt with our name on it. Not going to happen."

Chuck's phone rang before he could respond to Kurt's diatribe.

"Uncle Walter, do you have some good news for me? What?" Chuck spent some time on the phone listening and, for once, not talking.

"What is it Chuck?" asked Kurt, with Brian looking on wondering that himself.

"Kurt, you're not going to believe this. My uncle said that my ex-wife took my son to South America today. She said that I'll never see him again."

"I'm sorry to hear that, Chuck."

"Well, I guess I can invest now."

"Geez, Chuck, what about your son?"

"I'm sure I'll be able to force her to let him come visit me… You know, all that international treaty stuff. She must have been really mad when the judge wouldn't increase the child support. Trust me, I already pay a lot of child support. Too much, especially with most of it going into her personal account. Now I can move on without her trying to take all my money."

CHAPTER 10

A Regular Einstein

During the three weeks following Brian's barbeque, Kurt, Brian, and Frank brainstormed various ideas and plans to raise money. Some opportunities were more like hazards than anything else. Others seemed tailor-made to what they wanted to do. Just how lucrative any of them would be remained to be seen. With that in mind, the four of them flew out to Southern California to check firsthand on a couple of investments with very real possibilities.

The first investment involved an actual inventor by the name of Norman Einstein. None could answer whether or not he was, perhaps, a distant relative of Albert Einstein, and he hadn't offered that information. What they did learn during the three weeks spent recovering from the barbeque debacle was that Norman held the patents to a lot of the software that was needed for the new Sportsfan Chronicles Internet projects. Some were redundant to programs already in use, but owning those would keep them out of competitors' hands—an easily (and often) forgotten fact.

They were still strategizing and talking over one another as they walked toward Norman Einstein's office. Frank in particular was voicing his imperatives—what must be done and why it must be done. Invariably, the reason was money. *Of course*, thought Chuck, *Why else are we here?* But for once, Frank was more about avoiding outflow than income. He was still about making money, no doubt, but he was obsessed by the excessive costs of making that money. Two of them looked a little blank and one was anticipating Frank's idea. While Brian and Chuck were thinking *whatever*, Kurt said one word, "Patents."

Frank nodded. "Exactly, patents. Listen you guys, we need to convince this guy to sell us his patents, because we are constantly paying his middlemen to use his intellectual properties."

Brian didn't see how they could avoid these fees. "Frank, that's not going to happen. A patent is where the money is for these guys. For us, it's the cost of doing business. Didn't you say earlier that it's a penny or so every time we use his intellectual properties?"

Now Chuck was showing concern; they were almost at the office door, and they still hadn't formulated an approach. "And you waited until we're about to walk in to mention this, Frank?"

Brian was still not getting the significance of owning the patents. "Hey, guys, who cares? Let's just get in there and close the deal." Frank was getting frustrated and that sometimes spelled trouble.

As usual, it fell to Kurt to keep the conversation focused. "Brian, Chuck, just let Frank outline everything. We'll close the deal, but let's hear this first. We'll go over it afterwards."

Brian, still confused, repeated, "But you agreed it's the cost of doing business."

Frank's frustration was obvious. "Yeah, yeah, yeah. It's a cost of doing business, not the cost of…forget it, numbskull. It is not a one-time cost for us. It's ongoing. Every time we use them, we pay for that damn patent. Over and over and over again. Apparently, we use them a lot and those pennies are adding up to mighty dollars. Get it?"

Brian, as tenacious as ever and in fear of losing the deal, wasn't giving up. "Pennies? Geez, Frank, what does that matter? You know we already have a high margin on all our products."

"Okay, I admit, I regret not bringing this up earlier. But it's very simple, " said Frank, reigning himself in. "Brian, we need to watch the pennies so the dollars can take care of themselves."

"Did Napoleon Bonaparte used to say that one, too, Frank?"

Kurt was growing weary of Brian's refusal—or was it inability—to see something so obvious and so elementary. "I agree with Frank on this one. If we own the rights to the intellectual properties, we can save on those costs. Big time. It adds up fast. On top of that, our competitors will have to pay us every time they use them. Poetic. We'll be collecting from the competition. Gotta love it!"

Brian was not giving up and, for whatever reason, continued to challenge Kurt. "If this is so logical, why, then, haven't our competitors tried to buy them?"

Kurt smiled, glad that Brian had managed to accidentally steer the conversation exactly where he'd wanted it to go. "Who said they haven't? As a matter of fact, they have tried to buy them, but he doesn't want to sell just the Internet properties. That's where we have the edge. He wants someone to buy or invest in all his inventions. The patents that we and our competitors want are only a small portion of his inventions."

"Okay, so what's the game plan?"

"Geez, knucklehead, that's what I've been trying to tell you."

Kurt could see this easily going south. Bumping heads resulted in both sides having headaches. "Frank, let me—"

"No, Kurt, I would've had this settled by now if we hadn't stopped to hold these guys' hands. Chuck, you, Kurt, and Brian listen up. We're going to take a look at some of his other inventions. Remember, most of our competitors focus on a single industry. We are a conglomerate. Get that? Look the word up, puleez. *Conglomerate.* We can focus on any kind of business, no matter what industry it's in, as long as it makes us money. Mr. Einstein here will see we are not the idiots that usually show up at his door."

"So we might be able to use some of these other inventions?"

"Oh, God, Brian, really? Brian...even if we can't use them, buying all of them will get us the ones we need and allow us to charge competitors for access to those we don't need. Get it? We've got a number that we think he will take. We just need to

seem interested in his other crap. And appearing genuinely inter-
ested is key. It's not all about the money with these creative types.
Appreciation! Just let us do the talking, and you look interested.
That's all, final word on the subject."

And it had to be the final word, because they were at the front
desk of the building where Norman Einstein's office was located.
After giving their names to a bored security guard, they waited in
the lobby for less than a minute before an elevator bell rang, and
Mr. Einstein emerged.

Kurt had expected a man in a lab coat. Because he was an
inventor. Because his name was Einstein. He'd expected frizzy
hair and a lab coat.

Norman Einstein, who couldn't have been a day younger than
sixty, stood at five-foot, two inches; was completely bald; and had
a smile that seemed in danger of splitting his face in half. He was
dressed in blue jeans and a button-down untucked shirt, looking
more prepared for an afternoon in the park than what could be
the most lucrative business deal of his life. His voice echoed off
the walls of the lobby. "Kurt!"

No sooner had Kurt stood up than he was shaking hands with
the man. "Norman Einstein?"

The short man nodded vigorously as he released Kurt's hand
and shouted, "Brian!" and similarly shocked Brian with a handshake. In due course, there was a "Frank!" and a "Chuck!" as well.
Kurt noticed that he wasn't the only one rubbing his hand after
shaking it with the inventor. His grip was surprisingly strong.

It was Brian, of all people, who tried to get the conversation
moving. "We're very excited to see what you've been working on,
Mr. …I'm sorry, is it Doctor Einstein?"

He shook his head, chuckling as he turned back to the elevator.
"Nope. Not 'Doctor Einstein.' That's my brother. Not 'Professor
Einstein' either." The elevator doors reopened before he added,
"That's my sister. Me? I'm just a regular Einstein." He laughed at
what Kurt imagined was some sort of private joke.

The five of them packed into the elevator, and as they made

the trip up, the boisterous man seemed to go suddenly still, like a cuckoo clock whose springs had snapped in midcoo. Only Kurt was close enough to hear that Einstein was still muttering. "Bullet trains. Magnet rails. Elevator cars. Magnet tunnel. Smooth ride. Skyscrapers. Pacemakers."

And he realized that Norman Einstein was thinking out loud. He wondered if he even realized that he did it. It suggested a man who was constantly thinking, which was encouraging to someone who was considering investing in whatever fruits those thoughts yielded. On the other hand, it also suggested a social awkwardness that might explain why he'd never managed a whole package patent deal with any other investors.

And it suddenly occurred to Kurt that the display in the lobby might have been a very shy man overcompensating. Kurt remembered the sales persona he'd adopted early in his career at Pointy Foods, before the true confidence that came with accomplishment had replaced the false bravado of a young man desperate to impress everyone. The door to the elevator opened on the sixth floor, leading to Norman's office.

There were four initials stenciled onto the door: J.A.R.E. Those letters immediately set off red flags with Kurt. Looking to the others, he wasn't surprised to see that Chuck and Brian were oblivious to it. Even if they'd noticed the letters, they'd no doubt failed to see the implications, but Kurt knew those four letters could be a game changer.

It could be a game changer because they'd come here to do business with an individual. And if Norman Einstein was part of a corporate entity, even a small one, then the whole strategy had to change. So on top of everything else, Kurt had to find out what J.A.R.E. stood for. He tried to direct the conversation toward it subtly and not let on that they'd thought Norman was just a private inventor. And not give away that he had them at a disadvantage.

As Norman opened the door, Frank asked, "What's J.A.R.E. stand for? I thought you worked on your own."

Kurt sometimes wished he didn't need partners. Things would have run smoother in so many ways if he'd just bought that lottery ticket on his own. If Brian hadn't left their chosen numbers in Frank's office. If Frank hadn't appropriated those numbers (as he'd appropriated so many other ideas over the years) and played them on a ticket of his own. So many ifs and some regret.

Norman smiled, as he invited them all into his office. "Oh, I do work on my own. I maintain a small staff of assistants, but everything here is owned by myself. The letters on the door are, well, just a little joke."

Kurt smiled not only from relief, but because he suddenly got the joke. "J.A.R.E.: Just a Regular Einstein."

Norman offered a wink and a nod for confirmation. "It's what Dad used to call me. Thing is, I never heard him say that to my brother or sister. Never did figure out if it was supposed to be a compliment or an insult." He shrugged off his own question and then began guiding them through the various rooms of his facility, which encompassed not just the sixth floor but the fifth and the seventh as well.

The guys toured through the facility, pretending to be interested in everything, even the weird and seemingly useless stuff.

Each man had bitten his tongue more than once, holding back what would have been an almost reflexive, "What a waste of time." As well as dangerous. Impractical. Insane. It would be easy to imagine that Edison heard the same thing when he invented the lightbulb.

Still, Kurt finally broke down when they were taken into an all too familiar test area. "I don't get it. Why are you taking us into this bathroom?"

"Well, Kurt, this is not your normal bathroom. It appears to be just a regular bathroom, but in reality it is another one of our testing facilities." Norman pointed to a toilet inside a stall. "This toilet tests your waste every time you use it. Just imagine the possibilities. Anybody can check for medical conditions every time he or she uses the toilet."

Bathroom talk perked Chuck up. "Like what? Running low on your Viagra levels, Frank?" Chuck's inevitable snarky laugh was audible, while everyone studiously ignored the adolescent remark. Except Norman.

"Close enough. One example is a woman can see if she's pregnant. Or parents can check to see if their teenager is using drugs. It could even recommend what vitamins a person should take for the day."

Chuck was looking around, mulling over the claims when his attention was diverted once again. "Hey, guys, look at this one over here."

After they all walked over to another stall and saw a giant toilet, Norman explained, "This particular toilet is high enough for the tallest people in the world. I would love to have some NBA basketball player pitch the product for us."

Kurt mulled the idea of a toilet that a basketball player could endorse, perhaps something reinforced for extremely heavy people. With the nation's obesity epidemic, a supertoilet might be… Then he shook his head. He'd been in the facility too long, seen so many crazy inventions in one afternoon that even his own crazy ideas were starting to sound marketable. So he just nodded appreciably and then turned toward to the next display. Even if half this junk was never used, it would still be worth owning the world's biggest toilet if it meant getting control of the rest of Norman's creations.

Chuck, on the other hand, wasn't letting the absurd invention go with a simple nod. "Seen something similar years ago, but it's still so funny looking," he muttered. He started laughing hard, and while Kurt was familiar with the way his friend's mind worked, some of the others present were not familiar at all.

With a discreet but still audible clearing of his throat, Norman continued. "Come on, guys, let me take you to my sports department."

Kurt bristled just a little at the mention of a sports department. *Why didn't he take us there first?* he wondered. With no additional prompting needed, the guys walked over to another area where all sorts of sports items were displayed. Some of these appeared to be regular sport items, but by now they had come to expect the unexpected, and a quick glance revealed some items not so familiar.

Heedless of the potential danger of handling experimental equipment, Brian grabbed a seemingly familiar orange-and-black ball. "What's the deal with this one? It looks like a regular basketball."

"Brian, take another look. Go on, look again. Notice there is no hole for air. Because it never needs to be refilled."

"And this, what's this?" asked Brian, as he held up a long pair of gloves.

"Those are basketball gloves."

"Okay, basketball gloves for basketball players. Is that why the fingers are so long?"

"No, that glove is designed to fit someone your size."

Brian put on the gloves. "They do fit me, but why are the fingers so long?"

"Finger extenders. They are finger extenders for someone your size. Wearing these, anybody can palm a basketball." Norman was clearly pleased with his inventions, as well he should have been.

Kurt's cell phone broke the spell when it rang, Kurt having forgotten to put it on vibrate mode. He looked at the caller display and let out a whispered curse. "It's Chuck," Kurt said to everyone and to no one in particular. Taking the call, he hissed out, "Chuck, where the hell are you? What do you mean you're still in the bathroom? Hold on, we'll be there in a second."

Frank was ominously silent, while Brian asked, "What now?"

Kurt sighed. "Chuck said he's still in the bathroom, and he wants us to go in there."

And so they did. Upon entering, they looked around and couldn't believe their eyes when they saw that Chuck had climbed onto a supersize toilet and was sitting there with his trousers around his ankles requesting they take pictures.

While Kurt was not entirely surprised, he had hoped for a

modicum of good behavior from Chuck. "What exactly are you doing? You look ridiculous up there. You just couldn't keep your pants up, could you?" hissed Kurt.

All, without exception, were laughing at the improbable sight of an average size man perched on a toilet designed for the exceedingly tall man.

"My feet can't touch the floor. Take a picture of me. I want to post it on my Facebook page."

Happy to oblige in hopes of ending the farce, Brian took a picture of Chuck, who was indeed looking ridiculous on the giant toilet. Chuck's pants were beginning to slip over his ankles and feet—all of which were dangling in the air above the floor. Norman didn't seem at all bothered by Chuck's behavior as he walked over to a computer screen and intently gazed at the readout. "It looks like you might have a bladder infection, Chuck."

Even Frank didn't know what to think. "Geez, Chuck, you peed in his toilet?" The men were eager to leave before the unplanned "reveal."

"It's a toilet, Frank. People pee in toilets! Uh, guys, I might need help getting down."

Kurt, Brian, and Frank listened, heard, turned, and left.

"Norman, they left me here. Could you pass me the toilet paper? I can't reach it."

They left Norman's laboratory after having verbally agreed upon a price for all of his patents.

Not sure if he was still on edge after Chuck's display or experiencing buyer's remorse, Kurt offered a sincere-sounding encouragement, "Well, troops, I think we got all for fair price, even though we won't use most of his patents," more to convince himself than anyone else.

Brian, at least, was still impressed and not convinced that they wouldn't use others. "Actually some of that stuff was pretty cool."

Kurt offered a reassuring smile. "You never know. If any of

the other patents do something, it'll be a bonus. Now let's get over and see Skip's reality television studios. I hope this is not going to be a waste of time, but I just know that it is. I can't stand Skip, he's been a thorn in my side ever since I started dating Darci."

Of course when he'd started dating Darci, Kurt was just starting as a salesman for Pointy Foods, and Skip was on his way to becoming a big television star. Now, Kurt was a wealthy investor, and Skip was a disgraced has-been who needed Kurt's funding. The more Kurt had thought about it over the past few weeks, the more it had made him actually look forward to the meeting. Skip needed Kurt. And if that meant Kurt might be able to make him squirm just a little while a deal was still up in the air... Well, he'd never pretended to be a saint.

CHAPTER 11

The Cabinet

There was no doubt that Kurt, Brian, Frank, and Chuck had arrived at the right place when they saw that the large numbers on the gate matched the hastily written numbers on the palm of Brian's hand. If there had been doubt, it would have soon been dispelled when they saw "Reality Frenzy" in larger letters occupying almost every square inch of the giant sign over the entrance.

"Geez, I bet this could be seen from space!"

"What did you expect, Frank? A business card stuck to the light post?"

"Your annoyance underwhelms me. Get a grip, Kurt, and you two, stop standing around like looky-loos."

Brian and Chuck brought their attention back to Frank and followed him to the front gate where they checked in with the security guard. A brief moment later, another representative, a younger man who introduced himself as Mano, took them to Studio A in the golf cart parked to his side. Mano was a wall of a man, an impression only enhanced by the brick-red shirt he wore. He looked almost comical behind the wheel of the golf cart, his bulk taking up both front seats, with Kurt and Brian seated behind him and Chuck and Frank seated behind them. There was no doubt that this giant could have easily broken all four of them in half without working up a sweat, yet he seemed to be the one who was nervous.

Perhaps sensing his discomfort as well, Brian tried engaging

71

their unlikely chauffeur in some small talk. "Hi, I'm Brian. We were told we'd be meeting Jimmy."

Mano turned a corner as he nodded. "You are. I'm Jimmy Manokowski. Everybody just calls me Mano. Skip wanted me to be your guide today, because I grew up in Chicago."

"I'm Frank. What, if I may ask, is your job description here, Mano?"

"I share various duties with a few other people in Skip's cabinet."

"Okay, then tell me what 'Skip's cabinet' is?"

"You know, like the president of the United States. He has his cabinet of advisors and so does Skip."

"Great, just great, Skip thinks he's the president," mumbled Kurt.

"Zip it, Kurt," snapped Frank. "So, you're one of Skip's advisors."

"Not really, Skip won't take advice from us...or anyone else, for that matter. We're more like trusted employees. You guys have never met Skip in person?"

"Chuck, Frank, and I never met him. Kurt knows him."

Kurt shrugged as if he'd almost forgotten ever meeting Skip. The gesture was meaningless, since Mano wasn't looking at him. "Yeah, I've met the guy a few times...years ago. He was friends with my fiancée. They knew each other growing up."

"Oh, yeah? Her name wouldn't be Darci, would it?"

"Um, yeah... Why do you ask?"

"That's the only person he ever brings up from his childhood."

"That's nice to know."

"I just think it's interesting. Everybody in America has heard of you guys, and Skip's closest employees have all heard of Darci. None of us knew the connection."

"Also nice to know, Mr. Manokowski."

"Please call me Mano. Here we are. This particular studio is filming some of our shows right now. So follow me and don't get alarmed, because most of what you see is staged."

Kurt smirked. "It's fake." He was so obsessed with Skip Bower that Brian, Chuck, and Frank might as well have not been there. Kurt had a fleeting moment of satisfaction in hearing that Skip's reality shows were not real. Mano was the unwitting target of Kurt's ire of all things Skip and of all shows fake.

Mano was quick to correct Kurt. "No, not faked. Skip creates a unique environment, one where he gets the most out of his host and guests. Spontaneously, of course."

"Whatever. Staged, then," Kurt insisted. Not giving Mano a chance to argue further, Kurt shifted his focus. "Tell me, are any of these shows on television?"

"No, most of them are on the Internet, but he is planning on getting them on television. That's why we thought of you."

A skeptical Kurt suspected "thought" had nothing to do with it. He would have been gratified to know that Mano nearly said just that, but had mentally regrouped before "need you" had escaped his mouth.

"Okay then, so tell me, why aren't they on television now?"

"Oh, that. I'm sure you know that Skip was blackballed from all the major networks a few years ago."

"Blackballed? Oh, do tell." Kurt had heard something but wasn't going to let Skip's infamous fall from grace go without airing it again for all to hear.

"Well." Mano hesitated just a moment or two. "He was the producer on that famous singing show a few years ago. You remember the one. It hit the airwaves like gangbusters! Anyway, he was accused of cheating by doctoring the votes to get higher ratings."

For once, Kurt wasn't disappointed to hear Chuck's laugh as he chimed in. "Yeah, I remember that…but his name wasn't Skip. It was Johnnie Johnson, aka JJ from the Bronx."

"Yeah, one and the same. He was known as JJ from the Bronx, because it sounded more cutting edge."

Kurt and the rest of the guys started laughing, with Kurt's voice rising above the others.

"So, JJ from the Bronx is really Skippy from South Bend, Indiana." Kurt was thinking that this was getting better and better.

Until he heard Frank's voice. "Kurt, could I have a word? Gentlemen, please excuse us." Kurt had known Frank long enough to know he better be on his toes.

Once the two men were out of earshot, Frank whispered, "Listen, Kurt, I know the history. I know what's going on, but first and foremost this is business." Frank was talking so fast it was hard to keep up. He couldn't second-guess Frank because he had no idea where Frank was going. "This guy? Guys like JJ or Skip or whatever…they take short cuts like the vote thing. You, you… you're giving him the keys, you look weak, and if I notice that, you can bet your bottom dollar this obsessed nut job will, too. Get a grip and don't mess this up! Darci? That's just a fantasy. So do yourself and us a favor, get a backbone and look like your usual annoying self or get out."

"Shut up, Frank. This is not Pointy Foods."

"Damn right it isn't. We're in this one together, and I'm not going to let your jealousy ruin a potential moneymaker." If Kurt had timed it, he would have seen that Frank's diatribe took twenty-nine and one half seconds. A record. "Now get your ass moving. I'm here to make money!" Thirty-two seconds.

Mano, after nearly revealing too much, continued, "When you're young and successful, Hollywood can be very good to you, but with just one little mistake, it can also be very cruel. Skip was the top up-and-coming producer in Hollywood, and next he's on the outside looking in. He sued for all his royalties and got a pretty nice settlement, but nobody would hire him after that, still won't, and that's why we have to go on the Internet now. But, as they say, success is the best revenge."

Kurt was wondering who "they" were, and revenge for what? He'd cheated! Plain and simple.

The group moved on, entered Studio A, and witnessed what resembled more of a three-ring circus than a reality show studio. By the first stage, they could see what looked like an operating room with large windows on one side, separating the judges from the contestants on the other side, while affording them full view of the procedures.

They were judging three separate and different plastic sur-geries. The prize? The winning "rookie" surgeon got a portion of his student loans paid off, and the patients got free plastic surgery that they could ill afford otherwise.

Brian was wondering what kind of people would sign up for surgery by rookie surgeons. Especially the kind of surgery that almost always had visible results. Not voicing his question, he instead said, "Mano, you mentioned that this is one of your newer shows and these surgeons are right out of medical school."

"Yeah, that's true, and you can tell we've had a couple of botched nose jobs, and it's not uncommon for one patient to end up with two different breast sizes. But we figure the patients know that is a possible outcome."

"Wow, they can win first and third prize in the same wet T-shirt contest."

"Nice, Frank, I heard Larry the Cable guy say that same joke before, but nice anyway." Kurt was not amused, especially since Frank had voiced what he had been thinking.

Frank seemed to ignore Kurt's comment, pressing on with the questions. "What about liability? There's got to be enormous liability associated with slicing and dicing on air. And not even by regular surgeons."

"We spend a lot of money on insurance, and we also make every person associated with any of our shows sign waivers—hard copy and holograph."

"Holograph?" Frank was doing the actuarial computations in his head, finding little to convince him that insurance and waivers was enough of an answer when he latched on to Mano's reassur-ances. "Is that loony California-speak or what?"

"No, sir, not at all. Hard copy is the standard medium, and holograph is taped. You know, videotaped so the parties are seen and heard. It doesn't hurt to be redundant when dealing with security and guarantees."

"Redundant, Huh? I can think of one or two here who are redundant...without their money, of course," Frank muttered.

Kurt was inwardly pleased that Frank had inadvertently given him a moment to digest the guarantees and waivers by pursuing Mano's grandiose way of putting things. On the other hand, Frank had opened that particular door, so Kurt was not taking his advice to let things go. He now wanted to and resolved to see as much as possible, with the thought that he may well discover a major flaw in Skip's operations...and he didn't mean the onstage surgeries. "Hey Mano, what's going on in this area? It looks like there's a large, live audience."

"There is. This is one of our most popular shows. It's called Wall Street Wally. The host, Wally Schwartzman, was a successful Wall Street money manager...indisputably one of the best."

"Wally Schwartzman?" Kurt knew the answer, but he had heard that red flag word again: "was." It was a favored tactic of Kurt's to get information by diversion. Usually worked like a charm. "So what happened that he ended up here?"

Mano's face was too neutral for the lack of expression not to be forced. Kurt could tell that he was asking all the wrong questions. Wrong for Skip and his cabinet, anyway. "Wally went crazy when he caught his wife cheating on him with her podiatrist. Turns out she had a foot fetish, and the doctor used his knowledge to seduce her. It happened right before the 2008 financial meltdown. Skip tracked him down in a mental institution a year later. He helped Wally get back on his feet, and in return Wally helped Skip make a lot of money in the stock market. Wally hasn't fully recovered mentally, but he is somewhat functional, and he is brilliant. I guess you can say he's an eccentric person."

Kurt smirked. "Hmmm, I see, because Wally makes you lots of money, he's not crazy. He's eccentric."

Mano either didn't catch or chose to ignore Kurt's sarcastic tone. "Exactly. And our goal is to keep him busy twenty hours a day on his reality show."

They quickly peeked from the back where the audience was seated. Wall Street Wally was dressed in what could only be called a 1970s disco suit.

"Wally likes to wear strange outfits. Each day, he picks a different theme and today must be disco day. That means sometime next week, he will dress in a hard rock, '80s outfit. Tomorrow, he might wear combat fatigues or a wet suit or a tuxedo. You get the picture." Kurt and Frank were each thinking that this guy would get along just great with Chuck.

"Yeah, he's a nut job." Frank had no patience or inclination to mollycoddle nutcases, and it was obvious to all four of them that this guy was a major nutcase.

"He may be that, but the fans love him, and he really knows how to pick great stocks. Besides, being eccentric in dress choice doesn't make him a major nut job... Yeah, well, I guess he is, but he has a tremendous following, and that counts in this business."

The group walked past many other stages on the way to Skip's office, seeing, as they passed, a variety of strange shows being filmed.

"Let's see what Skip has to say." Kurt wasn't eager to hear but was eager to get this over with.

The men entered a fancy conference room, where they were joined by some of Skip's employees. After the tricky-to-follow, back-and-forth introductions, they all sat down.

Mano started the meeting with a cookie-cutter opening, "Welcome, representatives from the Sportsfan Chronicles. It is my pleasure to introduce to you to our founder and boss, Skip Bower."

With obviously rehearsed timing, Skip entered the room dressed in a very expensive suit. It was completely white and perfectly fitted to his slim frame. His blond hair was thick and gelled back in a style that Kurt didn't believe had been fashionable for at least twenty years. He was probably going for some sort of retro-eighties look, but his first impression was Mr. Roarke from *Fantasy Island* becoming a televangelist.

And it seemed Kurt wasn't the only one who was less than impressed. He heard the start of Chuck's familiar snickering behind him, followed immediately by a yelp. Turning, he saw Chuck rubbing at his shin, a glaring Frank beside him. He offered Frank the briefest of nods and returned his attention to business. Chuck never took anything seriously, and Brian might be too easily impressed by the no-doubt persuasive pitch that was about to come. Frank would keep a steady head and a well-aimed foot. Kurt knew that he was counting on him to do the same.

All of Skip's employees boisterously clapped and cheered, reminding Kurt of a dictator and the requisite response from all those under his control.

"What's with all the hoopla?"

"It's not hoopla, Kurt. It's the way I roll," Skip responded as he walked over to Kurt to shake his hand. It didn't escape Kurt that Skip walked over to him first.

"How's Darci been?"

"Oh, brother... She's fine, Skippy."

Skip sensed some tension in Kurt's voice and decided to ask more personal questions, giving value to the concerns Frank voiced earlier.

"Great, that's good. Did she make the trip?"

"No, Skip, she did not make this trip. She's in New York City."

"New York City? Are you two still together?"

"Yes, Skip, we are still together, but she occasionally works in New York City. Now can we get down to business?"

"Okay, okay, sorry, too much small talk."

Skip then went around and shook hands with Brian, Frank, and Chuck. "Guys, everybody in America is following you! You guys won the largest lottery jackpot in history. Now everybody wants to see if you will be able to raise the additional capital needed to purchase that football team. My sources say that you guys have done a great job so far, but you have only half the money needed. Am I not right about that?"

"Tell us something we don't already know." Frank was wondering why this dipshit was wasting time on small talk and on what everybody already knew. Why else would they be here? "Cut to the chase. What's your angle, Skip?"

"No angle, Frank, I want to help you reach your goal."

"Of course you do. Every con artist in America has already approached us. So we're used to smelling bullshit," said as only Frank could (or would) say it.

"Well, I may be a lot of things, but I'm no con artist, and look around you, I do know how to make money."

"So who are you, Skip? You dress like you're a Fortune 500 CEO. A far cry from your Indiana days." Kurt felt a kick he guessed was from Frank.

"This is the real me, Kurt."

"Really? And yet you surround yourself with the craziest looking characters I've ever seen."

"That's Hollywood, baby!"

"Okay, Hollywood, how are you going to make us money?" Frank voiced some of Kurt's thoughts, reminding him that Frank's abrasive manner had its uses.

"I want you to invest in my company."

Frank cut in with, "I told Kurt here and our partners that I thought you wanted us to do an infomercial."

"That's true. I do want you to do the infomercial, and I'm planning on giving you a large sum of additional stock for doing it."

"There's more than that." This, extracting information, was Frank's métier. "What else?"

"You'd be right. I'm hoping you will invest in Reality Frenzy."

"Ha, I knew it! I knew that there was more to this." Kurt had said all along that there was more to this proposal. Frank agreed but wanted to follow up anyway, thinking there might be an angle beneficial to their fund-raising efforts.

"Listen, I needed to get you here in person, so that was a teaser. You're here now. Might as well just watch my presentation and concentrate on our company's financials."

Over the next few hours, Skip impressed most of the guys with his presentation, and Frank voiced that, too.

Kurt almost conceded. "I have to agree with Frank that it is impressive...if it's true. I think you probably cooked the books." Brian and Chuck didn't disagree but neither did they voice an opinion.

He was surprised that Skip was neither angered nor even surprised by the accusation. Which only served to confirm his suspicions further. "No, Kurt, I didn't. You're welcome to have your accountants audit my company's financials."

"Well, gee, thanks, old pal, and trust me, we will. Just make sure our accountants get more than the one set of books, if you get what I mean."

Brian couldn't quite appreciate Kurt's suspicion. After all, the guy offered up his financials. "It looks good to me. It's a no-brainer."

"Yeah, spoken like a no-brainer, Brian."

Frank was also surprising in his even tone, giving Kurt pause for thought that, as usual, Frank had something else in mind. "No, Kurt, it does. It does seem like a lucrative deal..."

This, coming from Frank of all people, shocked Kurt. "Perhaps it does, but we aren't moving on it until our accountants verify the numbers. I'm just a little surprised, Frank."

"That's because you didn't let me finish. It seems like a lucrative deal, and no doubt his financials will show that. So I, too, want both sets of books from your accountants before we leave today. You wouldn't respect me if I failed to request that, would you? They are certified accountants, of course? Am I right?"

Skip's smile never faltered. "That's fine and, yes, certified. You'll have all we have." Which, in essence, confirmed Kurt's suspicions regarding doubled bookkeeping.

Chuck said little. He was still in his imagination mode, seeing himself going through the program on camera. Besides, the best person to take care of that end was Uncle Walter, who could find the most elusive discrepancy, mainly because it took one to know one. "Are we still going to do the exercise video?"

"Yes, I wasn't lying about that."

Kurt made it clear he was not going to participate in the video, but Skip had other ideas. "But you have to. You and Brian are the main focus of the video. You guys are the sports fans who won the lottery. This is a video for regular guys who need to just get in or stay in shape."

"I am in good shape."

"Not as good as you think you are." Brian threw out at Kurt's claim.

"Okay, a little rusty, maybe, but in good shape nonetheless. Maybe I am a little rusty."

Skip persisted. "The deal is, Kurt's in the video or there is no deal."

Chuck couldn't imagine anyone not wanting to do this, but Kurt had his suspicions about Skip's insistence and decided to play it out.

"Come on, Kurt, say something. Say yes."

Finally, just to keep things moving, Kurt coughed out a "whatever."

CHAPTER 12

That's No Treadmill

Three weeks after the guys purchased all of Einstein's patents, followed by the road trip to Los Angeles where they agreed to Skip's terms, they were packed once again. This time, they were flying straight to Los Angeles to film the exercise video.

Chuck and Alice had spent the night at Kurt and Darci's. The limo service was picking Darci and Alice up at 7:00 a.m. for their flight back to New York City for Fashion Week. Chuck was planning to go with Kurt to the office, although no words had been exchanged regarding the arrangement. It was, however, assumed. Then, after the meeting, as agreed, Kurt, Brian, Frank, Chuck, and Bernie were scheduled to depart for LA.

Little had changed. Chuck had just ruined Kurt's breakfast again by drinking all the cream and leaving him only burnt toast. Chuck, a master at rationalizing everything, justified his behavior because he thought Kurt should have awakened much earlier.

Chuck was already showered, dressed, and ready to go. Aggravating Kurt in the kitchen was what he thought Kurt deserved. By now used to Chuck's shenanigans and disgusted by his lack of respect for others, Kurt skipped breakfast in favor of getting ready in peace in the downstairs bathroom near the front door. That Chuck followed him into the bathroom should have been no surprise. "I'm just saying, you two woke us up this morning."

"Chuck, there's no 'you two' about it. She was on the treadmill this morning."

"Yeah, right, at five thirty in the morning?"

"Yes, whatever time it was, it was the treadmill that was making the noise."

"LOL, Kurtis, LOL!"

Kurt grabbed Chuck by his arm to push him out the door, but before he could shut the door behind him, Chuck pushed back against it. Kurt tried again to shut the door, but Chuck was determined to have his say. "Fine, just tell me what kind of vitamins you're taking because you two were going at it for quite a long time."

"Out! Out! Get out now!"

"LOL, Kurtis."

"Quit saying LOL, quit calling me Kurtis, and quit acting like a buffoon!"

No sooner had the words exploded out of Kurt's mouth than Darci was back in the kitchen with a small suitcase by her side. Upon hearing her place the suitcase on the floor, he wrapped a towel around himself, so he could see her and embrace her before she left.

"What's the matter? You don't like my breakfast?"

"I love your cooking, but I don't like Chuck ruining it. Let's not waste time talking about it. You look beautiful. Do you really have to fly to New York again?"

"You know I do. I have to prep for fashion week. You knew that once I took this promotion I would to have to travel a lot. Especially to Manhattan. In fact, we should consider moving to New York City. At the very least, get a place there."

"What, and leave Chicago? Are you crazy? I love Manhattan. Hell, I was born there. But I haven't lived there since I was a little kid."

"Hmmm, that's right, I keep forgetting that you were born there."

"My parents met each other when they worked for Howard Cosell at ABC. Nowhere near where you'll be. It's a big city. First they were on Broadway across from Lincoln Center and then in the new building on Avenue of the Americas."

"Actually I believe one of the events is near there. On Sixth Avenue. That's on the Avenue of the Americas, right?"

"Yep, that's right." Kurt grabbed Darci, pulled her close to him and did an imitation of Howard Cosell. "There he goes! He could go all the way." Kurt never tired of his Cosell imitations and was convinced each was funnier than the last. Darci was usually of a different opinion.

"Why did you have to get promoted, anyway? And why did you have to hire Alice? When you earned this promotion, I never thought Alice would be by your side, more like on your coattails, getting a free ride."

Darci pulled away from Kurt. "Not this again. Alice and I started in the business together. Her resume is as good as mine, and she is loyal. She should have been promoted, too."

"Operative words: 'Started *in* the business,' as in not starting the business together. Besides, she'll never get promoted, and you will always be carrying her..."

"Stop. Why would you say that?"

"Why? Why would I say that? Because it's true. As many men as women are in positions to promote. She routinely offends any and all men with her all-men-are-dogs attitude. Only an embittered woman would promote her. Loyal? She's loyal to you, but she hates men."

"Well, she's dating Chuck."

"Exactly! She hates men."

It was obvious that Darci didn't want to leave Chicago in a lousy mood. Changing the subject seemed to be the best thing to do, so she asked, "What time is your flight to LA?"

"We have to be at the airport in six hours. We'll be leaving for the office soon...better to keep Chuck out of mischief; then we'll head out for the airport and then on to LA to do that stupid video."

"Kurt, I hear your tone. Be nice to Skip. He's an old family friend."

"You mean your old childhood boyfriend."

"Kurt, that is so blown out of proportion. He was my boyfriend when I was in middle school. We kissed when I was thirteen years old at the skating rink. We were little kids. Skip is a family friend."

"That makes it weirder. Every so often he creeps around. I think he still has a thing for you."

"Kurt, throughout Skip's adult years, I think he has asked out every one of my sisters."

"Did any of them ever date him?"

"Date him? I don't think so. Well, perhaps. There is a rumor that one of my sisters actually had a short fling with him."

"Aha! Thought so. Which one was it?

"I'm not saying because it was a long time ago, and I don't think it was anything serious."

"Was this before or after he called himself JJ from the Bronx?"

"Before."

Darci rolled her suitcase to the front door and turned around to give Kurt, still in his towel, a good-bye kiss when Alice and Chuck joined them by the front door.

"Good morning, Kurt. I see that you got up early enough to see Darci off. I'm impressed. I thought you would have slept in even longer. Well, at least you managed to see her off in your towel."

"Nice haircut, Alice."

"Kurt! She didn't get a haircut. She put her hair up in a bun."

"Figures. Could have sworn it was cut, but the bun makes more sense."

Alice's hands rose to the bun, perhaps without her even realizing it. "What is that supposed to mean? Nothing good, I bet."

"Nah, it's all good. You kind of dress like a guy. Figured you got a cut to go with the duds. Let's face it, you act like a guy!"

Alice was wearing a stylish, designer woman's suit that only a beautiful woman could carry off. Kurt enjoyed making fun of her, because she gave truth to the adage that beauty was only skin deep. He figured everything else was only skin deep, too—everything but her vile spirit and hatred of men in general. He knew those qualities were the core of the woman.

"Kurt, she looks great, and we're going straight to a business meeting from the airport. The meeting is not far from our hotel on Central Park South, I believe, so it all works out thanks to Alice making the arrangements."

"You mean, thanks to Alice's secretary, don't you?" Kurt couldn't resist a smirk when he saw Alice's expression.

"Kurt, enough. You have our itinerary. Everything is there, except the meeting upon arrival. Admit it, Alice looks lovely, and we'll call it a day."

Chuck finally came into the conversation with, "Yeah, Kurt, you need to dress nicer when we go to our business meetings." Chuck might have fit the metrosexual description of clothing, had it not been for his penchant for oddities and imitation.

"Okay, Mr. Hoodie."

"I'm not wearing the hoodie anymore."

Alice nodded. "He promised me he wouldn't dress like that anymore."

"Well, thank you, Alice, for clarifying the situation. And Chuck? You are such a wussy."

Kurt's criticisms were much like water off a duck's back. Chuck just routinely shook them off. "I like to keep Alice happy, and I also miss dressing nice."

Kurt pointed at Chuck's clothing. "Sorry, Chuck, but if dressing nicer means wearing that, then it's not happening."

Chuck looked down at his suit. "What? What's wrong with the way I dress? I am happening, absolutely!"

"Glad you asked. First and foremost, you always have gadgets sticking out of your pockets. You also wear funny jackets."

As if Kurt hadn't said a word, Chuck continued his prior comment. "Dude, you got lots of money now. Why don't you upgrade to the latest fashions? I don't get it. Our girlfriends are the head buyers for the department stores, and you can't keep up with the latest fashions?"

"First of all, Darci is the head buyer for the department stores. Your girlfriend here is her lowly sidekick. And if wearing that fedora on your head is the latest fashion, then I'll stick to wearing my Chicago Bears cap."

Alice cleared her throat, both to indicate disgust and to indi-cate that her participation in this conversation was over. "Come on, Darci, let's go. We have to get to the airport, and the limo is waiting."

When Alice turned around and moved to kiss Chuck good-bye, he dramatically took off his fedora and held it behind her back. As Chuck kissed Alice, he opened an eye, winked, and gave the thumbs up sign to Kurt and Darci.

So much for unadulterated passion, thought Kurt. Keeping the comment to himself, he said, "I think I am going to puke." He actually meant it.

Darci pulled Kurt's arm and gave him a quick kiss good-bye, but Kurt was still annoyed by Chuck's stupid comments and was not convinced that all was said.

"Yeah baby! Here they go again! Kissy, kissy!" Kurt hated being right.

Darci squeezed past Chuck and headed toward the limousine, but not before Chuck could ask her one last question.

"Hey, Darci, do you think it's wise to use the treadmill right before you go on this three-hour flight?"

"What? I didn't use the treadmill this morning."

"Ha, ha, ha, of course you didn't. I knew you didn't."

Alice was laughing as she pulled her suitcase toward the car, meeting the driver halfway.

Darci looked from Alice to Chuck to Kurt. "I don't get it. What's with the treadmill?"

"Come on, Darci, I'll explain on the way to the airport."

CHAPTER 13

Taken for a Ride

As Darci and Alice pulled away in the limo, Chuck, in character as always, was dancing and waving at them apparently not caring that he looked like a clown. The girls gave one last wave, and Chuck took off his hat and gave them a courtly bow. He then spun around and tried to enter Kurt's front door. Kurt was blocking it and had no intention of letting him through.

"Aw, come on, dude, let me in. We have to get to the office and then fly out of here. Why do you look so pissed off?"

"Because I am. Okay Chuck, here's the deal. Go across the street to Brian's and give me a few minutes to get ready. I'll come get you on the way out." Not waiting for a response, Kurt shut the front door.

"Come on, Kurtis, at least let me have my briefcase. All my essentials are in it."

"Tough. I'll get you in a few minutes. Now let me finish getting ready."

"Whatever."

Kurt packed and finished getting dressed in record minutes. He grabbed Chuck's briefcase and suitcase, then took them with him into the garage. He taped an envelope with Chuck's name on it to his front door. It contained a twenty-dollar bill and a note that said, "Take a cab, and don't worry, I have your briefcase and your suitcase with me."

As Kurt opened the garage and started driving off, he noticed

Chuck peeking through his neighbor Mary Lee's bedroom window. Victor had left his car parked in Brian's driveway again. Chuck was spying and laughing at Victor through the window. Kurt had known all along that Chuck couldn't wait at Brian's house, because Brian had left earlier to pick up Bernie.

About ten minutes later, Chuck showed back up at Kurt's house and found the envelope on the door. "I'm calling his ass up!" He dialed Kurt's cell phone. "Kurtis, turn around and get your sorry ass back here now!"

"Take a cab."

"Why? Because I disturbed your breakfast? For making that joke about the vitamins? Come on. You have my wallet in my briefcase."

"I saw you peeking in Mary Lee's bedroom window, you pervert."

"No, no, Kurt, it's not what it looked like. Brian wasn't home, which you probably already knew. When I saw Victor's car parked in the driveway, I decided to see if I could see Victor and talk to him about a ride."

"Yeah, I bet you did."

"I did. I did see Victor, and he saw me, but he was trying to wave me away. Victor didn't want Mary Lee to see me as they were getting intimate. So I couldn't resist making faces at him. He was getting so mad, but he didn't want to say anything so he tried to ignore me. It was funny, really funny."

"You are funny, Chuck. A real funny guy. I left you money in the envelope. Enjoy your ride."

"You left me twenty bucks for the cab when I need at least thirty to get to the office."

"No worries, Chuck. If you're short, I'll send Kalia down with the rest. Your cab should be there any minute."

"I see him. He just pulled up. This is bullshit." Chuck put on his fedora and strolled out to the cab.

The driver barely looked at Chuck as he asked, "Where to, bud?"

"Park Ridge, um, take me to the Pickwick Movie Theatre in Park Ridge." The Pickwick Movie Theater, one of the oldest theaters in the country, was only about three miles from their office, and Chuck was giving himself a mental pat on the back for thinking of it.

Chuck was initially mad at Kurt, but as the minutes in the cab dragged on, the driver began to annoy him as well. He'd tried explaining the situation—how Kurt had locked him out of his house and taken his wallet, briefcase, and suitcase. The driver had seemed momentarily concerned about the missing wallet, but only insofar as he wanted to know how Chuck intended to pay him. Chuck opened the envelope just briefly enough for the cabbie to see there was indeed money in it, though not how much. But except for the wallet, the driver seemed completely indifferent, saying little more than the occasional "yeah" to Chuck's ranting. He didn't sympathize. He didn't ask any questions. He didn't even tell him to shut the hell up (the way his friends did). Thirty minutes later, the cab pulled up to the Pickwick Movie Theater, and Chuck didn't feel in the least bit guilty about the prank he was going to pull on this disinterested man.

Tapping the meter and still not looking at Chuck, the driver said, "That'll be thirty-five dollars."

"Yeah, right. From your mouth to God's ears." Chuck took off running into the Park Ridge Library. He then sneaked out the back door and jumped on a bus that would drop him off right in front of their office.

As Chuck exited the bus, he talked to himself out loud. "Hasta la vista, cabbie!"

As he walked toward the office building's front door, he made the mistake of turning around at the sound of a car door opening and slamming behind him.

The cab driver was actually much larger than Chuck had imagined. It was like those circus clowns who would topple out of a miniature car—one after the next. Only there was just one man, dressed in a camouflage shirt and faded slacks. His hair was pulled back in a tail that left his weathered face exposed. The bland expression was gone as he leapt from the open door. "You rotten son of a bitch!"

"Oh, shit!" Chuck knew this could be trouble. He raced toward the entrance but fell as he was about to reach for the door handle, giving the cabbie time to catch up and put him in a headlock.

"Okay, buddy, okay, you got me. Let me pay you." Chuck waved $18 at him.

"Not good enough. You now owe me fifty instead of thirty-five."

Instead of handing the cabbie the $18 and negotiating a settlement, Chuck threw the money at the cabbie's face, quickly grabbed his fedora off the ground and made a run for his office front door.

This was no longer about the money. This was about the disrespect Chuck habitually heaped on service people. The cabbie ignored the money and tackled Chuck in front of the office door. Chuck struggled to extend his arm and eventually was able to pound on the front door and yell for help. People passed and no one tried to help. In truth, no one even questioned why a man would be trying to tackle him. They all knew Chuck, after all.

Meanwhile, Kurt sat comfortably at the conference table with Frank and Brian. Brian was showing impatience. "I wish Chuck would get here, so we can get this meeting started. And finished."

It was on the tail of Brian's last word that they heard Chuck's voice as if from a distance. "Get this buffoon off me!"

Kurt couldn't help but laugh, "I believe Chuck has arrived."

Kalia entered the conference room, wearing an expression of concern. In her hand was a battered fedora hat. "Chuck tried to take an early exit from his cab ride without paying. The cab driver is very angry. Enough so that he roughed Chuck up a little bit."

Brian now joined Kurt in laughing, although not really knowing why, except that Chuck was in the middle of something clearly not to his advantage. Frank reached for his wallet and asked Kalia to bring the cab driver in so he could be compensated.

The cab driver apparently accepted the invitation, shoving Chuck in front of him with every step into the conference room. There were some tears, stains, and missing buttons in his once flawless suit. But there didn't appear to be any bruising on Chuck himself.

"He tried to rip me off!"

Frank offered a thinly veiled apology. "I hope this will take care of his bill." He handed the driver a brand-new $100 bill.

The driver's dour expression didn't change, but he released Chuck and accepted the bill. "That will take care of it. Thank you."

As the cab driver turned to leave, Chuck grabbed a glass of water from the table and poured it on the cab driver. "Now get out of here."

Before the cab driver could retaliate, Frank reached in his wallet and handed him another $100 bill. "Please take this money. Now. And please leave because I've run out of one-hundred-dollar bills."

"Apology accepted. Thank you, sir."

"Here's your hat, Chuck." Chuck thanked Kalia as he took his crumpled fedora and placed it on his head. He then turned to see Kurt and Brian laughing uncontrollably.

"Not cool, Kurtis, not cool!"

"And, what exactly was that all about?" asked Frank, who had a history with and an appreciation for cab drivers.

Chuck seemed to realize that he would not come out looking good in this story, so he shrugged off the question. "Nothing. It was a misunderstanding."

But Frank had just paid $200 of his own money to an irate cabbie, so the dismissal wasn't good enough. "Please explain to me, explain to us, what that means. A misunderstanding?"

"It's not my fault. Kurt left me behind this morning, and he took my briefcase, which happened to have my wallet in it."

"Really? Kurt did that? Why did you do that, Kurt? Why did you not wait for Chuck?"

Before Kurt could reply, Chuck started in. "Let me tell you why. Kurt couldn't take a joke about him and Darci…"

Kurt stopped laughing to cut Chuck off. "First of all, I'd watch what you say, Chuck. And you, Frank, this is not Pointy Foods and you are not my boss. If I did anything, I did it for a reason and with forethought. Chuck, do you really want all the morning's details revealed here?"

Chuck waved his hands as if that was all it took to brush away the event. "Okay, it's over; let's get on to business. I would like to start with the charity auction for Chicago's most eligible bachelors."

"You, Chuck, are trying my patience by talking in riddles. What charity auction? And how are we going to make any money on a charity? What's it? Some sort of tax write-off?"

"No, Frank, it's not a write off, but it will get some of us guys some free positive publicity. The participants will be auctioned to the highest bidder next weekend. Then, sometime later, they're going to have a photo shoot, and the most handsome bachelors will be featured on a calendar."

Frank looked from one man to the next, then asked, "How come nobody contacted me? I'm available and I'm rich!"

"Now that's funny, Frank; that's really funny!" Kurt couldn't believe that Frank actually asked why he was not part of the auction.

But Brian put it into words. "Sometimes money can't buy everything, Frank. For one thing, you have to be handsome."

Chuck was jumping around and pointing, in his own childish way, at Frank, who was ignoring the possibility that a contestant might be expected to have more than money.

"I may not be a pretty boy like you, Chuck, but lately I've been getting a little action. The ladies seem to like me a lot more now that they know I am worth a lot of money."

"How can they tell, Frank? You wear the same wrinkled suits every day. And according to your nephew, your penthouse is a mess." Kurt knew this to be true by virtue of the reports from Frank's nephew.

"Well, Meathead doesn't know everything, now, does he? He doesn't always drive me around at night. Sometimes I take a cab and show the ladies our corporate offices. I like to show the ladies our corporate offices. I like to do that. They really like Chuck's office, with all of his fancy gadgets."

"My office? Be careful. That's high-tech stuff in there." Chuck got up and headed to his office.

Kurt knew he should just let Frank have his bragging moment, then get on with the meeting. Calling him out on his "ladies" would accomplish nothing productive. But there was too much history between them, and he couldn't let it go. "I know you do, Frank. Last Thursday night, you scared the new cleaning lady when you walked into the hallway half-naked at ten. Ten at night, Frank. Half-naked."

Frank seemed genuinely surprised. "I did? I don't remember that. I must have had to use the bathroom."

"Of course, Frank, you were too drunk to remember."

"Okay, I see your point, but how the hell did Bernie make it on this calendar? He isn't actually a pillar of fitness lately. In fact, he gets winded walking up a flight of stairs."

Brian answered, "He didn't make it. The committee said that they didn't have a spot for him."

"Where is Bernie?"

"Kurt, I'm surprised you had to ask. He's in the bathroom again. He's been working out every morning this week. He was hurt when they rejected him, so he started working out. Now he wants to ask out the physical trainer he hired. She's got Bernie eating a lot of fiber and other health foods that make him shit and fart a lot."

Steering the conversation away from Bernie's bowel movements, Frank asked, "Who's in this bachelor thing? Or more to the point, who, like yours truly, isn't?"

Brian answered. "Just Victor and myself are doing this. Kurt and Chuck declined the invitation, because they're dating Darci and Alice…respectively, of course."

Chuck reentered the conference room holding a DVD. "Umm, I'm in, because Alice doesn't care."

"Yeah, right. Alice would kick you to the curb if she knew you were in the bachelor auction. Darci doesn't care if I do it. I just think it is stupid. It's not my thing. What's with the DVD?"

"So glad you asked. It's a recording from the motion-activated hidden security camera in my office."

Chuck walked over to the big-screen television affixed to the conference room wall and started playback of the security recording just as Victor walked in.

Chuck, having learned nothing (as usual), was back to his smirking, idiotic self. "Hey, it's the Italian Stallion. We're glad you could join us for work this morning. Sit down and watch the show."

Victor was not smiling. "You, I should hurt you, Chuck. You almost ruined my morning with Mary Lee. You stoppa laughing right now. Itsa not funny."

"Sorry, Victor. I couldn't resist. I thought you weren't going to Los Angeles with us."

"Yes, I want to for first day, then to New York City for fashion week. Neva' miss a year. Every year I go."

"You would." Frank found it hard to understand what Victor was all about and going to Fashion Week voluntarily was beyond Frank's frame of reference.

Chuck was busy setting up the security DVD player. "I think I have the video of Frank and that woman in my office."

And the smile returned to Victor's face as he turned to Frank. "Oh, good for you, Franco, that you gotta lucky."

"I guess." Frank was wondering, on so many levels, whether he did get lucky.

Chuck hit the play button, and the laughter was immediate upon seeing Frank stumble into Chuck's office wearing nothing but underwear and a tight tank-top-style undershirt with a bottle of booze in his hand. His words were hardly original, but the intent was clear.

"Come in here, darling... look at all my...my fancy electronic...eh...stuff."

Brian didn't know what to think. "Real smooth, Casanova. Let's see this pretty girl of yours."

Frank mumbled to himself. "Dear God, I hope she was pretty."

"Come over here and take a sip, darlin'. A pretty filly like you deserves the best."

Frank was holding the bottle up in the air as someone entered Chuck's office. Whoever Frank had let in with him was possibly a woman. They saw a tight skirt that ran well above the knee and across her razor-stubble thighs that seemed, in all fairness, more muscular than fat. She was stumbling a bit on high heels and had stepped out of one shoe without seeming to realize it.

"Let me have a swig of that, Frankie." The husky whiskey voice was probably female.

The blouse was as tight as the skirt, and it was clear that she was straining against the buttons across the stomach. Her hair was wadded up in a bun that had come half-loose. With the smeared makeup, it was impossible to tell for sure from the footage if she was, in fact, a biological woman or a cross-dresser.

No one in the conference room watching this was holding anything back. The laughter was loud and raucous.

"Wow, Frank you sure know how to pick them."

"Thanks, Kurt, I don't remember what she looked like? Okay? I had a few drinks in me."

"You must have been really drunk."

"Yeah, Brian, probably so. Can't deny it. They all look beautiful after a few drinks."

"Franco, mio amico was that even a woman?"

"Come on, yes, of course it was a woman. I think."

Frank put his face close the video screen. His expressions were of disbelief and disgust.

Frank was relieved to see her partially undressed. Her bra looked in danger of bursting as well, but at least she was clearly a woman. "Thank God."

Chuck was the first to concede. "I guess it is a woman."

The woman sat on the floor, staring all around at Chuck's surveillance junk. Her attention returned to Frank only when he began heading back to the door. "Where're you going, Frankie?"

"Hold on, darlin', I have to use the bathroom first."

Frank was seen grabbing his bottle of whiskey and stumbling out of Chuck's office.

"That is if I can find the bathroom first."

"You are funny, Frankie; it's down the hallway."

Frank stumbled down the hallway and apparently entered the bathroom at the same time the cleaning lady did. She screamed at the sight of Frank.

Back in the conference room, Frank walked over to the video recorder and hit the stop button. "Oh, boy. Well, that was one night to forget."

"Who was that woman that you brought into Chuck's office, Frank?"

"Sorry, Kurt, I have no idea. I don't know. I think I called her Olga."

"Okay, then, what about the poor cleaning lady? Is she going to sue Frank for sexual harassment?"

"What are you talking about? She walked in on us."

Brian shook his head. "Let it go, Kurt. I already took care of her. I gave her a bonus, and she knows that Frank is one of the owners and a top executive with our firm."

"Top executive! Kurt, I think I like the way that sounds."

"Good, maybe you should start acting like one."

Kalia interrupted the awkward topic. "Excuse me, your ride to the airport has arrived."

CHAPTER 14

Panic in the Sky

The guys arrived at the airport for once eager to get away. Putting some distance between themselves and the nuisances that had been occurring here and there seemed to be just what the doctor ordered. Actually they were happy...except for Chuck and Bernie. Chuck and Bernie were downright cantankerous. Being stuck in narrow seats in the tail of the plane will do that, especially when the other members of the group were up front, way up front in first class. Not being in first class was one thing, but the "great divide" of first and rear came with dramatic differences, not the least of which was the feeling of turbulence when there was none. Discontent was high because they reserved the better seats, thought they paid for the better seats, and expected the better seats, yet here they sat. Bernie in a middle seat and Chuck on the aisle.

Bernie was more passionate in his attempts to change seats because of his size. Even changing to an aisle seat and staying in the tail section would be better. Making the situation worse was Chuck's refusal to switch seats. His reason to Bernie was that he could at least stretch his long skinnies sitting on the aisle, but the real reasons he refused to give up his seat was, one, he wanted to make his way to first class and, two, Bernie wanted to change seats.

When they boarded, Kurt sat next to Brian and Frank sat next to Victor. They didn't bother to hide their amusement when

Chuck and Bernie boarded with coach passengers, arguing with each other every step of the way.

"Come on, Chuck, give me the aisle seat. I'll never fit in the middle seat."

"No way, big boy, the aisle is mine, deal with it! The seat is mine. See what my boarding pass says. It says twenty-two *D*. Yours says twenty-two *F*. Can't argue with the boarding pass."

It might have quieted down then and there had it not been for Chuck's invariably bad behavior of waving his ticket with the prized seat assignment in Bernie's face. Actually Chuck was waving it in and against Bernie's face. Back and forth, up and down, the ticket brushed every part of Bernie's head and face.

Chuck never seemed to grasp that one can push another only so far. Bernie grabbed the offending ticket from Chuck's hand and ripped it in half, and then in half again. And again. Their friends sitting in first class had difficulty keeping their faces straight, and the rest of the boarding passengers, in a state of mounting anger and impatience, wasted neither words nor time in telling them to move on. They actually started shoving the two men forward. Chuck reached down and picked up each little scrap of the paper that was once his boarding pass and ticket.

"This doesn't change things. The aisle seat is mine. Deal with it and you…you guys stop laughing, because you've got it made in those big seats. I'm stuck back there with big boy."

"Come on, you dipshit, just give me the aisle seat."

"Not going to happen!"

"Two of you could sit in that seat with room to spare. Me? I'm stuck in blood clot city here!"

Chuck's final words on the subject: "Sucks to be you."

<hr/>

The plane finally took off without incident, and Kurt settled back, stretched his legs out, and discussed the upcoming deal with Brian, who himself had stretched out for the duration of the flight. Kurt's concerns were more to do with Skip than anyone or anything else.

"Brian, I'm not sure we should be doing this fitness video. For one thing, there's definitely a weird factor about this. I can't put my finger on it, but trust me when I say something is not quite kosher. And it has nothing to do with Darci. The Darci thing is just a nuisance that neither Darci nor I need, but that's all it is. A nuisance."

"Gee, Kurt, you're saying this now?"

"Not really saying anything, just telling you I feel something's a little off-center. Maybe it's okay, and it's Skip who is off center. Just saying."

"I get that, but even without your feeling that it's not quite right, I don't understand why Big Bro Ken isn't in on this. Your brother is nuts with this stuff. He's all over the place. Can't miss him on YouTube. And that Skip, aka JJ…how come he never even mentioned your brother once? You'd think his name would've come up."

"First of all, the only name this idiot remembers is Darci. I, myself, didn't come to mind until that story blasted—"

"What story are you talking about?"

"The lottery thing. Not so much the largest win in history, but that the other unknown winner had the same hand-picked numbers, same city, same zip code as my boss had. No surprise JJ popped up. Darci is his main thought, but the luck issue is seductive. A few people seem to think that luck rubs off. That and the connection with Darci is what got this guy going."

"Good point in theory, but it doesn't mean that's all there is to this, Kurt. That doesn't explain why he never brought up Ken's name or, more interestingly, why you didn't. Ken not being in on this seems a little weird, considering who he is and what he does."

"Listen to me. I would never suck him into this silly venture. My brother is simply Ken to us, but he's Sergeant Ken to the public. He's known all over the country for his fitness boot camps. He doesn't need to do business with a guy like Skip. Ken is not tight with gimmicks. Skip? I can't wait to see how far this arrangement strays from the initial concept to the gimmicks we saw on those stages. Telling you, Brian, it doesn't feel good."

"I checked it out"

"Wait, Brian, if you thought it was such a great idea, you would've said something. You know Ken."

"I wasn't sure about it, and there's the whole boot camp thing he's got going. I did check out his YouTube clips. I checked them all. Kurt, he's *the* fitness guru to go to. Over a million hits. Come on, that's big time."

"Well, leave it at that. I don't see him associated with anyone whose credentials include the word *blackballed*."

"But still, a million hits."

Mention of a million anything was more than enough to get Frank's attention. "A million hits! Sign him up now!"

"Why, Frank? He already has his videos for sale on his website. A trilogy set, no less. Why would he need JJ? Answer: he doesn't need JJ."

Frank wasn't going to let go without a good fight, and immunity for family meant nothing. "What's the name of his website, and why don't we own it?"

"What, startfitness.com? We don't own it, because it's not for sale, Franky. He started it in the late nineties. He doesn't need to even think about selling anything." Kurt's justifiable exasperation was beginning to show. It always did when he was, in effect, talking to a brick wall.

"I'm going to have to check it out. Everything's for sale, and nothing's not for sale. Keep that in mind, Kurt. Yeah, I think I'll check it out."

"Sure, Frank, you do that. You'll have a heart attack after the first five minutes."

"What a lunkhead," Frank murmured. "I said I want to check it out, not do it. I'll give it to Meathead for his birthday. If anybody needs to go to boot camp, it's Meathead."

"I heard that, Frank! Do you get that it's an exercise boot camp?"

"So what? I'm still checking it out, and if I like it, he might be just what we need for this venture."

"Never happen. You're lucky that I'm doing this video. Besides, if JJ messes with Darci, Ken and I will break the idiot in two. How will that work out in your financial plans?" Except for his tour in Iraq, Ken was the most nonviolent guy Kurt knew, but Frank didn't know that."

Bernie suddenly appeared next to them, and he wasn't happy about his seat. Chuck was the focus of his discontent and wasn't about to hide it. "I tell you, Chuck can be such a prick!"

"You think so? How are you two getting along back there?" Kurt was biting his tongue so as not to say more. Bernie was right, but adding fuel to the fire in a small, enclosed place was not a good idea.

"It would be okay being back there in those narrow seats if I had the aisle seat, but he refuses to give it up. I have no room back there, and he thinks it's funny to make me climb over his legs when I get up to use the bathroom. All those fiber bars are wreaking havoc on my stomach. And he knows it."

"He knows it and doesn't care, and that, Bernie, my friend, is the essence of Chuck. How many fiber bars are you eating every day, anyway?"

"A lot. I'm eating around twenty per day. I need to lose weight, and they are supposed to help." Kurt just stared. "But I keep farting all the time."

"No shit, Sherlock."

Brian couldn't help but add, "On the contrary, my dear Watson. I bet there is a lot of shit."

"Well, gee, thanks, Brian. It's easy to make jokes while you sit up here in first class. I feel like I'm going to blow up now. Plus, I had explosive diarrhea in the bathroom in the back."

"That explains it. No wonder everybody from the back keeps using the bathroom up here. The stewardess said that they had to close one of the bathrooms in the back." Kurt had been wondering about the parade of people in and out of the front bathrooms.

"Yeah, well, pretty soon they're going to have to close the one in front, too. I gotta go again." Bernie started moving toward the front facilities.

Kurt was still laughing for a handful of seconds before he realized what was about to happen. "No! No, come on, Bernie, use the bathroom in back. You're going to stink up our bathroom."

"Well, Kurt, and I mean this from the bottom of my heart, tough shit!"

Brian had no intention of breathing foul air. "Stewardess, stop that man! He's about to drop a bomb."

The stewardess's face went white. "What did you say?" Several of the passengers around them had also gone quiet, suddenly turning to look at them.

Brian shook his head. "Nothing, I was just kidding. Not that kind of a bomb"

"Sir, you can't say that."

"Well, ma'am, I'm sorry, but he's the guy who stunk up the back of the plane."

Her head spun to face the bathroom. "Oh shit!"

"Exactly, ma'am."

The flight attendant had no intention of enduring the foul odor for the remainder of the flight. Unable to stop Bernie in time, she was left with nothing to do but pound on the door. "Excuse me, sir!"

"Whadaya want? I'm kinda busy right now."

"Sir, please stop what you are doing, and go back to the bathroom you used earlier."

"You're kidding me, right? You have to be kidding."

"No, sir, I am not kidding! Please stop before you smell up the front of the plane."

Meanwhile, the guys sat back in their comfortable and not yet smelly seats laughing.

"Ma'am, with all due respect, how do I know the other bathroom is not being used right now?"

"Trust me, I know! No one has gone near that bathroom since you last used it! You need to stop and leave right now."

"Okay, fine, but only if I get an aisle seat."

"Yes! Fine, sir! Now!"

Bernie finally unlatched the door and exited. The guys were still laughing as he was led out of first class toward the back of the plane.

He took a moment to stick his head back through the curtain dividing first class from the rest of the seats. "It's all yours, boys."

"Good luck with that twenty-fiber-bars-per-day diet. I hope it's worth it to you."

"Thanks, Kurt."

Frank grumbled, "I'm glad she got him out of there before he could use it. I really got to go. All those drinks are catching up to my bladder." Then he made his way to the front of the plane.

Frank opened the bathroom door, slammed it back shut and yelled, "It's too late, damn it! Bernie pulled a fast one on us, and he didn't even flush!"

Brian sounded truly distressed. "Shut that door! The smell is spreading everywhere up here."

By now, everybody in first class was moaning as the awful smell spread across the whole section, permeating walls and clothes and hair.

Kurt, too, was uncomfortable and trying not to breathe. "Shut the door, Frank!"

Pulling the front of his shirt collar up over his mouth and nose, Frank muttered, "I'm going in, boys. I got to go." Nature called, and Frank entered the bathroom.

Kurt shook his head. "That's sick. I'm going to see if there's an empty seat elsewhere." By the time Kurt made his way to the middle of the plane, he found Bernie already there in his new aisle seat. Kurt then looked up and saw Chuck in an aisle seat in the last row of the plane, trying to put the oxygen mask over his nose.

Hoping everyone on the plane could hear him, Kurt screamed, "Bernie, you stunk up both ends of the plane!"

As planned, all eyes were turned to Bernie, not Kurt. Even the attendants weren't bothering to order Kurt back to his seat—so angry were they with Bernie. Not that he seemed to care what anyone thought. "Yeah, well, now I'm laughing at you. One could say it was karma."

It was no surprise that the remainder of the flight continued without event. The unfortunate incident was said and done in a short time, because bathroom humor is humorous only as long as one is not involved. The foul odor that had permeated all, but the middle passenger area, had dissipated. Chuck kept a tight hold on the oxygen mask. Bernie finally had his aisle seat…in the middle of the plane.

CHAPTER 15

Chuck Leaves His Mark

The six of them left the airport and arrived at the Reality Frenzy studios, where they were immediately escorted to a locker room. With few words between them, they hurriedly changed into their exercise clothes. Kurt, still not eager to participate, was wondering why they felt the need to hurry. After all, nothing was going to start without them, but hurry they did.

Five of them were dressed and ready. Chuck, on the other hand, was dressed but not ready. He had disregarded the dress rules and attired himself in workout clothes he brought with him. His workout clothes were adorned with logos from other companies, and other company logos were contrary to everything they were doing. It was left to Skip to run out and make sure Chuck had something else to wear, something, anything without the logos.

"Here you go, Chuck. These should fit you."

"Thanks. I forgot about the logo rule. These look like they'll fit."

"Yeah, sure. Just hurry up."

Chuck took off his shirt, and it was then that Kurt and Brian got some sorely needed comedic relief. Chuck had a tattoo on his chest. If there was anything to laugh at, it was this.

Pointing to a tattoo of a very muscular man with Chuck's head on it, Brian bellowed, "Who the hell is that?"

Staring down at his chest, Chuck answered, "Who do you think it is? It's me! Alice helped me come up with it."

"Sorry, Chuck, that's not you. That's your head on somebody else's body."

"Well, it will be me! After we make these videos, that's exactly what I'll look like!"

Everybody was laughing, including Chuck himself. "Okay, okay, I'm in good shape, but I will admit that this picture is a little stretch."

"A stretch? A more accurate picture would be your head on a stick."

"Well, gee, thank you, Brian, for the assessment of my physical stature. If you like that, then get a load of this," continued Chuck, as he turned around and showed everyone the tattoo stretched across his lower back.

Even though nothing should have been a surprise where Chuck was concerned, Kurt couldn't hide his reaction. "Oh my God, you got a tramp stamp!"

Everyone in the room broke out into even wilder laughter, including Kurt.

Chuck was now turning his neck as if he could somehow see the name etched onto his lower back. As if he'd thought it might have changed from when he'd had it done. "What? What do you mean a tramp stamp? That's *Alice* on my back." And indeed it was. The large, left-to-right tattoo said *Alice*.

Kurt summed it for him. "You're right, you freaking idiot! Alice is on your back. You didn't have to put her name on your lower back for anyone to know that. You put Alice's name on your back! What were you thinking, Chuck?"

Kurt's response had changed the mood, and Chuck was genuinely angry. "Come on, guys. Give me a break. I'm getting into body art."

"Body art? You look like an idiot. Let me ask you this, Chuck, did Alice get any tattoos with your name? No need to answer that. I know she didn't."

"You're right, Kurt, she didn't. This is something I wanted to do for her. End of story."

Chuck tried to ignore them, while he continued to change, but ignoring them became impossible once he dropped his pants and revealed he was wearing a jockstrap. The laughter was deafening.

"Okay, okay, what now?"

"Dude, you're wearing a jockstrap. On top of that, you wore that on the plane."

"Give it a break, Kurt. You know I like to be prepared."

"No, I don't know that. Not to this extent, anyway. Go back in the stall and change."

"Why? We're all men here."

Bernie managed to stutter out between laughs, "Apparently some of us are more men than others."

"Bernie's right, and nobody wants to see your white, pimply, bare ass. Now go back into the stall and finish changing."

"Whatever." Chuck took his clothes and finished dressing in the stall to the relief of everyone present, most of all Kurt.

With Chuck's reluctant cooperation, they finally made it to the studio, where several cameramen and an aerobics instructor by the name of Shannon were busy setting up. Shannon was dressed in a black and pink spandex outfit and was clearly the only person in the room with any business wearing such a thing. With her cropped hair and headband, she reminded Kurt of Pat Benatar, which immediately depressed him because he was sure she hadn't been born before the last time Benatar had, had a hit song. He wouldn't commit to even saying she was old enough to buy her own drinks.

But it wasn't simply her youth that he found depressing. It was the way she looked at him. The way she looked at all of them. All six of them were millionaires, some even famous. She looked at the lot of them as if they were all her favorite uncles. She smiled, but there was an ease of movement that let them know she didn't care what they thought about her. Skip followed and was already talking before the door shut behind them. The *Fantasy Island* suit was gone, replaced by some equally absurd-looking khaki outfit that made him look like he was preparing to go on safari. "This is going to be great. Regular guys around the world will be able to identify with this workout video. You'll be on infomercials everywhere, but instead of athletes, it will be regular, out of shape guys trying to get into shape."

"Speak for yourself, Skip. I work out all the time."

Kurt was already annoyed, but before he could go on, Briar chipped in. "Yeah, me, too. I'm in good shape."

"*Sì*, as am I. For the ladies."

Victor's comment was followed by Chuck's declaring, "I'm the cardio king!"

"You guys are average, I guess, and some of you? Let's just say, under average," said Skip, pointing to Bernie and Frank.

"Hey, don't lump me in with Frank."

Shannon walked up to Bernie and took his hand. "It's okay, you're going to be fine." Bernie's blush was obvious as he watched her walk away. In fact, except for Frank, all of them watched her walk away. She was certainly petite but still curvy enough to make them glad she was wearing spandex…and that they weren't. And while every man there was at least momentarily thinking the same thing, Bernie knew there was only one of them who might have a chance. He looked toward Victor and whispered, "You stay away from her, lover boy. She's going to be mine."

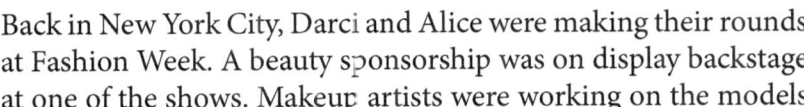

Back in New York City, Darci and Alice were making their rounds at Fashion Week. A beauty sponsorship was on display backstage at one of the shows. Makeup artists were working on the models seated on a row of director chairs, facing a wall of mirrors.

Darci's mind was flooding with ideas. Her forward thinking had gotten her to where she was and would likely propel her even further.

"It's not just about selling clothes, Alice. We need a wider platform. I've talked corporate into letting us take over the cosmetics department, too. We need to start selling more beauty products.

It should go hand in hand with selling the clothes. Think of cosmetics as another accessory…an accessory that no woman will go without."

"Oh my God, Darci, we'll be charged with buying half the retail product for the company."

"Exactly."

Neither had given a thought to their respective boyfriends since arriving. There was so much to do and so much more to plan. They looked forward to the changes and embraced their expanding roles.

<center>~~~~~</center>

The men, on the other hand, were second-guessing the decision to participate in the video venture. Once in the studio, it couldn't be denied that creating the video was far more difficult than Kurt and his friends had expected.

Shannon was putting them through their paces with no holds barred. She had them working on parts of their bodies that had never before been worked on. To make things worse, they looked especially awkward during the stretching portions of the routine, and stretching seemed to be part of every movement.

Kurt's reluctance was now validated, but victory was not sweet. "I am not physically capable of doing this yoga—this crazy stretching yoga! I knew it, Brian. I told you so!"

Brian could only gasp back, "Yeah, yeah, so what? None of us are."

"Speak for yourself, Kurtis."

When Kurt and Brian turned around in response to Chuck's comment, neither was surprised to see him with his legs positioned in a complete and perfect split.

"That's just so wrong looking."

"You mean it's so right looking! I told you guys I'm the Cardio King, and I'm also Mr. Yoga."

Brian looked away. "Whatever. I've seen enough."

Kurt pointed in the other direction toward Frank and Bernie, who confirmed his opinion that not one of them, with the exception of Chuck, was quite right for this video. All that came to mind was that they simply looked pathetic as they tried to stretch their legs and touch their toes. For all the obvious effort they exerted, they still reached only their knees.

Frank noticed the scrutiny and, Frank being Frank, wasn't bothered by that, but he did show some annoyance toward an all-but-inert Kurt standing there.

"Come on, Kurt! Get that skinny ass of yours moving. Do something. At least get ready. Rehearsal is over. The next round will be with cameras rolling."

As usual, Kurt blew off the order. It was an old habit from the bygone Pointy Foods days, but it really had to die once and for all. Until then, Kurt could only respond by humiliating the man. "Right, Frank! Get yourself a towel. You're covered in sweat… dripping is more like it."

Brian agreed, but couldn't resist adding that a towel would not do it. "Frank, you need, I mean really need, to shower before we film this routine."

Frank shrugged. "Okay, fine! I'll take a quick shower. Gotta look fresh for the camera."

Kurt was a little surprised by Frank's agreeable response but not for long. He watched Frank walk over to the table and pick up his towel, pulling a flask out from under it as he did so. Kurt continued watching as Frank opened the flask and poured the contents into his Gatorade. "Adding a little something to your Gatorade, Frank?"

Another shrug from Frank. "Of course I am. Need you ask?"

"No, Frank, that's what's called rhetorical, and—oh, geez, Frank, puleeze don't put that sweaty headband back onto your head."

Frank continued walking and left the studio, turning in the direction of the locker rooms with Gatorade in his hand and sweaty band on his head.

Sometimes actions do indeed speak louder than words. Frank's exit was more than enough to remind Chuck that he, too, could use a shower and change of clothes. Of course nothing in Chuck's world could go without saying, and he announced his intention loud and clear for all to hear, prompting Kurt to address Chuck's habit of leaving a trail of discarded items behind.

"Chuck, do not leave your jockstrap lying around where we will see it!"

"Don't tempt me, bro. Slightly used and fragrant? What's the problem?"

Kurt calculated his silence so as not to encourage Chuck on this line of conversation further.

Bernie, too, was headed to the bathroom, but not without announcing his intention apropos of nothing. "I'm going to the bathroom and—"

Brian cut him off, prompted by Bernie's problems with flatulence. "You better!"

Bernie's eyes flashed on Shannon, then focused back on Brian. "Hey, don't say anything."

Before he could say a word in response, Kurt cut him off. "Forget it, Brian, I think he's trying to impress the workout instructor."

"Probably. She does seem to like him."

He'd presumed the earlier bit of reassurance had been pity, but now that he thought about it, Kurt supposed it could be something more. Of course Bernie being true to form, maybe pity was his best bet, as far as attracting women was concerned.

But, truth be known, Kurt couldn't care less about Bernie's issues. He was still annoyed with himself for even being here. He sounded more annoyed at his friends. "I don't know how you guys roped me into doing these videos! Especially you, Brian. You know full well how I feel about it."

"Aw, come on. This is going to be fun. Relax."

"Relax? All I can say is that Victor got this one right. He has only this one video to do tonight, and then he gets to leave first thing in the morning, while we'll still be stuck here making fools of ourselves all week long. This is not my thing."

Forty-five minutes later, Kurt saw one of Skip's assistants walking by the studio. "Ah, the ubiquitous Manokowski, aka Mano, just who I want to talk to," he whispered, and intending to do just that, Kurt headed down the hallway, passing Frank and Chuck returning from the locker room as he did so. "Hey, you guys don't smell like shit anymore."

"Yeah that's right, Kurtis, and don't I look good, too?"

"Sorry, Chuckles, can't go that far—"

"Enough. Stop right there, Kurt. I'm going to cut you off before you make fun of me again. Where are you going, anyway?"

"I need to talk to Mano."

"Oh, Mano? I thought you were going to the locker room."

"Unlike you, I don't need to take a shower before I work out. I hope you didn't leave your nasty jockstrap on the floor near my locker."

"Don't worry. I didn't leave it on the floor near your locker because I know how you feel about that. You say it enough!"

A dubious Kurt continued down the hallway and caught up to Manokowski. "Hey, Mano, come here. Gotta minute?"

Mano had been looking anxious, but he quickly adjusted his expression to something that better simulated ease. Obviously for his benefit. "Hey, Kurt. How are the videos coming along?"

"Glad you asked. That's what I need to talk to Skip about. Where is he?"

Another hint of the anxiety before the false calm returned. "Skip? He just left, but I can leave him a message."

"That's okay, when is he coming back? I want to talk to him in person."

"Sorry, buddy, it'll have to wait. He's going to be gone until next week."

"Skip's going to be away for a week? What are you talking about? He was just here a couple of hours ago. He never mentioned that he wasn't going to be here this week. Where is he?" Kurt was beginning to get a bad feeling. He was also a bit annoyed, considering that he didn't want to be here in the first place and that Skip had insisted. "Where is he, Mano?"

"He's on his way to New York City. He said he's doing research for his new show. Don't worry. I can take care of things here. I always do."

And that, at least, was a way to explain his nervousness. Skip had left Mano in charge, but to leave a subordinate, even one of his top subordinates, in charge of a project on which he had so much riding made no sense. What could be so important to Skip? In New York? "Worried? I'm not worried. Just exactly what kind of research?"

"Design. He said it has to do with designers, so he'll be at Fashion Week. I think he said he wants to spend time with the buyers from department stores. *Buyer* being the operative word when you want to do sales."

What else was in New York? Kurt didn't mean to speak, but he nevertheless hissed out his girlfriend's name. "Darci."

"What?" And now the nervousness was giving way to a full-blown panic. Mano had realized too late that he probably wasn't supposed to tell Kurt about the trip to New York.

"I said Darci!" Kurt felt his blood pressure rising as he headed for the locker room. He was already at his breaking point with the video and now this. Skip was sneaking away to New York City, and he knew it had little to do with sales. He also knew he had to do something.

Turning back for a moment, he shouted, "Mano, wait here! I'm going to need your help." Kurt was not going to do the first video or any other video. He was going to catch the next plane to New York City. "Mano, I'm dead serious. Don't budge. I'll be ready in ten minutes."

"Ready for what?"

Kurt didn't bother to reply, but instead went into his locker. He was horrified to see Chuck's nasty jockstrap under his towel and on top of his nice clothes. Kurt, already in a high state of annoyance, yelled so loud that everybody could hear him all the way back to the studio.

"CHUCK, YOU FUCKING ASSHOLE!" It was so loud, it seemed to reverberate against the cold walls and uncarpeted floor.

The rest of the guys were together talking in the studio when the sound of Kurt's raw anger hit them.

Brian was the first to respond, and he knew full well to whom. "What did you do now, Chuck?"

Chuck burst out laughing. He was laughing so hard that he fell to the floor.

"What did you do, Chuck?"

"I stuck my sweaty jockstrap in his locker."

Everybody started laughing.

"Yeah," Chuck tried to continue. "I um…" But he found he couldn't finish the sentence. He was his own greatest fan and truly believed that his comedic talent was exceeded only by his fashion sense.

Brian had no such illusions. "Spit it out, Chuck."

"Okay, okay. I strategically placed it under his towel. So when he lifted the towel, he would see it on top of his clothes."

While they all resumed their laughter, Brian at least had the grace to say something. "Chuck, I gotta say, that's just wrong…on so many levels."

Back in the locker room, Kurt, now in a rage, punched the locker and bruised his hand and yelled again.

"YOU'RE AN ASSHOLE! A complete asshole, Chuck!"

Kurt's words fell on deaf ears, while Chuck was lying on the floor, laughing even harder, but he went on. "This is freaking nasty."

Bernie, who was in a stall near Kurt's locker, finishing yet another bowel movement, leaned down and peaked under the privacy wall to see what all the commotion was about, suspecting it had something to do with Chuck, mostly because it always did. When he did catch sight of Kurt, he saw that he was enraged. Seeing Kurt in what he called a red zone rage was more than enough inducement to lie low, and he decided to do just that. He remained seated, quiet and invisible, and, above all, out of it.

At that point, with little time to spare, Kurt carefully grabbed his wallet and keys. He came too close to touching Chuck's jockstrap and decided to skip the shower and leave everything else in the locker, including his nice clothes.

Mano, still very curious about Kurt's request for assistance, entered the locker room with more than a little trepidation in light of the raucous laughter and the lone angry voice.

Kurt wasted not another minute on Chuck's shenanigans, so intent was he on getting out of there. "Hey, Mano, I need you to get me to the airport."

"Okay. You want to go the airport, but what's with all the yelling?"

"Don't worry about it. Just get me out of here."

"No can do, buddy, you're supposed to be doing the video. I don't want to get into trouble."

Kurt knew screaming at this man would accomplish nothing. He took deep breaths as he explained, "Mano, you seem like a nice guy, so listen very carefully. I am going to cancel my investment in this company if I don't sit down and have a face to face talk with Skip now. And that would be real trouble! And as far as the exercise video goes, I'm not going to be in it. Now you can save your company's investment by helping me now, or I promise you, I will pull the plug. Your choice: hero or the alternative?"

"I hear you, but I don't know what to do."

"And I'm telling you... Just get me to the airport. It's that simple."

"But don't you want to get cleaned up first?"

"Nope. I'll go like this." Kurt's voice brooked no disagreement.

"Okay, I'll take you, but could you at least grab a towel? I don't want your sweat to get on my car."

"Fair enough. Now let's go." And so they headed straight out to the parking lot, Mano with keys in hand and Kurt with a towel.

CHAPTER 16

Eyes on the Prize

About fifteen minutes later, everybody was still standing around, waiting for Kurt and Bernie to return, so they could start filming.

Brian's impatience surfaced first. "Where the hell are they?"

Frank's hasty response was that he would go and bring them back, but then Bernie appeared and joined them in the studio.

"Don't waste your time, Frank. He already left."

"Left? Left where?"

"New York City."

"What?"

"I don't know, and I wasn't about to ask. He just left and said he's not doing the video, grabbed his wallet and stormed out of here. He left all his clothes in his locker."

And that started or, to be more accurate, restarted Chuck laughing at what he regarded as comedic brilliance. "Yeah, I'll just bet he did."

On the way to the airport, Kurt realized he had left his phone in the locker, giving him another reason to be angry at Chuck. "Hey Mano, let me use your phone. I left mine in the locker." Kurt wasted no time in calling Kalia at the Sportsfan Chronicles' corporate office.

"Hey, Kalia, I need your help."

"Kurt? Is that you? I didn't recognize the number."

"Yeah, it's me. I'm using Manokowski's phone. He's Skip's assistant."

"I know Mano. He's the one I was faxing all those contracts to last week."

"Okay, well, here's the deal. I need you to help get me to New York City ASAP."

"Okay."

"Wait, there's more. After that, I need you to get me tickets for the New York football game this weekend."

"Which game?"

"I don't care. Giants or Jets, whoever is playing this weekend. Just get me tickets."

"I said okay, but what if there are no tickets available?"

Kurt had the loose framework of a plan in his mind now. Planning his trip distracted him from thinking about Skip, so he just stayed focused on the plan and kept his voice steady. "Listen, Kalia, there is always a way to get tickets. I don't care if you have to get them from Eli Manning's or Rex Ryan's relatives, just get me the tickets. Find a way."

"Okay, Kurt, you got it. I'm on it."

He smiled for a second. There were still people he could count on. "Call me back at this number, because I left my phone back in the locker."

Beside him, Mano whined, "No, Kurt, I need my phone."

"Don't worry, Mano. I'll make it worth your while."

"Yeah, well, thanks. I have a feeling I don't have a choice."

"Mano, you are learning!"

Mano's phone, with perfect timing, rang just at that moment, and Kurt wasted no time in answering the call.

"Okay, Kurt, I've got you a first class ticket, but you have to be at the airport quickly because it takes off in ninety minutes. Ninety minutes, Kurt. No time to waste!"

"Good. Send the information to this phone. I'm already on my way."

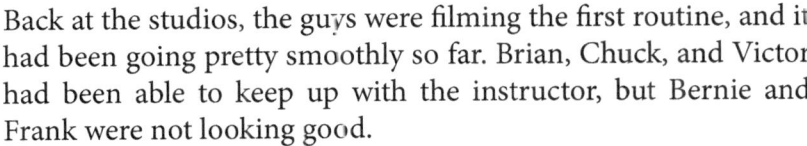

Back at the studios, the guys were filming the first routine, and it had been going pretty smoothly so far. Brian, Chuck, and Victor had been able to keep up with the instructor, but Bernie and Frank were not looking good.

Shannon instinctively knew that the filming was not going well. "Stop filming...cut...stop the cameras for a second." She thought this was as good a time as any for the guys to get a pep talk...from her! She'd noticed all of them staring at her. All except for the sweaty drunk, Frank. "You guys are doing great, but this isn't working. We need a different strategy. Frank, I know you're struggling, so I want you to slow it down."

"Struggling? What do you mean I'm 'struggling'? I am doing great and you..." Frank interrupted himself with hacking so explosive, he was forced to bend over almost double, causing him to hack even more. Shannon wasn't certain, but she thought she saw something solid come out of his mouth.

"My point exactly. Frank, you're having trouble breathing. That's bad for you and hardly motivational for any viewer. I want you to stay in one spot and march in place."

He wheezed with indignation. "What? Are you kidding? No way!"

"No, Frank, just listen. Don't waste time feeling embarrassed, because in sixty days, you might be able to keep up with the rest of them. Remember, these videos are to show where you are today and where you'll be in sixty days when we film again. Get it? We intend to show progress. Progress is motivational. Real guys watching real guys struggle and prevail."

"Soooo why do I have to be the one struggling?"

"Because you are struggling, Frank. This is real. Take it as a gift. Besides, I'm not budging."

Frank thought Shannon was being a bitch for singling him out when all of the guys were struggling. But, Frank being Frank, deciding she was a bitch actually made her seem more attractive, so he gave in. "Okay, but I can still jump in here and there and join the guys."

Brian wasn't so sure. "Frank, I haven't seen you move that much since the Pointy Foods basketball game."

"Oh, yeah, the good ole days…when my skyhook helped stick it to Marcus. Great game; that was a great game."

Shannon didn't know what they were talking about and didn't really care. Did they actually play basketball? She could picture Victor and Chuck easily enough, maybe even Brian and the guy who'd left after the warm-up. But Bernie? Frank? They'd be dead if they had to run a lap.

Still, thinking about it was just wasting time. "Okay, glad that's settled. Now, Bernie, it's going to get a lot faster. Remember, we're going to have lots of kicks and jumps. Don't be embarrassed if you can't keep up. Just modify the exercise and march in place with Frank. See where this is going?"

"Yeah, I see, but here's the thing. I may look like I'm out of shape, but that's just because of my gut. It's misleading."

Chuck laughed. "That's an understatement!"

"Shut up, Chuck, I can keep up."

Shannon had seen this sort of thing happen with other workout sessions. For some reason, people never got so tired from exercise that they couldn't work their mouths. She'd seen more than one session degenerate into a bitching contest, and she wasn't going to let that happen this time. Getting these "average guys" into shape was about more than getting some free publicity for the Sportsfan Chronicles.

Shannon had her own deal riding on these sessions, after all. If she impressed Skip with this project, he would be all the more likely to green-light her own reality show: *Pet Workouts*. People working out beside their dogs and cats, who could be trained to mimic the same stretches their owners made. She knew the show would be a hit, even if it was only on the Internet, and the money she got from product endorsements would be enough to pay her way through veterinary school.

She just had to keep these five motivated. "Okay, everybody, get a drink because it's going to get more intense. Hydrate!" Shannon had no intention of engaging. Letting them have the last word was no problem for her as long as they did as she directed and as directed, they walked over to the cooler.

Four of them were lost in their own thoughts. Frank was angry for being singled out. Victor was already daydreaming about the New York fashion show. Chuck was dwelling on Kurt's reaction to finding a jockstrap dripping sweat on his suit. Brian was worrying about his friend. Only Bernie's eye was on the prize, and the prize for him was Shannon. "Listen, guys, I think she likes me, and face it, she's a really hot-looking woman!"

"Oh no, Bernie's going to get a stiffy."

"Very funny, Chuck. Why don't you just shut up and stop dancing around like an idiot while you're at it?" Bernie unwrapped a fiber bar and ate it while unwrapping a second.

Brian had something to say about that, because Bernie's dietary habits were affecting not only each of them, but any and all others in close proximity. "I think you're supposed to eat only so many of those a day. How many have you already eaten?"

"Ummm, just a couple of boxes since we landed."

"Geez, Bernie, no wonder you're having bowel problems. You're gonna be the inspiration for the Fartsville app. Hey, maybe you can get the app royalties."

Bernie punctuated Brian's joke by lifting his leg and farting. "Don't you worry, Brian, it's out of my system. I feel fine now."

"You're never going to be able to keep up with us. Do we really want you to, anyway?"

"Very funny, Chuckles! Cut me some slack here. I have to keep up. I have to impress her."

It was Chuck who put a hand on Bernie's shoulder. "Well, okay, I feel sorry for you, Bernardo, so I'll help you get through this, but there's nothing I can do about the foul smell." Shannon called out, directing everybody back to his spot. "Okay, everybody, give me a spirit yell before we start!"

Of course Chuck was the only one to give out a yell. Most of them didn't even know what spirit yell meant, and they weren't sure they would join Chuck if they did know.

"Come on, guys, is that the best you've got? Again give me a spirit yell!"

This time, everybody did yell, but of course Bernie was the loudest. "Let's do this! Cue the music!"

The music started and everyone was once again in rigorous movement...for the moment, anyway.

CHAPTER 17
A Bit Too Much Reality

As the cameras rolled in California, Kurt had just landed in New York City, hailed a cab and was on his way to a clothing store to purchase all that he had not brought with him.

While in the dressing room, he noticed that Mano's phone signaled the arrival of a text message. From Skip. And of course Kurt was going to read it. This was war, and the text was intelligence. Little of value was revealed other than Skip's hotel name and room number. What followed, however, was that Skip intended to track down an old friend and that snippet of information confirmed what Kurt had suspected.

Kurt left the dressing room and instructed the clerk to total the purchases and check him out. "Here, I'll take all the clothes, shoes and the suitcase. No bag. Just put the things in the case."

"Very good, sir, would you like to open a charge account today? Ten percent discount if you do so."

"Sorry, not now. But I'll give you an extra twenty if you finish up fast and help me track down a cab."

"Yes, sir. I'll take you up on that and do you one better. The car is on its way."

"Another ten if you get it done in sixty!"

"Yes, sir, almost done. And there he is, sir, the black car by the curb. A pleasure doing business with you. Do come back." The clerk's final words were lost as Kurt rushed out the door toward the waiting car.

Meanwhile, Shannon had started the cardio program in the LA studios with cameras rolling once more. "Run in place. Raise your knees. Come on, come on, get those knees up."

Bernie was trying his best but was struggling just to keep up with the guys, so Chuck moved in next to him.

"Whatchya doing, Chuck?"

"Helping. Keep up with me. I told you I was going to help you."

"Help me? Go away! You're just making me look bad."

Chuck's hysterical laughter confirmed that was what he had intended. "Come on, big boy, lift them legs higher. Don't worry. The camera isn't filming us right now. They're focusing on Victor. Lift those knees up and pick up the pace."

Bernie squinted in pain. "I can't. I've got gas! And stop laughing! Just leave me alone. I think they're about to start filming this side of the room now. Just go away."

Chuck jogged back to his spot directly in front of Bernie's position. Frank was marching slowly in place, directly behind Bernie, and when the camera turned toward them, Frank tried to pick up his pace.

Shannon noticed what he was doing and reminded him, "Careful, Frank. Don't overdo it. You viewers at home who are out of shape, just follow Frank and work your stamina up over time. So Frank, please just march in place for now for the viewers." It escaped nobody's notice that, of all of them, only Shannon didn't appear to be sweating at all.

Frank had no choice but to slow down once he started coughing.

Shannon kept her voice loud enough to drown out most of the hacking. "Rome wasn't built in a day and neither was your body. Beginners, stick with Frank. Everybody else, try to keep up with us."

The music pace increased as Shannon started yelling instructions. "Get ready for three direction kicks."

The camera zoomed into the area where Chuck, Bernie, and Frank were exercising, and it was then that Bernie's worst nightmare came true. He couldn't control his body and broke wind very loudly on every kick with perfect timing.

"Front kick, back kick, side kick…front, back, side. Keep your legs straight, Bernie. Front, back, side…front, back, side."

Every kick was accompanied with a loud fart. Some were brief, like gunshots. Others rumbled like rolling thunder. Bernie tried to suppress them, but it seemed the harder he tried, the more forceful they were and the louder they came out. At one point he was actually afraid one of those farts would blow a hole straight through his pants. Bernie's face was red as he blushed with embarrassment. Between the blush and the exercise and the lights of the studio, he felt like he was slowly roasting. But he simply could not stop. The worst part was that the cameraman walked right up to him when the barrage of farts started.

Frank couldn't take much more of it. "Come on, Bernie, you're killing me back here."

The guys kept exercising and couldn't help laughing as they did so. Shannon was too busy watching everyone for signs of fatigue, her head filled with nothing but the sound of her own pulse and breathing, to dwell on what she assumed were sounds from an adjoining studio. Was a car backfiring outside? Was a gun being fired next door? Was someone training a team of barking seals? She had no idea about the strange sounds nor what everybody was laughing at, but as long as they kept up the movement, she didn't care.

Kurt, in New York City without his phone, had no idea what was going on in the studios and that was fine because he did not care. He had finally caught up to Darci at her hotel.

She was actually getting off the elevator, so lost in her own thoughts that she strode right past him with only a passing glance. She stopped a dozen paces later, turned back and gaped. "Oh my

God, what are you doing here?" She ran up to him, giving and getting in return a big hug.

He'd put some thought into what he would say to her and decided, until he knew exactly what Skip was planning, that the truth might…complicate things. "What else would I be doing here? Surprising you, of course."

"Well, mission accomplished. But what about the video?"

"What about it? I decided to not do it. If those guys want to do it, fine, but it's not for me. So I decided to catch up with you."

"Great, glad you did, but I have to work this week. Do you want to come with me to some of the events during the day?"

"Not really. But how is it going?"

"It's been great. Thakoon's embroideries were incredible. Tory Burch showed a collection with batiky patterns. SUNO had some interesting prints. Michael Kors had lots of bold stripes and blocks of color."

Kurt knew less about fashion than Darci knew about sports. Her enthusiasm was nonetheless infectious. "Wow, it sounds like this has been a good week for you. You sound as excited as me on NFL draft day. Well, don't worry. I won't disrupt your flow. I'm going to do some work while I'm here, and Kalia is getting tickets for this week's football game. I'll hook up with you when you're not busy."

"I am excited! It's been a good week, though some of America's designers are playing it safe with consumers. Everyone is still doing color blocking. Thank God that there's enough variety in New York to make it a successful buying season."

"Wonderful! Your company is lucky they have you. Hell, I'm lucky I have you. When are you leaving for your next gig?"

"Aw, sweetie, I have to go right now, and you just got here. Are you sure you don't want to come with me?"

"No. I don't want to interfere with your work. I'm just going to take care of some business while I'm here in New York."

They took five minutes to stop at the front desk, get another key so Kurt could get into her hotel room, kissed again, and parted ways. While he was rich enough that Darci never needed to work another day in her life, he knew that her work truly made her happy. No matter how many millions this deal or that deal brokered for him, Kurt knew none of it would ever make him as happy as his girlfriend was feeling right now, rushing off to another fashion show.

She was so excited, she hadn't noticed the new suit he was wearing nor the new suitcase he was carrying.

———

The guys had made it through the first day of shooting. Victor was heading to the airport to catch his flight to New York City, leaving the guys in Los Angeles to prepare and continue filming for the rest of the week.

Brian was exhausted and hungry. "Let's get something to eat. Now. Fast. Did I say *now*?"

"Heard you, but let's get something to drink first."

Brian was clearly ignoring the warning signs on Frank's face. But Bernie had noticed. "No, no, no. Come on, Frank, we have to work out tomorrow. Besides, we're all hungry."

"So what, you friggin' lightweight."

"Really, Frank? We don't get to stand there and march in place like a little lady. Like you."

"Somebody has to do it for the slower viewers. It was easy."

"You looked like you were struggling, Frank."

"Okay, okay. But for the record, I was fine. I'll order my drinks while we're eating. Brian, you, too, let's get going."

"Fine, Frank, but you also eat some food and no more fiber bars for Bernie!"

"Talk to me, Brian, not to Frank! And don't worry. I learned my lesson. No more than two fiber bars per day."

Brian's face pulled into a scowl just at the memory of the stench. First on the plane. Then in the studio. He decided that they'd find a restaurant with outdoor seating, just in case the bars hadn't finished working on Bernie's system. "You better hope they're able to edit those farts out. Thank God it's not Smell-O-Vision."

"Very funny, Brian! And sure they can. The cameraman said he will tell the editor to listen for them. And there's no such thing as Smell-O-Vision, stupid!"

All the guys were laughing and wondering why Bernie would even address the issue. It was what it was. No unringing this bell.

As they were heading for the door, Shannon stepped out of the women's locker room. The spandex outfit was replaced with a fun, little blue skirt and blouse, along with matching heels. The sort of thing one would wear to a party. She was also wearing a deep red, almost black, lipstick. Before anyone could comment, Shannon walked up to Bernie and told him very firmly, "No more than two fiber bars per day."

Bernie blushed again. "Sorry, Shannon. I hope I didn't ruin your video."

"It's okay. You did good today."

"I did? I mean, I did. Yes, I did."

Shannon just smiled and wished him a good night's sleep. Bernie got more from her than he would have imagined and less than he had hoped. He prayed for a fartless tomorrow.

And while Bernie was thinking about the embarrassing events of the day, Kurt was back in New York City. He decided to track Skip down and find out more about his real agenda. He knew it was more than the video series. Kurt spotted Skip in the hotel lobby and guessed that he was heading back to his room. He was dressed in a muted gray suit, something simple and elegant, as opposed to the more garish outfits he'd worn earlier. It was the sort of thing that would impress Darci. Kurt tried to catch up to him, but Skip was already on the elevator, so Kurt caught the next available one, no mean feat in NYC, where elevators were as crowded and as few as the cabs. At least Kurt knew which floor button to press. Skip was just opening his door as Kurt exited the elevator and approached him. "Skip, hold the door."

Skip was frozen at the door long enough for Kurt to close the distance between them. When he finally spoke, he gasped out, "What are you doing here? You're supposed to be at my studio, filming the exercise video."

"Not any more. I quit your stupid video."

"You can't. We have a contract."

"Trust me, I can and I did. You don't think Frank would put us in a contract with you without our having an exit clause, do you?"

Skip shook his head. "Impossible! My lawyer looked at it and said I was protected."

"Your lawyer sucks. Our lawyer is still laughing at the fact that you agreed to our contract."

"That can't be. My lawyer has got me out of a lot of jams before. I trust his ability. He—"

Kurt cut him off before he could babble any further about his lawyer. "Skip, you don't want to mess with me. Don't waste your time or my time arguing about lawyers. I have lots of money and the best lawyers in America. Those same lawyers are helping us build up our company, and believe me, exit clauses are their specialty. First and foremost. Sorta like checking fire exits in a crowded—"

"Geez, quit with the exits. If you hate me so much, why did you agree to do business with me?"

"Why? Primarily because I agree with my friends that your studios and reality shows can make us a lot of money. But I can put up with only so much. We've invested in lots of other companies that are doing pretty well. So I need you to come clean with me. What's up your sleeve? If I detect an ounce of bullshit, I will cut ties with you."

"Okay, okay, not out here. Come on in, and I'll explain everything to you."

Said the spider to the fly, thought Kurt as he entered Skip's hotel room. And saw Darci. Photographs of Darci. Pictures of Darci lay spread out on every flat surface of the room. He was immediately alarmed upon seeing the ones on the table. Some looked familiar, shots taken of her at various fashion events. Some were taken in connection with Kurt and Brian's winning of the lottery. Others appeared to be candid shots, seemingly taken without her noticing. *Just how the hell did Skip get close enough unseen to take those pictures?* he asked himself.

Kurt grabbed Skip and threw him against the wall. "What the hell is wrong with you? Are you stalking Darci?"

Some of the anger drained out of Kurt when he saw the look on Skip's face. It wasn't fear. It wasn't anger. Skip was pinned against the wall and was staring at him with a calm indifference. His tone of voice was closer to annoyed than anything else. "Get your hands off of me. It's not what you think."

Kurt released him. This wasn't going the way he'd rehearsed it in his head. Skip had gotten over his initial shock too quickly, had invited him into the hotel room, knowing what he'd see, knowing what he'd think. Something wasn't adding up. "Really? Then what're you doing with all these pictures of her? This better be good."

Skip brushed down his suit, seeming genuinely concerned that Kurt might have damaged it. "I purposely came up with the idea of having you do the videos, so I could get you away from her for a few days."

"No shit, Sherlock. You're just making things worse."

"No, I wanted to get you away from her for a few days, but not for what you think. I want her to be in one of my new shows."

"What? You gotta do better than that." But the tone of voice, the calm indifference to Kurt's anger, the whole setup... The explanation did answer a lot of questions.

"No, it's the truth. I want her to be a judge on a fashion reality show. See, look at this."

Skip opened a file folder containing promotional fliers. Kurt looked at the top one and saw Darci's name on it.

"See, it's the truth. I was going to pitch it to her this week, while she's here and you're away in LA. I didn't want you to inter-fere, and I knew you would because you think I just want to be with her. I want her for this show. She would be perfect for the show. It's just about the show!"

He looked through the file folder, then at the table, no longer focusing on Skip's face as he spoke. "Okay, so you're saying you don't want to be with her?" Kurt's head turned in order to take in every last one of the pictures as he asked.

"You want me to be honest, or do you want me to bullshit?"

Still not looking up, Kurt muttered, "I think you just answered the question, dumbass."

"I've had a crush on her since I was a kid. I know she doesn't think of me that way. Honestly, I know I don't have a chance with her."

Finally, Kurt turned his attention back on Skip. "Think of you that way? She doesn't think of you at all! I don't get it. You can get almost anybody, so why don't you just let it go? She's with me."

Skip nodded. "I know and I agree and I promise I will never cross the line. What do you think of her becoming a judge on the show?"

"Skip, the problem is you don't see a line. That's why you are always out of line! Ahhh, give it over, let me see the flyer." Kurt pulled the flyer out of the file folder. It looked good. Polished. Professional. As if a lot of time and thought had already been put into it. And Kurt had missed it. He'd been saying all along that Skip was up to something, had spent the last few weeks considering every angle that a con man could have worked. He knew Skip, knew how he thought and how he worked…and still he'd missed it. "It does look interesting, but it's up to her. But I really don't see her going on the Internet to do a show. She loves her job."

"That's the beauty of it all. She wouldn't have to change her job. That's what I'm talking about. I would work around it. Look, she knows what the buyers want, and she would be perfect for the show."

"I just don't see her on the Internet."

"Well, umm… That's the other thing I should probably tell you."

"What now?"

"Well, it won't exactly be on the Internet. It'll be on a major network."

"Network? I thought you were banned from network television."

"I am. Or was. But I still have friends in high places, and they remember how much money I made them before the scandal."

"You mean low friends in high places, don't you?"

"No, really, I've been in secret talks with some of the major players. They like what I've been able to do on the Internet, and they're close to accepting my proposal."

"And the video? What about our video? Is that all bullshit?"

"Yeah. I mean, no, it's not bull, and yes, it's legit. We will try to sell the videos on infomercials, thanks to a little loophole in the ban."

"Yeah, Skip, and that's what worries me. 'Loophole' should be your middle name."

"Whatever. Truth be known, I honestly wanted your brother and his *Sergeant Ken Boot Camps*, but he's not interested. So I concocted this idea to keep you busy for a week. And I do need you guys to invest into my company. The investment was not bullshit. Are we good?"

"I don't know." He'd contacted Ken. Of course he'd contacted Ken. Why hadn't Kurt thought to call his brother before signing up for this thing? Probably because he would have gotten the same let-it-go lecture he'd gotten from Darci, Brian, and Frank about his suspicions. Everyone had thought he was crazy not to trust Skip, and that had pushed him to deal with it alone. Which is why he hadn't bothered to even tell the guys why he was leaving before catching a flight.

Still, it did sound like a good deal. Kurt suspected he would regret what he was about to say, but said it anyway. "Yeah, we're good...but don't ever bullshit me again. If there's anything else out there I should know, now is the time to tell me. You go down, you go down alone. Everything I do is on the up and up. I mean it, Skip! My group is not part of your little cabinet."

Skip put the file folder back on the table and nodded. "On the up and up. I promise." He held out his hand to Kurt, who took it after a second's hesitation.

Still holding Skip's hand, he pulled him in closer to hiss out. "One more thing. About the up and up part. And Darci. Do not, I repeat do *not*, even think about anything that would compromise her. No loopholes. Up and up only. Take this as your chance to redeem yourself."

Skip still didn't break his calm veneer. He just nodded again. "I get it, Kurt. Enough already."

The week ended up being a lot of fun for everybody. For one thing, the guys successfully completed the video in LA. Bernie's wish came true when Shannon and he said "so long" and not "good-bye." The guys were not the least bit surprised when the two embarked upon a long distance relationship. They joked relentlessly that long distance was the only way it would work as long as Bernie continued his heavy fiber diet.

CHAPTER 18

Skip's Proposal

Darci would never come out and say as much, but she was glad that Kurt had skipped the video shoot to be with her in New York. She didn't expect him to understand what she was doing, as long he understood that it was important to her. And this week …oh, this week would change everything for her. If everything went well, by this time next year, everyone would be watching what she bought instead of the other way around. She doubted that even Alice could appreciate what was happening beyond the increased income it would bring to both of them. They would soon be trendsetters.

Not that she'd had much time to tell him. She suspected that Alice had blocked out eighteen hours of time for each day they were scheduled to be in New York, so that even when one appointment fell through, another seemed to materialize in its place. By the time she'd gotten back to her hotel room, it had been past two in the morning. Kurt had been fast asleep, not even bothering to sit up or open his eyes when she'd entered. He'd simply mumbled a "howditgo?" followed a minute later by a "luvyootoo" before falling back to sleep.

They'd shared an early room service. Kurt had begged off her second invitation to join her for some of the events, saying that he had some friends he wanted to look up. She'd thought it a bit strange that he'd traveled all this way to be with her and then didn't seem very interested in spending any time seeing what she was doing, but maybe he just felt uncomfortable in her environment.

Out of his own element. It didn't really matter to her, and after all, he had been born here so there probably were old friends he hadn't seen in years.

She'd had a 10:00 a.m. appointment with one of the leading leatherware designers on the East Coast when, ten minutes before he was meant to arrive, his assistant had called to cancel. *So sorry. Couldn't be helped. Maybe next year.*

She'd said it was fine, and really, she'd grown used to the last minute brush-offs over the years. Of course if everything went just right, in six months he'd be cursing himself for skipping an appointment with her. And she wasn't in the least surprised when, once again, another appointment seemed to manifest itself within a minute of the cancellation.

Of course at first she hadn't realized it was a business call. Looking at the caller ID, she saw that it was Skip. "What the hell," she muttered as she picked up. *Was he looking for Kurt? Why call her?* "Hello?"

"Darci! It's Skip. How have you been?"

"Great. I've been doing great, Skip."

"Wonderful. I was wondering if we could get together, maybe for a cup of coffee."

She smirked, wondering what Kurt would think if he could overhear them. He'd always suspected that Skip still had feelings for her. Skip certainly had not been shy about telling everyone about it. And while she always liked to deny it, she knew that there was something there, some irrational hope on Skip's part. But she also knew that nothing would ever come of it. Not just because of Kurt, either.

There was just something about Skip. Something...pathetic. Something no amount of fame or money could erase. A part of him had never grown up, never would grow up. In a way, she supposed she let the flirtations continue, because she felt a little sorry for Skip. It was probably the reason one of her sisters had dated him (although she had been honest with Kurt when she'd said she couldn't remember which).

Still, she really couldn't encourage this sort of thing. "I can't, Skip. I'm not even in Chicago today. I'm—"

"In New York. I know. I am, too. Look, I just want to talk with you for a few minutes. Fifteen. It's a business proposal."

"How did you know I was in New York?"

"It's Fashion Week. Where else would you be? I've got something that...it kind of ties in with that. Fifteen minutes."

"Look, Skip, it's... I'm booked solid with meetings and appointments and...maybe we can talk when I'm back in Chicago."

"I know you have a sudden opening in your schedule. Pete from Marianna Leathers cancelled, and there's no way you've had time to book another appointment to replace him yet."

Darci felt suddenly cold as she stammered out, "How did you—?"

"Fifteen minutes."

She nodded for several seconds before her mouth caught up with her neck. "OK. I'm at the—"

"The Starbucks across the street from your hotel." Then the call ended. Just like that. For a second, Darci thought that he'd gone through a tunnel and lost the connection. Then Skip's voice returned, just behind her, as a hand came to rest on her shoulder. "I know."

Wow, now I know what it feels like to have a stalker, thought Darci.

She would follow through with this meeting but knew that she would never look at Skip in the same way again. This is what stalkers do. She couldn't hold back her thoughts. "Skip, your actions are way beyond what I regard and know to be acceptable. You virtually stalked me. You interfered with appointments and the people with whom I had those appointments. Your acceptance of this behavior as being okay or being normal is a great concern to me. I cannot trust your judgment on anything. Apparently what you think is okay to do is okay for you...you don't question it. You can't just want something and then maneuver and manipulate everything and everyone in order to make it happen.

Where is your sense of proportion and concern of what another person may want? Who are you?"

I'm sorry, Darci, I didn't think—"

"Well, that's obvious, you just didn't think. You are so egocentric; you just do whatever comes to mind."

"What I meant was, that I didn't think you would take it this way."

"Skip, that's worse."

"I guess I didn't see it that way, but now I can. I am truly sorry. I was so excited about my plan that I got ahead of myself. I swear I will never do so again."

"Skip, one more chance, that's all, one more chance. You mess up like this again, you act presumptuous enough to act as if you are the only person in the world, you will surely know about it! You know, all this time I thought the guys were wrong in their opinions, but I have to admit they sensed the true nature of you and your intentions. Basically, if it is good for you, nothing else matters."

"Not true, Darci, I didn't think it would look this way. Actually I just didn't think."

She was disturbed, because as Kurt had said on more than one occasion, Skip had entertained romantic thoughts of her. She was more disturbed upon realizing how influential she had become. She knew that this weekend would mark some changes in her life—but she didn't realize that facets of her life had already changed some time ago.

———

The five minutes after finishing the initial pitch were spent fielding the obvious questions. How much time? How much money? Why her? All answered to her satisfaction.

So at the end of fifteen minutes, Darci was seriously considering the show. It would dovetail nicely with her own plans for expanding her influence in the industry and the timing couldn't have been better. But there was still one question that nagged her. "How did you know about Pete canceling his appointment?"

Skip could obviously tell that Darci was seriously considering his offer. He was relaxing into his seat, his measured sips of triple espresso growing less frequent. He was still nervously brushing at his suit, as if there'd been something on it earlier that he hadn't quite gotten off, but otherwise he looked like a man very much in control of his own world. "I have my sources. Let's call it secrets of the trade."

Darci shook her head. "What trade? Television? The Internet? Come on, Skip, you called less than a minute after Pete hung up. And you were already on your way here when I was talking with him, which means you knew he was going to cancel before I did."

He shrugged and offered an impish grin, but Darci just continued to stare at him expectantly. She wasn't letting this thing go. Finally, he sat up in his chair, looked down into the sparse grounds of his espresso. "Well, Pete is kind of a friend of mine. So I asked him if he could do me a favor and cancel his appointment with you at the last minute."

The smile remained as Skip nodded. "Well, *associates* might be a better word. You see, Pete's doing a show with me as well, and I convinced him that it would in the best interest of Reality Frenzy, and thus his own show as well, if I met with you as soon as possible."

"You threatened to drop his show if he didn't go along with it?"

Another shrug. "Six of one, half a dozen of the other. Regardless, it worked."

She nodded. "Yeah, I guess it did; and that says a lot about you." She didn't clarify. Let him take that any way he wished. "What kind of show could an East Coast leather merchant do anyway?"

"The kind that can't even get on cable. Let's leave it at that. But you, on the other hand…"

"Yeah, well, this is… Why didn't you just wait until I was

back in Chicago? You wouldn't have had to go through all this sneakiness."

"I wanted to see you alone."

"What does being in New York have to...Kurt. You were afraid Kurt would...what? Stop us from meeting?" She decided not to mention that Kurt had actually come into New York the previous night to surprise her. He'd probably figure it out when he learned how Kurt had skipped out of the video shoot.

And Skip's face tightened as he sat up. She could see now, for the first time, that just the mention of Kurt showed that Skip was genuinely afraid of him. "I'm not... Let's say he never ceases to surprise me. I don't want him to try to influence this deal."

"You mean influence me?"

He let out a single laugh. "No. I mean influence *me*. Sportsfan Chronicles is working on a big deal with my studio, remember."

"Yeah." She wanted to say that Kurt wouldn't be the sort to tank a deal out of pointless jealousy, but she didn't actually know that to be true. Gathering the material back into the folder, she slipped it into her briefcase. "Well, I'll look over all of this. I'm really in no frame of mind to make a major decision on this right now. But I'll get back to you."

He nodded, rising as she stood to leave. "I just wanted fifteen minutes of your time, uninterrupted, to make my pitch, like I said. Look at all of it. Call me after you recover from this week."

She promised to do just that as they shook hands and parted ways.

Darci tried to focus on Fashion Week, but Skip's offer just kept coming back to her. A television show. She'd never even considered such a thing, but the more she thought about it...and that was the problem. She kept thinking about it. She had to tell someone, get a second opinion, just share the moment. Alice could tell she was distracted but so far had just chalked it up to nerves.

Once they recovered from the exercise video debacle, Frank and Brian had spent most of the next day with Mano familiarizing themselves with the studio's other shows, as well as future projects in the pipeline. They were also brainstorming ideas for new shows, although at that stage, Brian imagined that Mano was just humoring them.

Nevertheless Brian was convinced that Norman Einstein had the sort of quirky personality that would fit right in with Skip's oddball programming. He imagined a show where every week the man would talk about another one of his inventions. From what they'd seen, he had enough to fill at least a year's worth of programming. And some of those shows would be de facto advertising for Sportsfan Chronicles–owned merchandise.

That Victor flew out to New York City for his annual presence at Fashion Week was no surprise, but detouring to Chicago on the way was another matter. Victor was usually solo at the annual event, with the intention of not remaining solo while there. Picking up Bulldog's girlfriend to accompany him to the event added a different texture to it all.

Equally unsurprising was that Bernie had planned to join a gym and commit to spending an hour a day there until he got back in shape. Again Brian didn't think that Bernie had ever been in any shape that he could get back to, but like Mano listening to reality show ideas, he thought it best to humor the man. Anything that got him to stop his steady diet of fiber fart bars could only be a positive thing.

Brian was in the middle of telling Mano the giant toilet story when he heard a muffled ringing sound. Looking around, he saw that it was coming from a suitcase propped against a wall. He hadn't noticed it earlier. "What's that?"

Mano's face seemed to open up from feigned polite interest to genuine concern. "Oh, that's Kurt's suitcase. I brought it here for when he came back."

"Is that his phone?" Brian had tried a half-dozen times to reach Kurt since his departure, every time getting sent to voice mail. Eventually, he'd given up, thinking that Kurt was a grown man and would get in touch with him when he was ready.

Brian got up, ran to the suitcase, popped it open, and dug through it...muttering, "I can't believe he went to New York without a phone."

"He's using mine," Mano explained. "He was so worked up, I didn't—"

Brian shushed him with a wave of his hand as he answered the call. The readout said it was from Darci. Trying to sound calm, so as not to worry her, he managed a weak "Hello?"

CHAPTER 19

Darci's Answer

Kurt was enjoying his impromptu vacation a lot more than he'd expected. With Skip settled out, he was able to relax, look up some old places he used to frequent, get in touch with some old friends, and make plans for later in the week.

Of course he hadn't really come to see the city. He'd come for Darci. He thought that maybe tomorrow he'd actually tag along with her. Most of the time, he could barely follow what she was saying when she talked fashion, but he imagined she was the same way when he began talking about sports. On second thought, to be fair, she knew more about sports than he did about fashion and retail.

Besides, there was a chance he'd see Victor at one of the shows. He wanted to ask how the shoot went after he'd left, but he hadn't quite worked up the nerve to call anyone. He imagined that anyone calling his phone would just assume he wasn't picking up. Unless Mano had told them everything…which Kurt rather doubted, given how scared the assistant had seemed by the time he'd left. No, probably everyone just assumed he'd gotten pissed off at Chuck for his jockstrap stunt and stormed off. That was fine with him. Time enough for the truth later.

He'd gotten back to the hotel early, just after nine, and settled in for a nap. He wanted to be awake tonight when Darci got back. He reached for the TV remote when he awakened shortly after midnight, intending to take advantage of the exceptional cable package in the hotel. Fifteen sports channels was too much to ignore. He enjoyed ninety minutes of basketball before he heard the click of the hotel room door. He muted the sound and looked up. Darci was the most welcome sight he could imagine, and yet she looked a little different.

There was something about her tonight that seemed just a bit…off. It was as if something was about to happen, and he was the only one who hadn't a clue what.

"How…did it go?"

Darci smiled a bit too broadly as she answered, "Great. Everything went great. I actually met with Skip today." *Ah, that was it,* he thought, she'd met with Skip and she was worried how Kurt would react when he found out. He knew better than to play it too cool, so he tilted his head and said a bit louder than necessary. "Skip! What did he want?"

She put down her briefcase and kicked off her shoes as she answered. "You'll never believe it. Guess."

"What? I…I don't know."

The smile was still there as she approached him. "Go on. Guess."

Kurt just shrugged. He hadn't expected Skip to meet with Darci so quickly. He hadn't really thought through what he would say to her when she broke the news.

He got up off the bed to meet her halfway. He kissed her briefly. *Uh-oh,* was all that came to mind. *Something doesn't feel right. I don't know what, but I'm about to find out.* Kurt and Darci had been together long enough that he knew not to trust this particular smile.

"Skip wants to do a fashion show for one of his reality programs. And he wants me to be the judge."

Kurt offered her a wide smile. "That's…wow, that's wonderful. I mean, is it something that you'd want to do?"

"Yeah. It really is. The more I think about it, I think it could be really great. But I guess I'm just worried how you'd take it. I mean, after all, you've made it pretty clear that you don't like Skip."

There was no point in denying it. "That's true. But I think

you can trust him. I mean, as far as the show goes. He seems to be really committed to getting this reality programming off the ground."

"Well, of course you agreed to do the workout video, so I figured you'd be okay with it. But that's you and Skip. And Skip and I would be something different. Right?"

Kurt shook his head, choosing his words carefully. "Don't... just...don't worry about me. If this is something you want to do, I think it'll work out great."

She was still standing inches away from him, the smile starting to drop at the edges, the voice suddenly becoming too soft, too sweet. "Really? It's okay with you? You'll let me do it? I mean, I have your permission?"

Since when does Darci have to ask permission? Kurt wondered. Something was most definitely wrong here. He took a step back without realizing he had done so. "Um?"

"Because, you know, if it wasn't okay with you, well, who knows what you might do. You might kill funding to his studio. You might catch the first plane you could and track him down. You might steal his assistant's cell phone, stalk him back to his hotel room, and physically assault him! I don't know, Kurt! I guess I'm saying I don't really know what the hell you'd do! What you're capable of doing! "

Kurt could remember every fight he'd had with Darci over the many years of their relationships. First, because they were so rare. Second, because when they did happen, they were things to be remembered. "Look. I was worried about you. When I found out that Skip had set up the workout video to coincide with Fashion Week, I guess I just...I don't know."

"You were worried about me?"

He nodded, knowing that any answer he gave would be the wrong one.

"And you were so worried that on your way to the airport, during the flight, on your taxi ride to the hotel, and when you were standing right next to me, it never once occurred to you to say, 'Hey, Skip's going to try getting in touch with you? Hey, I think Skip's up to no good? Hey, Skip's trying to keep us apart?' Anything? Not one single word to indicate that you trusted me?"

"I do trust you. Darci, it wasn't about you. It was about Skip and his lack of judgment. You? Never you. I was worried. I didn't know what he'd try." He sat back down on the bed, hoping that Darci would join him.

Instead, she remained standing. She was nodding in understanding, but the scowl remained unchanged. "I don't need you to ride to my rescue."

"What?" Kurt had never been one of those guys who was threatened by intelligent women. He'd loved the fact that a woman as intelligent as Darci had been attracted to *him*. But sometimes, the roundabout way her mind worked baffled him. How could his protectiveness turn into such a bad thing?

Reading the question in his eyes, she continued. "When you thought there was a problem, your first reaction, your only reaction for hours, was to keep it from me, to take care of it yourself, because you didn't trust me to take it as seriously as you. And when it turned out to be something else, you still needed to be convinced it was a good deal before you gave Skip permission to talk to me about it."

"I didn't..." And Kurt found that he couldn't say anything in his defense. It was exactly what he'd done. He hadn't realized it, hadn't stepped out of himself for even a moment in the last two days to consider what an outsider would make of what he'd done. He whispered, "Is that what I did?"

He hadn't really meant to say it out loud, but Darci answered nevertheless. "Yes, that's what you did."

"I'm sorry." He'd said it so softly, he wasn't certain she'd heard him. "It's in my nature to protect you. It has nothing to do with your ability to take care of yourself. I'm sorry. I know you have never been a damsel in distress type. I was reacting, not thinking."

"I called you. I wanted you to be the first person who knew, and I called you and Brian answered the phone, and he told me what happened at the workout. Then I talked to Mano. Then I called Kalia. Then I called Skip. Did you really think that with all those people would knew that I wouldn't ever put together…that you…what do you think…I felt like a fool not knowing what was going on." She paused for thought before going on.

"Every time I think you're being sweet, that you're just doing something nice, it's something else entirely.

Kurt continued reassuring Darci, letting her know that he was sorry, that he would never keep her out of the loop again… Well, he'd try hard not to.

He offered a slight smile, was gratified when she laughed in response. "So, are we good?"

<hr>

Skip woke to the sound of someone knocking at the door of his suite. A moment's glance at the nightstand clock told him it was just after three o'clock in the morning. Staggering toward the door, he didn't bother to look through the peephole before opening it. He was so tired that thoughts of safety were far from his mind.

But those thoughts quickly returned when he saw that it was Kurt standing in the hallway. "Kurt?" he croaked. What could Kurt possibly want with him at three in the morning? Without thinking, he snapped out, "I didn't touch her."

Kurt didn't seem to hear what Skip had said. He didn't seem to be fully aware that the door had been opened, and Skip was looking at him. "Are you okay?"

"Yeah. Darci threw me out."

Skip wasn't sure why Kurt had come over at three in the morning to tell him this. "I'm sorry."

Kurt brushed past Skip, walking into the suite. Skip was suddenly aware that Kurt was carrying a suitcase. He was trying to wrap his sleep-addled brain around what had just been said. Darci had thrown Kurt out? "You broke up?"

He took a step back as Kurt spun around, his face pulling back into that same rage-filled grin he'd shown Skip the previous day. Skip realized that he must have sounded hopeful, when he'd meant to sound surprised. Of course he actually was hopeful, but he'd meant to sound surprised. "I, um, I mean, I'm sure it's nothing that—"

"We didn't break up, you douche bag." Kurt dropped his suitcase beside a couch and stretched. "She threw me out of the hotel room, that's all. After she found out we'd talked, she was pissed... thanks to you." He collapsed onto the couch. "Really pissed."

Before Skip could offer an opinion, Kurt continued with, "So as I said, I'm blaming you, asshole."

Still not sure why Kurt had chosen to tell him all this at three in the morning, Skip tried to explain. "Look, by the time Darci called me, she already seemed to know most of it. I'm not the one who—"

"Not about her finding out. Darci's smart. I should have realized she'd figure it out sooner or later. I mean it's your fault I came down here in the first place. If you'd just kept everything up front, it wouldn't have set me off when I found out."

Skip could only shrug, seeing no reason in debating with Kurt at this hour. "Well, I already told you I was sorry, but I think Darci is honestly interested in the project, if that's worth anything."

Kurt nodded, stretching out on the couch and closing his eyes. "Oh, she's definitely interested. And like I said yesterday, if you try anything shady, I'll have a flock of lawyers descend on Reality Frenzy and pick it clean."

"Nothing shady," Skip promised, already worried about what Kurt would do when he found out how Skip had secured fifteen minutes with Darci the previous day. "So, um, what now?"

Kurt mumbled, "Now, we get some sleep, and I will smooth things over with Darci in the morning."

"You're sleeping here?"

Kurt's eyes opened to little more than slits. "It's three in the morning. I wouldn't know how to find a decent hotel with vacancies if it was daytime. And Kalia's asleep. It was either here or sleep in the park. Figured you owed me."

Before Skip could tell him whether or not he did, in fact, mind, Kurt had begun to snore.

There was no point in waking him up again, and if he called

security…well, it wouldn't sit well with Darci because Kurt was right. They hadn't broken up. If Darci had been the sort of woman who broke up with a man when he did something stupid, she'd have dumped Kurt years ago. He'd heard stories of Kurt's various exploits, even after he had the money to clean up the consequences.

It was best to let Kurt sleep, then politely invite him to leave in the morning.

By the time Skip settled back into bed, Kurt's snoring had grown from a dry wheeze to something like a locomotive. Pressing a pillow over both ears, he reminded himself that this was why he preferred call girls to a girlfriend. You could have dinner, talk a bit, finish with some business, and then part ways. Call girls didn't spend the night and keep you up with their snoring. Or their problems. Despite his feelings for Darci, Skip knew that he was far too busy to maintain a relationship the way Kurt did.

CHAPTER 20

Aches and Pains

Kurt awakened the next morning with a stiff back and cramping legs. The price of sleeping on the couch. Someone was lightly shaking him by the shoulder. Without opening his eyes, he mumbled, "Fuck off, Skip. You got me into this mess. Can damn well let me sleep."

"You got yourself into this mess." It wasn't Skip's voice. He opened his eyes to see Darci standing beside him, dressed in a pantsuit similar to what he seen Alice wearing a few days earlier. But it looked good on Darci.

He'd considered telling her as much, but settled for, "How'd you know I was here?"

"I didn't. I called Skip to let him know I was doing the show. He told me you were staying here."

He winced as he sat up. "Where is Skip?"

"Hiding in a café in the lobby. I told him I was coming up to collect you."

"So… We're good now."

She shrugged. "What's good? I love you, and I'm not leaving over something like this. So you'll just have to learn to trust me a little more."

He nodded. "Okay." There were several loud pops as he stood up. He smiled as he thought back to the Sportsfan Workout he'd walked out on to be here. Maybe he did need to get in better shape if one night on the couch could do this much damage.

Darci wrapped an arm around his waist, not so much to hug as to support him. "Stiff?"

He nodded.

"I think someone needs a back rub."

He smiled a little as he took his suitcase. "That would be great."

"Well, I'm sure the hotel has a masseur on duty. You do that, while I go back to work." And after a kiss on the cheek, she let him go and walked out the door.

———

Things were fairly quiet for Kurt during the rest of the fashion show. As a goodwilled gesture, he'd invited Skip to the game Kalia had gotten tickets for. He tried to remain on his best behavior, even when Alice was around.

He'd literally bitten into his tongue when he found out that Alice had also signed up as a judge for Skip's fashion show. There were so many things he could have said. That Darci would represent fashion, and Alice would represent the opposition. That Alice would be there so the losers wouldn't feel bad. That telling women what they should wear wouldn't be as easy as telling Chuck what he should wear. But he kept it all to himself. At least until they got back to Chicago, he'd promised to keep it to himself.

———

The following week Brian, Bernie, and Chuck were in Kurt's man cave watching the Bears game. It was good to be home. Kurt and the guys didn't notice the presence of Darci and Alice until Darci asked how the game was going.

Kurt was usually distracted and nonresponsive when his favorite teams were competing. "This is unbelievable! The Bears' defense is playing great. But Bulldog is just throwing people around right and left. He playing like he's possessed."

Brian was not as amused as the carnage went on. "Yeah, he's

throwing everybody around, but his penalties are killing us. He was just called for roughing the passer again. It's not funny any more. Awwww, Chuck, did you see...?"

"Yeah, saw it. Couldn't miss it! Damn! He just tackled the fullback so hard he knocked his helmet off."

"Isn't he supposed to tackle the fullback?"

Chuck's eyes never left the screen as he answered Darci. "Yeah. The other team's fullback! Not his own teammate. He got mad when the Bears' fullback fumbled the ball, so when the guy went over to the sidelines, Bulldog knocked him to the ground."

Brian added, "The referees don't know what to do because they're teammates. Can't call unnecessary roughness, so they called delay of game."

"I know something's bothering him because I've never seen him play this angrily before." Kurt had the feeling there was more to this. Bulldog was known to be a no-holds-barred player, but this was extreme even for him.

As if to put Kurt's feelings into reality, Bulldog, on the next play, leveled the tight end and forced another to fumble. After the play, the other defensive players tried to congratulate him, but he pushed them away in response.

"He's definitely pissed off about something."

"You're right, Brian, I wonder what's making him so mad? Aren't you glad it's not you? Chuck, you got any idea what's going on?"

"Maybe he knows that Victor is banging his girlfriend right now."

"Nice, Chuck." Either Chuck had forgotten that Alice was there or perhaps he didn't care. He had a habit of saying whatever came to mind either way.

"What do you mean? I thought that whole thing was over."

"No, Bernie, not over. In fact, Victor flew her out to New York City last week for Fashion Week," answered Kurt. "I'm thinking that Victor shouldn't have stayed there for as long if that's what's going on with Bulldog."

"He parked his car at my house a few hours ago. So it is possible that he knows," Brian said.

Darci touched Kurt's shoulder. "Kurt, maybe you guys should go talk to him."

He nodded, squeezing his hand. He knew all too well how crazy a man could get in this sort of situation. In Kurt's case, he'd flown across the country to terrify a media mogul. "Let's wait until halftime before we attempt this conversation. We know that Bulldog will be busy at the game, so we have time." Timing was important, but so was self-preservation.

Brian pointed to the screen. "Hey, look. They benched Bulldog! They probably want him to calm down."

"They need to calm him down because he's playing with reckless abandon," said Kurt. "But I'm thinking the venom is building with reflection. He's not going to calm down."

When halftime came around, the guys decided to walk over to Mary Lee's house and talk to her and to Victor. Mary Lee invited them all in with a smile. They followed her into the living room, sat down, and waited for her to join them.

Apparently, Victor didn't hear the doorbell or the greetings because he came out half-dressed and definitely looked surprised to see them all there, seated one next to another and saying nothing.

"So what's this? You can't see I'm busy?"

Kurt wasn't comfortable in the role of interloper but reminded himself that Victor's welfare could very well be at stake. "I'm sorry, Victor, this won't take long because we want to be back before halftime ends." *And before Bulldog arrives*, Kurt deliberately omitted.

"So, Kurt, what is it? What is so important you all come without—"

It was Mary Lee who interrupted him. "I think I know why your friends are here, Victor."

"You do?" asked Brian, as if he himself did not know.

"Yes, I do. I think you guys are worried about Bulldog finding out about Victor and my special friendship."

Chuck's unfiltered responses were often a source of annoyance but no one, for once, stopped him. "I'd say it's more than a friendship…wouldn't you?"

"Well, yes, we are friends with betterments."

"That's friends with benefits."

"Thank you, Bernie, but that'sa whata said! Betterments."

"Benefits, it's benefits!"

"Okay, that, too."

"Oh, why do I ever try to correct you? You're the one with the gorgeous girl again." Bernie's frustration showed as he entertained the thought that Victor was never going to get it.

Mary Lee, though, did get it. "Thank you, guys, for your concern, but Bulldog has two other girlfriends. Two can play at this game. If he wants me all to himself, then he needs to get rid of his other girlfriends."

"Yes, *si*, she give him an alteration."

"A what?" Bernie looked confused, and Chuck's inappropriate and ill-timed guffaw went unnoticed.

"An alteration. Bernardo, you know…he makes commitment or she's sees other people."

"Oh, okay, you meant to say *alternative*. The word is al-tern-a-tive, Victor, alternative, but you mean *ultimatum*."

Even Chuck could see this was going nowhere and for once went straight to the point. "You guys have been hot and heavy for a while."

"Victor, Chuck's right, and I think Bulldog might be catching on. And since you parked your Ferrari in my driveway, I think he might take it out on me."

"Brian, you don't worry. We are careful; he's at the game. You no worry."

"Not worry? Victor, your car is out in the open in my driveway. You are not at my house. So where are you if not with me at my house?"

"This is silly. I am here. You know that."

"Exactly, Victor, you are here and your car is there, so who do you think Bulldog will go after first? Old Brian here, that's who! And why? Because you are..."

Mary Lee's voice broke through the men's back-and-forth discussion. "I'm going to break up with him if he doesn't make a commitment."

"Well, I think this love triangle needs to end." Kurt feared that Bulldog would arrive before he said what he had to say. "Here's the problem: Bulldog is getting penalized for unnecessary roughness. The coaches are getting pissed off! I hope he calms down before the game is over. If not, you might not have the chance to say anything before he goes wild on all of us, including Victor here."

And, speak of the devil, Mary Lee seemed to lose her breath for a second as she gaped out the front window. Before Kurt could turn to see what had scared her so badly, she shrieked, "Oh my God, Bulldog is here!"

Although they were expressing fear that Bulldog would arrive shortly, everyone was nonetheless surprised to hear Mary Lee announce just that.

"What?" was Kurt's only response. He turned to look out the window and there was Bulldog's SUV coming down the street.

Chuck followed that with, "How can he? He was just at Soldier Field at halftime."

Brian was next with, "No, no, no! They benched him in the first quarter. He must have left the stadium."

"He's not allowed to do that," was Chuck's superfluous and inane comment.

"Well, he did." Kurt was looking around for a means of escape.

Mary Lee seemed to have regained her composure enough to start giving orders. "Come on. You guys need to hide."

"What?"

"Just go hide. Kurt, I'll get rid of Bulldog."

Kurt and Brian wasted no time in following Victor back to the master bedroom, where the three of them went into the walk-in closet and quietly closed the door behind them.

"Guys, hurry up. He's almost at the door."

Chuck ran to a window, knocked out the screen, and climbed out. Bernie panicked and tried to follow Chuck. The window was opened high enough for skinny Chuck to slither through but not high enough for larger Bernie to follow. Bernie's frame was not only too large, but in his panic he didn't think to raise the window higher so he kept getting stuck. At the last minute, Bernie decided to hide behind a couch. And not a moment too soon as the front door opened with a crash and revealed Bulldog, still wearing part of his uniform.

Mary Lee exclaimed for all to hear, "What are you doing here?"

"Where is he?"

"Who?"

"Come on, Mary Lee, playing dumb? You know who. Victor, that's who!"

"How do I know?"

"His fancy car is parked next door for one thing."

"So go next door."

"If I find him here, I'm going to put a spur in his saddle."

"Calm down, Bulldog."

"Don't tell me to calm down, Mary Lee! Now, where is he? He's slicker than owl shit. He's probably hiding. I know he's here, and when I find him, I'm going to knock him into the middle of next week, looking both ways for Sunday!"

Bulldog began to go through the house, room by room, opening closets as he did so. Bernie was still behind the living room sofa, hiding there and waiting until Bulldog reached the master bedroom. When he did so, Bernie started to crawl from behind the sofa toward the front door. Mary Lee stood in front of Bulldog and tried to prevent him from opening the master closet door.

"You just stop this. Now!"

"Move!"

Bulldog opened the walk-in closet and became even angrier upon seeing Kurt, Brian, and Victor huddled together, hiding there in plain sight.

"Now hold on, big guy, it's not what you think," said Kurt, in his most placating tone. It might have worked, had Bulldog not seen Victor in there, too, but he did see him, and as soon as he did, he tried to get him.

"I'm going to cancel your birth certificate!"

Kurt and Brian tried to hold Bulldog back, but he made his living pummeling men stronger than them. They succeeded only in getting themselves whipped around instead as Bulldog tried to get at Victor.

Meanwhile Bernie had reached the front door, opened it and was almost free to leave unscathed. But his adrenaline had kicked in and obliterated all common sense as he turned back to join his friends and grab on to whatever flailing limb came within his reach.

"Bulldog, stop this before somebody gets really hurt."

Bernie's plea was ignored as Kurt was tossed against the wall with horrific force. He looked over to the window and was appalled to see Chuck laughing hard. Laughing he expected, but filming the incident on his cell phone was a new low, even for Chuck.

It was apparently Brian's turn to receive Bulldog's wrath. "Kurt, for God's sake, help me!"

Kurt was experiencing his own adrenalin rush and, in the back of his mind, wondered how much pain he was going to be in tomorrow morning…right before he jumped on Bulldog's back and tried to tackle him. Bulldog simply tossed Kurt around, swatting him off as if he were a fly.

While Mary Lee's "stop it now" went ignored, it caused a nanosecond pause…enough for Kurt, Brian, and Bernie to at least hang on to Bulldog, all at the same time. It didn't stop Bulldog from going after Victor. It just slowed him down, enough so that

Victor grabbed his shirt and ran out the front door (instead of the side window, for a change), escaping in his Ferrari.

Mary Lee's anger was increasing. "He's gone! Now stop it!"

Kurt tried placating once more. "Bulldog, you're killing us here. Give it a rest."

When Bulldog finally paused, everybody fell to the floor beaten and bruised. In fact, they all had bruises everywhere.

That welcome pause, however, gave Bulldog just the moment he needed to see Chuck standing at the window filming everything. He grabbed a picture from the dresser and threw it through the window. The broken glass barely missed Chuck.

"If you don't stop, I'm going to post this video on YouTube right now, and you'll be in big trouble."

Instead of ignoring Chuck's whining (as he almost reflexively did these days), Kurt thought maybe he could follow up on it. "Listen to Chuck. He will send it. Don't ruin your professional football career over this." Bulldog's eyes were almost glazed as he looked at Kurt and then refocused on Mary Lee.

When she spoke, it was more like a mother to a disobedient child than a woman to her lover. "Come on, baby. I warned you. I told you if you didn't make a commitment, I was going to move on. You told me you were going to break up and quit seeing your other girlfriends. It's time to move on."

Between them, Kurt, Brian, and Bernie hadn't managed to land a single punch or kick. Bulldog hadn't even been bruised by their combined efforts. But Mary Lee... She had made him cry. Just a couple of tears, but still more than one would expect from Bulldog. "And I did that! I broke up with them yesterday. I was a wreck last week while you were gone. I've been so confused lately, I don't know if I should check my ass or scratch my watch."

"You did break up with them? You did that?"

"Yeah, I realized I only want to be with you, only you."

"Oh, baby, come here. You finally did it."

When Bulldog took Mary Lee in his arms, Kurt winced. He'd just experienced the strength in those arms, and he feared that

Bulldog might crack his girlfriend's ribs he was holding her so tight. Still she didn't seem to mind, and he guessed the tears in her eyes were from joy. "I know I deserved what you did to me. I've been a very bad boyfriend. I'm ready to make things right."

When he finally released her, her tone returned to that of a disapproving mother. "All right. I'll give it another try, but no other girlfriends, Bulldog. Just me. I'll stop seeing Victor, but you've got to leave him alone."

"I wouldn't walk across the street to piss on him if he was on fire."

She shrugged, perhaps as baffled by some of his sayings as the rest of them. Between Bulldog's weird turns of phrase and Victor's constant butchering of idioms, Kurt wondered when the last time was that she'd had a totally comprehensible conversation. "Good, as long as you stay away from him."

"Okay, but you really need to cover up more. We can see clear to the promised land!" Bulldog grabbed a very large bra lying next to the bed. "Here, go into the bathroom and put on your over-the-shoulder boulder holders."

Brian started coughing, perhaps a delayed reaction to the injuries he'd sustained. "Bulldog, are we good? We tried to talk sense into them."

"Yeah, Brian, we're good. Now that I got Mary Lee back, I'm grinning like a possum eating a sweet tater."

"You know you're going to get into trouble for leaving the game." Kurt was back to business in no time. "I don't think I've ever seen that happen before. Ever!"

"Yeah, I may be the first, Kurt. I'll probably get kicked off the team for this. If I do get cut, I'm moving Mary Lee to Florida before winter. No point staying here. Chicago gets cold enough to freeze a tit off a frog."

"Maybe it won't come to that. Hopefully you don't get cut." But as they left, Kurt had to admit, if only to himself, that he certainly wouldn't miss them if they left.

CHAPTER 21

The New Neighbors

The guys headed across the street back to Kurt's house. Chuck joined them on the way. "Holy shit, Kurt, you guys got your asses kicked big time." He said it as if he hadn't just seen the whole thing happen, as if he hadn't just seen it and done nothing.

Kurt wondered, not for the first time, why he was friends with Chuck. He had no doubt that if he suggested beating the shit out of Chuck, right then and there in the street, that Brian and Bernie would go along with him. They could be each other's alibis and could certainly hire decent lawyers if Chuck decided to press charges. Instead, Kurt just muttered, "Yeah, thanks for helping us out, Chuck."

"I wasn't dumb enough to try to stop Bulldog Williams."

The four of them walked down to the man cave, where Darci and Alice were waiting. Darci was the first to see them. "Oh, dear God, what happened to you guys?"

Kurt and Bernie had various visible injuries, including black eyes, torn shirts, and plenty of scrapes and bruises.

It was Chuck who answered. "Bulldog left the game and surprised everybody at Mary Lee's house. We tried to keep him from killing Victor."

Brian snapped back, "We? Are you kidding, Chuck? You crawled through a window and didn't try to stop Bulldog. Don't deny it! You don't have a mark on you, you cowardly shit!"

Chuck started laughing as he always did. The man had no shame. Of course his trusty sidekick Alice would see it differently.

"Good thinking, Chuck. You still look good compared to the rest of them."

Kurt added a sarcastic, "Yeah, thanks Chuck. And Alice? I would expect no more from you! You don't care about other people, do you?"

Darci took advantage of Kurt's justified tone to divert his attention away from Alice. "Is Victor okay?"

Brian shook his head. "I don't think he ever touched Victor. He escaped while Kurt and I tried to hold Bulldog."

"You guys are really beat up. Do you think you should go to the hospital?" Darci knew Kurt would slough off the idea of going to the ER but felt the need to put it out there.

"I feel like I've been eaten by a wolf and shit over a cliff, but I think we're going to be okay." Kurt, feeling raw from head to toe, meant every word. "Besides, it's over now. Bulldog and Mary Lee are back together, but I think he's going to be in a lot of trouble for leaving the game."

Kurt was thinking that "in a lot of trouble" was a masterpiece of an understatement. How right he was.

After the game, the Bears announced that they intended to kick Bulldog off the team. Later that night, the Bears were able to work out a trade with the Miami Dolphins instead. One team's loss is another's gain.

"I'm going over to tell Bulldog that he's been traded to the Miami Dolphins."

"No, Chuck. I don't want you going over there by yourself. It might be dangerous." Alice said no more after Chuck leaned in and whispered to her. He left by himself to tell Bulldog the news.

Kurt was well used to Chuck's Byzantine thought processes and was a little concerned that his visit to Bulldog might restart the fracas. "What exactly does Chuck have up his sleeve, Alice?"

Alice offered a thin smile. "Nothing yet, but hopefully we'll have a surprise for you. Really. Just wait till he gets back."

A little more than an hour passed before Chuck returned in one piece. Of course his return would be dramatic with an equally dramatic statement.

"I've got great news everybody! Alice and I are moving into Mary Lee's house. Bulldog and Mary Lee have agreed to sublease the house to us. What do you think about that? We're going to be neighbors."

Kurt felt a fresh pain in his gut that had nothing to do with the beating he'd suffered from Bulldog. "I think I'm going to puke."

CHAPTER 22
The Auction

Two weeks after the fight with Bulldog, Victor and Brian were in the bachelor auction. Kurt, Bernie, Chuck, Darci, Alice, and Frank had all decided to sit in the audience to support or laugh at them. As the auction began, Frank had failed to show up, but only Bernie seemed to care. His worry for Frank was summed up by "where is that prick?"

Kurt shrugged. "Probably stopped for a drink. Or, more likely, was already drinking and never started for here."

Bernie shook his head. "I told him there was a bar here." There was, in fact, a bar in the hotel where the auction was being held, but the drinks were grotesquely over-priced, and Frank preferred his drinks to be rotgut cheap or complimentary. Kurt wouldn't put it past him to walk in with a six-pack.

Chuck was already smiling, no doubt prepping himself for one humiliating quip after another for each of the men who'd volunteered for this event. The fact that all the proceeds were going to benefit a network of animal shelters meant nothing to him. In fact it seemed he decided to practice on Bernie before the event even began. "What's wrong? Worried that, without Frank here, you'll be the homeliest guy in the room?"

Darci glared at Chuck, but he didn't seem to notice. Alice, on the other hand, couldn't help but offer an approving smirk as she patted her boyfriend's arm. In fact she hadn't let go of Chuck's arm since they'd arrived. Kurt knew that Alice was still worried that Chuck might enter the auction at the last minute. Her presence was more to stake out her territory and rein Chuck in than to laugh at any of the men presenting themselves.

Sometimes Kurt thought he wouldn't wish an obnoxious jackass like Chuck on his worst enemy. But then he'd think of Alice and realize that, no, in fact, he had already wished Chuck on his worst enemy, and God had answered that prayer. Although he couldn't tell what the two saw in one another, he also believed that they truly deserved each other. The fact that Alice was scared that any other woman would want Chuck just made the whole thing funnier to him—not to mention bizarre.

Kurt reassured Bernie. "I'm sure Frank will be here, probably drunk, and make a complete jackass out of himself. Don't worry. In the meantime Chuck will pick up the slack."

If Chuck caught the insult, he ignored it, instead yelling, "Hey, it's starting." He reminded Kurt of a child waiting to see Santa in the parade. Laughing at others seemed to be the only thing that truly made him happy.

Several of the women in the audience turned to gape at Chuck for several seconds before returning their attention to the main stage. When they stared Kurt noticed Alice's grip on Chuck's arm tighten. For a woman who seemed to hate every other man on earth, she was completely oblivious when that hatred was turned toward her own man. It didn't help that Kurt, Bernie, and Chuck appeared to be the only men in an audience of one hundred women. Not that they were at any risk of being approached—even if any of them had come alone.

Kurt had noticed several brief appraisals of himself—just a quick look up and down—while he was looking for a row of seats. But once it was clear he wasn't going to participate in the auction, every woman who'd looked him over had lost interest. There was something about the auction itself, about the process of bidding, of openly competing against one another, that appealed to them. He'd noticed that the women seemed much more interested in one another. It was almost like a ritualized catfight, where the object of the fight didn't matter so much as the fight itself. The auditorium was fairly quiet, save for a few whispered conversations here and there. The calm before the storm.

There was some polite applause when the event began and the auction mistress came on to announce the event, thank everyone for coming, and remind one and all that this was, first and foremost, a fundraiser. She then outlined some basic rules of bidding etiquette that sounded to Kurt like a referee reminding two boxers that he expected a good clean fight. And then the first bachelor came on.

The applause was loud but didn't seem terribly sincere. It almost completely drowned out Chuck's first insult of the evening. "This one looks ready to bury, not marry." He wasn't particularly old, no older than forty-five, but the dark suit he wore did seem a bit reserved for the event.

One of the women sitting in front of them spun her head around so fast Kurt immediately thought of *The Exorcist*. She screamed at Chuck, "Will you shut the fuck up, jackass!"

This was followed by a much louder, and far more sincere, applause. Even the bachelor on stage joined in, which seemed to endear him to several of the ladies, because the bidding went on for several minutes before capping at just over $500.

Bernie was sitting beside Kurt and his mouth was slowly falling open as he listened to the bidding escalate. After the winning bid had been made, he whispered to Kurt, "Do you believe this shit?"

Kurt could only shrug. "It's for charity."

"Yeah, but for homeless animals, not homely bachelors. Why not just give five hundred dollars to the shelter?"

Kurt shook his head. "I don't know, Bernie. Some women like homely guys."

"I could have gotten five hundred," he muttered.

Kurt didn't want to make Bernie's day any worse. But he also couldn't bring himself to lie. If Bernie cleaned himself up, got a decent haircut, a nice suit, lost twenty pounds...it still wouldn't make a difference. There was a schlubbiness to Bernie that couldn't be covered up. It was something that went beyond his looks. There were bound to be uglier men on the stage, but none of them would have the weird antimachismo that Kurt's friend exuded.

When the next bachelor took the stage, he stood a clear head shorter than the auctioneer. Chuck began to sing the opening lines to the song "Short People" by Randy Newman before *Exorcist*-head stared him into silence. Meanwhile Bernie whispered, "Christ, they'd be better off just auctioning the dogs."

That guy went for $420. Bernie muttered, "This is insane."

"Why did you come?" Kurt whispered back. "If you're just going to get upset, why stay?"

Bernie looked genuinely hurt by the question. "I'm here for Victor and Brian. Same as you."

Kurt shook his head. He knew that wasn't the reason. Bernie wanted to see who had made the cut when he hadn't, and he wouldn't be happy until he'd torn every other bachelor down.

The next two bachelors received obnoxious quips from Chuck and more hushed appraisals from Bernie, so that Kurt was hearing it from both sides. At one point Darci whispered, "If Chuck doesn't shut up, we're all going to get thrown out." Apparently she couldn't hear Bernie.

Kurt could only react with a shrug. It was more out of a sense of duty than anything else that had brought him here, and if circumstances out of his control forced him out, such was life. And when had anyone been able to control Chuck's mouth (including Chuck himself)? No, as long as Chuck kept his voice down, no one really cared what he said (again much like every other situation in which Chuck found himself).

When the fifth bachelor took to the stage, Darci offered a much louder and more enthusiastic applause. It was Victor, dressed in a pair of designer jeans (that had probably cost more than a tuxedo) and a tight shirt with the top two buttons undone. It looked corny to Kurt, who thought it was missing only the gold chain to complete the '70s swinger ensemble, but the crowd seemed to eat it up. Kurt knew that Darci was only applauding because Victor was a friend, but the rest of the women seemed to genuinely like what they saw. All except Alice, of course, who waited for Chuck to say something appropriately shallow and cruel.

"Jesus, he looks like a pimp in that suit." Chuck began laughing at his comment, always his own best audience.

Again several of the women turned to glare, but it was Victor himself who spoke up. "Charles? Il mio amico, is that you? You come to see me raise the money?"

Chuck was still laughing and could only nod in agreement.

"And Bernie! You come, even though they say you not a good bachelor? You are a good friend for this." Kurt didn't have to look at Bernie to see he was blushing as women turned to look.

Victor waved to the five of them and then the bidding began. The bidding was going much further than it had gone for any of the bachelors who'd taken the stage so far. Even Darci let out a gasp when it passed $1,000. Since Kurt was seated near the back of the audience, he couldn't get a clear look at who was actually bidding. He could tell by the voices that they were all women, of course. He could also tell that, past the $700 mark, the bids seemed to come down to three separate women. Curiously as it continued, Kurt could see that Victor was beginning to look uncomfortable. It couldn't be modesty.

At first the bids would start at $50 and then move up in $10 increments. But after a thousand, the bids went up by $25 amounts. "Thousand twenty-five," came a thick Russian accent to Kurt's left.

Before the auctioneer could say a word, "thousand fifty" squeaked a couple of rows ahead of her.

From somewhere to Kurt's right, there was a harsh "thousand seventy-five."

The Russian went to "thousand one."

There was a pause and the auctioneer raised her gavel, then the gravelly voice croaked out, "Thousand one twenty-five."

The Russian immediately countered with "Thousand one fifty."

But gravel-voice snapped back, "Thousand two fifty."

There were several muted gasps from the women. But no

other response. No opposing bid. After the count of three, the auctioneer brought down her gavel.

The winning bidder (in clear violation of the earlier stated rules of decorum) immediately leapt from her seat and shouted, "Woo-hoo! In. Your. Face." She was dressed in a red blouse and white slacks. Her skin was tanned, weathered to the point where it was difficult to confidently guess her age, but Kurt would offhand hazard somewhere in her seventies, if not early eighties. Her white hair was cut short and almost belied her age as she cheered for herself. Even from four rows back, he could see the blue veins in her arms.

Chuck had nearly fallen out of his chair upon seeing her. "I wonder if Victor will have to cut her food for her. Hey, maybe he'll luck out, and she'll forget even winning this thing. Maybe he can take her on a double date with his grandmother."

The event was nearing its end, and Frank was still nowhere to be seen. Alice seemed finally comfortable enough that she actually released Chuck's arm and stood up to leave long enough to use the ladies room. Kurt noticed that Chuck began to stand up as well before catching himself and sitting back down. Had Alice conditioned him to stand up whenever she rose to leave a room? Or was he like a dog that would instinctively follow his mistress wherever she went?

Again he knew those two deserved each other.

Alice was still gone when Brian took to the stage. The applause was nowhere near what Victor had received, but it was still loud enough to bolster his friend's ego. The bidding was less frantic than what Victor had inspired, but the number was slowly going up, past $300, past $350, all the way to $370, where it stalled.

The auctioneer raised her gavel. "Three seventy going once, going twice."

"Four hundred."

Half the women in the audience turned to glare at Chuck, whose hand was still in the air. That old familiar grin was splitting across his face. Kurt hissed, "Chuck, what the hell are you doing?"

Chuck just ignored him, repeating his bid. "Four hundred."

Brian stood on stage, unable to appear shocked, because honestly it was far from the most obnoxious thing Chuck had ever done. The auctioneer, on the other hand, was not so resigned. "Sir, the bidding is restricted to women. I'm afraid you can't—"

"Four hundred!" he screamed.

"Sir, I'll have to ask—"

From several rows up, a woman yelled, "Four ten."

Chuck immediately snapped, "Four twenty."

Again the auctioneer tried to explain, "Sir, will you *please* stop—"

"Four thirty," the other woman yelled.

Chuck countered with, "Four forty."

The auctioneer was waving toward giant men in suits who seemed to appear out of nowhere. As they approached Chuck, the other woman yelled, "Four fifty."

Kurt stood up to let two of the large gentlemen pass him as they made their way toward Chuck. Darci and Bernie did the same. Before Chuck could offer another bid, the men were on him, one hand clamped over his mouth, while thick hands took hold of his arms.

As Chuck was being dragged to the exit, the auctioneer tried to regain control of the room. "I believe the bidding ended at three seventy. If we could start from there."

The other woman repeated her last bid, "Four fifty."

The auctioneer shrugged, raised her gavel, and after "going once, going twice," brought it down hard. "Sold." The rest of the women began to cheer. Kurt turned to watch Chuck being dragged out the door, smiling to see that Alice had returned from the bathroom in time to see her boyfriend being taken away. The applause drowned out whatever she was saying to the security team, but Kurt could guess based on her expression.

The remainder of the auction was uneventful. In fact the only other incident occurred about fifteen minutes after the auction was finished, as the room was clearing out and Kurt, Darci, and Bernie were waiting for Victor and Brian to find them in the thinning crowd. They heard the problem before they saw it—an all-too-familiar voice slurring into the microphone. "You don't know jack about what women want. None of you women know jack about women. I know about women. It's not about pretty boys or sensitive touchy guys. Women don't care about that. They like guys with money. Power. That's all it is. Power. Napoleon could have any woman he wanted. You think that short little bastard could have gotten any action if he wasn't the most powerful—"

Kurt shook his head as he saw Frank, having lost his jacket somewhere between the office and the auction, standing on the stage in an untucked shirt. He was clutching the microphone as three of the giants in suits surrounded him. One tried to pull the microphone from his grip, while the other two were lifting him by his shoulders. "Hey, you can't pull me out of here. They saved the best for last, that's all. Hey, ladies, it's the encore. Last chance for—"

There were several boos from the surrounding ladies as the microphone was finally pulled from Frank's hands, but his voice was loud enough to carry over it all. "No way does Brian get in this thing, and I don't! Or Victor! Are you kidding me?"

As the security team dragged Frank from the stage, he continued shouting. "Last chance!"

The last thing Kurt heard as Frank was taken out the door was a garbled cry that sounded suspiciously like "take me to Pointy Foods."

CHAPTER 23
Victor's Date

Victor always found it annoying when his friends repeated what he said, as if he hadn't said it. He knew that his accent was a bit thick, but surely it wasn't that difficult to understand him. Still they were his friends and he knew they always meant well. So when Bernie had stopped by his restaurant on the night of his auctioned date, Victor knew he wasn't there to make fun of him.

"You might have reminded her of someone she knew years ago. She's probably a widow who got tired of sitting at home every night."

Victor smiled as he watched Bernie finish a second beer. Against his friend's advice, Victor had decided to remain sober for his date. If nothing else, he refused to make a shameful spectacle in front of the woman who'd spent a sizeable amount of money to share an evening with him. "Yes, I think it is old memories and loneliness. And the money is for a good cause."

Bernie nodded. "Yeah. A good cause. What was it? Cancer research?"

"Animals, Bernardo. Shelters where no one will eulogize them."

"Euthanize."

Victor sighed, again reminding himself that his friends meant well. "Yes, as I said, eulogize. Dogs and cats are given to families and not killed." Victor had a dog himself, a German shepherd

170

named Benny, who invariably drew the attention of women when he walked him. Benny was a good dog who always knew what Victor was trying to tell him and was the best kind of listener—the kind who didn't interrupt. He'd picked Benny up at one of the shelters that would benefit from the auction. It was the least he could do.

Bernie shook his head. "So… You said she was coming here?"

Victor nodded. "Yes. We spoke on the phone, and she said she wanted to pick me up here. At four. I guess she wanted to start early."

"She probably doesn't want to stay out too late."

Victor sighed as he looked at the clock. It was five after four. For a Wednesday afternoon, business was decent. Wednesday nights were usually decent nights. Not terribly busy, but worth keeping the doors open. At the very least, it was doubtful he'd be needed.

"Well, try to just get through it, Victor. I know there were some really gorgeous women bidding, but—"

Victor raised a hand. "I know, Bernie. This is the way it goes, and beauty is in the eye of the beholden, I guess."

Bernie opened his mouth, perhaps to repeat something else that Victor had just said, when a woman's voice boomed from across the restaurant. "Victor!"

Victor turned, as did most of the patrons and staff, to see his eighty-three-year-old date for the evening advancing past the door. She was dressed in black slacks and a purple blouse. Her white hair was cut short, and he was surprised once again to see that she wasn't wearing glasses. Contacts, then, surely. He'd also expected to see her limping or moving in that baby step shuffle that his grandmother had always employed (or, at least, for as long as he'd known her). But she was taking long, confident strides toward him.

She seized one of Victor's arms. "Ready to go?" She smiled with teeth too even and too white to be real.

Victor nodded, then turned to Bernie. "Bernardo, this is Olivia. Olivia, this is my dear friend, Bernardo."

Olivia nodded to Bernie. "Yeah, I remember you. You were there with the loudmouth."

Bernie laughed. "Yeah."

"Your friend should learn some manners."

"Well, if he hasn't by now..."

Olivia cackled her understanding, then took Victor by the hand. He almost cried out when he felt her grip. She tugged him along toward the door. "Come on, Vic. I'm double-parked."

"Where are we going?" he asked as they left the restaurant.

"I told you, it's a surprise. Don't you like surprises?"

Many of the surprises in Victor's life involved boyfriends and husbands that his lady friends had failed to mention to him. "Surprises are not always so good."

"That's no way to go through life. Shit!" Victor followed her line of sight and realized she was panicking over a police officer walking toward them. She reached into her pocket and the beige SUV in front of them beeped to life. "Get in!"

Victor was pulling himself into the passenger seat but apparently wasn't getting in fast enough for his date's comfort. She pressed a palm onto his behind and gave him a quick shove, stealing a brief squeeze before slamming the door shut and running around the front to get in the driver's side door. Gunning the engine, she swore under her teeth, "Bastards aren't going to ticket me again this week."

But the officer, a doughy man in his late forties, was running up to the SUV, tapping on the driver's side window before Olivia could shift gears. She turned to glare at Victor, hissing, "You're my grandson, and we're on our way to the grocery store."

Victor shook his head. "That is not such a nice date. And why would the officer—"

There was more tapping on the window, and Olivia shook her head. "Just be quiet and let me do the talking, cutie." She turned to face the officer, bringing down the window. "Problem, officer?"

"Miss, have you been drinking?"

Olivia paused before answering. "Why would you ask me something like that?"

"Well, miss, mostly because you are double-parked and you are about to drive off in this car after walking out of that sports bar."

"Oh no, officer. My grandson here was in the sports bar. I was just picking him up so we could go grocery shopping."

The officer raised an eyebrow. "Grocery shopping?"

"Oh yes, I can still push the cart myself, but unloading all those groceries, well, I need some help these days."

Victor just nodded slightly, uncertain whether or not he was breaking the law.

But the officer didn't seem to think much of him as he asked Victor, "You make your grandmother pick you up at a bar?"

Victor was about to say something, when Olivia popped in with, "Oh no, you see, he works here. He's just finishing his shift."

Victor nodded. "It is true. I am shiftless now."

The officer raised an eyebrow. "You two are related?"

"He's adopted," Olivia snapped. "My daughter, she couldn't have children, and it took her years to adopt, and I guess maybe sometimes I do too much to let my Victor know that he is a part of this family." She reached out and squeezed Victor in a hug. "I know he'd rather be out with his friends, but the fact that he still takes the time to help his grandmother, well..."

Victor heard Olivia gasp and realized that she'd begun to cry.

The officer just shook his head. "It's all right, ma'am. Just... Try to be more careful how you park." He put away his ticket pad and wished them both a good evening.

Olivia rolled the window back up and shook her head. "Donut-sucking killjoys. That's all cops are."

The SUV jolted in reverse, then forward, and Victor thought he heard glass breaking as Olivia pulled into traffic, grinning at the officer as she passed him. The officer's eyes went wide as he watched Olivia dart into traffic. He shook his fist and began screaming curses that Victor couldn't hear through the window.

Not meaning to be heard, Victor muttered, "I should have known not to judge a book by its color."

But Olivia heard him just fine as she squealed around a corner. "Yeah, my husband used to say the same thing."

———

The drive out to Lincoln Park took forty-five minutes, and Olivia consistently stayed at least ten miles above the speed limit the whole way. Of course the drive might have taken half that long, but she insisted on only taking side roads.

After twenty minutes on the road, Victor had asked, "We should be taking an excessway. It is faster than—"

"No expressways!" she'd screamed, as if Victor had been passionate about it. "People don't know what America looks like anymore. The neighborhoods. The little shops. The slice of god-damned life stuff. They just get on the highways and look at all their billboards and think that's it."

Victor raised his hands in surrender. "I understand. Don't yell at me. I'll just watch life slices." He turned to the window but noticed no shops or neighborhoods. He saw only the angry faces of the motorists whom Olivia was passing. Curses that could only be inferred through the glass…and gestures, which didn't need to be heard to be understood.

Many horns honked at them, but the noises were always receding behind them, and Victor imagined Olivia had grown rather accustomed to the sound over the years. Hoping to change the topic of conversation from the decline of America, Victor offered, "I know many nice restaurants in Lincoln Park. If you like the French cooking, there's—"

"I got someplace picked out already. And don't worry, we've got all night." She rested a hand on Victor's thigh, squeezing gently. "First, we just need to build up your strength."

———

A half hour later, the two of them were sitting down at R.J. Grunts. Despite being a Wednesday night, every table was filled. Olivia had requested the table facing the Lincoln Park Zoo. It was almost seven o'clock, and Victor had to admit that the long ride had worked up an appetite in him. "You have eaten here before?"

Olivia nodded. "Oh yes, my Eddie used to take me here all the time. It was our place." Her eyes seemed to glaze over just a little at the mention of her husband.

"That is nice. Your husband, he was a good man, I am sure."

Olivia closed her eyes, smiled faintly. "Oh yes. We met in Saigon. He was a general and I was a journalist.

"Years ago, this publisher started asking for copies of my articles. And just like that, we were rich." Wiping a stray tear away, she added, "Two years ago, Eddie got diagnosed with a brain tumor. Inoperable. Three months after that...gone."

Victor winced as he reached a bruised arm across the table to take hold of Olivia's hand. "I am sorry."

She shook her head. "Don't be. Eddie told me not to mourn. He said we had a great life together and that I should just keep on living." She turned from Victor to speak with a passing server. "Two hot-and-spicy chilis."

"Hot and spicy? Is that... Perhaps I should get something more—"

"Relax." She waved a hand to dismiss his concern. "I eat here all the time. It's just a name they give to the house special."

"Tonight's house special is hot-and-spicy chili?"

She nodded, reaching across the table to squeeze his hand again. He looked down and marveled at the blue and purple web-work of veins crossing the back of her hand. Each of her knuckles was a thick knot in otherwise spindly fingers, but the strength was unbelievable. "Five different kinds of pepper and a blend of fifteen spices. You don't mind...spicy?"

Victor could see that Olivia was also getting quite hungry, the way she was licking her lips.

Again Victor shook his head. "Oh no, I think virility is the spice of life."

Olivia's smile widened. "I'm...so glad you said that."

Missing the entendre, Victor tried to change topics again. "So, after we have eaten, what did you want to do? A movie? Or dancing?"

Olivia shook her head. "No movies... And dancing...well, there are plenty of men my own age who can give me dancing. I was hoping we could try something a bit more adventurous." She squeezed his hand again.

Victor pulled his hand away. "An adventure? I am not much for dangerous things." He thought about the various husbands and boyfriends he'd dodged over the years—most recently a maniacal football player who'd skipped out in the middle of a game just to pummel him.

His date licked her lips once again. "Oh, an adventure doesn't have to be dangerous. It just has to be something you've never tried before."

"Ah. Yes. I see. Like going to...ah, the Botanic Gardens?"

"I was thinking something more animal than vegetable." He felt her foot under the table, slowly making its way up his inner calf to his inner thigh. It continued traveling up his thigh until—

"Oh, here's the chili. And our beers."

Victor shook his head. "I did not order beer. I am keeping my head on the level tonight."

"The beer's for the chili. You'll need to drink something to cool you down and water really doesn't help."

Victor insisted that he could handle the chili. After all the dishes in his own restaurant were plenty spicy. But after two spoonfuls... "Perhaps a sip."

The "sip" emptied a third of the glass and two more "sips" finished it off. And after finishing that first drink, Victor didn't think a second would be that much of a problem. After all Olivia was the one driving, so it wasn't as if having a few drinks would be irresponsible. And they'd established that just because Olivia had made a sizeable bid for an evening with Victor, it wouldn't entitle her to anything more than dinner and perhaps a walk through Lincoln Park. It was a beautiful night.

And except for the flirting, she did remind him of his grandmother.

Victor was feeling much more relaxed when the second drink arrived. He'd been dreading this date, but now it seemed like everything was going to go just fine.

The next morning, Victor awoke to the feeling of his dog's cold nose nuzzling his face. "Away, Benny. I am a dying man." The headache struck him the moment he opened his eyes, blinking in the dawn's light. He was lying on the floor of his bedroom.

When he tried to brush his dog away, he realized that his wrists were bound in red, silk-padded handcuffs. Looking down at himself, he noted that it was all he was wearing. He could see his pants, underwear, and socks piled up on the bed. On the floor were two stretches of fabric that had been his shirt, now torn in half. His skin was covered in red blotches. Scratches. And bites.

Wobbling over onto his side, he managed to bring his face level with the bed. There was a note resting on it, written in a shaky hand.

Victor,

I had a wonderful time last night. Keep the hand-cuffs as a memento. And if you ever want to be a little adventurous, give me a call.

—Olivia

CHAPTER 24

Brian's Date

At a quarter to five the next day, Kurt peeked his head into Brian's office. "Got a minute?" It was a strange tone of voice, one that Kurt had been affecting a lot more since becoming part owner of a business. It was a tone of voice that said that Brian would, in fact, be sparing a minute even if he didn't think he had one to spare.

Walking in, Kurt closed the door behind him and sat. Despite being the one seated behind the desk, Brian recalled his various trips to the principal's office. He quickly replayed the events of the day, trying to recall what he could have possibly done today to earn another "talk" from his friend.

"So, your date's tonight." There was nothing casual in his tone.

Brian nodded, not sure where this was going.

"How do you think it will go?"

He smiled lazily at the memory of the auction. "Should go great. I mean, did you get a look at the woman who won?" Thick blonde hair, a curvy figure barely contained in the dress she'd worn that night...and best of all, she'd bid on him, so he already knew she was interested.

Kurt shook his head. "I only saw her from the back."

"How did her back look?"

"Brian." There was a drawn out sigh, then, "You're not getting lucky tonight. You do realize that, right?"

"Not... Come on! With what she paid, no way she's not interested in—"

"If that's what she wanted, she could go to any bar and have

her pick of guys if she's as beautiful as you say. Those women...
They were looking for something else. They're used to being hit
on, to the guy making all the moves. This woman is probably
looking for a date that's more on her terms, and she was willing to
pay a lot of money for it."

"On her terms?" Brian could tell there was some sort of coded
language here, like when Kurt spoke with him about respecting
female coworkers and all he meant was to not let them catch him
staring. But where was this conversation going? Then... "Oh! Oh,
I understand. You mean she'll want to be on top. I'm fine with
that."

"I don't mean she wants to be on top. I mean she wants to
spend an evening with a gentleman. The way you carried yourself
when you were at the auction. You seemed like a nice guy, easygoing, polite—"

"I *am* easygoing and polite."

"To the men, yes. And any woman old enough to be your
mother."

"Speaking of old enough to be my mother, have you heard
from Victor? I've been trying to reach him all day to see how his
date went. He's not picking up."

Kurt winced, an unconscious habit that Brian didn't think he
even realized he had, one he'd picked up shortly after starting the
Sportsfan Chronicles. It was something he did whenever the topic
got changed. "I'm sure it went fine. The fact is that Victor doesn't
really flirt all that much. He just, I don't know, exudes something
that draws women to him. Besides he's not a co-owner of this
business, so it's not really my business what he did. You, on the
other hand—"

"Wait, what does my date have to do with Sportsfan?"

Again the wincing. "It has everything to do with it. When
you're out with, um—"

"Madison," Brian offered.

"When you're out with Madison, if you start getting obnoxious or...touchy...it will come back to haunt us all. This is not a

personal date, and you bid as a personal representative of SFC. So just…take her out to dinner, go to a movie, take her home, and if you must, one kiss. I don't want to read about your date in the gossip column tomorrow."

Brian nodded. "Okay, fine. Wait. There's such a thing as a gossip column? What paper is that in?"

"It's called the Internet. And all our competitors follow it." Kurt stood up and left.

Before he was fully out the door, though, Brian stopped him. "Kurt." He turned back, looking only a little annoyed. "How do you know so much about why women go to bachelor auctions?"

Closing his eyes, his friend whispered, "Darci explained it to me," then left.

Two hours later Brian was at the door of Madison's condo complex. Not sure how much he should take Kurt's advice to heart, he decided to prepare a date that would be "on her terms" if she wanted it. He had a couple of restaurants in mind. He'd offer her a choice of three and let her decide. The movie would go the same way. That's about as far as he was willing to go on the matter, though. Giving over much more control than that and he might as well let her drive.

They'd planned to meet at 7:00 and it was 7:04 when he rang the doorbell. Brian was prepared to wait the obligatory twenty minutes while his date got ready, but instead the door opened before he could ring the bell a second time. And Madison was ready to go. Red dress with a neckline that just naturally drew the eye, matching shoes, little black purse in hand. And an expression of wide-eyed joy that held so many promises for Brian.

But he remembered what Kurt had told him and decided that he would at least try to keep tonight's date platonic. And if, after a drink or two, she made a move on him…well, then he could always say he tried. "You look great." It was standard boilerplate for starting a date, but he did mean it. She did look great.

Madison tilted her head. "Thank you. You look good, too. So, what were you thinking for dinner?"

"Ah, well, there's Sayat-Nova. It's a Middle Eastern place, not too far. Never been there, but I've heard good things. Or we could go to Gino's East or Giordano's it's some of the best pizza in Chicago. What were you in the mood for?"

Brian was always surprised how many of his dates, given the choice, would opt for pizza. The Middle Eastern place was mostly to give a sense of variety.

"Sayat-Nova! Absolutely. I've been meaning to try more Middle Eastern cooking. Eric would never go. No Chinese. No French. Not even Italian."

Brian let her walk past him toward the car, partially as a gentlemanly ladies first gesture and partially to see how she looked from the back. He took in a quick breath as she swayed past him, her hips swiveling with an ease that...

He had to focus. Not stare. Actually talk with her about something. Without thinking, he asked the first question that popped into his mind. "Eric?"

"Ex-husband," she offered. "Seven dull years stuck with him. The divorce was finalized three months ago, and I'm ready to live."

"Well...let's go."

And Brian offered a silent apology to Kurt. No way he was passing up this gorgeous blonde on the rebound from a long, dull marriage. "Ready to live" was pretty much divorcee code for "ready to get into all the freaky bedroom stuff my husband would never try." As long as he let her do most of the talking and threw in the occasional compliment, he was in.

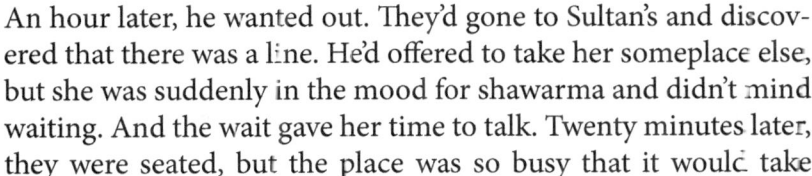

An hour later, he wanted out. They'd gone to Sultan's and discovered that there was a line. He'd offered to take her someplace else, but she was suddenly in the mood for shawarma and didn't mind waiting. And the wait gave her time to talk. Twenty minutes later, they were seated, but the place was so busy that it would take

another half hour for their meals to be ready. Again she didn't
mind, snacking on pita bread and talking. When the meals finally
arrived, she ate slowly, clearly enjoying her meal and taking her
time between bites to talk a little more.

And what did she talk about?

"So as soon as Eric would finish one contract and I'd think we'd
have some time together, he'd go right into negotiating another.
And he'd work late and always be tired, and I'm sure he used his
job as an excuse to avoid sex the last couple of years. I mean, you
want to think it's not a big deal, but when the sex goes, there's just
no way the relationship is going to survive."

Brian was mostly just nodding and nibbling at his beef...
something or other. He'd just pointed to something on the menu
with beef and rice as ingredients. Even when their server had told
him the name, he'd immediately forgotten the pronunciation. At
first he'd tried to stay focused on her eyes, fought the urge for
his gaze to repeatedly drift down to her chest. But eventually
he stopped staring at her eyes and her breasts entirely and just
watched her mouth. It just kept moving.

"So I told Eric one night, look, if you're not interested in me
any more...oh. Oh, I'm sorry. Here I am, going on and on about
my ex. You probably don't want to hear me carrying on like this."

Brian offered a weak smile. "It's okay. I was just thinking about
what you wanted to do after dinner. Maybe a movie?"

She nodded. "Sounds good. What did you want to see?"

Again the man-woman gap had to be bridged. There were
guy flicks and chick flicks and the droning wasteland of alternative cinema in between. Taking her to an action film would
make him look like an insensitive jerk. Taking her to a romantic
comedy would make him look like a wussy. There were no neutral
comedies currently playing. Fortunately he'd done some research
beforehand. "How about that new one about the psychic who
goes looking for his dead parents? That looked kind of good."
Scary could be good, as long as it wasn't gross.

Madison smiled. "That sounds wonderful." She leaned across

the table, offering him an unintended view of her cleavage as she took hold of his hand. "You've been great tonight. I can't tell you how long it's been since I've just been able to go out to dinner with someone who wasn't yapping away on his cell phone half the time. Guys who don't know how to keep their jobs at work."

Brian nodded. "Oh, that's never a problem with me. Hell, I barely work when I'm at the office."

She laughed just a little. "That really is refreshing. Eric always told me that I was being a baby about it, that I had to understand that we wouldn't be able to go anywhere nice if it hadn't been for his job, but I knew that was bullshit. One time we took a cruise together, a real romantic trip down to the Caribbean. Or it would have been. He actually packed a fax machine. What kind of sick bastard packs a fax machine on a second honeymoon?"

Brian went back to smiling and nodding. He just had to get through the meal. Once they were in the theater, she'd have to shut up.

Or as it would turn out, she would just have to bitch more quietly. "I can't even remember the last movie Eric and I went to see," she whispered over the coming attractions. "I'm sure it must have been while we were still dating. Once we were married, forget it. He had me; why bother after that? But that's how guys are. It's all about the chase. Once they've got you, it's off to the next conquest.

"I'm sure he would have cheated on me, too, except he was impotent. And he always brought that up like it was my fault. Like I wasn't attractive enough. And for the longest time, I believed him."

Brian was no longer even bothering to nod or add the occasional "uh-huh." He just let her ramble on, barely listening.

"I mean, you'd fuck me, right?"

As the movie began, Brian slowly turned to face his date. She was smiling in the dark, running a popcorn-buttered hand over his. He nodded.

Holding hands, they watched the movie without another word about Eric.

Ten minutes after the movie was over, Brian couldn't remember a damn thing about it. The trip back had been much quieter. By the time he found a parking spot near her complex, both of them were all but sprinting for the door. Madison cursed once under her breath as she fumbled through her purse for keys. He rested a hand on her back, which froze her for a second.

Turning back to look at him, she grinned as the key slipped into the lock.

Once the door was closed behind them, he was ready to take her right in the front room, his hands already working both ends of her dress, one sliding down between her shoulders and the other sliding up her thigh. Between kisses, she muttered, "No... bedroom."

Without thinking, he scooped her up and growled, "Which way?"

She waved in a leftish direction, and he found his way through the dark room as they went back to kissing.

Laying her down on the bed, she immediately slid out of her dress. Even in the dark, what he saw of her was...breathtaking. He pulled off his shirt and then began pulling down his pants as she leaned across the bed for the nightstand, offering him a nice view of her behind.

She picked up a telephone that was beside the alarm clock, and Brian couldn't help but laugh. "You're checking your messages?"

"No" was all she said as she dialed, then put the phone back down in its cradle.

Brian kicked off his shoes as he stepped out of his pants. He crawled onto the bed until he was on top of Madison. He began kissing the small of her back, working his way up her spine as he heard the phone buzzing. She was dialing a number and putting it on speakerphone. He barely thought about it as he moved up her neck and began kissing her ear. "What are you doing?" he asked.

Then a man's voice answered, "Hello?"

Brian said nothing, stopped kissing. Madison was also silent. Again the man's voice asked, "Hello? Is someone there?"

After a few more seconds, Madison whispered, "Eric."

The voice on the other end repeated, "Hello? I can barely hear you."

She spoke a little louder. "Eric."

Silence on the other end for ten seconds…then, "Maddie?"

"How are you?"

There was a deep static-laden sigh, followed by "I'm fine. What do you want? It's late."

"Not for all of us. It's only late for old men who'd rather make love to their jobs than their wives."

"Maddie, the divorce is finalized. You got everything you're going to get out of me. You won. Okay. Just let it go and move on."

"Oh, I'm moving on. I just got back from a date with a gorgeous guy who couldn't take his eyes off me all night. He's in bed with me right now and I'm going to let him do all the things you were too busy to do to me. How do you like that?"

"I think you're delusional."

"Say something."

Brian was so disoriented by the whole thing that at first he hadn't realized she was talking to him. Madison was glaring at him now, hissing, "Say something."

Brian shook his head. "I don't… What do you want me to say?"

She turned her face back to the speakerphone. "You hear that! He could hardly wait to pull my clothes off! He almost took me right in the doorway, he was so ready to go!"

"Jesus, Maddie. This is sick."

Brian looked away from Madison and the phone, suddenly wondering where he'd left his pants. "Maybe I should—"

"No!" Her fingers sunk into arms, making him cry out. "Don't go. You want me. I'm yours. Tonight, I'm anything you want me to be." She turned back to the phone. "You hear that, Eric? I'm going to be this guy's sex slave tonight. Just think about all the depraved things I'm going to let him do to me."

"Yeah, I can hear. It sounds like he's trying to get away. Where'd you meet this guy anyway? Singles bar? Park? Shelter?"

"Don't you wish? He's a CEO."

"Sure he is."

"It's true. He's one of those Sportsfan guys. The ones who are going to own a football team?"

"The lottery winners? Oh, that's a good one."

Feeling a need to defend Maddie, Brian added, "It's true."

"Yeah." Brian could hear typing through the phone line. Eric was on a computer while they were talking. "Let's see." He started laughing.

"Don't you laugh at me, Eric! Don't you fucking laugh at me!" Her fingers dug into Brian's arm again. He could feel the trickling of either sweat or blood.

"No. It's just... I'm looking at a screenshot of your new boy-friend right now. Jealous doesn't...begin to tell you how I feel. Hi, Frank."

"That's not his name, asshole! It's Brian."

"Oh. Okay." More typing. "There you are. Sorry about all this, Brian. Maddie does this once in a while. I know you're probably tempted to leave right now, but believe me she's absolutely worth it. Maddie's probably the best one-night stand you'll ever have."

"Fuck you!"

"Yeah, yeah. Fuck me. Fuck him. Fuck...oh, oh this is just... um, Brian? Were you part of a bachelors auction about a week ago?"

Brian could only say, "Um?"

And Eric began laughing again. "Oh, this makes my night. You had to pay a guy to go out with you?"

"Shut up!" she screamed.

"This is better than the one who couldn't speak English."

"Shut up!"

"Or the time it was just you making your voice really deep, like I wouldn't notice."

"Shut the hell up!"

"Or when your brother—"

Madison picked up the receiver, then slammed it back down, ending the call. She was shaking, gasping for breath. When she turned to face Brian, the moonlight falling through her bedroom window cast long shadows over her near-naked body, adding a surreal, nightmarish look to her.

She grinned with a feral intensity, shrugged, and asked, "So, you ready?"

CHAPTER 25
Bicycle Safety

In the couple of weeks following Bulldog's trade to Miami, he was staying very close to Mary Lee. He was taking no chances while Victor was around and leaving her alone in Chicago was not something he intended to do. Under the guise of relieving her of the pressures of packing, he hired movers to pack for them. The house was emptied in mere days of his Chicago to Miami trade.

Chuck and Alice, too, wasted no time and were moved into the house almost on the heels of Bulldog and Mary Lee's departure. Not a day, not a minute was wasted in becoming Kurt and Darci's neighbors…once again. At least they were not sharing a thin condo wall. That experience was a reminder that familiarity does indeed breed contempt. Not that Kurt didn't already have contempt for Alice.

Sometimes new surroundings have an energizing effect, and this was so for Alice. Darci and Alice decided it was the perfect day for a bicycle ride around the neighborhood.

The two fashion perfect women, of course, had outfits for every occasion, and thus it was that they were waiting at the end of Chuck's driveway wearing what could only be described as cute bicycle outfits.

"Darci, this is terrific! We're going to have so much fun. Well, we will if the guys ever get here. Where is Kurt, anyway?"

"I believe he had to pump up the tires, because he doesn't ride that bike too much anymore. Hey, here he is now."

No sooner had Kurt reached the girls, than Alice had to make her presence known even though she was unfortunately standing in plain sight, "Kurt, we're dressed for bike riding. Just what are you wearing?"

"Aha, you may well ask. Vintage. I'm wearing a classic, vintage concert T-shirt. And, just in case you don't get it, that's Ozzy Osbourne holding Randy Rhoads up in the air. It's from the Blizzard of Oz tour. It's a genuine classic."

"Sharon Osbourne's husband? That Ozzy?"

"One and the same. What other Ozzy is there?"

"And the other guy? Who's the other guy?"

"Randy Rhoads. One of the best rock guitarists that ever lived."

"Right. Never heard of him."

"Not surprised. He died in a plane crash a long time ago."

"Nooo, Ozzy died in a plane crash?"

"Geez, Alice, no. Ozzy's guitarist, Randy Rhoads, died in a plane crash."

"Oh, yeah, I remember once you said that the greatest guitarist that ever lived died in a helicopter crash."

"Oh my God, it's like 'Who's on First?'... I did say something like that, but about a different guitarist. The great Stevie Ray Vaughan. His helicopter crashed into the side of a mountain just before an Eric Clapton concert."

"Sounds like your favorite guitarists should start taking the train."

"Sometimes the great ones are taken from us too early," said Kurt, in a controlled voice.

"Whatever. You look like a bum in that T-shirt."

"Sorry, Alice, that's the way I roll."

It was then that Brian rode out of Chuck's garage on a recumbent bike. Never had such a ridiculous sight appeared more welcome to Kurt. "What are you riding, Brian?"

"A recumbent bike. Chuck is letting me use it. Isn't it cool?"

"Cool? I'm not sure that the word *cool* comes to my mind. I see that you're also wearing a little outfit. A little, cute matching outfit."

"Hold the sarcasm, Kurt, you're the only one not wearing an outfit. Wait till you see what Chuck's wearing!"

"I can only imagine." But imagine is exactly what Kurt did. Images were passing through his mind like a montage of runway designs never intended to be worn in public. Just as Kurt was questioning his decision to join in on the bike ride, Chuck appeared riding down his driveway in the most over-the-top cyclist outfit ever seen.

"Who do you think you are? Lance Armstrong?"

"Exactly, minus the performance-enhancing drugs." Chuck pulled his bike next to Kurt's and tipped his designer sunglasses down to the end of his nose. "Really, Kurt? A concert T-shirt? Is that really the best you can do?"

"Exactly. Yes, I feel more comfortable in this shirt. That bike of yours looks like it cost a small fortune."

"Wrong, *kemosabe*, it didn't cost me a small fortune. It cost me a large fortune. This is top of the line. Try to keep up with me."

"No problem. That shouldn't be hard."

"Ha, wanna bet?"

"Not going to waste my time, Chuck."

The five of them started the ride together, with Chuck making fun of Kurt's bike with every turn of the wheel. "Nice bike. What old man did you steal that from?"

"Funny, Chuck, laugh away. I can still whip you and your fancy bike."

They rode for a while and found themselves further out than expected when they decided to turn around and head back. Chuck's mouth was going the whole time, taunting Kurt with every one-liner he could come up with. At least it wasn't his usual incessant laughing, although the day was still young.

Still sometimes Kurt just took the bait. "Okay, Chuck, I'll race you back!"

"Fine… What's that over there?" He pointed down the street

they had just come on. His face was pulled into an expression more resembling concern than shock.

As soon as Kurt turned his head to look, Chuck took off for an early jump on the race, but it wasn't long before Kurt caught up with him.

Meanwhile, Brian was pacing himself and enjoying the ride along with Darci and Alice. "Hey, are they racing each other like that all the way back? That's crazy."

"Yes, they are, and Chuck is going to win." What else would Alice say?

Brian thought about the two of them racing back. He knew that, no matter what kind of bike Chuck was riding, there was almost no chance he was going to beat Kurt in a long-distance race. Kurt was going to make him eat his words, and when he did…Brian wanted to be there. "I want in on that action."

He started to chase them but was too far behind to get even a little closer. He continued the rapid pace anyway. About thirty minutes into the race, when Kurt and Chuck were neck and neck, Chuck turned to Kurt and smiled. "Watch this."

Chuck went for his gears and started playing around, adjusting this and that, then blew past Kurt. Chuck then slowed down long enough for Kurt to catch up with him. "Just stopped to say good-bye, Kurtis, old pal."

And with that, Chuck stood and pedaled, using the weight of his body, such as it was, to gain maximum momentum. Even though Chuck took an enormous lead, Kurt tried his best to keep up with him.

As the two of them approached the neighborhood, Chuck was surprised to see that Kurt had caught up with him. "Shit! Holy Shit!" Chuck grabbed his water bottle and threw it at Kurt, but it bounced onto the street, a foot away from him. He still kept on coming and stayed right behind Chuck.

Kurt, keeping his head up just enough to see ahead as he pedaled, was suddenly shocked to see a large deer bound out of the forest preserve and smash into Chuck.

Kurt stopped his bike next to Chuck, who was lying flat out

on the street, unconscious. Kurt looked at the deer and looked at Chuck, wondering whether either was dead or alive. His concern for Chuck was all about his medical condition, and his concern for the deer was that it would awaken and ram both of them.

As he was checking to see if Chuck was okay, he jumped in surprise when the deer did indeed awaken and take off running. "Oh my God, what just happened? Chuck, Chuck, wake up! Are you okay?"

By then Brian had reached them and was asking virtually the same thing. "He looks awful. Is he okay?"

"I don't know if he's okay. I don't know! I'm calling for an ambulance now." Kurt fumbled for his phone while continuing to check for some sign that Chuck would wake up.

But Brian was still trying to figure out what he was seeing. "What happened? I didn't see a thing. I just rode up and here you are with Chuck laid up flat on the road. What the hell happened?"

"He got hit by a deer is what happened! A big, crazy deer hit him!"

And just like that, the panic left Brian's face. Kurt watched his friend's eyes narrow. "Yeah, right. You better come up with a better story than that."

"Better story? That's what happened. Who would make that up?"

"Come on, Kurt, that sounds ridiculous. Deer don't run into people on bikes. People in cars run into deer. Better come up with something better."

"Brian, I'm telling you, a deer came out of the forest and slammed into him. That's what happened."

After Kurt made the call, he continued arguing with Brian about what had happened. Brian was looking over Chuck's bike as if looking for clues. The sound of a siren momentarily interrupted the bickering, and the ambulance pulled up a minute later. The paramedics carefully immobilized Chuck's neck and placed him on the stretcher, then moved him into the vehicle. "Can anyone tell me what happened? Did either of you witness the accident?"

Kurt nodded. "I did. He collided with a deer."

Again a three-second pause then narrowed eyes. "Come on. What really happened?"

"I just told you what happened. He was racing me, and he collided with a deer."

The paramedic took a couple of seconds to look around, as if thinking the deer was still hanging around to corroborate the story. "Yeah, sure he did. Have it your way. Let's get him into the ambulance."

Alice and Darci arrived as Chuck was being placed into the ambulance, and the round of questions and disbelief started all over again.

Darci asked what had happened, and Kurt, once again, explained that Chuck collided with a deer.

Alice was in attack mode. "You liar! What did you do to him?"

"I didn't do anything to him. You think I caused this?"

"Of course you caused it. He was probably beating you, and you knocked him over."

Kurt was about to ask Alice how he could have knocked Chuck over if he'd been ahead of him, when the paramedic joined in and asked if that was what had happened.

"No! I told you, he collided with a deer. Or the deer collided with him. I had nothing to do with this. Look at his bike damage and look at my bike. I had nothing, nothing, to do with this!"

Alice was diverted as Chuck started waking up. She ran over and held his hand. "Oh, Chuckles, what happened?"

Not opening his eyes, Chuck whispered, "I was racing Kurt, and I want my mother."

"Oh, honey, your mother has been dead for years."

Kurt screamed, "You collided with a deer, Chuck!"

Chuck tried shaking his head, then winced. "I don't remember any deer."

"Come on, folks. Move back so we can take him in for observation." The paramedic closed in on Kurt. "Have you been in an accident lately?"

Kurt couldn't even follow this new line of questioning. What was the paramedic trying to say now? "No, I haven't been in an accident lately or otherwise. Why?"

"I noticed you and the guy on the recumbent have some old bruises. Do you guys have a history of violence?"

"No, of course not. Those were from Bulldog."

"Those wounds are from a dog? Dogs usually bite, not punch. Your stories don't add up. You want me to believe that you guys keep getting beat up by dogs and deer?"

"Yes to the deer and no to the dog, kind of. Just forget it. You're not going to believe me anyway."

"Let's just say he fell off his bike, shall we, sir?"

"Whatever! Just take him to the hospital."

As they loaded Chuck into the back of the ambulance, he wheezed, "Kurt, you owe me a new bike."

"No, Chuck, I don't! I don't owe you shit!"

And that bickering was ended by the doors closing and the ambulance taking Chuck to the hospital. Darci, Alice, and Brian headed back to the house. Kurt remained there with Chuck's broken bike. Brian yelled, "Don't worry, Kurt, I'll be back with my SUV."

Kurt sat down near the sidewalk, exhausted and on edge. He looked across the street and noticed somebody's window shades closing. Shaking his head, he muttered, "This is unbelievable."

Later that evening Kurt and Darci walked across the street to look in on Chuck, who was lying in bed, wearing a neck brace. It was Darci who asked, "Are you feeling any better?"

"No."

"Well, at least you don't have any bruises on your face."

"Thanks, Darci, but my neck hurts. That's why I'm wearing this brace. Thanks, Kurt."

"I had nothing to do with this. Nothing."

"Yes, you did. Nobody believes that dumb deer story. It's okay. I know you couldn't handle the fact that I was beating you, and you knocked me over."

"I was going to beat you, and you were the one panicking. You threw your water bottle at me."

"Funny. I don't remember that."

"You have selective and deliberate amnesia!"

"Just make it right, Kurt, and we can move on. Leave this behind."

"What do you mean 'make it right'? I have no reason to make anything right, because I didn't do anything wrong."

"Come on, Kurt. That deer story is ridiculous. Nobody believes you. Just make it right, and I won't bring it up again."

"You honestly think I knocked you over so I could win a stupid race? You think that?"

"Let's just say it was a very suspicious accident where the only known witness claims it was caused by a deer."

Darci was tiring of this, and she had no reason to believe Kurt would do such a thing, no matter how ridiculous it sounded. "Chuck, what exactly do you want from Kurt?"

"My bike! I want him to replace my bike."

"Good, he will. Let's just call it *goodwill*."

"Oh no, I won't!"

"Come on, Kurt. Just end it."

"Really? How much, Chuck? How much is the 'goodwill' gonna cost?"

"Four thousand dollars."

"Sorry, no way!"

"Why not? You're filthy rich. You can afford it."

"Yes, I can and I won't! It's not the money. It's the principle. You and Alice know what that is, don't you? Principle?"

Darci sighed. "Honey, just do it."

"Fine."

"And…?"

"And what, Chuck?"

"I'm going to need you to drive me to work Monday."

"Okay, fine. I'll drop you off at one of your delis."

"No, not at one of my delis. I'll be happy when I sell the rest of those delis. I'm talking about SFC corporate headquarters. We can go together. In fact, since we live across the street now, it's not a big deal."

"Whatever. You're one of the many faces of tyranny…you and Alice!"

CHAPTER 26
Let's See That Again

On Monday morning, Kurt drove Chuck to work as agreed. Chuck was still wearing the neck brace, but he was happy nonetheless because Kurt had given him a check to cover the bike.

"Hey, Kurt, how do I go about getting a handicap sticker for my car?"

"No."

"No what? I asked how to get a sticker for the car."

"And I said *no*. No to using a handicap sticker, no to helping you get one, no to telling you how to get one."

Chuck played his part and played his injuries well. Kurt carried Chuck's briefcase through the lobby even though he was well able to do so himself.

As they walked through the lobby, Kurt noticed a lot of smiles and giggles. All directed at Chuck. Chuck noticed as well. "That's really weird. The employees seem to think my wearing a neck brace is funny."

Things got worse when they walked past the Pit. Everyone was laughing, and no one was bothering to hide the laughs. Chuck asked Kurt, "What the hell is going on? Why are they laughing?" as if Kurt would somehow know.

"I have no idea, Chuck. Maybe something on the news."

"It's... They should be working." He took his briefcase out of Kurt's hand and turned away. Chuck was still confused as he headed to his office.

Kurt, too, was confused, but decided to find out what was going on. Normally, anything that made Chuck uncomfortable was okay with him, but there was something wrong with the way the laughter was directed at Chuck. The employees generally liked Chuck, and even if they had loathed him, Kurt didn't want to think they'd be the sort to laugh at another man's injury. He headed back to the Pit, where he heard the loudest and most raucous laughter, and wasted no time in calling up the group by Mitch's computer. Mitch was actually wiping a tear out of his eye as he looked up at Kurt. "Hey, boss, how you doin'?"

"I don't know yet. Tell me why everyone is laughing."

His smile went so wide that Kurt thought his face might split open. "Ooooh, you haven't seen it yet?"

"Seen what?"

"Chuck's video. Somebody filmed the bike accident. Someone across the street was filming everything. It went viral. It's the hottest thing on the Internet." Mitch waved over several of the other workers as he brought up the video. "Hey, Kurt hasn't seen it yet."

And then Kurt saw it. Flanked by a half dozen of his employees. Shocking and vindicating all at once, he remained silent as he viewed the replay.

Mitch and his friends couldn't contain themselves, even though they had been playing and viewing the film over and over again. They burst again into uncontrollable laughter as the deer was seen colliding with Chuck.

Mitch pointed to the monitor. "This is the best part, Kurt. Whoever posted the video actually caught the deer hitting Chuck and programmed it to run in slow motion over and over again. Here, watch, it's coming up."

Sure enough, the video Kurt was viewing showed Chuck very clearly sighting, looking at the deer, and saying "Oh, shit" right before impact.

Kurt didn't laugh, but he was smiling at indisputable proof that Chuck knew exactly what had happened. And he smiled even wider when he noticed a hit counter at the bottom of video. Since its posting ten hours ago, the video had been viewed 103,479 times.

He tried not to give away too much of what he was feeling as he spoke. "Mitch, do me a favor. Send this clip to Chuck's computer, would you? Wait, better yet, can you send it to every computer in the building?"

Mitch nodded. "No problem. Can do. Sure you want me to?"

"Absolutely. The sooner the better. Thanks, Mitch."

Kurt left the Pit and headed straight to Chuck's office, where he made him sit down and watch the compromising video. "Chuck, my friend, you knew the whole time, you knew from the beginning that a deer hit you. You knew and said nothing!"

Kurt wasn't naïve enough to expect remorse, but the unabashed laughter as Chuck reenacted the scene was beyond Kurt's grasp. "I want my mother. That was a nice touch, wasn't it?"

"Nice touch? Is that all you can say? You're unbelievable! Why would you do this?"

"Oh, come on, Kurt, why do you think? I wanted you to replace my bike. Plain and simple."

"And your neck... There's nothing wrong with your neck, is there?"

Chuck resumed his insane laughter as he removed the neck brace with a flourish. "At least I don't have to wear this thing anymore. But, no lie, I was bruised up pretty good. That part is true, trust me."

"Trust you? I don't think so."

"Oh, get real, Kurt. You're super-rich. I knew four thousand dollars wouldn't put a dent in your wallet. I turned my accident into a funny gag, and it almost worked."

"Chuck, you never cease to amaze me. That, by the way, is not a compliment."

"Wasn't that crazy...how that deer collided with me?"

Kurt's nonresponsive answer was to demand the return of the check.

"Okay, it was worth a try, but at least I'm going to be famous now. Hell, I am famous now."

Chuck's self-congratulatory speech was interrupted by Kalia's entrance with news much more foreboding than a deer heading toward Chuck. "Kurt, this is serious. Nobody knows where Frank is. He hasn't been heard from since Thursday night."

Beyond Chuck's office, there were fresh bursts of laughter as the last few employees who hadn't seen the video opened the company-wide e-mail.

Kurt tried not focus on the laughter. "What do you mean? He hasn't called? Come to think of it, I don't recall seeing him at all on Friday. Call Meathead and ask him where his uncle is. Don't ask if he knows where, but ask him straight out where he is. I'm going to check his office."

Kurt suddenly saw shades of the past; although, he couldn't understand why Frank would repeat that history now when all was going so well.

When Kurt opened the door, he was surprised to see Meathead sitting at Frank's desk. He was dressed in an unbuttoned flannel shirt with a Black Sabbath T-shirt underneath and several days' worth of facial hair. He was sifting through a dozen pieces of mail that were strewn on his uncle's desk when he looked up. Kurt asked, "Hey, where's your uncle?"

Meathead shrugged. "He left. He went to Vegas for the weekend."

"And why aren't you with him? You know he's not supposed to be by himself. Your job is to make sure he's not by himself too long. That's your job, yet here you are, knowing he is in Vegas alone."

"No, sir, he's not by himself. He's with his lady friend."

"What lady friend?"

Meathead held out one of his hands, and with his other hand, he rubbed his thumb with his first two fingers in what Kurt called the gimme-money gesture.

"What are you doing?" Kurt just stood in front of the desk, staring at Meathead's hands.

"It's the universal sign for money for information."

"I get that, but you watch too many movies, Meathead. I mean—"

While still gesturing for additional money, Meathead cut him off. "It's okay. You can call me Meathead. Uncle Frank has called me that for the last year. It doesn't bother me. I think it's kind of funny, actually." And the hand gesture continued.

"Meathead, please, enough with the hands. Just tell me who your uncle is with."

"Uncle Frank hasn't paid me this week."

Kurt was somewhat amused by Meathead's single-mindedness, but retained his unsmiling expression as he reached for his wallet, pulled out two twenties and handed them over. It seemed no sooner had he gotten his $4,000 back from Chuck, than someone else was trying to mooch off him. "Now that that's settled, just tell me what's going on."

Before Meathead could answer, his phone rang. Slipping it out of his pocket, he answered it before the second ring. "Hello. Oh, hey, Kalia. Uncle Frank? He left on Thursday. No, he left his telephone."

Enough was enough, and Kurt interrupted by grabbing the phone out of Meathead's hand. "Kalia, it's Kurt. Meathead is here in Frank's office right now. Frank's in Vegas, and I have no idea why Frank is in Vegas. I have no idea who he's with in Vegas, and I have no idea why Meathead is sitting in his uncle's office and not in Vegas!" He clicked the phone off and then turned his attention back to Meathead. "Why are you here?"

"I assumed I was going with them, but on the way to the airport, his lady friend said, 'Two's company and three's a crowd.' She said I couldn't go with them. The last thing he said to me was no slacking while he was gone. I haven't heard from him, so I figured I'd come here and wait for his instructions."

By then, Kalia had joined the two men in Frank's office.

"Why didn't you call me, Meathead? How tough would that be?"

"I didn't think I was supposed to."

"I don't buy that. You know your uncle can't handle his liquor and a weekend with some woman, who nobody knows, could be dangerous. What's her name, anyway?"

"Umm, Linda. I think it was…yes. That's it, her name is Linda."

"Okay, does Linda have a last name?"

"Davis. I think. Linda Davis."

The response produced a mixture of anger and horror in Kurt's eyes. This couldn't be happening! "Davis! Her name is Linda Davis? Are you sure about that? Are you sure her name is Linda Davis?"

Another shrug. "Yeah, that's the name she gave me. So what's the problem?"

"What does she look like?"

"Umm, short hair, pale skin, medium build, and her eyes were kind of spooky. They were dark, almost black."

Kurt could feel his skin go cold. "That's her, all right. Meathead, I need you to get to Las Vegas and find out what the hell your uncle is doing. In all the years I've known Frank, he's never missed work."

"Sure, I'd love to, but how?"

"Kalia, please book him a ticket and a room at the same hotel where Frank's staying. You know where he's staying, right?"

"Yeah, but the front desk was instructed to not take any calls for him."

"Then you really have to get out there. Why am I not surprised? That Davis bitch thinks of everything!"

So much for the $4,000. Kurt endorsed the check that he had originally made out to Chuck and handed it to Meathead. "This is more than you need, so bring me back whatever you don't use."

"That's great, Kurt, but what am I supposed to do with this check? I don't have a bank account."

"What do you mean you don't have a bank account? You gotta have a bank account."

"I'm part of the Occupy Wall Street movement, and I'm not giving the banks my business."

"Oh, give me a freakin' break—that's ridiculous! Everybody needs a bank account! How do get your paychecks cashed?"

"No paychecks. Uncle Frank pays me cash every week."

"That's… You know, forget it. I don't care. Kalia, make sure he stops at my bank on the way to the airport, would you? I'll call my personal banker and ask her to convert the check into a prepaid debit card. But just get him there fast. Meathead, you have Frank call me as soon as you see him and not a second later. I mean it!"

CHAPTER 27

What Should Have Stayed in Vegas

Five hours later, thanks to Kalia, Meathead was in Las Vegas and Kurt, Brian, and Chuck were in the conference room. The three of them were brainstorming theories on what Linda Davis might be planning, since it was unlikely she'd just looked up Frank for a good time. Nobody looked up Frank for a good time. The theories ranged from trumped-up harassment suits to an attempted corporate takeover to a flat-out ransom. Each theory was punctuated by a string of profanity from Kurt and Brian.

Chuck had never met her and after thirty minutes observed, "You guys really hate this woman."

Kurt shook his head. "Hate doesn't begin to describe how we feel, and in this case a healthy hatred is self-preservation. She's vicious in every way. She's the one who got us fired when we were working at Pointy Foods."

Brian corrected him. "Speak for yourself, Kurt. Technically you got fired and I quit."

"Whatever. She was a beast when Frank dated her. Oh my God, she made Frank a bigger ass than he already was back then. She's a cold, calculating, sociopathic bitch." He'd forgotten how much of his hatred he'd put away, until the news had brought it all back.

"Yeah, Kurt's on the money there. She is a mean, tough, nasty woman. I thought I would never have to hear that name again."

Before Kurt could respond, Kalia called on the intercom and said Frank just walked into the building.

Brian screamed, "He's in the building?" After a brief, violent burst of fresh profanity, he followed up with, "Find him and bring him back to the conference room." A few minutes later, Frank entered the conference room but not without assistance from Kalia. She'd propped herself against his shoulder so that he could use her as a support. At first Kurt thought Frank was bleeding, but then he realized that it was just a dried wine stain on his shirt. Like Meathead, Frank had clearly not shaven in several days. His eyes were thoroughly bloodshot.

As he entered the conference room, Frank seemed suddenly aware that he was being propped up and pulled away from Kalia. "Let go of my arm. I'm fine. I don't need help." He stumbled further into the room, catching a chair and leaning on it.

Kurt nodded to Kalia. "Good job, Kalia." She took the cue to leave the room. "And you, Frank? You have a seat. We need to talk."

Frank fell into the chair. "Nah, no way. I don't need to hear any crap from you guys." Frank's hair was drenched with sweat. Sweat was dripping from his armpits, and the smell of booze was oozing from his pores. "I had a long weekend."

"Yeah, Frank, we know."

"Gimme me that water." Without waiting for an answer, Frank grabbed Kurt's water bottle and began chugging.

Kurt tried to keep his voice level. Cooler heads had to prevail, at least until they could figure out exactly what Linda was doing. "Frank, we know you were with Linda Davis in Las Vegas."

"Yeah, I was. So what?"

"Frank, you know better than anyone that woman is no good."

"She contacted me and said she wanted to get together. One thing led to another. A few drinks later, I was in Vegas with her. Do you guys know where Meathead is?"

"As a matter of fact, I do know where your nephew is. He's most definitely not with you where he belongs! I sent him to Vegas to look for you."

Frank paused, apparently letting that piece of information sink in; then he shrugged again. "Don't worry about me and Linda. I can handle her. Brian, gimme your water."

And again without waiting for an answer, Frank took Brian's half-filled bottle of water and began chugging it.

"Frank, you need to end this thing with Linda and the sooner the—"

Kalia was shouting at someone. "You can't go back there without their permission." Kalia was trying to block the door from somebody, but she was shoved to the side. When the woman walked in, the men were rendered speechless to see none other than Linda Davis herself stride in.

Dressed in black pants and a white jacket, black heels and spinster glasses edging down her nose, she looked as if she'd returned from a board meeting rather than a Vegas weekend. The edges of her pitch-black eyes squinted in annoyance, but otherwise there was no hint of emotion on her face.

Kurt, on the other hand, was horrified, and it showed all too clearly on his face.

Linda's voice was a bark that seemed far too big for her body to produce. "Move!"

Frank slurred out, "It's okay, Kalia."

"But, Frank, she just—"

"Let it go." Frank rose from his seat and met Linda at the door.

Kalia gave Linda an angry look, and Linda left her with some parting words in return. "I'll have Frank deal with you later. Count on it."

More vague reassurances from Frank. "It's okay, Kalia, just go back to work."

Linda whispered to Frank, "You've been a bad boy, Frankie, you left me in Las Vegas last night while I was sleeping. You know what happens when you've been a bad boy."

"I recall telling you very clearly yesterday that I had to get back to work."

Linda smirked. "Back to work? You own this large company.

You can do what you want. It's okay; we're together now. But tonight I'm going to give you an extra hard spanking."

Frank seemed oblivious to the fact that Kurt and Brian were still in the room, hearing far too many personal details about him. "I really don't like it when you do that."

Kurt had, had enough. "Quit whispering over there. We need to talk. Now."

Linda put her finger up to Frank's face and gave him a stern look. She then straightened her St. John business suit, shuffled her Jimmy Choos, and took the seat at the head of the table while instructing Frank to sit next to her.

"Yes, Kurt, you are right. We do need to talk." She then turned to look across the table at Chuck. "I'm Linda Davis. Who are you?"

"I'm Chuck Jennings, founder of the Chuckles Deli chain and minority owner of the Sportsfan Chronicles."

Kurt needed to keep this conversation on topic. And any conversation that included Chuck was doomed to digression. "Enough of the small talk, what are you doing in my conference room? Who do you think you are, barging in, acting like you own the place?"

Linda didn't seem in the least put off by his outburst. "I don't own your company, but my husband owns half of it."

"What?" asked Brian, in his most incredulous tone.

"Your husband?" Kurt couldn't believe what he was hearing. Slipped off to Vegas for a weekend. His de facto chaperone left behind. Add that to his usual intake of alcohol, and it made sense. It made a horrible sort of sense. "Oh no, Frank. Please tell me you didn't marry her."

Frank was looking down at his hands, seeming to notice for the first time that he was wearing a ring. "I guess I did, so I can't tell you that."

Linda looked directly at Frank while, at the same time, waving a sheet of paper around in front of everyone's faces, making sure each had ample opportunity to glance at it. "This is our marriage license. Now, if you don't mind, I would like to finish our honey-moon. He's taking the rest of the week off. Come on, Frank. Let's go. Now. I mean it."

Frank stood up and followed his horrid wife. "I guess I will take a few days off."

Kurt was trying for damage control even as they walked out of the conference room. "Don't sign anything else, Frank. Linda, stay away from our company." But he had no confidence that Frank would heed his advice.

After they left Kurt asked if any of them managed to get a good look at the paper Linda was waving around. "She said 'license.' License, not certificate. Maybe it isn't legal yet."

Brian thought about that, but dismissed it. "Kurt, everybody says license. They're married. Little doubt about that, despite your hopes. Time to think about what we can do about this."

CHAPTER 28

One for the Team

Nothing was done that evening. They were mentally whipped and ill equipped for a battle of wills with Linda Davis. The next day, after a restless night of tossing and turning, Kurt was in the office. Kalia had Meathead fly back and sent him into Kurt's office as soon as he arrived. Meathead had found time at least to shave and put on some decent clothes and was looking appropriately contrite, although Kurt didn't think anyone had told him about the marriage. Perhaps contrite was just a default expression for Meathead whenever he got called into someone's office. Shaking his head, Kurt broke the news. "Apparently, your uncle got himself married in Las Vegas. To Linda Davis. I have a feeling she got him drunk and tricked him into marrying her. You know what that means, don't you?"

"She's my aunt now?"

So much for contrition. "Noooo, Meathead. It means we need to get rid of her...fast!"

"How do we do that?"

"I need you to get close to her and get information. Anything you can do to help us protect your uncle."

"Well, if you want me to turn on Aunt Linda, it's going to cost you a little bit of money."

"Aunt Linda? Give me a break. I'll let you keep the rest of the four thousand dollars, but I need something to help get rid of her."

"I don't have that money anymore."

"Didn't I tell you not to gamble while you were working on this assignment?"

"I didn't gamble, but since I got there so late, I decided to check out that famous strip club. I've never been to one before."

"You spent four thousand dollars at a strip club? This was a work assignment. What were you doing? Research?"

"I figured I was off the clock for the night. I guess I did spend it at the strip club. I'm sorry. As I said I've never been to one of those places before."

"No wonder your uncle calls you Meathead."

"I really am sorry, but I'm broke. I'll do this for you, but can you slip me two hundred dollars walk-around money? Kurt, I promise I'll get you information that will help get rid of Aunt Linda."

It was like throwing money into a black hole, but right now Meathead was the best plan Kurt had for Linda. "Fine, but I need you to cozy up with your new aunt. Make her believe that you're happy your uncle got married and get her to keep you as your uncle's driver."

"Yeah, I can do that. I'll send you whatever information I find."

Kurt was sure that his lack of confidence was showing as he pulled four fifty-dollar bills out of his wallet and handed them over. Black hole.

During the following days Kurt received regular updates from Meathead who assured a doubtful Kurt that he was doing what had to be done in order to gain Linda's trust. He hastened to add it was very difficult, but he forged on knowing he was acting to save his job, as well as his uncle. Kurt's opening line during those conversations varied little from, "Do you have anything for me yet?" and this was no exception.

"Yeah, Kurt, I can tell you that she's kept my uncle's glass full with alcohol all the time. I mean all the time! She's also been trying to get him to meet with her lawyer, but he hasn't been in any condition to go anywhere. Keeping his glass full has its drawbacks."

"You can't let that happen, so don't count on drawbacks. He's been known to function while under the influence. Trust me, I know! She will doggedly wait and seize the moment."

"I've convinced her that he needs to sober up a little. She thinks I'm going to help her get my uncle to sign some documents."

Kurt shook his head. "And why would she think that you would betray your uncle? It doesn't make sense."

"Well, in a way, it does. She knows how... Well, you've seen how Uncle Frank can get mean. The way he is around the office... When he's at home, he can be even worse. Some of the things he says to me when no one else is around, I've learned to just shrug it off. But Linda's heard enough that she's, well, not surprised that I might hold a grudge. She trusts me now, and she promised that she would take good care of me. She's going to be gone for a few hours tonight, so this would be the time for you to come and visit."

"Good job! Let me know when she's leaving. I don't trust her and neither should you, so call!"

"Don't worry, Kurt. I'll be careful."

A few hours later, Meathead did indeed call. Kurt and Brian, knowing the full importance of details, listened to what Meathead had to say without interruption. He had arranged to take Linda Davis out to dinner under the guise of giving her a well-earned break. He convinced her that Frank would be okay "resting" for a couple of hours.

Kurt and Brian went to the building as soon as they saw Linda and Meathead leave. Meathead had left the key to the front door under the doormat, and they entered without incident.

Upon entering, they were surprised at seeing the condition of the penthouse apartment. While Kurt and Brian didn't really know what to expect, this was not it. Well kept, tidy, clean were not words they associated with Frank. Their surprise stayed with them as they went from room to room.

"Geez, Kurt, look at this place. For Frank, it's in perfect shape. Hell, it's in perfect shape for anybody. Who would've guessed?"

"Not me! He usually neglects keeping up with his place. Are we sure this is the right place?"

"You know it is, but I get what you're saying. Remember when we saved him and how long it took for us to clean his old house?" It had been before the three of them had started the Sportsfan Chronicles. Frank had gone on a depression-fueled bender that had ended with him almost dying from alcohol poisoning.

"Never forget it, and I wish I could! Remember how many times he used to say 'clean all that shit off your desk'? Seeing the squalor he lived in was the ultimate irony. And I do mean squalor. His place was toxic."

"I hear you, Kurt, but this place is way too clean for Frank. Or for anybody else, for that matter. What's wrong with this picture?"

"What's wrong is this has Linda Davis written all over it. She doesn't want to give the appearance that Frank is incapacitated or being taken advantage of. Where is he anyway?"

"He's over here on the couch, hiding in plain sight. He's got an empty bottle of whiskey next to him. At least that's in character."

"Come on, Brian, let's try to wake him up and—" The ringtone of Kurt's phone interrupted his thought. "Hey, Meathead, we just got here."

Meathead whispered, "Linda is using the bathroom right now. I'm calling to give you a heads up that we're heading back to the penthouse in a few minutes."

"A few minutes? I thought you were taking her out for dinner."

"So did I. That was the plan, but she decided to get carryout instead. I don't think she wants to leave Frank alone, that's what I think."

"Meathead, you gotta get her to trust you and—"

"I'm trying, Kurt, but she does what she wants, when she wants."

Kurt couldn't fault Meathead on that point. He doubted there was anyone on earth who could make Linda Davis do anything she didn't want to do. He doubted there was anyone who wouldn't regret trying. Still he couldn't help venting a little into the phone. "But you haven't given me anything that I can use yet, except that you're coming back with takeout. I need you to get her to let her guard down. I know she's a beast, but you've got to take one for the team. Don't forget, I gave you four thousand dollars, and your uncle needs your help."

"Oh, God, here she comes. I've got to go. We'll be back shortly. Don't worry. I'll get her to trust me."

"Yeah, well, the sooner the better for your uncle...for all of us."

Kurt got off the phone and started to work on Frank. "We've got to do this quickly because they're heading back. Come on, Brian, help me; time is running out."

Brian immediately set to shaking Frank. "Wake up, Frank, we need to talk. Come on, Frank, get up now." Nothing he did or said was working as Frank simply mumbled and continued to sleep. He was dressed in a pair of stained sweatpants and an oversize Chuckles Deli T-shirt.

In turn Brian continued shaking and pleading. "Come on, Frank, get up."

Kurt decided it was time to try a different tactic, a tried and true tactic, and approached the two men with a glass of cold water in his hand. He said, "I love this part" as he dumped the water on Frank's face. "I really do love it."

Frank's eyes shot open. He looked around the room but wore the expression of a man who didn't quite know where he was. "Hey, what the hell? What are you doing?"

"Don't complain, Frank, I could've just stuck your hand in warm water instead."

Mindful of the time limit, Kurt tried to get right down to business. "Frank, we need to talk."

"What? Huh? I didn't do it. I don't think I did. "What happened?"

Brian kept glancing toward the door. "He's not making sense, Kurt, and we've gotta get out of here."

No sooner had Brian uttered the words than Kurt's phone rang once more. Meathead was sending a text message that he and Linda had arrived. "Shhh, Brian. Meathead is talking to Linda."

"Why isn't he talking to you if he called you?"

"Just be quiet. He is talking to me. He's talking to Linda, but he's texting me, and it sounds like they're here!"

"Oh, I get it…here? Whaddaya mean they're here? We took too long trying to wake him. Should we kidnap him?"

Brian and Kurt decided to do just that. Kidnapping was the only solution, and they tried to pick him up, but picking up Frank in a drunken stupor was no different than picking up a dead body. Frank was dead weight, so Brian decided to throw him over his shoulder in a firefighter's hold, and Frank obliged by vomiting all over him.

"Aw, damn it, Frank, you puked all over me. Kurt, do something!"

"Just put him back down on the couch. Grab a towel. Clean up the mess."

Brian went into the kitchen, grabbed towels, and started cleaning up the mess. The possibility of imminent disaster if Linda walked in on them had Brian moving in double time.

Meanwhile Kurt tried to get through Frank's alcohol haze.

"Frank, you've got to listen to me. Don't let Linda know we were here. You've got to be careful. She's trying to get your money. Don't sign anything without showing us first. Please, Frank, you have to listen to me. Linda is taking advantage of you and intends to keep on doing so until she gets everything you have!"

Brian hissed out, "Kurt! We've got to go now! I hear the key going into the lock." And with that Kurt and Brian made their getaway down the fire escape.

Meathead looked up and saw them and made a split-second decision to distract Linda with a surprise kiss. Giving the woman a kiss had not been his intention, but he had heard that desperate times called for desperate measures.

Her lips were cold. And hard. Muscular. Linda Davis had muscular lips, as if holding them in a perpetual neutral line had built them up...or something else. When he pulled away, there was a glimmer in her eyes. Just a glimmer. A little shock, but also...

Linda Davis smiling made his skin crawl. But he smiled back. "I'm sorry about that, Aunt Linda. I know I shouldn't think of you like that, but I just...I just can't help myself."

"Is that why you wanted to take me out to dinner? To get me away from your uncle?"

Meathead shrugged and nodded a little.

"That's why you got so panicky when I said I wanted to head back. It ruined our evening together?" He said nothing in response nor when she wrapped one arm around his waist, the other across the back of his neck. "Well, you should have just said something earlier." And she kissed him.

Meathead wasn't sure how he should kiss Linda. It didn't feel sexy or passionate or loving. Kissing her felt like a test he could never pass. Her cold lips moved open and shut, demanding entry into his mouth. The hand cradling his neck moved up into his thick hair. The hand wrapped around his waist went...down.

"We...shouldn't. Out here." They were still on the street. He was still holding a bag of Chinese takeout in each hand.

She whispered in his ear. "You're right. Let's go back inside."

"No! I mean, Uncle Frank is—"

"You know perfectly well that your uncle is so hammered, he wouldn't wake up if you were in the next room screaming your head off. Which, come to think of it, you will be."

And Linda Davis led Meathead back into his uncle Frank's penthouse, her new lair.

CHAPTER 29
Ninja Chuck

Kurt and Brian had managed to slip away without getting caught, thanks to Meathead's quick thinking. Six hours later Kurt was still on the couch in his man cave, where he had fallen asleep, something he often did when Darci was out of town. Kurt was awakened at 4:00 a.m. by someone pounding on the window. "Geez, now what?"

He grabbed his baseball bat and walked upstairs to the window next to the front door and tried to peek outside. Kurt's face was a scant few inches away from the glass, because he couldn't see who was out there, and it was then that a shirtless Frank jumped in front of the window, yelling, "Let me in!"

Kurt was so startled that he swung the bat at the window. The broken glass set off the alarm and peppered the front porch floor (as well as Frank himself) with shards. It was only moments later that Kurt realized it was Frank who had been pounding on the window.

As he opened the front door to check on Frank, he was yelling back, "What the hell are you doing, Frank? You scared the shit out of me! Are you cut? I don't see any bleeding."

Frank had sat down on the porch, absentmindedly brushing glass off his chest and shoulders. "No. At least I don't think so."

Brian heard the still-ringing alarm and came running across the street, wearing nothing but boxer shorts and sandals.

He hadn't even made it to the porch before yelling, "What's going on?"

"Frank scared the shit out of me. Get him inside, would you, while I turn off the alarm."

As Kurt was turning off the alarm inside the house, a barely clothed Brian was trying, for the second time in one day, to lift a shirtless Frank up. "Come on, Frank, just put your arms around my shoulders while I lift. And no puking this time."

Brian and Frank were virtually hugging each other as a grunting Brian lifted a very weak Frank.

"I didn't know you two were a couple." Chuck's appearance was inevitable, as was his callow attitude and accompanying laugh. At first Kurt thought he was wearing black pajamas, but the sword strapped to his back revealed something much dumber.

"Very funny, Chuck, and why the hell are you dressed like a ninja?"

"I'm surprised you even ask. I heard Kurt's alarm go off, so I decided to throw on my ninja outfit. It's perfect for home defense. They can't see me coming."

"Except for that giant, shiny sword."

"Yeah, and I was ready to use it until I found out it was just a lovers' quarrel."

Brian gasped out, "Give it a break and put that thing down. Help me get Frank inside."

The three of them carried Frank to Kurt's couch. Kurt managed to stop the alarm and give the security company the okay on the phone. With that settled, he turned and got the full impact of Chuck's appearance.

"What the hell are you wearing, Chuck? What? Are you practicing to be a monk?"

"Ninja." Chuck withdrew his sword and shut the front door.

"Not in my house! Put that thing down before somebody gets seriously hurt."

Chuck put the sword down on an end table as requested but then surprised everybody by pulling out Japanese nunchakus, which he promptly began to twirl.

"Come on. Put the nunchucks away before you break something."

Chuck seemed to shrug it off as he turned his head and focused on the bat still stuck in the broken window. Of course he started laughing again. "You're the sloppy amateur, not me. And its proper name is *nunchaku*."

Chuck grabbed the nunchakus—a traditional Japanese weapon requiring more than a little skill to effectively wield against an opponent. Of course that didn't deter Chuck, who first saw the awkward-looking weapon in his beloved Bruce Lee movies and had been a fan of them since then. Consisting of two sticks connected at one end with a short rope, the nunchakus in Chuck's hands were maneuvered with finesse as he spun, turned, and leaped against the invisible opponent. "I am an expert at home defense!"

Chuck was not deterred by the absence of an intruder, and he continued leaping around Kurt's living room, swinging the nunchakus and coming dangerously close to destroying everything in sight.

"Cool it, Chuck! Quit swinging those nunchakus around!" Before he could stop as Kurt had requested (not that he would have), he accidentally let the nunchakus slip from his hand. The men stood frozen as they watched the weapon fly across the room with dead-center aim at the glass pane of a window.

The sound of shattering glass and shards flying in the air mobilized the men into protective positions behind sofas, chairs, tables, and any other solid surfaces available.

"I'm sorry! I'm really sorry. I thought I saw an intruder trying to get through that window."

"Oh yeah, you saw nothing but didn't hear something! Bullshit! I told you to put the damn thing down. You're paying for that!"

Chuck's laughing response was ominous and Kurt was not surprised to see yet another weapon fly from Chuck's hand right into the wall.

"Chuck, stop damaging my house! I hope that Japanese star was your last weapon."

"It was, and the proper name for that weapon is *shuriken*."

"I don't care what it's called. If you pull out one more weapon, I'll grab my baseball bat and turn you into a Popsicle!"

Chuck kept laughing. He always laughed. Never seemed to stop, yet Kurt felt compelled to turn and see the object of Chuck's humor. "Geez, Frank, what the hell is going on?"

Kurt threw a couple of T-shirts at Brian and Frank. "Put these on. Come on, Frank, what have you got yourself into?"

When Frank opened his eyes, he seemed to be staring at the ceiling, as if he couldn't quite make out where the other three men were standing. "You were right about Linda. I think she's trying to get my money. It's a conspiracy, and my nephew Meathead is trying to help her."

Kurt shook his head. "Not exactly, Frank. You're right about Linda, but Meathead is not helping her."

And Frank's eyes regained a manic focus as he tried to sit up, only to collapse again. "Wrong, Kurt. I have proof. I woke with a wet shirt. I must have spilled water on it."

This time Brian interrupted. "No. That was us. Kurt and me. And how is a wet shirt proof of anything? We snuck in your penthouse and poured water on you, trying to bring you around. But you were out for the count! We just tried to wake you up and warn you."

"Yeah, well, I also must have vomited on my shirt."

Brian was nodding in agreement. "Yeah, you did. We didn't have enough time to clean it up."

"Whatever. I went into the bathroom to clean up, and I caught Meathead and Linda going at it. Whaddaya have to say to that, Kurt?"

"*Going at it* as in getting it on?"

"*Going at it* as in having sex. On my bed. While I'm in the next room. And they weren't even trying to stay quiet about it. Yeah, exactly what I mean. It figures he sold out. He wants my money, too."

Kurt was shaking his head, unable to get his head around what Frank had told him and, just as important, trying desperately not to conjure an image of the slacker and the beast in bed together. "No. Meathead is loyal. I told him to take one for the team and get her to trust him. But I didn't mean for him to sleep with her."

"Whatever, Kurt. When I saw them together, I decided to get out of there. I didn't have my wallet or my keys..."

"Or your shirt."

"Nah, Kurt, I just took off."

"How in the hell did you get to my house anyway? If you didn't have your keys or any money?"

"I hitchhiked. Well, I tried, at least, but nobody would pick me up. So I walked here."

"You walked all the way here from your penthouse without a shirt on? That's got to be at least five miles."

"It took me hours."

"Yeah, but it sobered him up, Kurt. More than you and I were able to do. Frank, this might have been the best thing you could have done for yourself. You now have a clear mind. And you're gonna need it."

"What am I going to do? What can I do? I'm married to her. I don't remember it, but I married her in Las Vegas."

"Are you ready to get back to work?"

"Of course, Kurt, always, but what about Linda?"

"We have a company meeting later today. The best thing you can do is to be there around lots of people. We can call our attorneys and see if we can get this marriage annulled."

"Sounds good to me. But I'm going to need some clothes."

CHAPTER 30

One Way to End a Marriage

The first order of business the following morning was to get Frank dressed. Kurt took him to Chuck's favorite clothier, commonly referred to as "Chuck's Suit Store." Kurt gave the clerk his credit card, because Frank didn't have his wallet, and Chuck wouldn't take out his. For once Kurt didn't care. He just wanted to pay, leave, and get a head start on the machinations of the beast.

Meathead called Kurt just as they were completing the purchases, and Kurt answered without giving the man a chance to even say hello. "Did you sleep with Linda Davis?"

"Maybe. Do you know where Uncle Frank is?"

"Yes, I do. Your uncle is with us, and what do you mean 'maybe'? Either you slept with her or you didn't. Which is it?"

"I did. And I clearly recall your telling me that I might have to take one for the team. That's what you told me. So now you're sounding all indignant?"

"Meathead, I was trying to make a point. I wasn't pressuring you to sleep with that beast."

"Actually it wasn't that… Well, I had to distract her from seeing you two. If I saw you going down the fire escape, she was bound to see you, too. I knew that would be a problem, so I made a move on her. Didn't know what else to do."

"Well, we appreciate your commitment to the cause, but it did kind of freak everybody out when your uncle told us."

"Uncle Frank knows I had to sleep with her?"

"He saw you two last night."

"Aw, geez, Kurt, I hope he's not mad. I hate it when he gets mad."

"Forget about it. Just get information, and don't let her leave. Better yet don't let her out of your sight."

"How do I do that?"

"Easy, just keep pretending you want to help the beast."

———

After getting Frank outfitted, they went straight to their attorneys' office, where Frank was royally lectured by the legal team about prenuptial agreements...or the absence thereof. They then ruled out any chance of a postnuptial agreement, given what they knew about Linda Davis. The only course of action left was divorce and, ideally, an annulment.

Kurt, Chuck, and Brian, along with Frank, arrived at the SFC headquarters for their company meeting as planned, but Frank's head was still wrapped around nullifying a marriage he had yet to recall.

"I have a feeling that this little marriage is going to cost me some money."

Kurt tried to calm him down. They needed Frank in control, at the top of his game, for the coming fight. "It is going to cost you some money, but not as much as it would have if we hadn't acted quickly. Hopefully she accepts the hundred-thousand-dollar offer from our legal team." Kurt was thinking that hope was but a thin thread, because Linda never did what one hoped, only what one feared.

Despite Frank's preoccupation with his present state of affairs, the meeting was going along great and, with the couple of guest motivational speakers present, it went even better.

Frank, who decided for once to take a back seat, had also taken a smaller role. He was not only exhausted from the events of the night before, but he was also trying to come to grips with not recalling that he had married someone. He remained a presence at the meeting only to announce the employee of the month.

"I am pleased to announce that our company had another great month. To say we're on a roll would be an understatement. I would especially like to thank our employee of the month, John Harling. Come on up here, John, and take your plaque and bonus."

John Harling joined Frank and the others on the stage to receive his award and to be photographed during the obligatory handshake with Frank. As the photographer was shooting the picture, loud yelling was heard from the lobby. Frank's swift "oh no" didn't bode well at all.

Of course it was Linda. She was in the lobby, Meathead at her side. Kalia was trying to pacify the woman, which would have been laughable under better circumstances. Neither Kalia nor Meathead was able to calm her and neither could they stop her. Frank watched in frozen fascination as Linda advanced like a Panzer tank in war. If she noticed that she was interrupting a company-wide meeting, she gave no indication nor did, Kurt imagined, she care.

Her usual ice-queen stare was gone, replaced by a red, rage-filled face. Kurt imagined this was what Linda looked like when things didn't go her way—a situation he had never before witnessed (or even heard of). There was small satisfaction in knowing she was angry over some sort of denial, since he wasn't certain she was unprepared to kill someone. With her money and her legal team on retainer, he imagined that Linda Davis could probably kill someone in a conference room full of witnesses and not suffer more than a few hours in a cell before bail was posted and charges dismissed.

She was dressed in gray pants, a black blazer, and a pair of leather boots that rose to midcalf. Her face was a deep red and her eyes were twitching as she screamed to the whole room, "Where is he? Frank, I know you're here! Show your face, Frank! I'll be easier than if I find you!"

Apparently Frank's lawyers had already contacted Linda, and she didn't appear to be too happy with what they had said to her. She pushed through the crowd of employees and made her way to the stage.

She pushed John Harling aside with such force that he actually toppled off the stage. She didn't even bother to glance his way. "Frank, let's go now! I mean it! You are leaving here now!"

To Kurt's gratification, Frank remained unmoving and speechless. He whispered, "Don't you budge, Frank. Don't move." Then he ran toward John, to see if he was all right.

Meanwhile Linda waited for Frank. Again Kurt imagined that waiting was something she was not accustomed to doing. Frank's lack of response just enraged her even more so. Linda's anger was so intense that Kurt could hear her breathing. It was a ragged sound, as if she were trying to suck all the air out of the room with each breath. Sweat oozed out of her pores and saturated her skin, staining her clothes.

"Frank! Don't you ignore me, Frank!" was followed by one last harsh breath before she collapsed on the stage.

———

People rushed to her aid, but Linda Davis was dead by the time the ambulance arrived. The paramedics stated initial findings to be death by cardiac arrest, then placed her body into the ambulance and drove off. Under the circumstances Kurt decided it would be best to call an end to the meeting and suggest everyone return to their offices.

Frank was unmoving and looked stunned. "She was so mad she had a heart attack? Is that right? She had a heart attack?"

Brian answered Frank with a terse, "That woman went crazy."

Frank just muttered, "I gave my wife a heart attack."

———

Days later they gathered at Linda Davis's funeral. Kurt, Brian, and Frank stood in front of the casket, talking to each other. None of them were crying.

Frank shook his head and whispered, "I really dodged a bullet. You hear me, Kurt, I dodged a bullet."

Kurt nodded, trying to look solemn. "You sure did. More like a grenade, though." The open casket allowed each of them a clear view of Linda. They turned to Brian to say something prosaic, and he didn't disappoint. "She still looks like she's pissed off at you." Kurt was in the same frame of mind as Brian. "They couldn't put a smile on her face?"

It wasn't a surprise to anybody that Frank had addressed the burial issues. "The funeral director said they tried everything, but they couldn't get a smile on her face."

"What's with her bosom?" Brian looked confused. "I don't recall her being built like that."

"I gave them a picture of her when she was young. I told them to prop those babies up. Actually I think she would have wanted them that way."

"Eh, nice idea, I suppose, but I think they went a little too far."

Frank shrugged. "Yeah, that's what her mother said."

"Her mother? Which one is her mother?" responded an uncharacteristically curious Brian.

By way of answering Brian, Frank turned to a couple sitting in chairs behind them. A man and woman, both in their seventies, slim, sharply dressed in black. Both wore expressions that were a blend of anger and grief.

Frank asked the woman, "You need anything, Mom?" The woman simply glared at Frank.

Brian let out a brief whistle. "She looks just like her daughter."

Frank rolled his eyes. "You have a keen sense of the obvious, Brian. Anyway, the lawyers say that I get a portion of her estate. So not only do I not have to pay her alimony, it turns out I will be getting a couple hundred thousand dollars. Not too bad for a couple of weeks of marriage."

Meathead appeared out of nowhere. "I can't believe what happened to Auntie Linda. It is always sad when we lose a family member."

CHAPTER 31

My Second-Favorite Team

Two weeks later the guys were meeting with the top executives and officers of a very large investment bank that been aggressively pursuing them. Still working toward and hoping for additional funding toward their goal of owning a football team, the guys explored all possible avenues of financial resources. This was one of the better ones.

Even with such heavy matters at hand Brian couldn't resist giving Chuck a hard time about Linda Davis's burial...or in this case, Linda Davis's almost nonburial. "Chuck, I still can't believe you dropped the casket. Chuck, you dropped the damn casket!"

"What do you mean? That wasn't my fault. I was stuck on the same side as Frank and the lady's father. Those two were useless. I was carrying all the weight. I don't know why we were carrying the casket in the first place. Can you tell me that, at least?"

"You know why!"

"No, Brian, I do not know why!"

"Because we were the only ones who would. Did you notice that hardly anyone was there? And no tears from anyone who was there. Not one tear. Do you get that, Chuck? It's weird! No one was crying. I mean, no one. Everybody knows you're supposed to cry at funerals. That's why we had to carry the casket. She sure as hell wasn't going to climb out and bury herself."

"But why did we have—"

Brian shouted, "Chuck, someone had to! She needed to be buried, preferably with a stake through her heart, but thank God there wasn't, because that would have been something. A body with a stake through it."

Frank was uncharacteristically appalled. "That's just sick! For all I know, she could be crunched up in the corner of the casket."

"Aw, come on, Frank, so the casket took a tumble. It wasn't that bad."

"Yes, Chuck, it was that bad."

"Okay, it was awkward."

Frank let out a deep sigh. "Whatever. At least it's over, and now we can get down to business. These bankers really want our business." And with that the ever-pragmatic Frank ended the conversation.

Kurt entered the conference room on the tail end of the conversation and heard just enough to be grateful that he missed it.

"Okay, time for business. I was just with the investment bankers. They're here…just waiting for a couple more of their guys to show up. Kalia will let us know when the rest of them arrive, *so if* you don't mind, no more casket talk."

Brian didn't have to be convinced to put the rolling casket talk behind him. The bankers were the reason for this meeting, and he hoped they would be responsible for even more after the conference. "How many of them?"

"There are going to be five of them and they—"

"Yeah, yeah, yeah, Kurt. These guys have been sniffing around here before. I hope they're serious."

Brian answered, "Yes, Frank, I believe they are."

"What the hell do you know, Brian?"

"They must be, because it's usually just two of them asking questions. Now they have their boss with them."

Kalia's voice on the intercom, letting them know the bankers had arrived, brought the sniping to a halt. Kurt asked her to escort them to the conference room and, just as quickly, told Frank to zip it. Presenting anything less than a united front would put the guys at a serious disadvantage with potential investors. Even Frank grasped that, and so it was that they did, indeed, appear to be united as Kalia opened the door and led the men into the conference room a few minutes later.

Kurt wondered how long that would last as he looked up and saw the five buttoned-up investment bankers enter the room. After an introduction and some small talk, Daniel Jones, the vice president of the firm, started his pitch.

"Good morning, gentlemen. We really want to be part of putting a deal together. We're confident we can get you the additional funding needed to purchase an NFL football team. No doubt in our minds about that."

As one of the bankers passed out the financial proposal packets, Frank felt an under-the-table kick from both Kurt and Brian, who had deliberately placed themselves on either side of him.

They felt rather than saw the all-too-familiar look on Frank's face. He virtually vibrated with belligerence. They had privately agreed that if this failed, it shouldn't be because one of them couldn't exert self-control just long enough to listen and hear the proposal. Perhaps blundering in with empty, corrosive challenges was a result of being with the late Linda Davis too long. Whatever the reason, Frank could be the loose cannon that brought the walls tumbling down.

Silenced before a sound could escape him, Frank looked to Daniel Jones standing before him across the table. The energetic vice president detailed the history of their various large companies, along with some of the well-known deals they had structured and underwritten.

That the bankers could do this was not in question. Mr. Jones needed to convince them that he wanted to do this. Experience had shown him that company hierarchy doesn't always dictate business protocol. His private research prior to the meeting indicated that one of the men would be a particular challenge, and so it was that he met Frank's eyes first.

"You know that we want to put this deal together."

Having secured Frank's attention, he addressed the group at large.

"You guys are doing great. You will eventually reach your goal, of that there is no doubt, but why wait for the other three to four hundred million when we can get this done now? In fact, we're prepared to get you even more than the amount you think you'll need."

Kurt offered, "Well, what we think is that it's going to cost between seven hundred fifty to nine hundred million to get an NFL team. We have over four hundred million."

Mr. Jones nodded, already knowing as much. "We want to get you the rest of the money now. As I said, why wait?"

As expected, Frank uttered the first challenge. "And just how will you do that?"

"Let me ask you this. Did you ever consider taking your company public?"

Kurt responded before Frank could say anything. "Yes, considered but dismissed. We don't want to answer to public shareholders right now. Perhaps down the road, we'd consider going on the stock market. But now? I don't think so. We want to stay a private company."

"Understood. That is considering the amounts usually and commonly offered in a situation such as this, I understand. But we are far from usual or common. We're prepared to participate in lending up to one hundred million at a very good rate, providing we get collateral."

Kurt stifled a sardonic chuckle. "Ah, yes, the Big C—collateral. Just how much collateral and at what interest rate?"

"I understand your caution, Kurt. Actually I respect that. I have little confidence in the fella who jumps in without asking how deep."

"How much, Daniel, and at what rate?"

"Well, we can get you a great interest rate depending on how much collateral you're willing to put up. We have a lot of options here. I'm confident we can work that out."

Emboldened by Kurt's obvious suspicion, Frank jumped in. "That's great, but you still haven't answered Kurt's question, and either way we'd still be short a few hundred million dollars."

"We have options, Frank, but if you want to stay a private company, then we need to bring in additional private lenders and banks. The other banks probably won't offer you the great interest rates that we are offering you on a larger amount."

Frank nodded in his get-on-with-it way. "Okay, what private investors are you talking about?"

"One in particular… The one we have in mind is Pierre La Fontelle. He is extremely wealthy. We're working on additional investments for him right now, as a matter of fact."

Mindful that percentage rates, among other things, appeared to be deliberately ignored, Kurt's BS radar was giving him cause for pause. "Is he from France?"

Mr. Jones smiled. "No. With that name, you would think so, but he's from Wisconsin. He's a cheese mogul… His family is known for producing cheese."

Frank straightened up at the familiar reference. Frank knew the food industry and had no hesitation in letting that be known. "La Fontelle cheese! Remember we used to distribute La Fontelle products at Pointy Foods."

Kurt nodded. "I knew that name sounded familiar."

Mr. Jones took some confidence from their familiarity. "Well, there you go, that's who I have in mind, and he's in town as we speak. In town and very interested. He loves football, and he wants to talk. This guy is the perfect fit."

"When can you set up a meeting?"

"How about today. Frank? How's that sit with you?"

"Where?"

"Here. How about we meet back here in a couple of hours?"

It was slightly out of character for Frank to look to Kurt and Brian, but he did so before agreeing to the time and place.

———

And so it was that, two hours later, they were back in the conference room. While Kurt and Frank were familiar with the company, it was not at all unusual that they had never met Pierre La Fontelle.

Larger than life was the first thought that came to mind when they did meet. He fit their preconceived and stereotypical idea of Wisconsin and large, brawny men. Even sitting down, he clearly was the tallest man in the room. But more than just physical size, there was a presence to the man that seemed to fill the room. He instantly appeared at ease in the unfamiliar office, as if he'd been dealing with the SEC for years instead of minutes. That inexplicable level of comfort was contagious, and very quickly, everybody appeared to hit it off.

By the end of the meeting, Pierre had made it very clear that he wanted in on the deal. It was such a good fit they could almost have done without Daniel's group. Almost. Introduction was golden, and the one thing the guys couldn't have easily managed by themselves. The investment banker was justifiably confident that he could facilitate this deal in record time.

Pierre agreed to invest $100 million in return for a ten-percent stake in the team. He had a separate agreement in mind should the guys decide to seek additional funding for a stadium. Pierre, good businessman that he was, felt it to be a distinct possibility.

Meanwhile based on the success of this meeting, the investment bankers were confident in their ability to bring in other investment banks to the deal.

All in all it had been one hell of a great day! A celebration was in order, and the guys knew just where that would be. After all what was Kurt's man cave for, if not celebrating success?

———

And so it was that Kurt, Darci, Brian, Chuck, and Alice were watching Monday night football on the big screen and shooting pool when Meathead and Frank showed up.

"Whoa, Kurt, those are nice pinball machines!"

"Why, thank you, Meathead," Kurt answered with mock

formality. "They happen to be not just any pinball machines. These are classics. Chuck always, without fail, plays pinball when he comes over. Hey, if you're a gamer, I just happen to have Madden's latest video game set up on the other big screen. Interested?"

Meathead continued scrutinizing the pinball machines. "I know my generation loves the video games, but me? I'm into pinball."

"That's my nephew," Frank said with barely concealed derision. "My nephew here thinks he's going to be the world champion. All he does is play pinball at the bar around the corner from my penthouse. That's all he does."

"World champion? I didn't know there was such a thing."

"Well, there is, and Meathead thinks he's an athlete."

"Well, it is a sport! Do you mind if I play a round or two, Kurt?"

Kurt shrugged. "Fine with me, knock yourself out. Just let me turn down the volume. These machines are beyond loud."

Chuck stood up. "You want to be a world champion? How about trying to beat me first?"

"Go for it, Chuck. I've got five hundred dollars on my nephew!"

"You're on, Frank. But he's not gonna beat me. Never happen."

"Don't be so sure. Hold onto that bet, Uncle Frank. I've been training for a long time. I train so much I get sore in my legs and shoulders. I've been building up my pinball muscles."

Years spent around Chuck and Frank had honed Kurt's bullshit sense to an almost superpower. "You've got to be kidding me. Pinball muscles?"

"Yeah, Kurt, no joke. I started playing a few years ago. I practice three to four hours a day. Not hard to do. It's addictive. You start thinking about when you're going to play next and where. Sometimes I actually dream about the ball going to the out lane at twelve inches away, and I know I have to do something ASAP. My dream is to go to the World Pinball Championship."

Chuck waved a hand as if to dismiss Meathead's dream. "Whatever, you ain't got nothing on me, bitch."

Darci snapped, "Chuck, that was plain rude!"

Alice surprised everyone in the room by being the one to blow off her boyfriend's bravado. "Forget it, Darci, he's trying to intimidate. Look, he's got his game face on." Alice was all too aware of Chuck's looks when he went into his pinball world.

"Game face, Alice? Are you serious? He looks angry and constipated."

"Brian's right, Chuck. You do look angry and constipated."

"Wrong, Kurt, I'm intimidating."

"Right, Chuck, you look real intimidating in those skinny jeans. Actually Brian, you hit the nail on the head. He does look like he's straining to take a shit when he tries to look tough."

Chuck had no problem with the familiar ribbing he got from the guys because he was adept at ignoring it all while sticking to his point. "Oh yeah, Meathead, I like the machines, too. When I play pinball, I've got this dance thing going on. I will pop it and change my stance, and then I can control the tempo. Frank, you are crazy if you think I am going to let your nephew come into my house and beat me at pinball. You might as well kiss the five hundred dollars good-bye."

"Hey, hold on a minute. Your house, Chuck? You mean my house. You and Alice live across the street. And that's more than close enough!"

"Aw, come on, Kurt, you know what I meant. Anyway, I'm the only one who uses these pinball machines. You and Brian are always shooting pool or playing darts. Not to mention playing Madden video games. That's what I meant when I said 'my house.'"

"Say what you want, I think it was more than a Freudian slip. You two guys are turning my cool man cave into the nerd cave."

As if to confirm Kurt's assertion, Chuck and Meathead started playing pinball, while the rest of the group turned their attention to the football game they had been watching.

Having finally settled down, Kurt was more than a little tempted to let the ringing phone go unanswered. Recalling the events of the day, however, was enough for Kurt to pick up.

Pierre was calling to say he was heading back to Wisconsin and asked if he could stop by Kurt's house on the way out. He indicated that he wished to present a new proposal, and a couple of hours later, he and his assistant showed up to do just that.

≈

Kurt, Brian, and Frank went upstairs to the living room to discuss this new proposal. Chuck decided to skip the meeting because he and Meathead were tied up in pinball, and he didn't want to chance losing his $500.

"Pierre, if you don't mind my saying, this must be very important to you if you had to see us tonight, so why don't we cut to the chase? What's on your mind?"

"Well, first of all, I am very glad that the investment bankers brought this deal to me. The fact of the matter is that they usually try to get me to invest in Internet start-ups or something else I really don't know much about. For generations millions of people have eaten cheese from my family's business. I know everything about cheese; that's why I'm good at it. I also know football. I've been a die-hard NFL fan my entire life. I'm passionate about football, and that's why I want to up my offer."

"So, let's hear it."

"Fine, Frank, that's why I stopped by. I want more than ten percent. How about four hundred million for fifty percent of the team? That gives us eight hundred million dollars to buy a team. If we need more money, then we will use the investment bankers."

Kurt didn't even bother to pause out of courtesy, to give the illusion that the offer would even be considered. "No. Sorry, Pierre, but we aren't giving up fifty percent ownership, no matter what the deal is."

"But we will counter that offer," said Frank, taking Kurt by surprise.

Before Frank could say more, Kurt repeated, "Pierre, we aren't willing to give up majority ownership."

Pierre persisted. "Kurt, just how much are you willing to give up, may I ask?"

He had given the matter some thought, more as a hypothetical. "Maybe we would give up fifteen percent, but even that's a stretch."

Frank listened and for once said nothing.

"You can do better than that. Come on. You guys need me."

"Yes and no. We're doing pretty well on our own. All our investments have been winners. You can't really expect us to give away the store."

"You guys are millionaires. But I'm a billionaire. You don't have to wait to raise more funds, because I have the money now. I probably have enough money to do this by myself."

Frank used his oiliest tone as he addressed the investor. "Mr. La Fontelle, the fact that we are negotiating millions of dollars with you in Kurt's living room right now is quite an honor. Now I am willing to increase—"

"Frank, sit down and shut up. We aren't increasing our offer. This is a good deal as structured, and it's the best we're going to offer. Final word."

But Pierre wouldn't let the matter go. "I want at least four seats on the board of directors, and I want the option to purchase stock if you decide to sell more shares."

"You can have two seats on the board, not four, and Chuck gets the first shot at buying more shares of the company. That's a given."

"What? This guy Chuck gets the first shot of buying more shares?"

"You can get your fifteen percent for an additional fifty million. We made a deal with Chuck when we were a much smaller company. Chuck is getting a total five percent once he pays us the money we agreed on. We honor our agreements and that works both ways, Mr. La Fontelle."

Pierre closed his eyes, sighed hard. "I guess I respect that. Okay, I'll do this deal, but after Chuck gets his five percent, then

I want the opportunity to purchase any additional shares if you decide to sell more."

"We aren't planning on selling more."

"Of course you'll sell. Everybody says that and everybody sells. This is a good deal for you guys."

"And for you, too."

"So verbally we have a deal. Let's have the lawyers draw up the paperwork."

"I'll have our lawyers get with your lawyers," said Frank, before anyone could change his mind. "Mr. La Fontelle, you look as if you have a question."

"Really? Well, actually, I do. Does Chuck need to know about this?"

"Yeah, but he's downstairs. We'll fill him in later."

Pierre turned to Kurt. "Why isn't he up here?"

"He isn't up here because he's playing pinball."

"What?"

"He gave us proxy on this matter."

"Well, let's go down and talk to the man."

And so Kurt led them down the stairs. As they entered the man cave, Pierre commented on Kurt's murals. "Whoa, is that a picture of you and Michael Jordan? It can't be."

Kurt shrugged. "Yeah, well, almost. I had the artist replace Scottie Pippen with me passing the ball to Michael Jordan."

"And this one? Is this one a picture of you standing between Mike Ditka and Walter Payton holding the Super Bowl trophy?"

"The nineteen eighty-five Bears, baby! The Super Bowl champs and the greatest team in the history of the NFL. I had the artist add me to the picture. Isn't that cool?"

"How many Bears fans does it take to change a lightbulb? Fifty-one to change it and forty-nine to say what a great team the eighty-five Bears were." Pierre thoroughly enjoyed his own humor.

Kurt was not amused. "What's the matter with you? You're not a Bears fan?"

"Actually the Chicago Bears are my third favorite team. My

favorite being the Packers, and the second being any team that plays the Bears."

Brian was not amused, either. "You're a Packers fan, Pierre? I have a question for you. If a married Packers-fan couple divorced, are they still brother and sister?"

Pierre smiled, but it was not a pleasant grin. It was something a bit more predatory or perhaps retaliatory. Gone was the man who set everyone in the conference room at ease. "Very funny. Just remember the name of the trophy they're holding in your mural. It's called the Vince Lombardi Trophy, not the Mike Ditka Trophy. They named the Super Bowl trophy after Vince Lombardi, because Lombardi was the greatest coach of all time, and he coached the Packers."

Brian was still on track with his cheesehead jokes. "Why do Packers fans always smell so bad? So the blind can hate them, too."

Pierre had no intention of leaving without giving as good as he got. "You know why there was a traffic jam near Soldier Field last week? Because someone put an end zone on the street."

"Real funny, Pierre. Real funny. In my house, too!"

"Okay, enough about the Bears and Packers. Who gives a shit?" Frank now had the ire of both Pierre La Fontelle and his SFC partners, but was oblivious to that fact as he introduced the man to Darci and Alice.

Pierre was very cordial to the ladies as he asked about Chuck. "Those two guys playing pinball over there...which one is Chuck?"

Kurt nodded to them. "The one dancing around the pinball machine like a buffoon is Chuck. The one playing next to him who looks like he just smoked a joint is Frank's nephew, Meathead."

"Eh, thanks, Kurt, I think." Pierre was reminded by his assistant that he was scheduled for a morning appointment, and they needed to head back to Wisconsin. Pierre departed with a handshake and a promise to do the deal with them. After they left, Frank made another drink to celebrate the new deal. "That worked out great."

Kurt shook his head. "We aren't doing the deal with him, Frank."

"What are you talking about, Kurt? Nonsense as usual!"

"You don't understand, Frank, Pierre hates the Bears, and I'm not doing business with anybody who hates the Chicago Bears."

Frank's drink began to splash on the floor of the man cave as he trembled. "What? Are you crazy? Who cares if he hates the Bears? We aren't buying the Bears. Remember?"

"I don't care if we aren't buying the Bears. They're still our favorite team, Frank. How can you forget that? That's how we got here, in a sense. That team is our favorite, and don't forget that."

Frank's face was turning red. "Whose favorite?"

"Mine, Brian's, Chuck's, and, I thought, yours."

Frank was shaking his head as he spoke. "Aw, come on. Grow up, boys. This is business. I'm not going to let your childish alliances interfere with this opportunity."

"Sorry, Frank. It's called loyalty."

"Loyalty, shmoyalty! This deal is moving forward, and I don't care if I have to wear a cheese hat to close it. What? You got something to say, Kurt? Say it!"

"We're not going to sell out."

Frank put his drink down on an end table, undrunk. "Come on, Meathead, we're leaving."

Meathead didn't look away from the machine. "Aw, come on, Uncle Frank, I'm winning. You've got money on it!"

"Let's go. I said, let's go!"

Chuck piped in with, "You leave, you forfeit, Frank. This is my game, too."

Frank walked over to the pinball machines and unplugged them. "He's won. It's over. You owe me."

Meathead whined, "I told you I was winning, Uncle Frank. I was winning! Whatchya go and do that for?"

Chuck shook his head. "I am not paying. I am most definitely *not* paying."

"Yeah, yeah, whatever, Chuck. Come on, Meathead, let's go.

I'm calling the lawyers tomorrow morning and letting them start the paperwork."

Kurt didn't move as he spoke. "Frank, I wouldn't make that call if I were you."

"Well, you're not me!"

Chuck started laughing. "Sucks to be you, Frank! Hey, Meathead, you don't know how lucky you are. I was about to beat you."

"I don't think so. I had a huge lead, and you know it."

"What I know is I was letting you wear yourself out. Your uncle here stopped me from opening up your ass."

"Whaddaya talkin' about? Whaddaya mean?"

"I was reserving my energy. Just like Rocky did when he fought Apollo Creed. You didn't really think you were beating me, did you?"

"Of course I was beating you! You were dancing around the whole time! I even had to yell at you for reaching over and tilting the pinball machine."

"I was kidding around."

Kurt forgot the dropped deal for a moment. "Chuck, don't tell me you messed up one of my machines again!"

"Don't get your panties in a twist. Your machine is fine."

"It's 'knickers in a knot,' and answer my question. Did you screw up my machine again?"

"He's still got his game face on."

"Well, gee, thanks for that, Alice. I can't wait to see what his face looks like after I make him pay for repairing the damn machines."

And so the evening ended. Chuck was still dancing around, Alice looking on with amusement. In fact he danced all the way home across the street. Kurt was just glad to have his house to himself. He'd think about the damage later. He wanted to sit back, put up his feet, watch the game recaps, and deal with Chuck another day.

CHAPTER 32

Frank Makes a Call

Monday morning, Kurt was back at the SFC building, thinking Monday had come around too soon. The blinds in Frank's office were closed and everything was relatively quiet. Chuck was unaware that Kurt and Brian were in his office waiting for him, so he was understandably surprised to see them there.

"Hey, guys. What's the matter? Don't tell me it's about your pinball machine. I didn't spill that beer on the machine Meathead was using."

Kurt momentarily forgot the actual reason they'd been waiting for Chuck. "What are you talking about? What beer? Aha, that's why the bumpers are sticking. I knew it. Damn it!"

Brian rolled his eyes, not at all surprised. "Let me guess. Meathead was beating you, and so you decided to spill beer on the machine he was playing on."

"Uh, no, Brian, you got it all wrong. That was Meathead's beer. Wait a minute. What're you talking about? Is the machine not working now?"

"He doesn't have it wrong. Meathead wasn't drinking beer. He was drinking water. You creep, you did try to end the game so you poured beer on my pinball machine while we were upstairs, didn't you? Anything for a win. Right, Chuck?"

"No, it's not like that. I didn't mean to. I spilled it, and Darci came running over with towels. She cleaned it. I'm sure it works fine. She promised she wouldn't tell you."

"Well, she didn't tell me. She didn't have to. You know what, Chuck? I'm going to have it checked out, and you're the one who's gonna pay for it. The problem is you never mean it, or it's always an accident, and I don't, for one minute, believe that you are that accident prone." Kurt was ranting and showed no sign of stopping. "Why is it always you having accidents, Chuck? And now you're telling me you have five hundred owed you!"

"Whatever. Fine, just keep the five hundred dollars I techni- cally won from Meathead. Just keep it, but you'll have to collect the money from Frank, because they forfeited by leaving. Fair's fair."

"You know nothing about fair! And Chuck? You're right. It was a forfeit. Big difference. You did not win."

"That's what I said."

"Yeah, you did, and I pulled teeth to get it said."

"I also said you'd have to get it from Frank."

Brian didn't think he could take another minute of this his- tory repeating itself. "Guys, guys, enough. We aren't here for this." Chuck would always be in the center of chaos. They knew that. "May I remind you, we have work to do. Chuck, we need you to set things up, so we can hear what Frank's doing."

"What? In Frank's office? Why don't you just ask him?"

"Geez, Chuck. You know Frank never answers anything."

"So what? You want me to eavesdrop?"

"Noooo! We want you to set up his office for recording. We have to know what he's doing behind closed doors. Besides… when have you ever declined sneaky? Just set it up, so we know what he is doing!"

"Oh, I get it. You want to know what's going on—"

"Finally he gets it!"

"I can do that, but why? What's the matter? What's going on?"

Brian threw up his hands. "Kurt, you talk to him. I can't stand another minute of—"

"Chuck, listen with both ears and at least half your brain. We have to know what is going on in Frank's office. We have to know what Frank is not telling us. We know something is going on. We want to know what that is."

"Oh, why didn't you say so?"

Brian was tense, and this conversation wasn't helping, so he walked out, leaving Kurt to finish.

"Chuck?"

"Yeah, Kurt, I get it. You want me to wire Frank's office."

"Yes. Sight and sound."

"I can do that, but how? His blinds are shut, and his door is closed."

"We'll take him to lunch to discuss a potential business venture."

"Really, what is it?"

Kurt could start to feel the veins in his head bulging. "Chuck! We're just telling him that. We want you to wire the office, and we'll get him out so you can do that. Get it? Before you say anything… This has to be done. Has to be! Listen, you get this done, and I'll forget about the damage to my pinball machine. But only if you get it done while we're at lunch. Just nod, don't say anything." Kurt knew that Chuck was incapable of not speaking and wasn't surprised when he did so.

"I promise you I will get it done. No one will know. You promise I don't have to pay for any damage, damage I didn't do? Really, Kurt, you can be so petty for such a rich man."

"Yes, I promise, but you have to tell the truth, or I'll get someone else in here to do the job. The truth! Did you spill that beer on purpose?"

Chuck was already laughing hysterically when he answered. "Of course I spilled it. I wasn't going to let him beat me."

"Nice. You better get this done, Chuck, or this will never be over. As a matter of fact, if you don't get this done, you will never be over. Ever!"

Kurt didn't wait for a response. Chuck knew that Kurt was at the end of his rope, and contrary to popular belief, Chuck did know when to stop. He usually chose not to. This was not one of those times, and his mind was already in overdrive, thinking about the equipment and where to place it.

Kurt was halfway down the hall when Chuck heard the last ominous words. "Just make it happen."

A few hours later, Kurt, Brian and the ubiquitous Frank were walking down the hallway, returning from lunch. Of course Frank was mocking with great relish the "new" business deal.

"That's the best you could come up with? Exercise shirts with bright lights on 'em? I thought you guys were getting stale, but this deal beats all. I don't believe it, exercise shirts with bright lights on them."

Brian remained committed to the performance, still trying to pitch the ridiculous product. "Yeah, Frank, it's for people who like to exercise outside at night. It's a great concept and a proven one. Nobody's done shirts. Headbands and ankle bands but not shirts. This is lifesaving."

"Come on, Brian, lifesaving? You've lost your marbles."

"This will save people from being hit by cars."

"Yeah, yeah, whatever. Who works out at night, anyway? That's whiskey time, stupid. Another big mistake. We're making an obvious-to-all-but-you mistake by not going forward with Pierre. Thanks for lunch, guys. No to the shirts."

Kurt and Brian headed toward Chuck's office, while Kurt harped on Frank and the luncheon. "Brian, you said you had come up with a good decoy business venture. That was it? The only good thing about it is that Frank was focused on our stupidity."

"Hold on a minute. I did actually love the idea of bright-light exercise shirts. It even has a ring to it. Bright-light exercise shirt ads would grab everyone's attention. You really don't get it, do you? You're making it sound silly."

"I repeat, we're doing millions of dollars in business, and you come up with that."

"Yeah, Kurt, and it worked. We got him out of the office. And

I didn't hear you come up with anything better on the spur of the moment. It's a good thing I didn't come up with something that sounded halfway decent, or after three drinks, Frank might have gone for it."

"Good point."

Kurt opened the door, and they entered Chuck's office, looking for confirmation that something had been done. Chuck's laughing and dancing around indicated just that.

"Mission accomplished! Come on, look at my desktop screen."

"Desktop screen? Why not the dedicated monitors?"

"There's no password required on the monitors… You said, 'Secretly,' I recall."

Kurt paused, not quite believing that he was about to extend a compliment to Chuck. "Wow, good thinking. For once you surprised me." The three men hunched together over Chuck's desk and saw Frank picking up his phone. "Chuck, sound? I said we need sound."

Chuck waved him to calm down. "Give it a second. He's punching in the numbers. There is no sound yet."

Frank's voice was the confirmation Kurt and Brian were looking for. "This is Frank at SFC. Sportsfan Chronicles. I need to talk to Pierre."

The guys remained glued to Chuck's desktop as they listened for the incriminating evidence that Frank was indeed doing a backroom deal without them. They knew it. They just needed to prove it.

"Hey, Pierre. This is Frank. Thanks for taking my call. I'm going to cut to the chase. The Sportsfan Chronicles aren't going to do the deal with you."

This most certainly was not what they expected to hear. They had been certain that Frank was going to try to do the deal with Pierre and were surprised that he did not do so.

"Yeah, it is a pity, but we decided to go in another direction and nothing you can say will change their minds. I'm planning on retiring. The guys don't know it yet, but it's time for me to exit this venture and enjoy the good life. They've made it clear that they don't want to do this deal with you and that I have no say on this at all. I'm going make them an offer to buy me out. Sorry we couldn't do business with you."

Kurt and Brian couldn't have been more shocked. They didn't hear a backroom proposal, but they did hear that Frank intended to retire. Something wasn't right, but they heard what they heard and would have to take it at face value.

"I can't believe it. What about you, Brian? Can you believe what we just heard? He didn't try to do the deal behind our backs. That is so not like Frank."

Brian grinned, shifting his weight from one foot to the other in an almost dance. "I can't believe he's retiring and letting us buy him out. Finally! We can finally get rid of him."

"Don't get too high on the news. How much is it going to cost us to buy him out?"

"Uhhhh, I think a lot. He owns half the company because he put in one hundred million. What does that mean? We pay him back his hundred million, plus we throw in an extra thirty or forty mil?"

"Brian, you act like a hundred thirty million is nothing. That's a lot of money that will be depleted from our company."

"Yeah, but the company is now worth over four hundred million dollars. Actually we're worth a lot more."

"You don't really think Frank's going to settle for anything less than two hundred million?"

"So what, Kurt? We still have a growing company worth more than two hundred million. We have a chance to get rid of Frank, and we've recouped the other half of the money from the lottery. It's a no-brainer."

Kurt shook his head. "Frank's been behaving himself the last couple of years. That two hundred million will set us back. Plus, why would Frank want to give up all of this?"

"Who cares? Let's grab it before he changes his mind."

Kurt spent the next couple of hours thinking about the

situation and questioning what he had heard. There were so many questions. Nothing made sense. At least nothing made sense based on what they knew.

He was still ruminating later that afternoon when Frank called a meeting and announced his plan to retire.

Kurt and Brian made an attempt at looking shocked, while Chuck just sat there looking stupid as usual: the perfect poker face for him. It was Kurt who first asked, "Frank, I'm surprised. Why do you want to retire? You're living life better than you ever have before. The financial return is great. Better than great! And you want to retire? I don't get it?"

Frank stared at him and muttered, "Of that I have no doubt, Kurt."

"Okay, whatever that means. But why retire?"

"You guys stopped the deal with Pierre, because he doesn't like the Bears. What kind of reason is that? Don't answer, Kurt. I don't want to know. I don't need this anymore. I'm cashing out and going to enjoy the rest of my life."

"Cashing out? Just how much, exactly, do you think you're going to get? Can you tell me that?"

Brian apparently didn't want to wait for an answer, even if it had been rhetorical, and to Kurt's chagrin, he started negotiating. "We are prepared to offer you one hundred and forty million for your half of the company. That's a forty-million-dollar profit in less than two years."

Frank's mouth hung open in disgust. "Kurt, tell Brian here what you already know, that this is not up for negotiation. You know me better than that."

"Apparently I do, Frank, but do go on. Let's hear it anyway."

"Again it's not up for negotiation. It's black and white. When you allowed me to do this deal with you, you purposely put in the contract that you or I can walk away with half of the company if either party decides to part ways within the first two years. We are in the twenty-third month, and I'm ready to get out."

"And, how much do you want, Frank?"

"This company is worth over four hundred million dollars, but I'm going to make it easy for everybody. I want two hundred million cash, and I won't fight for the other twenty-eight million that I'm entitled to."

"Really, Frank, are you sure you want out? This is going to be a big financial setback for the company."

"Don't overplay your hand, Kurt. You guys will be fine. I'm leaving you guys in great shape."

"You're leaving us in great shape?"

"Of course I am. You think you'd be this successful if I hadn't been running this place? You think you'd have done this well alone?"

"Frank, this place was…is successful because we all contributed."

"Whatever you tell yourself. If that helps you sleep at night! No skin off my nose."

Kurt shrugged. "Okay, Frank, we'll buy you out."

"Immediately."

"Why immediately? Where did that come from?"

"Kurt, immediately. I have one month to take advantage of the contract. I want to start looking for a small island in the Bahamas to purchase. Always wanted to own an island. Forget the talk. You can't stop it, so let's move on. You should be happy that I'm ready to retire."

Brian simply said, "It's a deal."

CHAPTER 33

Frank Makes
Some Friends

Three weeks after finalizing Frank's buyout, he was gone and $200 million richer.

Kurt was feeling the loss, not of Frank, but the cash. He was a bottom-line guy, and this didn't sit well with him. It smelled funny, too, but the cash was the primary issue. "Great, guys. Now we have only one hundred and sixty million in liquid cash."

Brian was somewhat startled by the statement and looked confused. "One hundred sixty million? I thought we were worth around four hundred and sixty million before we paid Frank his two hundred million dollars. So we should have around two hundred and sixty million. Numbers don't lie."

"No, Brian, numbers don't lie, but you're talking cash, which isn't the same as value. Two hundred sixty million is what we have in assets...combined assets. We have the value of the various companies we purchased, along with the intellectual property and real estate we own. That, added to the cash, gives us a value of two hundred sixty million dollars."

"Oh. So we still have a hundred and sixty million in cash, and our business is a cash cow. We can just keep adding to it. Now we own all of the company."

"Yes, exactly, and it's time for Chuck to step up and invest the rest of the money he promised. We're six hundred million dollars short of being in a position to purchase an NFL team. I think we should have convinced Frank not to retire, but for some reason I don't think that would have happened."

"How much is Chuck going to invest?"

"He bumped it up to fifteen million last week. He's accepting an offer on the rest of his deli chain. Finally."

"Who would've thought his delis were worth that much? Hard to believe."

"Brian, it sometimes comes down to numbers. It's because he has so many of them. He has those sandwich restaurants of his sprinkled in almost every neighborhood in the Chicago area."

"Give me percentages."

"You and I own eighty-two percent of the company, and Chuck will own the other sixteen percent. Victor and Bernie will own the remainder. That's only two percent."

"Awesome."

"I hope so, because now we have to make it grow. Where is Chuck anyway?"

"Chuck is moving into Frank's office as we speak."

"Okay, Brian, good timing. Let's go find out when he plans to pay us."

Chuck couldn't hide his excitement about moving into Frank's larger office, and Kurt was about to seize the moment when Brian beat him to it. "Hey, Chuck, I think you should pay us before you move into Frank's old office."

"What are you talking about? It's happening, guys. We should be closing on that any day now. This is awesome. Look at the size of this office, would you?"

"This is me, Kurt, you're talking to... You make sure you come through with the money you promised if you want to keep enjoying it."

"I hear you. I want Frank's old job."

"His old job? You can have his office. As far as his old job goes, I don't know about that."

"Why the hell not, Kurt?"

"Because I don't think it's a good fit. I think you should focus on the marketing duties we gave you. Your marketing duties."

"I disagree. Come on, I want Frank's old job."

"For now his department heads will answer to me. We'll see how this new setup works for a while. Chuck, please. Just focus on finishing the sale of your restaurants. End of discussion."

Chuck finalized the sale of his restaurants a couple of weeks later. Just prior to having the bank wire the proceeds to the Sportsfan Chronicles' bank account, Chuck tried to chisel a larger amount of ownership.

Kurt tried to stay calm as he explained it. "Chuck, here's the thing. We gave you a good deal. You agreed to that deal, and why wouldn't you? You were getting sixteen percent for fifteen million dollars. That sixteen percent is worth way more than the fifteen million dollars we got from you."

"Yeah, well, things change. Like you getting all this additional money. More money, bigger percentage!"

"Not what we agreed. We aren't giving you twenty-five percent, so take it or leave it. But may I remind you, if you leave it, you can pack up your gadgets and move out."

It was a rare moment when Chuck wasn't laughing his head off like a buffoon. "Whoa, that's a little harsh."

"No more so than your blackmail. You know I mean business. It's time to shit or get off of the pot."

"Okay, I'm going to take a big shit! I'll take your sixteen percent for five million dollars. Deal!"

Kurt shook his head. "I don't think so, Chuck, get off of the pot. Sixteen percent for fifteen million dollars. Fifteen million, not five. Fifteen million dollars, and I'm not fucking around anymore."

And that had Chuck laughing. "Okay, okay, hold on for a second." Chuck was still laughing and remarkably nonspecific as he phoned his banker, telling him to wire the funds.

"Okay, it's done. I'm now a major shareholder in the Sportsfan Chronicles. I'm all in. This is the bulk of my assets. Now let me have Frank's old job."

"Okay, congratulations, Chuck, but not so fast. After accounting confirms that we have received the money—the correct amount of money—I will talk to Brian and see about letting you have Frank's old job. But before you start celebrating, you have to take it seriously. If I can say anything about Frank, it was that he took the job seriously."

The smirk was still on Chuck's face as he nodded. "Trust me, I'll take it seriously."

"Trust has nothing to do with it. I know you, Chuck."

"No, really, I have fifteen million reasons to take it seriously."

"You seem to have forgotten that Brian and I have over one hundred million dollars invested in this company. Sorta puts things into perspective, doesn't it?"

"Okay, I get that and I will take it seriously. Really I will. Let's make the announcement when I get back to the office."

"Good idea. Let's do that." If Kurt was worried or still dubious, he didn't show it. He knew that he could undo anything and everything if Chuck didn't come through with the full amount of money as agreed. More importantly Chuck knew it, too.

Later in the afternoon, Kurt, Brian, and Chuck gathered the staff around the stage in the Pit, where Kurt called for their attention.

"As most of you may already know, Frank has decided to retire from our company. We have bought out all of his shares, and we wish him well and hope he enjoys drinking his margaritas on some sunny island in the Bahamas."

For the benefit of the few who hadn't known, Kurt paused briefly and then continued. "With Frank's departure we had to consider how best to fill his position. We are confident that we have the right guy for the job. Chuck Jennings has decided to get out of the restaurant business entirely. Doing so allows him to focus his energies and expertise here at SFC full time. He will take on Frank's former duties. So effective immediately everyone who worked directly for Frank will report to Chuck. Let me add that Chuck has also become a larger investor in the company. So, everybody, let's give Chuck a round of applause."

Chuck was well liked by the staff. The applause was immediate and loud, and Kurt nodded as he beckoned Chuck and offered him the stage.

As Chuck walked past Kurt on his way to the microphone, Kurt stopped him and whispered, "Chuck, what are you wearing? What's with all the zippers on your pants?"

"I thought it would have been obvious. It's my new office look."

"This? This is your new office look? Are you serious?"

"Yeah, I'm serious. You know how Brian likes to dress like Steve Jobs by wearing all black, and how I used to dress like Mark Zuckerberg with the hoodies, except Alice doesn't like me to dress like that? Well, I've decided to bring back parachute pants from the nineteen eighties. It's going to be hip. And the best part? I'm probably the only person in the world right now wearing these babies."

"Some things should never be brought back, and those are one of them."

Chuck was laughing as he acknowledged the applause and moonwalked across the stage toward the microphone. By the time he took the mike in hand, all the employees had started cheering.

"Well, here I am. Out with the old and in with the hip!" He tried to start his speech, but the crescendo of cheers had grown even louder, and he was forced to wait a moment. The staff began to quiet, and Chuck began his speech.

Kalia took that opportunity to get Kurt and Brian's attention by waving at them. The two partners went immediately to her side, knowing she must have something important to say. She would not have interrupted them for anything less than ominous.

She spoke just loud enough to be heard over the cheers. "Listen, I got a weird message from Frank. Weird even for him."

Kurt shook his head. "Let me guess, he's drunk at the beach."

"No, Kurt, not at all. Actually he sounded sober. Come on.

Into the conference room so I can play it for you. You should hear this for yourselves."

As if a ghost was speaking from the grave, they heard Frank's voice speaking directly to them, "You miss me yet? I've got a little message for you people. Tune in to SSN at five today for a very important announcement. You won't want to miss this."

They were confused and had no idea what Frank was getting at beyond his suggesting that they tune into the SSN channel at five.

Kalia, too, was confused. "What's he talking about? Or do I not want to know?"

Brian shrugged. "You know as much as Kurt and I do, and all I can say is that it sounds ominous to me."

Kurt was eager to get to the bottom of Frank's cryptic message and asked Kalia to turn on the television and tune it to the channel. "What time is it? He said to do this at five. Is it five yet?"

Kalia nodded. "It's almost five now. That's why I interrupted. I thought you'd want to see or hear this firsthand." And so they stood in front of the flat screen, awaiting Frank's appearance without knowing why. "I want to see what he's talking about. Kalia, try to call Frank and find out what's going on." No sooner had he asked Kalia to call, than multiple broadcasters were seen talking on camera.

"Breaking news, ladies and gentlemen. Breaking news that can potentially affect the National Football League. It appears that a powerful group of wealthy investors is about to announce they are ready to buy an NFL franchise."

The picture switched to a press conference with none other than Frank at the microphone. Kurt had a sinking feeling as he saw Frank on camera, along with several prominent and very recognizable businessmen standing behind him.

By now, Brian, too, saw the scene. "What the hell is Frank doing up there?"

"Don't know, but I think he royally screwed us this time."

"Kurt, look. Isn't that Pierre La Fontelle standing by him?"

"Yeah, one and the same. I also see John Pointy the Third."

"Pointy as in Pointy Foods?"

"Yeah, none other. The largest shareholder of Pointy Foods. You know, the founder's superwealthy grandson. But... Why is he standing up there? Hey, Brian, any idea what's going on?"

"Haven't a clue. I remember his portrait hanging in Frank's old office at Pointy Foods, and that's as close as I've been." Their discussion was on hold, while they watched what was going on.

One of the reporters started with, "I'm John Mercado, pool reporter for the Sunrise Sports Networks. So, why are you choosing to make this announcement in such a big way? SSN has been told that you haven't actually purchased a team yet."

Frank was the obvious leader and spokesman, and as such he stood to answer the queries from various reporters, including those from Mercado.

"Purchased? Not yet but we are ready. We're ready in a big way! I wanted the country to know that we're ready to be the next owners of an NFL football team right now. We intend to be the next choice for the greatest league in the world." Just then Frank was interrupted by the ringing of his cell phone.

As soon as he saw the caller ID and knew it was Kalia, he smiled and shut off his cell phone. "Hold on a second. I'm sorry. I forgot to shut off my cell. Isn't it always the annoying people you know who have a knack for calling at the wrong time? Not to mention some people who every time is the wrong time, if you know what I mean."

Once again Frank smiled as he looked directly into the camera. The reporter smelled a story and was persistent and determined to get it. "Well, sir, weren't you going to do this with the SportsFan Chronicles? What happened to them?"

"Let's just say they're way out of their league. I can't wait any longer for them to raise the necessary funds needed to do this. I decided to leave them and start my own group. My new organization is called Franklin and Friends. Our sole purpose is to purchase an NFL team. I've surrounded myself with some of the most successful businessmen out there. People like myself with a proven track record. We have enough money to buy an existing team or start a new team, and if needed we can build a brand-new stadium, a stadium as incredible as Jerry Jones built for his Dallas Cowboys. We're the real deal. No waiting. We are ready now. With that I am ending this press conference."

Brian had the appearance of a man in clinical shock. He sat down and put his head on the conference table. Kurt was simply angry, very angry. "I knew it! I knew something wasn't right. After everything we did for him. The old Frank is back. What a lying bastard!"

At the sound of Kurt's anger, Brian raised his head from the table.

"Oh no, Brian! Do you have tears in your eyes?"

Brian wiped at his eyes, shaking his head. "No! Okay, yes, a little. Frank's been screwing us most of our lives. He's still screwing us."

It would have been so easy for Kurt to just agree, to pick Brian up, walk him to the nearest bar, and take turns ordering rounds. It's what they'd done more than once after Frank had screwed them over at Pointy Foods. But that was back when there hadn't been a damned thing they could do about it and when there was so much less at stake. "Later! We need damage control now. I don't want to lose morale among the staffers."

Brian wiped away the tears, gave himself a mental shake, and steeled himself for battle. "Don't worry about it. I'll let them know that Frank is going to buy a football team now before we do."

"You don't have to say it like that. We are going to find a way to purchase the team before he does. I don't know how, but we are. That cretin doesn't know anything about sports."

"Right. Right, Kurt. I'm going out there and telling them that Frank is attempting to buy a team before we do. How about that?"

They walked back out to center stage where Chuck was still giving his acceptance speech. Speech? It was more like a pep rally.

Kurt whispered, "Brian, just make sure you sound as professional as you don't feel right now."

Brian wiped his eyes one more time, mostly to confirm that

they were dry. "Don't worry, Kurt, I'm on it. And I do feel profes-sional!" Brian played his part well as he walked across the stage and took the microphone from Chuck's hand.

Chuck couldn't have looked more shocked if Brian had slapped him. "Hey, what're you doing? I'm not done yet. Wait a minute. Have you been crying?"

Brian ignored him, turning his attention to the employees gathered around him. "Listen up, everybody. Frank fucked us!"

Kurt was all but frozen as he looked at Kalia and shook his head. "Well, that was professional. At least he went straight to the point."

Brian spent the next few minutes ranting about what an ass-hole Frank was. Kalia tore her eyes away from Brian only when her cell started ringing. "It's Frank. What do you want me to do?"

Kurt said nothing as he reached over and took Kalia's phone and answered it. "Frank, you son of a bitch! What have you done?"

Frank's tone was neither gloating nor apologetic. "I did what I needed to do."

"Okay, Frank, why? We saved your life. A couple of years ago, we saved your rotten, good-for-nothing life! We got you on your feet again. Did I mention we saved your life?"

"Yes, Kurt, you did. Numerous times. You saved my life. Is that what you wanted to hear? You saved it, and I've paid you back over the last two years with my loyalty and good behavior. We're even."

"Loyalty? You call this loyalty?"

"No, not now. But prior to this, I was your very loyal leader. My business practices made the Sportfan Chronicles very profitable."

"But why, Frank? Things were going so well. Why did you do this?"

"I felt I had no choice. I knew I had to make a move when you turned down Pierre's offer because of your pettiness. When Pierre told me that John Pointy the Third wanted in on the deal, I knew I had to do this. I now sit on the board of directors of Pointy Foods. Of course the first thing I did was have my old nemesis Marcus fired—him and his trusty sidekick, Dwayne. Both of them. Gone on the spot!"

"And you call me petty?"

"Yes, Kurt, you are petty. Pierre introduced me to other powerful businessmen, and now I've created a very powerful company. I have the capital to do very big things right now. Things we only dreamed of before. Does that answer your question?"

"Frank, don't tell me you stole all of our ideas and our work toward the football team. Most of the football ideas came from Brian and me. Not you."

"Yes, although I wouldn't use those words. None of the football stuff that we were working on was protected. Deep down inside you know you're happy that I betrayed you. You now have Frank to hate again. Now you will be really motivated to get that company growing."

"Believe me, Frank, I have more meaning in my life than the need to hate you. You're not that important. What you stole, on the other hand, is. Intelligence. You stole intelligence, ideas, plans. Things you could never do or create on your own—"

"Call me what you want. I know you and Brian need to go up against me. Just like old times at Pointy Foods, but this time the stakes are a lot higher, and I have a huge lead. Good luck."

"You son of a bitch, you set this up."

"Well, it didn't take much. I knew Chuck would be recording me in my office. That was a no-brainer. So I decided to make it work for me. I pretended to talk to Pierre to throw off any suspicious thoughts you would have, and it worked, plain and simple. Now you'll have to excuse me as I have some very important phone calls to make."

"Frank, you might think that you've taken us out of the picture, but I think it's more than possible that you have overplayed your hand…as usual. Who's going to watch your back now? Have you thought of that, Frank? Have you?"

"Good-bye, Kurt." There was a feeling of the proverbial bad penny always turning up when Frank was involved. This time was different. There was an uncomfortable air of finality about the click on the other end of the line.

"Kalia, where is everybody?"

Kalia looked suddenly very uncomfortable. "Oh… I thought you knew. They went to Frank's penthouse. Brian said that Frank no longer has any business ownership in SFC. You know, Kurt, he's right. It's a company-owned complex. Frank no longer has rights to anything SFC. That they wanted to be the ones to throw him out is your problem."

Kurt shook his head. "Let 'em at it. I seriously doubt that Frank's still in the penthouse, but this could get out of hand. I'm heading over there."

CHAPTER 34

Meathead's New Suit(e)

Kurt arrived to see a virtual mob of employees against the door. Brian was already there, and far from keeping things under control, he appeared to be leading the mob. A vase lay shattered—its artificial flowers littered the floor. The pedestal it had been resting on had been turned on its side. Two of the employees picked it up and were swinging it toward Frank's door, apparently planning to use the pedestal as a battering ram.

Kurt tried appealing to the one member of the mob who might listen to him. "Brian, hold up! I've got the key. Don't you dare knock down that door!"

Brian rolled his eyes. "Aw, come on, Kurt. We need to send a message. This mob knocking down the door is it."

"Well, we could send a message, but doesn't it seem counterproductive? We own the building and the door."

Brian nodded to the ram bearers. "Yeah, I guess you're right. But I so wanted to smash down that door!"

"Brian, he's not even in there. I guarantee it. Why did you bring half the employees with you?"

"I didn't exactly bring them. Most of them live here in the complex, anyway."

"Yeah, right." Kurt was wondering, *What next?* "Okay, let's do this."

The door was opened to reveal a mostly empty penthouse. There was no furniture—only several crumpled-up napkins scattered here and there, an empty Jack Daniel's bottle, and some stains in the carpet.

"Wow, Kurt, look at this place. He took almost everything!"

Picking up the bottle, Kurt saw a framed photograph beneath it. "Not quite. Here… He left a picture of himself by this piece of paper. 'Suckers'. It says, 'Suckers.'"

"He got us, Kurt. He got us good. Just like old times."

"Stop. Brian. In the end we'll get him just like we always did. We always got him back."

They continued through the apartment to the master suite, where they were surprised to see Meathead sitting next to a sleeping bag. A pile of clothes (apparently Meathead's wardrobe) lay in one corner of the suite. There was an empty McDonald's bag lying beside him. He was dressed in a Who concert T-shirt and baggy jeans. If he had shoes, they were nowhere to be seen.

The mob didn't bother him, didn't care, moved on to other rooms once they realized it was only him. Only Kurt stayed in the bedroom. "Hey, Meathead, what's up? What's going on?"

"What do you think's going on, Kurt? Uncle Frank abandoned me. He up and abandoned me."

"I can see that. Did he say anything? He didn't just breeze out of here and say nothing. What did he say?"

"He said I was a distraction and that he didn't want to babysit me anymore. He left me five hundred dollars and said I could have his empty penthouse."

"Well, Meathead, the penthouse wasn't his. What he did was leave you with cab fare."

"What am I going to do? Five hundred won't get me anywhere. A motel until it runs out, I guess, but watching him was my job, so now I don't even have a job."

Brian overhead the exchange as he prowled the apartment, looking around for clues as if this was a mystery of grand proportions. He was thinking this was bad even for Frank.

"Brian, find anything useful?" At the negative response, Kurt returned his attention to a forlorn Meathead. He wanted to get as much information from him as he could before the shock diminished and the anger set in. "Meathead, listen to me. Where is Frank? Do you know how he can be reached? How can we contact him?"

Meathead seemed to put far too much effort into considering the matter. "Ummm, I think he's in Wisconsin."

"Wisconsin? Why do you think he may be there?"

"I don't know. I drove him up there a few times last week, but then he cut me off. Pierre's setting him up with a new driver and a bunch of new assistants."

"Hmm, the plot thickens..."

"Kurt, I don't know what I'm going to do. Can I come work for you?"

"Sorry, Meathead, I don't think we can use you."

He fumbled up to his feet. "No, Kurt, you can. Please. I can be your driver, your assistant, something like that. You know I can do it."

Kurt shook his head. "Meathead, I'm sorry. I don't need anything like that. Part of your job was watching your uncle Frank, and he flew the coop, gone, no longer here. I'm all out of people to watch."

"You don't have to pay me much."

"Sorry. I don't think it's a good idea."

As if he had been listening to them and waiting for the next pause, Chuck walked in and joined them. "Wait a sec, Kurt, I think I can use him."

Kurt was approaching a boiling point, and it showed. "For what, Chuck? You got someone who needs watching?"

Chuck brought up his hands. "Whoa, that's a little harsh. No, but I can use him. I told you I wanted Frank's job. Meathead, you can be my driver now."

"Chuck, you do not need a new driver. You don't need a driver, period!"

Chuck continued as if Kurt had said nothing. "I want you in full livery and—"

"For God's sake, Chuck. Full livery? Meathead, you know what livery is? Look, he doesn't know what you're talking about."

"Full chauffeur uniform. Livery. And you report to me whenever I need you. But you're not just going to be my driver. You will
be my personal servant. Got it?"

After all these years, Kurt could still be surprised by Chuck.
Every now and again there was a time and a place when Chuck's
bullshit just could not be less appropriate. "Geez, Chuck, livery?
Chauffeur? Servant? We've got real problems here. You can show
off later. We don't need more problems!"

Chuck again continued as if Kurt had said nothing. "As I
was saying, full dress uniform, on call at all times, gentleman's
gentleman duties...looking after my every need. Got it? How
hard is that?"

"I'll take it. I'll figure out what you're talking about later. You
got it, Chuck, sir." He put a hand to his forehead.

"Geez, don't salute him, Meathead. Where's your pride?"

"Thank you, sir." Meathead was perhaps a little bit sharper
than he let on as he pandered to Chuck's insatiable ego. Kurt took
note.

"Okay, you can stay in the penthouse this week until we can
get you into one of the smaller apartments. Just this one week."

"Thanks, Kurt."

"Typical. I give you the benefit, and you give him the 'sir'
treatment. Whatever!"

"No, really thank you, Kurt. I'll call you whatever you want."

"Yeah, yeah, you're welcome, and 'Kurt' will do just fine." So
they'd lost Frank but got to keep Meathead. "Just great," he muttered to no one at all.

By the start of the following week, Kurt and Brian had put together
task forces with the goal of stimulating faster growth and, at the
same time, finding ways to slow down Frank's new company.

How long of a head start Frank had was unknown. They knew
only that it was long enough for Frank to have covertly executed
his betrayal seamlessly.

Kurt started the meeting. "Okay, guys, listen up. We've really got to pull some deals together to raise more cash. I think it might be time to sell a few of our businesses. The ones that are peaking would be a good place to start. Brian?"

"Your chicken wings are being pulled from Pointy Foods distribution."

"That's okay. I expected that. They're under contract with us for the next six months, so we have that much time to find another distributor. We have the files on those so start vetting them."

Mary Johnston was the newest addition to the SFC team. For the moment, she was vital in dealing with the Pointy Foods issues that were part of the fallout of Frank's departure and as such was present and looking very confident and ready to go. "I've got good news about some of your intellectual properties. We researched all of the thousands of new patents you acquired a few months ago. It seems that La Fontelle Cheese and Pointy Foods are paying you for using six of your patents, including the new shrink-wrap.

"Yeah, we know."

"Okay, but do you also know that if you refuse to let them use those patents, it will cost them a fortune? It will cost an absolute fortune to change all of the packaging. We are talking about maximum impact here! On top of that, we found three other patents that they aren't paying for at all."

Kurt shook his head. "Can't be significant or Brian and I would have noticed."

"Perhaps but these are somewhat easy to slip by. They are related to the new cloud computing that they are using in their day-to-day business operations."

Kurt felt the smile fill his face as that bit of information sank in. "Well, this is great news. How about we send Pointy Foods a message? Pointy Foods and La Fontelle Cheese. Both of them."

Brian shrugged. "What's great about that, Kurt? I don't get how that's going to stop Frank from buying the football team."

"If we can start hitting his investors where it hurts them the most, which is on their core businesses, they might start to reconsider their arrangement with Frank."

"Nice."

Mary didn't let up. "Wait a minute, gentlemen. There's more. We have also reviewed three offers from buyers who are interested in purchasing your shares in some of those Internet start-ups that you invested in. The ones that are doing great, of course."

"How much are we talking about?"

"Kurt, let me first say that there has been a bidding war for the Internet cloud company. As you are aware, you own thirty percent of that company."

"How much, Mary? We just put some feelers out there for that one."

"It's up to two hundred and fifty million dollars."

The room went quiet as everyone absorbed the significance of the dollar amount mentioned. Kurt looked at Brian, making sure he had heard her correctly, and he must have as Brian was wordlessly sitting there waiting for Kurt to respond.

Mary looked worried as she asked, "Did you get that? I said two hundred and fifty million dollars."

"Yeah. We got that. That's…that's a big number, Mary. Brian?"

"It is, no question about it, but if Frank finds out, won't he say he deserves part of it?"

And just like that, Mary went from looking worried to her usual confident self. "Kurt, may I answer that? Brian, Frank no longer has anything to do with this company. He signed off on everything. Signed, witnessed, notarized, and recorded!"

Kurt added, "Ironically, Frank didn't even want us to invest in that company. He didn't know what cloud computing was."

"Kurt, Brian, I have to ask, are you sure you want to sell that company? It seems to be the one that everybody wants."

Kurt nodded. "It has the most potential. We need to make sure that we can live with the fact that these shares might be worth a lot more than two hundred fifty million dollars later on. We could be giving away shares that have the potential to be worth billions of dollars a few years from now."

Brian reminded him, "But, Kurt, we don't want to wait a few years to buy our football team."

Kurt closed his eyes and weighed both sides before speaking. "How about this? Tell them that we're willing to sell a twenty-percent stake in the cloud computing for two hundred fifty million. We keep the other ten percent. Tell the bidders the first one who takes the offer gets it, but we will rescind this offer in forty-eight hours. Make it clear they'd be ill advised to drag this out."

"Great idea. I hope it works." Brian clearly had his doubts, even in light of Kurt's enthusiasm.

Mary, on the other hand, seemed to have no doubts at all. "It is a great idea and a good strategy, and it will work. I will be meticulous in drawing up the papers, as always. No point in revisiting a problem. Get it right the first time around, and I'm not entirely sure that your former partner is as careful."

"Well, I can't say. He probably isn't, but this has been a costly lesson to not let down our guard and to not underestimate him. That still leaves us all the other investments for cash flow. Chuck? I've never seen you this quiet before. What's going on? You paying attention?"

Chuck was staring at the table and eventually whispered, "We are ultrarich."

"Yeah, well, just remember all this money is to buy a football team. And Chuck? You got in at the right time."

He looked up at Kurt, nodding slowly. "Of course. But it's still a lot of money."

"It's still a lot of money, but there is no more cashing out. Mary has added legally sound amendments to our corporation so that none of us can do what Frank did. We're in this together. No cashing out. We are going to buy a football team."

Chuck seemed almost hesitant when he asked, "Did you know that the cloud computing company was worth that much before you purchased Frank's shares?"

"Well, Chuck, let's just say that we had a hunch it was worth a lot, but I didn't think it would be so valuable at this stage."

Mary added, "And that, Kurt, is why I think you should reconsider and not sell any of those shares right now."

"Thank you, but no. We need to move forward so we can

replace Frank's capital, the capital we no longer have, may I remind you. We'll actually have more money on hand after this sale than we had when Frank was still with us. But just make it clear that we are keeping ten percent of the cloud company's shares."

"How much will our company be worth after we sell off those assets? That's what I'd like to know."

Mary looked down at her tablet, speaking as she sifted through data. "That's fine, Brian. Our due diligence, our estimates, put it at well over five hundred million."

"And how much of that will be liquid?"

"As I mentioned to you, four hundred thirty million dollars of that will be cash."

"Brian, we might be able to borrow the rest. I don't see why not." Kurt's mind was in overdrive, thinking of various resources.

"Should we call the investment bankers?"

"Unless Mary sees a pitfall, I think we should. First let's see if we can sell this cloud computing investment."

Although she was surprised that Chuck had little to say, Mary made a note that the three men were in agreement.

CHAPTER 35

The Mole

A few weeks later, Kurt and Darci were sitting in the living room drinking her special brew of coffee and discussing the latest events connected to SFC.

"Well, Darci, we did it. We sold off those assets and replaced Frank's capital. On top of that, we still kept ten percent of the Internet cloud business."

Before Darci could respond, they heard Chuck yelling across the street. *What now?* wondered Kurt, as he got up and walked over to the window.

Kurt just shook his head as he watched the scene unfolding in front of Chuck's house. Eventually he said, "Darci, you're not gonna believe this. It's Chuck. He's yelling at Meathead."

"Not surprised, Kurt. I bet Meathead forgot his chauffeur's hat again."

"You'd be right, but it looks like Chuck went and bought some extra ones. This is ridiculous."

"I'm afraid to ask."

"Chuck went back inside the house. What the...? He's making Meathead ring the doorbell again. Now he's making Meathead carry his briefcase to the limousine."

"Kurt, I still can't believe he purchased a limousine."

"Score one for us. He actually tried to get the company to purchase it. When we said no, he went out and purchased one himself."

"It is convenient when Chuck has Meathead drop us off at the airport. Alice and I haven't had to worry about getting there since he bought it."

"I'm sure it is convenient. I'd rather drive myself. I like being in control. I mean, look at this. Chuck is making Meathead start all over again, because he forgot to open the back door for him."

"You're not telling me that Chuck went back inside the house again?"

"Absolutely. He's making Meathead ring the doorbell. Now Meathead is carrying Chuck's briefcase..."

"Did he remember to open the back door to the limo for him?"

"Yes, but Chuck's yelling at him again."

"He opened the door, so why is he yelling again?"

"You had to see it. After Meathead opened the back door, he took off his driver's hat and held it out, expecting Chuck to put a tip in it."

"I wonder how long this setup is going to work out for them."

"Darci, you know that Chuck pays him hardly anything? Has Alice mentioned it? It's outrageous, but if Meathead goes along with it, then oh well."

"I'm surprised that Meathead is willing to put up with so much from Chuck and not get paid that much. Who puts up with that kind of treatment? It makes me think he may be a couple of small paychecks away from quitting."

"I don't know about that. He did put up with his uncle Frank's verbal abuse for months. Sometimes it becomes a habit or..." While he was still looking across the street, Kurt's train of thought was interrupted. "Now what's going on?"

"What is it?"

"You'll see. Meathead is walking up to our door." Even though Kurt could see what was going on, he waited until Meathead knocked before opening the door.

"Kurt Weichert, Mr. Chuck Jennings has asked me to ask you if you need a ride to work this morning."

Kurt shook his head. "Come on, what's with the formal bullshit?"

"I'm sorry, Kurt. Mr. Chuck Jennings yells at me if I don't conduct myself in this manner."

"You tell Mr. Chuck Jennings that Kurt Weichert told you to tell him to shut the hell up."

"I can't say that or he'll yell at me for insubordination. He says I still owe him for that pinball game we played at your house. He claims I forfeited. "

"Does Chuck treat you as badly as your uncle Frank did?"

Meathead shook his head. "Nobody was worse than Uncle Frank, even Mr. Jennings, but at least he was family."

"I will say something to him later today. It's just not right."

"I will tell him that you will not be needing my services today. He loves it when I say stuff like that."

"Oh, brother, I think all of this success has gone to that empty head of his."

Later that afternoon at the office, Kurt and Brian were discussing their plans with the focus on future strategies and actions. At one point Kurt shut the door.

Before Brian could ask what was going on, Kurt leaned in close to his friend and whispered, "Listen, Brian, we have to be careful, very careful about our next moves. We have a mole on the inside."

Brian screamed, "A mole? Inside?"

Kurt almost threw his hand over Brian's mouth. Instead, he just moved his hand up and down in a settle-down gesture. "Keep your voice down. Yeah. We have a mole inside our company. No doubt about it."

"Are you sure? How do you know that?"

"Absolutely sure. For one thing Frank has told me things that only a few of us know about."

Brian looked even more shocked at this bit of news. "Frank told you? What do you mean Frank told you? Have you been talking to him?"

"Yeah, every night for the last week...or more precisely, he's been talking to me."

"What? And you didn't say anything to me?"

"I am saying something, Brian. Now. I'm telling you now."

"Yeah, but why did you wait until now to tell me? I would have let him know how we are kicking his ass."

"Exactly, Brian, you would have told him that. I'm trying to get information from him, not shut him up. I knew if I had told you, something like that would happen. He doesn't remember calling me the next day because he's really drunk when he calls. But he sure would remember if you got him all fired up. He must be feeling the pressure if he's drinking that much again."

"What's he saying?"

"Sometimes he doesn't say much at all. He just babbles on about nothing and swears randomly. Frank's drunk when he calls."

"Drunk? How drunk?"

"How drunk do you think? He's really drunk when he calls. For one thing it's usually around three in the morning. I let him blather on, and I hang up when he falls asleep...usually when he starts talking Napoleon Bonaparte. When he talks about Bonaparte, I know I'm about to hear him snoring. I can almost see it. Chin on his chest, mouth open, and snoring. Probably drooling, too. I really thought those days were over."

Brian shook his head. "He's gotta be feeling the heat from some of his investors. We must be hurting their core businesses. It's better than I thought."

Kurt nodded. "One thing I learned last night is that we have a mole around us. He said a few things that you and I shared with only a few people."

"I'm not the mole."

Kurt rolled his eyes, almost laughed. "Of course you're not the mole, Brian. Would I be standing here discussing this if I thought it was you?"

"Sorry. I kind of lost my sense of reasoning for a second. Who is the mole?

"I know it's not you, and well, I don't think it could be Kalia..."

"No, no, no! It's not Kalia! It couldn't be. It would break my heart if it was." Kurt had momentarily forgotten Brian's deep feelings for the woman. Something like unrequited love.

"It's okay, Brian. It's not Kalia. She would never betray us. That much I know. Besides the information was from the meeting we had with Chuck yesterday."

Brian took a few seconds before he responded. "Chuck? Chuck screwed us? I can understand Frank but not Chuck."

"I don't think it's Chuck either, but I do believe Chuck's responsible for the information being leaked."

"What are you talking about? How can he be responsible if he didn't leak it?"

"Think about it. The only other person around and within earshot of our conversations was Meathead."

A moment of surprise, then Brian's eyes narrowed in understanding. He was nodding along with Kurt now, probably without realizing it. "Frank's nephew. Chuck has to fire him. Are you sure it's Meathead?"

"I'm sure, but we need proof. Think about it, Brian. Who in his right mind would put up with that much shit from Chuck and not quit his job?"

"Yeah, you're right. But we need to be sure it's Meathead before he loses his job. Of course even if it isn't, we'd probably be doing him a favor. Kurt, have you seen how badly Chuck treats him? It's beyond bad. Which reminds me, did you notice Chuck just put one of those elevated chairs you see at the airport in the lobby—the kind where people sit and get their shoes polished?"

"I know. I saw it. Only Chuck would put a shoeshine station in the lobby. You know why, don't you? So everyone can see him sitting there, reading the newspaper while Meathead polishes his shoes."

"That's exactly it. Yesterday morning when I got to the office, I told Chuck that he looked ridiculous. Listen, it gets worse."

"Brian, it can't get worse than that!"

"No, it does. Kalia said that when he's done, Meathead has to turn his hat upside down while Chuck tosses a quarter into the cap. Then he usually says, 'Not bad, but you missed a spot,' while Chuck points down to his shoes. She said Meathead then gets back on his knees and wipes the imaginary spot. It's the same thing every morning. He seems to have actually timed it, so most of our employees can see it as they enter our office."

"Kalia said that after Meathead gets his quarter, he has to say, 'Thanks, Mr. Jennings.' No one should be treated like that. Ever. I understand why he'd screw us over."

"Well, Kurt, I'm sure you have something in mind. What's the plan?"

"It's very simple. We're going to feed him information. We'll discuss things in front of him today. Specifically we're going to talk about the two hundred fifty million dollars we made from the Internet cloud company. We're going to say that we got paid yesterday."

"But we received that a few weeks ago."

"Brian, he doesn't know that, because Chuck doesn't know. Remember? We didn't tell Chuck yet, because we didn't want him going around bragging about it to everybody."

Just then, the door opened. Chuck must have finished the daily morning shoeshine routine, because he entered the conference room looking happy and smug, newspaper in hand. "Hey, what're you guys doing in here? Having a meeting without me?"

Kurt smiled, thinking about how much it would devastate Chuck to lose his personal slave. "Yeah, Chuck, I guess you can't spy on everybody anymore since I had all those cameras disconnected."

"Funny, Kurt. So what's going on?"

"What's going on is we just received the two hundred and fifty million dollars from the Internet cloud business sale. How about that?"

Chuck started to do one of his little dances, pumping his fist in the air and shouting, "Yeah baby! Show me the money! Show me the money! Two hundred fifty million dollars!"

"Hey, keep it down, Chuck."

Kurt walked over to the door and as expected saw Meathead within earshot. "Good morning, Meathead. Sorry, but I have to close this door. In fact, you don't have to stand in the hallway. Take a break and go get something to eat. It's on me. Chuck will call if he needs you."

Meathead didn't move. "It's okay, I'll wait here for Mr. Jennings. His orders. I'm on the clock, you know. I don't want to take advantage of my minimum wage salary."

Chuck yelled out the door, "Hey, Meathead, I heard that. Don't forget you get to stay in that studio apartment for free."

Brian's voice dropped to a whisper. "Chuck, the city code officer said we couldn't rent out that converted storage closet, because it wasn't up to code."

"Mind your own business, Brian. And so what? He's lucky he's got a place to sleep."

"We never even connected the heat to that space, Chuck. What are you thinking?"

"I'm not. It's only Meathead, and it doesn't matter anyway. I'm not renting it. It's free. Plus he gets tips all day long. You hear me, Meathead? Don't forget that!"

Kurt was disgusted. This was bad even for Chuck. If Meathead's spying was hurting only Chuck, he was fairly certain he would have let it go. But the fact was that the whole company could suffer from what he was doing. "Meathead, here's twenty dollars. Go get something to eat now."

"Meathead! Don't you spill food on your uniform, hear me!"

Kurt's face pulled back in disgust for a moment, an expression that Meathead caught. And that might work to their advantage, he thought, if Meathead saw that only Chuck was being abusive to him. "Go on, Meathead. You deserve a break." Kurt peeked out the door to make sure Meathead left and turned to address the business at hand, but Chuck wasn't finished swaggering.

"Why, may I ask, are you giving my personal assistant orders?"

"Chuck, Meathead is a mole."

He just stared blankly at Kurt, as if he didn't understand the term, as if he thought Kurt had just told him Meathead was a small burrowing mammal. "A mole? What do you mean?"

"We have suspicions…well-founded suspicions that Meathead is feeding information to his uncle Frank."

Chuck was shaking his head, and he began to pace the room. "No, no, he can't be! I mean, he's been loyal to me. I don't want to lose him."

"Well, whatever. It's him. He's the mole. That's why I told you we received the money yesterday. I said it when I knew he would hear it."

"You mean we didn't get paid yesterday?"

"No, we didn't. We got paid three weeks ago."

"Why didn't you tell me?"

"Come on, Chuck, do you have to ask? Okay, let's just say we needed that information kept quiet for a little while."

"Oh, because of Meathead?"

Kurt shook his head, deciding he didn't want to get into any more fights than necessary today. "Yeah, sure, that's it. That's why we didn't tell you."

Chuck for once was not laughing. He challenged Kurt about his course of action and launched criticisms at Brian for going along with the plan of secrecy. "So, does your grand plan include what we're going to do about this?"

"Drop the attitude. We did what we had to do to save ourselves, you included. To answer your question, I'm hoping that by tomorrow we'll have proof that Meathead is the mole. We need the actual proof, Chuck. Don't tell anyone else about the two hundred fifty million dollars."

The rest of the day was business as usual, and Chuck continued his daily abhorrent behavior toward Meathead. By five thirty, they were more than ready to head home and put their concerns aside for the evening.

Tomorrow promised to be interesting. Seeing the expected events unfold and effectively dealing with them would require sharp minds and a good night of sleep.

CHAPTER 36

That Scene from
The Godfather

Kurt and Darci were awakened by the sound of Kurt's cell ringing at three in the morning. Just as it rang early every morning.

Darci groaned. "Come on, Kurt. Not Frank again. I need my sleep. We need our sleep."

"I know, but this time, it is vitally important."

"Just start turning your phone off at night!"

Kurt was full of expectations as he grabbed the phone and heard Frank's irate voice. Darci started hitting Kurt with a pillow over the head before he could even start talking. He whispered, "Let the fun begin." He laughed, he understood, he left the room, he shut the door behind him.

"Frank."

"Don't you Frank me, you son of a bitch! What the hell! You stole half of my two hundred fifty million dollars."

"Why, Frank, you don't sound too drunk tonight."

"What do you mean, tonight?"

"Oh, I'm hurt. You don't remember that you've been calling me all week?"

"I haven't called you until tonight, you son of a bitch!"

"You've been drinking heavily again, Frank. How would I know that if you hadn't been calling me every night?"

"Whatever! You knew that company was worth two hundred fifty million dollars, and you withheld that information. You think that I'm sneaky? You guys are crooks. I should have known you would try to screw me over."

"Screw you over? Now that's a novel idea. Actually we didn't know. We didn't know those shares were worth that much until after you left. We found out when we needed to raise cash to compete with you."

"I am going to sue you!"

"I'd be disappointed if you didn't. You can sue, but you won't win because our new legal team has confirmed that you don't have a case. And you know why you don't have a case? Because you signed off on everything. It's karma, Frank. You got that?"

"This is war. I don't believe you didn't know. You screwed me out of one hundred twenty-five million dollars."

"I don't think so, Frank. You screwed yourself out of the one hundred twenty-five million. I believed you when you said that you were ready for retirement. I was also prepared to let you back in if you changed your mind. If we had known we were going to get two hundred fifty million dollars, we probably would have shared that. You thought you screwed us, but you really just screwed yourself."

"It was business."

"And so is this. We just evened the playing field."

"You know I won't let you guys beat me. The gloves are off."

Frank hung up the phone. A smiling Kurt returned to bed. "Ah, the sweet taste of revenge."

Darci had a pillow pressed over her head, but she was apparently still able to hear at least some of what had transpired on the phone. From beneath the pillow, there was a muttered, "Good night, Kurt."

Slipping back into bed, he closed his eyes, glad that tonight's call had not only been sweet but short. "Good night, Darci."

—————

The next night, everybody met at Victor's restaurant to celebrate Victor's birthday. The place was packed and people were shoulder to shoulder, especially in the bar area where not a seat was to be had. Kurt, Darci, and Brian were fortunate enough to find space to stand.

Kurt's mind was still busy going over Meathead's betrayal. He had serious concerns about Chuck and how he planned to handle firing the man. Brian, too, had concerns. "You don't think we should be handling this?"

"Perhaps. But think about it, Brian. Chuck brought Meathead into our inner circle. He was the one who brought him in and thereby exposed secret information to Frank. Now Chuck has to fix the problem."

"I get that. He wants to fix the problem, but he keeps telling me he's going to *Godfather II* his ass."

"What's '*Godfather II* his ass'?"

"In the second Godfather movie, Michael Corleone discovered that his brother Fredo was the one who was spying on him for their enemies. Darci, you saw it. Remember?"

Darci had barely been listening to the conversation and just shook her head. "No, I don't think I did. So what did he do?"

"He thought it would be a good idea that he'd swim with the fishes."

Darci nodded. "You mean he killed him."

"Yeah, he eventually killed him. They didn't want to do it while their mother was alive, but that's what happened."

"Wait. Chuck's going to kill Meathead?"

"Not exactly. Michael Corleone didn't kill Fredo right away. He brought him back and told him that he was forgiven, let him be part of the family again. But later on he had him killed on a rowboat."

"Well, let's make sure Chuck doesn't buy a rowboat. Kurt, you don't buy one either."

Kurt squeezed Darci's hand. "Very funny. Make sure Chuck doesn't buy a rowboat. Don't include me in on that. No, Chuck thinks he can convince Meathead that we forgive him. That part is true. You know how Al Pacino said in *The Godfather*, "Keep your friends close, but your enemies closer."

"Is that why you didn't want to ride in the limo with Chuck and Alice?"

"No. The truth is I try to avoid riding in a car with Chuck anytime lately. He's been acting like a bigger spaz than usual. Darci, he's too hard to be around. Being shut up inside a car with him is more than I can handle right now."

"So Chuck's going to let Meathead know that you know that he's the mole, and then Chuck is going to try to convince him to stay on as his driver?"

"Yes, at least that's Chuck's plan. He begged us to let him handle it this way."

Brian was suddenly distracted from the conversation by the appearance of a waitress. "Oh, look here… My favorite waitress is tending bar tonight." His favorite waitress was dressed in black slacks and a white blouse that maybe had one button too many undone. Blond hair was pulled back into a tail, and when she thought no one was looking, her face looked breathless.

The wait staff was working hard tonight for Victor's birthday. Kurt tried to sympathize, especially with the current object of Brian's affection. "Great. We all get to watch Brian strike out with the waitress tonight…again."

"Oh, Kurt, I trust you to remember that. Well, tonight she's not a waitress. She's a bartender, and I'm going to get her to like me. Look at her. She's beautiful."

"We shall see."

Darci had her doubts, too. "Come on, Brian. She's so young. She's probably fifteen years younger than you. If you were a woman, they would call you a cougar."

"More like a sugar daddy," Kurt offered.

"Sugar daddy? Thanks, Kurt, I'm not that old. Nobody has ever called me that before. You're going to give me a complex."

"I'm just saying she looks awfully young."

"Not really. She's at least twenty-one, maybe twenty-two years old."

"She probably is, but she looks younger than that."

Brian made no further comment to Darci on the matter, and he knew not to say anything to Kurt for fear of prolonging the discussion. Instead he waved her over. "Hi, Melinda."

"Hey, Brian, do you need me to get you another drink?"

"No, Melinda, I need you to please step away from the bar. You're so hot you're melting all the ice."

"Very funny. Do you need a drink 'cause I'm really busy. This place is crowded."

"Well, you owe me a drink, because I dropped mine when you walked past."

"What are you drinking?"

"Surprise me, darlin'." Melinda heaved a bored sigh and left to make Brian his drink.

"Brian, talk about laying it on pretty thick. I don't think she has any interest in you at all."

"Brian, Kurt's right, and she's definitely too young for you."

"Thanks, thank you both. You're making me sound like an old man."

Melinda returned with the drink, but her hopes of leaving just as quickly were not to be realized. "You know, when I saw you from across the bar, I fainted and hit my head. So I'm going to need your telephone number for insurance purposes."

Melinda smiled a bit wider. "Good one. That's a good one, Brian."

"No, seriously, where have you been all my life?"

"Well, I'd have to say for the first half of it, nowhere. I wasn't born yet."

"Ouch!" And that was about as eloquent as Kurt could be in this situation.

Darci reminded him, "Kurt, I told you she was too young for him."

Kurt and Darci might as well have not been there. Brian was oblivious to everything in his pursuit of Melinda. And relentless. "You have beautiful eyes."

"I'm surprised to hear you say that. Actually I'm surprised you noticed. All you ever do is stare at my chest."

"No, Melinda, not so. I was only looking at your nametag. Honestly."

"Sure you were. You know sex without love is an empty experience."

"But as empty experiences go, it is one of the best. Undeniably."

Melinda flashed another smile at Brian and simply walked away.

"Well, Brian, my friend, as experiences go, that really went well for you. I told you that you didn't have a shot with her."

"You miss one hundred percent of the shots you don't take."

Brian then recognized one of Victor's model friends across the room. Remarkably she appeared to be alone. But only for the moment. "You'll have to excuse me."

Kurt and Darci wordlessly watched Brian walk across the room to the model. "My friends bet that I wouldn't be able to talk to the most beautiful girl in the room. I propose we buy some drinks with their money."

Kurt looked at Darci in complete disbelief. "Whatever he said to the model must be working because she's laughing instead of pouring a drink over his head."

"He'll never change. By the way whatever happened with that auction date? Did he mention anything to you?"

Kurt was watching his friend continue to talk up the model, waving a server over to get her a fresh drink. "Yes. The day after. He came into work just looking...honestly he looked shell shocked. Like he'd been in a war. When I asked him what happened, all he said was that he was never doing that auction again."

"Good thing you're with me. Otherwise you might have gone on that auction, too."

Bernie caught sight of Darci and Kurt standing in the bar area as soon as he entered. He walked over and promptly took the spot just vacated by Brian in his pursuit of the beautiful model.

"Bernie."

"Hey, Kurt, Darci. What's with the standing? No seats for us? This place is packed like never before. Maybe I should throw myself a birthday party at one of my restaurants. I can do a different restaurant every month. What do you think?"

"Sounds like a plan to me."

"It looks like Victor has new bartenders. Is that chick old enough to work in a bar?" Bernie segued into loudly yelling for Melinda. "Hey there, little girl, get me a mojito. I need some service over here."

Kurt shook his head. "Let me get this straight. You're going to have a Mexican drink in an Italian restaurant. Tell me it isn't so."

"Who gives a shit? What are you, Kurt, the arbiter of ethnic beverage choices? And what are you drinking? A Peroni?"

"It's an Italian beer."

"Well, good for you, buddy, I don't want a beer, and I don't want wine."

Darci, silent during the exchange, had formed a mental bet with herself on how long this would go on. Past experience offered no indicators, but she did know it could stop as abruptly as it started. Or not.

"I'm surprised you're not drinking water. Aren't you worried about your girlish figure?"

"No, forget that crap. I gave up on that exercise and diet stuff after we got back from filming the exercise video. Not for my world, not for me!"

"What about the fitness instructor you're dating? The one from California?"

"It's a long-distance relationship, Darci. It's difficult. Anyway, she probably won't want to sleep with me again when she sees I've gone back to my old bad habits. Wait until she sees how much weight I put back on. Hell, I've gained so much in the last few months, I can't even get into my own pants."

"Maybe not, Brian, some girls are attracted to projects."

Bernie was way past the discussion, not happy to be regarded as a project and was not just a little impatient for something to quench his thirst and lift his spirits.

"Hey, sweetheart, I'm great friends with the birthday boy here. You know, your boss. How about some service over here?"

No sooner had Bernie stopped yelling than Melinda showed up. "Here's your drink."

"Listen, little lady, I'm Bernie, Victor's friend. You might have heard of me. I'm the guy who owns the comedy clubs and sports bars all over the city." Bernie lightened his tone by reaching into his pocket to give her a nice, well-earned tip. "Listen, Melinda, I'll make you a deal. You give us extra attention, and I'll keep these nice tips rolling your way. Got it, good looking?"

"We're really busy tonight, but I know who you are, and I know that you're Victor's good friends, so don't you worry. I'll keep a good eye on you tonight. And I appreciate the tips. I'm a full-time college student."

"Great! Tell you what, get us some of those delicious Italian appetizers, would you."

"What would you like? Anything in particular?"

"I'll make it easy. Get us one of everything on the left side of the menu and put it over there when it's ready."

Bernie ran around grabbing empty high-back chairs at the bar. The chairs weren't together, but he started assembling them in one spot at the bar. "Come on, Kurt. Get with the program and grab a chair."

"Where? Where are you going to put these chairs?"

"Listen and watch. Hey, everybody, move to the right." Nobody paid attention to Bernie, so he yelled even louder. "You, over there, move to the right. Come on now. It's not that hard. You people can't hog the bar. Now, you two, scoot your chairs over. You three are next. Pick up your chairs and move them over. Thank you."

Bernie moved the three chairs he already had taken from other areas and put them together at the bar. "That was easy."

It was inevitable that someone wouldn't be happy. A man came up and complained that Bernie had taken his chair while he was using the bathroom.

"Shuffle your feet, lose your seat." An unapologetic Bernie stood his ground, stood up, and yelled to Melinda. "I want to buy this guy a drink," then went on to explain Bernie's Rules of the

Crowded Bar. "Here's how it works. If a seat becomes available at a crowded bar, you have to protect it. Since you say you went to use the bathroom, I must buy you a drink, but you don't get the chair back."

The guy walked away with his drink, muttering "What the hell? Bernie's Rules of the Crowded Bar? Whatever."

"Kurt, Darci, how long have you been standing here alone? Where's Brian?"

Kurt pointed to Brian talking to the gorgeous model.

"Hey, you gotta be kidding. She's way out of his league. Damn it! Maybe I need to start dressing like Steve Jobs. But I'll wait until I peel off some pounds."

"Black is a slimming color."

"No shit, Darci. I never knew that. I'm going to start wearing all black. Why the hell did I ever work out? All I had to do was wear black."

"That and do some cardio every day and eat a sensible diet. Moderation is the key."

Melinda brought out a giant tray of appetizers.

Bernie stretched out his arms as if to welcome the tray. "Now this is what I call moderation. One of everything."

"Where do you want me to put all of this?"

Bernie turned to the people next to him. "Hey, give us some more room. You know the drill. Scoot, scoot, scoot."

The two people didn't just scoot. They got up and left the bar area. "Whoa, even better. Thank you."

Bernie moved over three of the newly acquired seats and had Melinda put the dozen plates of appetizers on the bar.

"Good job! Now get us extra napkins, extra silverware, and another round of drinks. Here's another big tip for college tuition."

"Thank you. Just let me know when you need something else."

A couple approached Bernie and asked if they could occupy the two empty chairs across which Bernie had stretched his legs. "Sorry, I can't. These chairs are for our friends." The couple left without another word. "Hey, guys, when is Chuck going to get here?"

Darci answered, "They're here now, Bernie."

"Right, Darci, I don't see them. More importantly, I don't hear Chuck's loud voice."

Darci pointed Bernie toward Chuck and Alice, but all he saw was Meathead clearing a path and creating an opening for them. And he was yelling. Meathead was yelling at people left and right. "No pictures, no pictures please. Any paparazzi will be removed from the premises and the cameras will be destroyed."

Chuck was wearing a Giorgio Armani suit with dark sunglasses. Bernie wasn't going to let this go without comment, even if it was an inane comment. "Look at the fancy suit."

Kurt yelled across the restaurant, "Yeah, Chuck, Where's your parachute pants?"

Alice pulled her face back in a grimace. "Yuck! Don't even mention those again, Kurt. I'm serious. Those nasty things are banned from our house."

"Here, you two sit down. Kurt and Darci here have been waiting long enough." Bernie was taking charge and apparently ignoring Chuck's social protocol, whatever that was this week.

"Come on, sit down, and I'll get another chair for your driver. Frank's nephew."

Meathead shook his head. "That won't be necessary. Mr. Jennings would prefer that I stand while I'm on duty. That way, I can make sure nobody tries to disturb him."

Bernie looked derisively toward Chuck, then back to Meathead. "Disturb him? Why would anybody try to disturb him? He's just a dork in a fancy suit."

"Nice shirt, big boy." Chuck had given Bernie a dramatic head to toe once over. Bernie dressed well, but his shirt was way too tight around his stomach, and it showed.

"Aw, come on, give me a break. I donated my old fat wardrobe a few months ago."

"You better go back to Goodwill and see if you can get any of it back. I'm scared to sit next to you. Those buttons on your stomach look like they are getting ready to explode."

"You're right. I'm going to unbutton my shirt. It's okay. I've got a T-shirt under my dress shirt. I'll just untuck it and give myself some breathing room. It's a casual look."

"A sloppy look," Alice corrected.

"Hello, Alice." While deliberately not wasting another second on Alice, Bernie stood up and yelled to get Melinda's attention once more. "More drinks and more plates." Melinda was by Bernie's side almost immediately and took care of Chuck and Alice.

Chuck pointed to Melinda. "You see that, Meathead? That, Meathead, is what's called good service."

Bernie laughed. "Good service? Yeah, right. It's called huge tips. Don't kid yourself, if I wasn't throwing all this extra money at her, she would be treating us like every other schmuck at the bar. Right, Kurt?"

"Yeah, probably so. Speaking of schmucks, what's with the expensive sunglasses and Giorgio Armani suit, Chuck?"

"What? You don't like my suit?"

"No, it's nice. Just a little overdone, and you can take off the sunglasses, because there's no sun in here."

"It's a look, Kurtis."

Bernie turned his attention back to Meathead. "Are you just going to stand there in your chauffeur uniform or do you want to eat some food?" Bernie had little patience for the star treatment Chuck was demanding. "So what is it? Eat or stand there doing nothing?"

"Sir, I'm not allowed to eat on the job, sir."

"So the answer to my question is that you are going to stand there with your arms crossed."

"Would you like me to stand by the door, Mr. Jennings?"

"That'll be okay, but make sure you stand where you can see me, just in case I need you."

And with that, everybody saw what only Darci and Kurt had seen until now. Meathead tipped his hat upside down, and Chuck tossed a quarter with unerring accuracy into the center of the cap.

"Last of the big spenders, aye, Chuck? Here, Meathead, take this." Bernie stuck a cannoli in Meathead's hat.

"Sir, thank you, sir, I love cannoli."

True to her word, Melinda kept her eye on Bernie, refreshing drinks and clearing plates as she tended bar and served food. On her way to place an order, she stopped to clear their area and no sooner had she collected the empty dishes than Bernie requested yet more.

"Hey, Melinda, I think we are going to need some more cannoli."

Kurt shook his head. "This poor girl, first Brian hits on her, and now she has to put up with you, Bernie."

"It's okay, Kurt, all for a good cause. You like me, don't you, little lady?"

"Actually yes, I do. You guys are fun."

"Good girl. Right answer, but we know you really just like the big tips."

"That helps."

"Seriously, Melinda, I don't blame you for not taking Brian's advances. He's too old for you."

"There is a slight difference in our ages."

Bernie attempted to translate the polite observation. "She doesn't want to do her dad."

Alice didn't hide her disgust at the comment. "Real classy, Bernie. You should act more like Chuck."

"Really, Alice? You want me to act like that inbred banjo-playing kid in *Deliverance*?"

"Are you saying Chuck is—?"

Brian walked up and joined everybody at the bar just in time to cut Alice off. He put his arms around Kurt and Bernie and yelled, "Hey, Melinda, do I get a gin and platonic or a scotch and sofa?"

"One gin and platonic coming your way."

With everybody laughing at Brian, Melinda walked right past him. "Don't stop! I don't usually get to see beauty in motion."

She was still laughing and shaking her head as she helped the people at the other side of the bar.

"I think I've just found the angel I'd like to be touched by."

"Brian, she's so young she probably wouldn't know that *Touched by an Angel* was a television show. You just aged yourself."

Brian ignored Darci's quip while he continued on in his bid to get Melinda's attention. "Hey, darlin', which pickup line works on you?"

She turned and sweetly smiled at irrepressible Brian.

"None of them work on me. Darlin'."

"You stole my heart."

"That's okay, he's got another one at home in the fridge."

Bernie's joke caused more laughter among the friends. "Weren't you over there with someone? What happened to the pretty model, Brian?"

"Since you asked, we actually hit it off pretty well. She went back to say good-bye to Victor. She couldn't stay, but I did get her telephone number. Huh, Huh? Bet you thought I couldn't score. How about that?"

Bernie shrugged. "You probably didn't. Bet she gave a fake number."

"Well, Bernie, you'd lose that bet. The number is real. I know 'cause I called it as soon as she gave it to me. Her cell phone started ringing right in front of me."

"That was smooth, but didn't you wonder about what she'd think? Come on, Brian, she gives you a number, and you use it right then and there? She's going to think you're insecure."

"I asked her for her telephone number. When she paused, I said, 'You can even give me a fake telephone number if you want, then at least the people in the room can think that I got the telephone number from the most beautiful woman in the world.'"

"Impressive."

"Yes, Bernie, it was impressive. She wasn't going to give me a fake number after that, and she'd expect me to try it out. It was a good move. Actually I'm impressed myself."

"Gotta hand it to you. Never heard of anyone calling a number like that."

"I did, and as I said before, it rang. In front of me! I'm taking Bianca out to dinner later this week."

"Bianca. That even sounds like a model's name."

"Enough. I'm hungry. Gimme some of that artichoke bruschetta."

Bernie shoved the plate over. "Have at it. Finish it off."

"So, Chuck, what's the deal with Meathead?"

Chuck took a moment to look to the door, where Meathead was standing attentively. "Ah, yes, Meathead. I'm going to try to turn him. I'm going to let him know that we know that he's the mole. I'm going to convince him to start spying on his uncle Frank for us. He can stay on as my driver, but the only information he'll get from us is misinformation. Actually it sounds like fun."

Kurt was about to say something about that when everybody started cheering. Victor was making his way through the noisy crowd of people.

"Oh, Kurt, just look at all the birthday kisses Victor is getting from those beautiful women."

"Why doesn't that happen to me?" asked Bernie, as he grabbed the tiramisu and ate it with his fingers.

"Maybe if you quit eating like a pig in front of people and took better care of yourself. Have you ever heard of moderation?" Alice snapped back.

Bernie shrugged. "Yeah, I know. I've kind of let myself go."

"And the clothes have got to go," Chuck added.

"What? You mean dress like you?"

Ignoring Bernie's remark, Alice continued. "And maybe some better cologne. I can still smell you, even in this crowd."

"What's wrong with my—"

"And those pickup lines you've been using—"

"Okay. Forget I asked."

"Use a fork, you slob," Chuck chimed in.

"Can't. I dropped it on the floor."

"Then ask for another. It's not like you're worried about bothering the waitress." Alice smirked at the barb about his failed flirtation.

Bernie reached over and grabbed Alice's used fork off her plate and continued to eat his food. "Happy now?"

Victor walked up to them while the guys started chanting "Victor, Victor, Victor." The rest of the restaurant guests joined in with the chant.

"*Grazie, grazie. Si prega di scattara uno foto.* I wanna picture with my *migliori amici*, my besta friends. These are my besta friends!"

A photographer took a picture of the friends posing together, a picture that was reminiscent of Frank Sinatra and Dean Martin's Rat Pack pictures. That particular photo would eventually be enlarged in black and white and end up in all of their restaurants. In their homes, too.

"I feela so good right now. *Oggi me sento bene.*"

Everybody started singing "Happy Birthday" when Melinda and several other servers wheeled out a giant birthday cake. At the end of the song, one of Victor's former girlfriends jumped out of the cake, wearing a sexy costume. The place erupted with laughter and cheers.

"Bene. My wisha come true. Thank you, everybody. Grazie. I wanna everybody to hug the person next to you and celebrate with me."

The music was loud and everybody in the place was either hugging someone or dancing to the music. Chuck waved and beckoned to Meathead.

"Yes, sir. What do you need, Mr. Jennings?"

Chuck approached Meathead and hugged him tightly. He then grabbed him by the back of the neck, pulled him in and kissed him.

Meathead pushed Chuck away, wiping at his mouth. "Hey, what the hell are you doing?"

Chuck spoke in his worst fake Italian accent. "I know it was you, Fredo. You broke my heart. You broke my heart."

"Mr. Jennings, why did you just kiss me?" asked Meathead. He clearly was not familiar with the character Fredo Corleone from The Godfather movies.

"I know it was you that betrayed us, Fredo."

Meathead stepped back and then pushed his way through the crowd. He paused to turn, then yelled at Chuck. "It was me! I'm the mole, and why do you keep calling me Fredo?"

"Ah, Fredo, come with me. It's the only way out tonight. Frank is dead. Meathead, come with me. You are still my driver."

Meathead turned around and ran from the building, with Chuck yelling after him, "Meathead! Meathead! Fredo! Fredo!"

CHAPTER 37

Meathead's Other Confession

The party went on for an additional five hours of drinking and cheering. Chuck was the only sober one, because Alice halted his drinks when Meathead took off.

Chuck became the designated driver. After they dropped Bernie off at his house, Chuck started annoying everybody who was sitting in the back of the limo. He thought it was funny to roll the windows down in the bitingly cold weather, and he aggravated them further by repeatedly doing so. He also kept his favorite techno music blaring, because he knew how much Kurt hated it.

"Chuck, I swear, I'm going to climb up there and kick your butt in a second."

Chuck just kept on laughing. He laughed on and on even in light of Alice's complaints. "Chuck! Watch the bumps. I have to use the bathroom." That was enough for Chuck to purposely hit every pothole on the road.

"Chuck, stop it now! I said stop it!"

Chuck just laughed all the way home.

Kurt leaned forward and whispered, "Hey, Chuck, your girlfriend really looks like she's getting mad right now. She sounds mad, too." Nothing changed until Chuck pulled in front of their houses. Then and not until then, he lowered the volume and rolled up the windows.

Kurt, as intended, was angry. "Chuck, you are the village idiot."

Darci said nothing as she ran inside wearing Kurt's jacket, because she was still freezing from the insane ride home. As soon as she opened the front door, she screamed. Everybody came running into the house.

Kurt took hold of her. "Darci, what's going on? Are you okay?"

It didn't take long for everyone to see that Kurt and Darci's house had been trashed.

"Oh my God! You guys were robbed!"

"No, I don't think so, Alice. It doesn't look like they took anything."

Everybody present was surveying the mess when Brian found a chauffeur's hat lying near Kurt's desk in his home office.

Chuck screamed, "Meathead did this! Fredo!"

Kurt shook his head. "No, not Meathead. Frank. I knew it was Frank as soon as I smelled his stale cigarettes and the cheap whiskey that goes everywhere with him."

"Should we call the police?"

"No, Brian. Put the phone down. Frank's just going to make Meathead take the fall. He'll deny ever being here, and Meathead will say it was all him. Trust me on this."

Darci was still walking around the house, picking things up. She didn't stop moving as she asked, "Why did Frank do this to us?"

"I'm sorry, Darci. He knew we were on to him, that's why. This was probably an attempt to try and find information, any information, while we were at Victor's birthday party."

Chuck was nodding in agreement, as if he'd worked it all out himself. "Meathead must have picked Frank up right after I told him we knew he was the mole."

"I've been leaving Frank messages on his phone." Brian was looking around the mess as they talked and saw it wasn't quite as bad as it appeared. "Look, Kurt, Darci, calm down. I can't speak to the feeling of violation, but it's not as bad as it looks, really. There's no breakage. Nothing is broken. I bet the mess wasn't deliberate. It's fallout. Frank was probably drunk again. Darci, really, don't be upset. This is Frank when he's drunk. He did this way back when we were at Pointy Foods. Right, Kurt?"

"Yeah, right, but I don't care. They broke into my house. They were in my house! They were too stupid to take something and at least make it look like a robbery. Violation is right, Brian. It's a violation and that is typically Frank!"

"How do we know he was drunk?"

"How? First of all, take a deep breath and sniff! Secondly, Meathead's chauffeur cap. How stupid is that?"

Darci was going around the room almost erratically, picking up items, and Alice was right behind her, telling her not to touch anything in case the police need fingerprints.

"Shut up, Alice. Did you not hear me say no police?"

For once, Alice was quiet, and Chuck was not laughing. The mess was nothing more than a sign of where Frank's head was and the odor was a sign that he was reverting to type. The difference was that a meaner, drunken Frank appeared to be on a mission, and judging by the mess, his mission was not accomplished but was planned well enough to leave a souvenir to implicate his nephew. *What next*, came to Kurt's mind.

No one noticed that Chuck had left for his house until he returned wearing a police equipment belt complete with night-stick and Taser. For once Alice didn't criticize his ridiculous attire and for once Kurt did not respond to either of them.

Brian spared only a second to glare at Chuck, who was doing what Chuck had done since the first time they'd met: making himself the center of attention. Even now in the middle of a crime scene, with Darci barely able to hold it together, Chuck had to make an obnoxious bid for attention. The best thing to do was ignore him. "Kurt, you're right, Meathead is going to take the fall for Frank, even if you don't call the police. You do know that, don't you? It's his hat that we have. Even if it wasn't, even if it was a plant, the finger would still point to Meathead. Who else around here has to work in full livery? Who even knows what it is besides Chuck here? No. Meathead is taking the fall for this." He was disgusted to see that all Chuck took away from what he said was the mention of his name, indicated by his eyes lighting up.

Before Kurt could say anything, Darci spoke up. "Who cares? Guys, help clean this mess if the police aren't going to be involved. Alice? Come on. I won't be able to sleep until—"

Kurt's cell phone rang. He took a deep breath before looking at it. "It's Frank." He was barely controlled when he answered. "Did you hear what happened in my home? Did you get all of my messages? Did you get any of my messages?"

"Kurt, I almost died in my sleep."

More Frank bullshit. Years of Frank bullshit, and now he was breaking into homes. At that moment, for one heartbeat, Kurt wished he'd left Frank to die. He didn't bother to acknowledge his latest lie. "In my home! In my bedroom where Darci sleeps! Downstairs in my man cave where my friends come and play and where you have been welcomed. In my home!"

Frank had apparently sobered since he'd left Kurt's house. "Sorry, but I had nothing to do with whatever happened."

"We have evidence! We found Meathead's chauffeur hat inside my house. The police are going to take fingerprints."

"Don't waste your time. Meathead did it. I had nothing to do with it. He was probably mad that Chuck fired him."

"Oh, well, that makes sense. Chuck fired him. He gets mad at Chuck. Then he breaks into my house! Really? Why didn't he break into Chuck's house? Can you tell me that?"

"Who knows? He's not the sharpest tool in the shed."

And just like that, Kurt knew how he had to handle this thing. And he knew he had the advantage, because while he knew what Frank was capable of doing, Frank still thought Kurt wasn't on to him. For all his talk, he would never really expect Kurt to do something underhanded. Holding onto his anger, he growled out, "I want you to help me take my revenge."

"Anything. You name it."

"I want your nephew in my house at nine o'clock this morning. Sharp!"

"Are you going to have him arrested?"

"Just have him here or else."

"Okay. And I will personally throw in a five-thousand-dollar check as a goodwill gesture. Just please don't call the police on my nephew. He made a mistake."

Kurt hung up. He knew without a doubt that Meathead would be at the door at nine sharp.

A clean-shaven and short-haired Meathead showed up a little after nine wearing a very nice suit (jacket, sweater, slacks, all properly fitted) and holding a sheet of paper.

When Kurt and Darci opened the door, Meathead started reading aloud from the sheet of paper. At first Kurt thought he was one of a door-to-door ministry group, the transformation had been so complete.

He'd made himself ready for anything, but Darci seemed genuinely thrown off-balance by what was happening. "Kurt, it's a speech. He's reading a speech."

"Shh, this should be good."

Meathead read the statement in a near monotone, never once looking up from the sheet as he spoke. "I am sorry for breaking in and messing up your house. As you will see, I did not take anything. I just made a mess. I would also like to state that my uncle Frank had nothing to do with it, but as a goodwill gesture he would like me to give you this check for five thousand dollars."

Darci turned and walked into the dining room to join Alice.

Alice was brewing coffee and offered Darci a cup as she sat down. "What did he say? I heard his voice but couldn't make out what he was saying."

"He apologized and said Frank had nothing to do with it. Which we all know is completely untrue. It was all written down. Every word. But the odd thing was, I didn't even recognize him."

"What do you mean?"

"What I'm saying is that Meathead is unrecognizable. I could have passed him in the street and not known him. He cleaned himself up, and he must have gotten a haircut this morning. His hair is cut! And no straggly beard. He must have gotten the works. And he's wearing a turtleneck and sports jacket."

"What's he look like? I keep thinking how scruffy he looked last night. How scruffy he always is."

"Actually he cleans up nice. Meathead is good looking."

Not willing to stretch her imagination any further, Alice walked out to the living room to see for herself and interrupted Kurt and Meathead.

Kurt shook his head. "Alice. Of course you'd walk in without being asked. Can I help you?"

"No, you can't help me. I just wanted to see what he looked like. Darci was right. He does clean up nice."

Meathead was keeping his attention more or less focused on his written statement. "Um, gee, thanks, I guess."

Alice walked back into the dining room and rejoined Darci. Kurt was not taking any chances that Alice wouldn't interrupt again, knowing that Alice does what Alice wants when she wants and so beckoned Meathead to follow. "Come on, Meathead, Let's go into the kitchen where we can talk in private."

When they entered the kitchen, Meathead was surprised to see Chuck sitting at the table. "What are you doing here?"

"What am I doing here? What do you mean what am I doing here? What were you doing here last night! You're in a lot of trouble."

"You're not going to try to kiss me again, are you?"

"Oh, that's good. Just keep joking around. You think this is funny, don't you?"

Chuck was really enjoying trying to come off as a hard-ass and keep a straight face as he did so. Kurt just found it annoying. They needed information, and they weren't going to get anything if Chuck insisted on stealing control of the conversation.

He tried shifting gears just a little. "So, what's the deal with your new look?"

"Well, Kurt, I figured if I'm going to be arrested, I better look respectable to the judge."

Chuck snorted. "You are so stupid, Meathead. You were stupid when you worked for me, and you're stupid now. Where you are going they really like pretty boys. You would have been better off keeping the scraggly look. Why, may I ask, couldn't you look like this when you were my driver?"

"I am ready for my punishment."

Kurt was sick of the scripted routine already. "You don't have to go jail if you tell me the truth. Why did you break into my house? What really happened?"

Meathead began reading aloud again. "I am sorry for breaking in and messing up."

"Put the speech away. I want to know the truth. Why did you break into my house?"

Chuck grabbed the sheet of paper before Meathead could start reading from it again and ripped it into small pieces and then started yelling at him.

"You, my man, are going away for a long time. No more lies. Tell us the truth."

"You want the truth? You can't handle the truth!"

The sound of Kurt's clapping broke the eye-to-eye, nose-to-nose tension between the two men. "Thank you, Jack Nicholson. This isn't a movie! It's my house! Just do the right thing and tell us what's going on."

"I'm sorry, Kurt. I don't have a lot to say. Believe it or not, I was kept pretty much in the dark. Frank always kept things close to the chest. You know that! I'm telling you! I didn't know all that much…and I sure didn't know he was going to make such a mess."

Kurt sighed, relieved at least that Meathead was now admitting that it was Frank who had committed the break-in. "Well, he did. You can at least tell us why you went along with it. Why did you go along with it?"

"Because he said that there was something in it for me."

"Something in it for you? My house! Darci's house? Because there was something in it for—"

"I have always taken care of you, Meathead!" Chuck was more centered on his imagined slight, but this was a Meathead he didn't know, whom he hadn't taken the time to know.

And just like that, the contrite face and the measured words were gone. Meathead stood up, slamming his hands onto the table and glared at Chuck. "Taken care of me? Taken care of me! You treated me like shit! Did you ever think about that? Make Meathead polish my shoes! Make Meathead beg for tips! Make Meathead stand at attention like a dog! Like a fucking dog! Shit. Shit—that's how you treated me! And the worst thing is everybody knew it. Sir, Mr. Jennings, sir!"

"It's the way I wanted it. If you didn't—"

"Shut up! You shut the fuck up! Here's a news flash, it's not the way I wanted it! I can handle things. I'm smart. Unlike what everybody says, I'm not dumb. I'm smart. I want respect! Sir, Mr. Jennings, sir!"

The outburst had no visible effect on Chuck. "Meathead, you're nothing to me now. You are not my driver. You are not my friend. I don't want to know you or what you do. I don't want to see you near our houses."

"Easy, Chuck, easy. Meathead has put up with a lot and you know it. Hell, everybody knows it!" Kurt turned to look at Meathead, his face red with rage, fists tightened and threatening to smash through his table. "We all know what he was doing to you...we know."

Chuck added. "Meathead was spying on us."

Kurt closed his eyes, already exhausted from a long day at only 9:00 a.m. He knew this was not going anywhere. Chuck was obdurate, and he never took responsibility for anything. He was also entitled and arrogant at times, and this was one of those times. Kurt wanted to, needed to get to the bottom of this, and Chuck, whose house wasn't trashed, was not going to back off.

"Meathead, you deserved to be treated better by Chuck and by your uncle Frank. That's a given. Is there anything at all you can tell me?"

Kurt was hoping that just hearing the injustice of his treatment acknowledged might pacify him. And, in fact, Meathead opened his fists back out and rested his palms on the table. After a few quiet seconds, he sat back down. He kept his eyes on Kurt when he spoke. "Last night Frank was in Chicago. When you told me you knew that I was the spy, I had a cab take me to Uncle Frank's hotel room. He was already pretty drunk when I got there. He made me drive him to your house. When we got here, he broke in and started searching for things."

"What was he searching for?"

"Anything he could get his hands on that would tell him what your next move was."

"I didn't have anything he could use."

"I figured. I tried to stop him, but he just got angry and started pushing me around. I knew it wasn't right, but he was drunk and acting irrational. His drinking has gotten really bad since he left you guys."

Kurt added only, "He's out of control."

"Yeah, but when he sobers up, he's back to normal. Doesn't remember half of what he did. He just tries to do damage control."

Kurt wanted to keep Meathead talking, but he couldn't abide with any more of Frank's excuses. "You can't blame his screwing us over on the alcohol. Sorry, Meathead, that won't fly. Look around you. You think alcohol did this? Frank did this, Meathead! And I want to know why!"

Meathead was angry at Chuck, angry at what Chuck had done to him over the last few weeks. And Meathead had probably not fought as hard against Frank as he could have, in part because of what Chuck had done. Kurt had mostly just let it happen, hadn't done much to stop Chuck. And while that didn't make it his responsibility, he also knew that Chuck probably didn't really give a damn about him one way or the other. So Kurt leaned in and quietly delivered a low blow. "Meathead, Frank did this to Darci. It wasn't just me. Look around. He did this to Darci, too, and she has nothing to do with this. She has always treated you with respect and kindness, and this is what she gets for it."

And there went the last of the rage. He saw Meathead suck in a deep breath. "I'm sorry. I am so sorry, and no, you're right. Competing against you was intentional, but when he drinks, things get out of control. Not blaming alcohol, but the problems are always when he gets drunk. He doesn't do this when he's sober. When he's drunk, he makes really bad decisions, and he seems to be drunk a lot lately. Really, Kurt, it wasn't intentional."

"Don't blame alcohol."

"No, Kurt, listen. Just last week, Pierre asked Frank why he fired all his advisors the night before. Frank replied 'I did what?'"

"It sounds like the old Frank has resurfaced."

"The problem is Frank's cracking under the pressure."

"Really. So things aren't going good for them?"

"No, they are going good. That's why I tried to stop him from breaking into your house, but he wasn't thinking rationally."

"How good?"

"Really good, Kurt. Uncle Frank and his partners are going to build a football stadium in Southern California. He said it's going to be the greatest stadium in the world."

"And when is this happening?"

"Not exactly sure but soon. Uncle Frank is going to Pierre's lodge in Wisconsin with John Pointy today to work out some final details."

"Where is Pierre's lodge?"

"Pierre's lodge is in the middle of nowhere in Wisconsin. And I do mean nowhere! Pierre's family own hundreds of miles of wilderness, and they have a lodge in the middle of it. It's so remote that Pierre flies his little airplane to a landing strip in front of the lodge."

"Interesting. I bet it's a nice jet."

"Not exactly. It's nice, but it's a little four-seat plane that Pierre likes to fly himself."

"So Frank is flying out to this ranch to finalize the stadium plans."

"Yeah, Uncle Frank is racing back to Wisconsin to meet them at the airport. He was running behind because of this fiasco."

"Meathead, before Chuck here chimes in, let me remind you this is more than a little 'fiasco,' *capisce*?"

Then Chuck chimed in. "What? You saying he's building a stadium?"

Kurt shook his head. Chuck was always two steps behind in the conversation, because his self-admiration was always two steps ahead of anything said. "It's not about a stadium. He's going to use a brand-new stadium to pressure the NFL to give them the next football franchise. It's about a team, our team. Isn't that right, Meathead?"

Focusing, as always, on the most trivial aspects of the situation, Chuck asked, "Does he have a name for the team?"

"They're going with the Warriors."

"That was going to be our name. He, your uncle, is using our name!"

"I know. That's why he chose it."

"And you're telling me all of this. Why, Meathead, why are you telling me this?"

"Because you've always been decent to me, Kurt. I wish my uncle would have stayed in business with you. At this point it doesn't matter. No one is going to be able to stop my uncle and his partners."

"I don't give up that easy. You should know that by now. We will get an NFL franchise. We will get that franchise!"

"My uncle believes you will eventually get one but not before he does."

Kurt couldn't help but laugh a little. "He always had to compete with us. My whole adult life, your uncle always had to compete with me."

Chuck added, "Kurt's right. It has always been competition, but you...you still were spying on us."

"My uncle said he would always take care of me if I was loyal to him and to prove my loyalty, this was one of the things I had to do."

"You should have been loyal to me instead, Meathead." Chuck's egocentric comment merited no response and none was offered.

"Are you going to throw me in jail? I promise I did try to stop him."

Kurt closed his eyes, shook his head. "You know what? I do believe you tried to stop him."

"I did, Kurt. I really did."

Chuck, channeling Dirty Harry, pulled out his police night-stick and slammed it on the table. Kurt opened his eyes again and just started to smirk. It was so ridiculous. Chuck was so ridiculous. Getting all worked up, because Meathead didn't appreciate being his slave. He looked at the nightstick, then at Chuck.

"What? We should teach him a lesson."

"Easy does it, Chuck."

Meathead looked directly at Kurt, "Thank you for your kindness to me."

Kurt swiftly reached out and grabbed the check. "I will keep the five thousand dollars for my trouble."

"Yes, of course. My uncle does feel bad about messing up Darci's stuff. He said he always liked Darci. He is really sorry, really sorry about Darci's things."

Kurt smiled, slipping the check into his pocket. "But not mine, right?"

"No, just Darci's."

"At least now I know you're telling the truth."

Chuck, unused to not being the center of attention, reverted to type. "Hey, Meathead, I believe in second chances. Do you want to be my driver again?"

"Absolutely not."

"Then get the fuck out of here. I don't want to see your miserable face again."

Meathead got up. Leave when the going was good was foremost on his mind, and Chuck was a little too erratic for him.

"Last chance to be my driver again."

And this time Meathead actually smiled when he whispered, "No."

Kurt just shook his head and laughed. "Give it up, Chuck."

Chuck was going to issue one last offer to rehire Meathead when the front door burst open, and they heard Brian yelling. When he made it to the center of the trashed room, he repeated what they couldn't make out from the kitchen. "Pierre is dead! Pierre is dead! Pierre died in a plane crash."

Not believing what they were hearing, Kurt, Chuck, and Meathead joined Brian.

"What? Say that again."

"I didn't know you were here, Meathead. Your uncle's business partner died. I'm sure that will be a big setback for Frank."

Meathead sat down on the living room floor, looking down. As Brian blundered on, Kurt was frantically trying to signal him to stop talking about it. Meathead was curling in on himself, his body beginning to shake.

Brian finally slowed down enough to realize that Meathead was crying. "What's the big deal? I didn't like Pierre anyway. Who did?"

Darci and Alice had deliberately absented themselves from the exchanges with Meathead, but the loud yelling indicated something else was going on. They cautiously entered the living room, expecting to see a fight or the police. They saw instead Kurt making faces and signaling, and Brian who was ranting.

"Haven't we had enough drama for one night, guys? What's going on?"

"I'm trying to tell you, but Kurt here is acting like a fool. Pierre died in a plane crash."

Meathead wept. And wept.

"Gee, he must really like Pierre. I didn't think he'd take it that hard."

"Enough, Brian, enough. Frank was on that plane." Kurt walked over and put his arm around Meathead in an effort to comfort him. "I am so sorry for your loss." Darci joined Kurt and together they hugged and comforted Meathead.

"I am so sorry. I know my uncle betrayed you, but he is all I have…had."

"You still have me, Meathead." Chuck again didn't get a response although, strangely enough, he had expected one. He chalked it up to grief.

CHAPTER 38

Dead Man's Party

Once the news really hit them, they were all in shock. They were trying to grasp that Frank, Pierre, and John Pointy had died in an airplane crash.

The snowstorm, low visibility, and ice on the wings were more than enough to bring the plane down. It exploded in flames upon impact, burning everything, including the remains.

Meathead was still sitting on the floor, just staring at the wall across from him. Darci was standing beside him, staring at Kurt. He wasn't sure what she expected him to say. What could he say?

Finally she looked down to Meathead and asked, "Do you have a place to stay?"

Meathead continued staring at the wall for several seconds, apparently unaware that the question had been addressed to him. When he finally did realize that Darci was speaking to him, he looked up at her in disbelief. "I don't...no, not really. I guess I'll just have to move back in with my mom. She's going to be pretty upset."

Darci nodded. "She's lost her brother."

"What? Oh, yeah, she'll feel bad about that, too. They were never really that close, to be honest. She used to tell me I reminded her of him, and well, it was never a compliment. I suppose that's why she finally just sent me to live with him."

Kurt was glad that Meathead was talking again, glad that Darci was able to get through to him, but he had to ask, "I'm sorry, Meathead, but…why would she think you were like Frank? You don't seem anything alike to me."

He shrugged. "Probably because I went to college like Uncle Frank. Most of the family didn't like him, because they thought he acted like he was better than them. Like that associate's degree made him something special. And I guess I always did think my uncle lived this great life in the big city, heading a major food vendor…then coming up with the Sportsfan thing."

"Coming up with… I came up with it!"

Meathead shrugged. "That wasn't the way he told it, but I'm sure you're right. Anyway, now that he's gone… I don't know."

Darci shook her head. "I mean do you have anywhere to stay today?"

Another shrug. "I guess not. Uncle Frank said he'd take my clothes with him when he left, that I'd be able to move in with him once this whole thing blew over."

Kurt asked, "This whole thing?"

Meathead waved his arm around the living room. "I mean, the thing with your house."

Kurt chuckled, shook his head. "You knew damn well we weren't going to call the police."

"Uncle Frank said you probably wouldn't, that the check would cover any damage, and you wouldn't want a long court battle. Bad publicity."

Darci glared at Kurt, no doubt warning him not to bring up the house wrecking again. And he decided that if she was willing to put it behind her, then he could do the same. With a deep sigh, he said, "You can stay here for a couple of days. Until you figure out what you're going to do." At least until the funeral, he decided.

Darci nodded her silent approval.

———

The memorial service was three days later. Without a body there were just a half-dozen photographs of Frank on a table, some cloth lilies flanking them on either side. Kurt was surprised at how many people were in attendance. The room was brimming with faces, most of whom he didn't recognize. At the front entrance to the visitation room was Meathead, dressed in a black suit that Darci had helped him pick out. He was greeting each person who walked in, shaking hands and nodding his thanks for their condolences. Men, women, young, old, clearly rich, clearly poor. He offered the same lazy smile to every one of them.

As Kurt approached he recognized the old couple currently speaking with Meathead: Linda Davis's parents. It was her mother who first offered a backhanded condolence. "It's no less than he deserved. Bastard drove our daughter to her grave."

Meathead didn't blink, instead speaking very softly. "Auntie Linda told me, the day before she... She told me she couldn't believe he loved her. She'd been alone for so long, I think she'd resigned herself to never finding someone to share her life. When Frank proposed...she couldn't believe it."

Linda's mother looked unmoved by the revelation. Linda's father only added, "I hope he burns in hell."

Meathead closed his eyes, nodding. "If he is at least they're together again."

Both parents stared at him, mouths gaping for several seconds.

Then both of them broke into laughter. It was a low, polite chuckle, but it seemed much louder in the funeral home. Linda's father nodded. "You're a bastard, just like your uncle."

Meathead opened his eyes. "And you raised a daughter every bit as vicious as yourselves."

The two of them walked into the room, seemingly satisfied with the exchange. Before the next attendee could approach, Kurt whispered, "You handled that well."

Meathead shrugged. "I'm used to people yelling at me. Sometimes they just want to vent and sometimes they won't stop until you snap back. It's just a matter of reading people."

"Yeah. So, how are you holding up?"

Meathead nodded casually. "Better, actually. I was talking with

Uncle Frank's lawyers, and it turns out he left me some money. They said that my uncle held me in high regard."

"Really? I mean, I'm sure he—"

"It's okay, Kurt. I know what you're thinking. I couldn't believe it either. And when I pressed the lawyers, they admitted that 'held in high regard' was more their words than Uncle Frank's. His words were closer to 'the only relative I've got who's worth a damn.'"

Kurt nodded. "That sounds…more like Frank."

"Yeah. Still… That's how he was with everyone. He always respected you and Brian, you know. I think part of why he left Sportsfan was he missed fighting with you."

"He said something like that to me, too, the day he went public with his new venture. How we did better when we had him to fight."

"Well, I hope he finds someone to piss off in heaven."

"Yeah… Look, um, are you still moving back in with your mother? I mean, is that your plan?"

Meathead shrugged. "Probably not. Like I said, Uncle Frank left me some money, enough to get a place in Chicago, take some time to figure out what I want to do, maybe go back to college and finish a degree."

"Really?" Kurt knew that rent in Chicago and college tuition could both be very expensive and worried that Meathead might sign himself into some debt before he realized what he was doing. "I don't want to sound crass, but if you don't mind my asking, how much money did your uncle Frank leave you?"

Meathead's eyes glazed over for a few seconds, and he began whispering numbers. After a few seconds, he answered, "I'm not real sure what the exact amount is going to be after the lawyers take their cuts and the estate tax and everything else. Something like um, a hundred seventy-five million. I think. I'm also the sole trustee and the sole beneficiary, so I don't have to wait for the estate to settle."

Kurt stood beside Meathead in silence as another attendee, a middle-aged man in a charcoal polyester suit, offered his condolences. He was followed by a pair of seventy-year-old women who took three seconds apiece to put down their cell phones, express their regrets, then go right back to talking to their respective clients. An eighty-year-old man in a motorized wheelchair cackled as he shook Meathead's hand, then withdrew a bottle of Jack Daniel's from out of his inside chest pocket, asking to christen the corpse.

Meathead dealt with each attendee with patience and ease. Kurt had been prepared to offer Meathead a job at Sportsfan Chronicles. He'd been discussing the matter with Brian and the job had been intended as some entry-level assignment, just something to give him some money until he figured out what he was going to do.

But no sooner had Kurt realized that they could actually use a man like Meathead than he'd learned that Meathead really didn't need them.

Once there was another lull in attendees, Meathead threw Kurt for another loop. "Actually I wanted to talk with you about the inheritance. I'm really not that good with money, as you probably remember."

Kurt did remember the fiasco of losing $4,000 in a Vegas strip club but just nodded.

"Anyway, I was wondering if I could talk with you about it. The money, I mean."

"Sure. Um, yeah, sure."

The rest of the service went without incident.

CHAPTER 39
Catfished

In the weeks that followed, Kurt and Brian met with Meathead repeatedly. And in secret. Usually the meetings were little more than lunch appointments or early evenings at a coffee shop. It was all done under the guise of checking in on him, making sure that he was handling things after the death of his uncle.

And, at first, that had been a lot of it. Meathead had come to depend on his uncle for so much in his day-to-day life, but it had quickly become clear to both Kurt and Brian that his problem was more to do with confidence than competence. When Meathead had come asking for advice on what he should do with his massive inheritance, it turned out that he already understood a lot of what needed to be done. He simply needed someone else to tell him he was on the right track. He still didn't trust banks with his money and wanted to invest in something, but where his money should go was just too vast a decision for him to make immediately following the death of his uncle.

In fact it wasn't until three weeks after Frank's memorial service that Meathead first suggested the obvious investment. "What about Sportsfan Chronicles?"

Kurt made an effort not to choke on his caramel latte. He just nodded calmly, as if the thought hadn't really crossed his mind. "Well, that might be a good idea. We're actually fairly close to our goal money. Depending how much you wanted to invest, well, that would determine how much of a percentage we would offer you."

Meathead nodded. "Well, it turns out that after everyone

else gets their cut, I'm left with one hundred seventy-eight million dollars. So I was thinking a hundred and fifty million. What would... Are you okay?"

Kurt was choking on his latte, his eyes tearing up as he waved a reassuring hand to Meathead. "Just... Went down the wrong pipe," he gasped. "I'm fine." He spent half a minute swallowing, getting his voice back, before continuing. "Yes, ah, that would be great. Brian and I could draw up some papers and...yes, we can do that."

"What sort of percentage were you thinking about, Kurt? I mean, offhand?"

Remembering the deal they'd been prepared to make with Pierre, Kurt threw out, "How would ten percent sound?"

Meathead nodded. "What about twenty? Are you sure you're okay?"

Kurt waved him off again, taking another minute to stop choking on latte. "Fine. I'm fine. Twenty's... No, we couldn't do twenty."

Meathead shrugged. "Okay. How about fifteen?"

Kurt was about to dismiss that number as well, but then he thought about it. One hundred and fifty million might take them just over the edge of what was needed. And Meathead would certainly be easier to work with than his uncle. Or Pierre. Which brought up another point that might be a problem.

Casually Kurt asked, "Did you catch the Bears game last night?"

Meathead nodded. "Never miss one. Why?"

Kurt smiled. "Just checking. I think fifteen percent would be workable."

The meetings had been done in secret for a reason. The reason was that, from the beginning, both Kurt and Brian had been hoping to get Meathead to invest some of his inheritance back in the Sportsfan Chronicles. And that was information better left private until the deal was done. The contracts had already been predrafted, and it just took some quick reworking to get them to the numbers that Kurt, Brian, and Meathead had found acceptable.

Meathead had shown up at the Sportsfan Chronicles offices early on a Monday morning, before most of the staff was present, with two attorneys. He'd been waiting in the main conference room when Kurt, Brian, and Chuck had arrived. By 9 a.m. the contract was signed, and one month after Frank had been declared dead, Meathead owned 15 percent of the Sportsfan Chronicles for $150 million. The fact that he'd paid 50 percent more than what Frank had invested for 50 percent of the company would have certainly galled his uncle. But such was life and business.

Another small revelation came when Meathead had signed all of the paperwork. Kurt and Brian exchanged glances to let one another know that, no, neither of them had known Meathead's real name before that day.

It was Kurt who first used it, extending a hand to their new partner. "Well, congratulations, Martin."

Chuck just muttered, "Fredo. Your name is Fredo."

Martin just smiled as he extended a hand to his former employer. After several seconds, Chuck took his hand. "Yeah, I finally watched *The Godfather*. Great movie. Kind of surprised I'd never seen it before."

"Part two was even better," Brian offered.

Martin nodded. "I know. And it teaches so much about life. I loved the part about keeping 'your friends close, but your enemies closer.'" And he offered just a little nod in Chuck's direction, squeezing his hand just a little tighter and letting Kurt and Brian know that the prospect of working beside Chuck was more of a bonus than a drawback.

The next few days saw Chuck and Martin settle into a sort of truce. Chuck had stopped calling him Meathead. He'd begun calling him Fredo instead, although that didn't bother Martin very much at all.

Most of the employees hadn't realized that Martin and Meathead were the same person. He'd cleaned up so well since ceasing to be Chuck's chauffeur that even Kurt and Brian had trouble accepting it at times. And it wasn't just the haircut and clothes. There was a new confidence to him, now that he was no longer under the thumb of his uncle or Chuck. In many ways Martin had been given a second chance to make a first impression, and he'd taken full advantage of the opportunity.

Martin had access to his uncle's vast Rolodex of contacts and, coupled with his new found confidence, had begun slowly working his way through it. He would sometimes hold as many as five meetings in one day. And while none of these meetings resulted in the sort of money Pierre La Fontelle had offered, the net result of $2 million here, $5 million there had soon taken them well past their initial goal of $700 million.

Martin's efforts had resulted in Kurt and Brian getting more of the one thing that money had seemed unable to buy: free time. For Kurt the extra time meant more hours spent with Darci between her increasingly frequent trips to New York. For Brian, unfortunately, more free time meant more opportunities for getting into trouble.

One month after bringing Martin onto the team, Kurt got his first hint of Brian's latest catastrophe-in-the-making. It was two weeks before Christmas, and Kurt was on his way to Martin's office to congratulate him on his latest deal. It was a walk he made at least three times a week, and while he never got tired of celebrating good news, he could tell that Martin was becoming increasingly embarrassed about it. No doubt he assumed that Kurt and Brian worked just as hard.

Passing Brian's office, Kurt heard a woman's voice through the closed door. "Actually I hardly ever wear panties."

Kurt stopped, immediately looking around the Pit to see if anybody could overhear the woman. Everyone else seemed oblivious, going about the late-afternoon duties. Pulling out his cell phone, Kurt pretended to check his messages while continuing to listen to whatever was happening behind Brian's closed door.

He heard Brian's voice next. "Well, this pair looks great on you. And you say you never did any modeling? Professionally, I mean?"

"No. I'd feel kind of guilty getting paid for doing something I enjoy that much. Besides, I mean, I like putting on little shows for my boyfriend, but doing that in front of a crowd of people…a bunch of strangers. I could never…"

"So… You have a boyfriend?"

"Oh no, I meant, when I had a boyfriend, I liked to do that for him. It's weird. Some of the boys I've dated, all they've wanted to do is look at me. But not touch. That's what I miss most…being touched."

"I think it's awful that no one touches you. If I were your boyfriend—"

"Oh, I think I'd like that, Brian. I think I'd—"

Kurt opened the door. He'd only listened this long because he wanted to place the voice, but it had been too faint, almost a husky whisper. Of course it could have been a friend of Brian's, someone he'd met at a bar who had come to visit him at the office. The more likely scenario, however, was that it was another Sportsfan employee. Another potential lawsuit… Now, when they were on the verge of achieving everything they'd set out to do.

"What's that?"

Kurt had expected to see the woman seated across from Brian. Or draped across his desk. Or sitting on his lap. In some state of undress.

Instead he just saw Brian, looking up from his desk phone with a guilty smirk. The two of them stared at each other in a silence that was finally broken by a woman's voice on speakerphone asking, "Is there someone else in the room?"

Brian nodded. "Yeah, my…partner just walked in."

"Partner?"

"Business partner. Kurt. You remember Kurt."

"Oh yes. Kurt. Um, hello, Mr. Weichert."

Kurt shook his head. "Hi, Miss…"

"Winters. Look, Brian, let's…ah, meet soon so I can show you that…thing. okay? I'll call you later?"

"Yeah, that would be… I'm looking forward to it."

"Bye." And the line went dead.

Kurt shook his head and sat across from his friend, deciding to milk the scenario. "So who was that?"

Brian shrugged. "A friend." He flipped down the monitor on his laptop computer, which had been turned away from Kurt, so that he hadn't seen what was on it.

"She seemed nervous about being overheard."

"She's shy."

"Yeah. Shy?"

Brian shrugged. "She's… Her name's Claire. She got in touch with me a week ago."

"Oh?"

"She was at the auction and…well, she liked what she saw"

"She was one of the bidders?"

"Yeah."

"But I thought the woman who won was—"

"Don't! Don't…mention her." Kurt had never been able to get any details about Brian's auction date, only that there wouldn't be another. "And, yeah, she lost, but that doesn't mean we can't go out on our own time."

"So this date's going to be on you?"

Brian smiled then flipped his laptop back open. "Let me show you what's going to be on me."

Turning it around, Kurt watched as the monitor faded back on. A woman in her late twenties with curly black hair was standing in front of a dresser in a Chicago Bears jersey and black lace panties. Her smile was less seductive and more playful. In the dresser mirror, Kurt could see what looked like a twenty-something douche bag in blue jeans and a wife-beater shirt, holding a camera. The mirror also offered a blurry view of her backside.

Kurt nodded. "Pretty. And you're sure this is the woman on the phone?"

Brian shrugged. "The picture came from her."

Kurt rolled his eyes, not believing that even Brian would be gullible enough to fall for this old scam. "But how do you know the picture is of her? She could have just pulled this off the Internet."

Brian shook his head then clicked on the photo to offer Kurt another shot of her. This shot was the same woman, now dressed in blue jeans and a red blouse, leaning against a railing in front of what looked like the Grand Canyon. The next photo was the same woman, albeit much younger, in a purple and blue dress, wearing a white corsage, on the arm of another douche bag (this one in a tuxedo) draped across her shoulder.

"Is that her prom photo?"

Brian shrugged. "I think so. She told me that she doesn't have a lot of photographs of herself. She's a network administrator and works mostly from home. Long hours. Not much of a social life. That's why she was at the auction."

Kurt shook his head. "There's something wrong. A woman that hot doesn't need to buy a date."

"Maybe she's just really shy," Brian offered.

"She didn't look shy in the picture. And she didn't sound shy on the phone."

"Yeah, well, she…wait. What do you mean?"

"You need a thicker door, Brian. I could hear everything you two were saying."

"You could… You were eavesdropping!"

"Just for a minute, lover boy. Don't worry."

Brian shook his head. "Eavesdropping on a private conversation… That's something I'd expect from Chuck."

"Well, you're just lucky I had him take out all that surveillance equipment or else Claire's little panty talk would probably have been played at the next board meeting."

"Oh, God."

"Relax. Just... Keep the office conversations PG. Even when the doors are closed. Oh...and be careful."

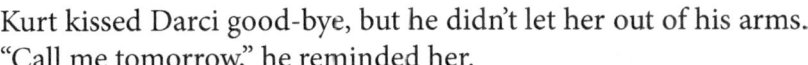

Kurt kissed Darci good-bye, but he didn't let her out of his arms. "Call me tomorrow," he reminded her.

All around them, people were scurrying past, boarding and departing on airplanes destined for every part of the world. Chicago's O'Hare International Airport was one of the busiest in the world.

Darci nodded. "Of course."

"And be careful."

"What?"

"Just...be careful." He smiled to think back on the advice he'd given Brian only a couple of hours earlier. It seemed to be all he could offer to anyone today.

"I will."

"Really. I know Skip seems harmless, but—"

Her hand slid across Kurt's mouth. "Two things. One, you do *not* want to start acting protective again. I don't want to leave Chicago mad at you. Two, I've seen what Skip is capable of doing. I know he's not harmless."

When Darci took her hand away, the first thing Kurt said was "capable? What did he do?"

The hand immediately returned to his mouth. "Nothing scary. Just...rude and insensitive. I've already told him that if he tries anything funny, if I see anything that might make me think he's trying anything funny, then I'm on the next plane back here, and I'll have my boyfriend's lawyers break the contract. Same as they broke the one you signed for that video shoot. Now when I take my hand away, we're going to kiss one more time, and then I really have to get on that plane."

She pulled her hand away a second time, and Kurt was smart enough to kiss the most beautiful woman he knew without saying another word.

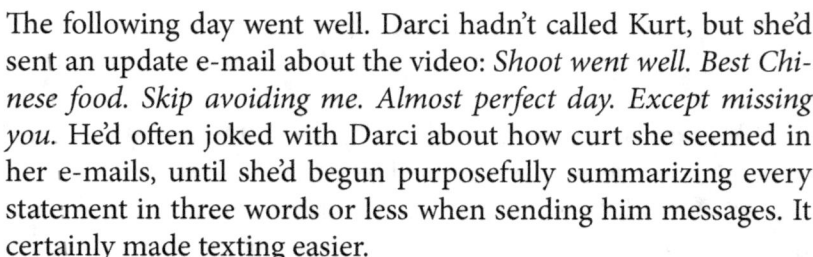

The following day went well. Darci hadn't called Kurt, but she'd sent an update e-mail about the video: *Shoot went well. Best Chinese food. Skip avoiding me. Almost perfect day. Except missing you.* He'd often joked with Darci about how curt she seemed in her e-mails, until she'd begun purposefully summarizing every statement in three words or less when sending him messages. It certainly made texting easier.

It was the kind of good mood that couldn't last, and so he wasn't really surprised to get a frantic telephone call from Brian just before five. "Kurt, could you come into my office?"

Kurt shook his head. "What's wrong?"

"Just... There's something you need to see. On my computer. I just... Could you come in here?"

He hung up and made his way through the Pit to Brian's office. About half the employees had already gone home for the day. Kurt and Brian had never been terrible sticklers for schedules, making it clear to their employees that, as long as the work was done, no one was going to fault them for leaving a little early once in a while. It was a policy of trust that had very rarely worked against them.

Brian's door was closed. Kurt was about to knock, when he recalled how ineffective it was at blocking sound. "Hey, Brian," he offered, not bothering to even raise his voice.

From inside the office, Brian offered, "Come in, Kurt. Come in."

Opening the door, he saw Brian and Martin, both seated behind Brian's desk, both staring at the laptop. Without looking away from the monitor, Brian waved Kurt toward him. "Close the door."

Closing the door, Kurt approached the two men. "So what's the problem?"

Shaking his head, Brian just turned the laptop around, so that Kurt could see the monitor. "Hey, that's—" was all he said before reading the headline. What Brian had been reading was a news article. The photo was of Claire, Brian's latest love interest. The headline read, "Black Widow Freed."

Sitting down, Kurt took the laptop in his hands and read through the article without saying a word to either man. Apparently Claire Winters, age thirty-three, had been accused of murdering three of her boyfriends. After two months of investigation, however, all charges had been dropped due to lack of evidence.

When Kurt had finished reading the article, Brian added. "We've been searching, and there's nothing more about her after she'd been freed. No one even seems to know where she's gone. It's as if she disappeared from the face of the earth."

"Are you sure..." Kurt didn't even bother to finish the sentence. It was her. They had the same face, and they had the same name. "Wait. Why would she give her real name if she was wanted for triple homicide? That doesn't make sense."

It was Martin who suggested, "Perhaps because she's insane, Kurt. But there's more. Look at this." He pressed a couple of keys on the laptop, and another article came up, this one with even more photos, including the prom picture Kurt had seen the other day. There were three different men in the pictures as well. The victims.

Kurt nodded.

Martin asked, "Notice anything about them?"

None of the men looked familiar to him. "I don't know. They all kind of look like assholes. That dumb, douche-bag smirk."

Martin cleared his throat and spoke a bit softer when he suggested, "I mean, um, that they all look like Brian."

Kurt looked up at Brian, but he was clearly too upset about the whole turn of events to be offended by the douche-bag remark. Looking at the photos again, he finally saw the resemblance. The men looked maybe ten or fifteen years younger, but there was a facial resemblance.

Martin continued. "She targeted men who looked like her father, would date one for a few months before...um, dispatching him."

Again Kurt stole a glance at Brian, who was looking sick.

Despite pitying his friend, a cold part of him thought, *Only Brian.* Sure Victor had encountered his own romantic mishaps, but at least those had been the standard jealous boyfriend or husband scenarios, where the risk was usually no more than a broken bone or some heavy bruising… Risks he could survive.

More to himself than anyone else, Kurt asked, "How did she kill three boyfriends before someone caught on?"

Martin answered, "She'd use an alias. The photos were all from her private collection that the police found after catching her. Apparently she got sloppy after the third murder."

"So if she used an alias, how did they link her to the other murders?"

"She, um, she had a signature, a trademark. She'd remove a… body part from each victim."

"What part?"

"What part do you think?"

Brian's head fell to his desk. "What am I going to do?"

"Don't answer any more of her calls."

"But she's already talked to me a bunch of times. She's expecting us to meet for drinks."

"Don't."

"But she knows me now. She's probably fixated, like a *Fatal Attraction* thing."

Again only Brian. Kurt put the laptop back on the desk. "Don't answer the phone. Don't erase any of the e-mails. Don't erase any of the voice mails. If she starts threatening you, you can turn them over to the police as evidence.

"You don't think I should—"

"No!" Kurt slammed his hand on the desk, bringing Brian's head up. "No, I don't think you should."

"But you don't even know what I was going to—"

"You were going to ask if I think you should go to the police now. So far all you have is a woman who saw you at an auction and wants to hook up. She hasn't been convicted of any crimes. And she's even using her real name now. There's nothing for the police to do if no threat's been made. Just… Break contact with her."

Brian nodded, no doubt having come to the same conclusion, although not entirely for the same reasons as Kurt. While everything he'd said about lack of evidence was true enough, there was another reason why he didn't want to involve the police. Thanks to Martin, they were closer than ever to closing a deal with the NFL, and Brian's extracurricular shenanigans could only screw it up, whether or not this particular problem was his fault.

Kurt tried to reassure his friend. "It'll all blow over. Don't worry."

CHAPTER 40
A Cure for Boredom

The weekend had been especially long for Kurt. Without any Chuck- or Frank-related disasters, fund-begging deals, or other major events, he had two days mostly to himself. Without Darci around it had just made the time drag even further. Brian had begged off coming over to watch the game on Sunday. Victor was going out with the new love of his life on Friday, followed by a date with one of his former waitresses on Saturday. Bernie was spending the weekend getting in shape, due mostly to Shannon coming to visit next month. From what Kurt understood, getting in shape would involve a half hour on a treadmill, followed by four hours passed out from exhaustion on the sofa, followed by another half hour on a treadmill, repeated for two days. And Martin… Well, he had his own plans. Apparently there was an Occupy Wall Street event downtown that he wanted to attend.

It was strange, not having anything to do, and Kurt found that he was looking forward to Monday. Darci would be coming back Monday afternoon. Martin wanted him to sit in on a couple of meetings with potential investors. Chuck was working with his team on some promotional plans. Brian was going to be interviewing for some extra assistants for the ever-expanding Sportsfan Chronicles team.

And Kurt? He'd probably go over the books. Check the progress reports for the last six months' worth of new hires. Then maybe spend the afternoon building a chain out of paper clips.

He had a talented staff, men and women whom he could trust

at their various tasks. He didn't have to micromanage them and didn't want to be that sort of manager anyway. But most of what he had to contribute involved ideas and, frankly, running a football team. So he was in a sort of holding pattern until something changed.

The call came at two in the afternoon. A representative from the National Football League wanted to meet with Kurt and Brian to discuss their plans to start a new team. He wanted to see their plans. Talk specifics. Get something together.

Kurt had sputtered through the conversation, barely registering anything that was said, scribbling notes about dates and phone numbers. Hanging up the phone, he looked down at his notes, letting it all sink in.

And, all of a sudden, there weren't enough hours in the day.

The first thing he did was gather Brian, Chuck, and Martin together to tell them the news. It had been a closed-door meeting, but everyone in the Pit had figured out what had happened thanks to Brian's screaming.

The second thing Kurt did was to make the official announcement to everyone in the Pit about the upcoming meeting. It wasn't a guarantee of having their bid accepted, but it was an extremely positive step in the right direction. He congratulated everyone for their hard work, and he then emphasized that there was still much to do. In many ways what they'd accomplished so far had been the easy part. The next stage (convincing the NFL to let them start a new team) would be even more challenging. And if they succeeded in that project, the next step would be establishing a team, which would bring even greater challenges.

After the announcement Kurt called Kalia into his office for a meeting with himself and Brian. They first told her that she was going to be promoted to senior office manager, with a healthy pay increase to accompany the new position. Next she was informed that a senior office manager title was fairly meaningless unless there was a junior office manager as well, so her first official act in her new position would be to draft out a job description for her new assistant. Finally they informed her that they would be giving every single staff member a bonus on their next pay check, just a little thank you for all the work they'd done so far, as well as an encouragement to keep it up in the year to come.

By four o'clock, Kurt was feeling better about himself, and his place in the company. There was so much to do now that all his ideas for a team were finally going to be relevant to their day-to-day operations. His dreams were just a little bit closer to coming true.

After a weekend in New York, Darci had probably been expecting a quiet night alone with Kurt. What she got instead was a small party in the man cave. Brian had followed Kurt to his place. Martin (still showing his newfound work ethic) had opted to stay at the office until six, not making it out until seven. Chuck and Darci had arrived shortly after Martin.

Chuck was wearing a cap with an ornamental *O* on it, wreathed on either side with garlands. Kurt had chosen to ignore the cap, but Brian had taken the bait and asked, "What the hell is that?"

Chuck pointed to the *O* and proclaimed, "This, my dear business partner, is the logo for the future greatest team in the National Football League: The Olympians!"

Kurt shook his head. "Let it go, Chuck. It's Warriors. You should...wait a minute. Is that what you've had the Pit working on? Olympians crap."

Chuck shook his head. "Not crap, Kurtis. This will be the name that makes our team a winner. Imagine fans waving foam lightning bolts and wearing foam garland hats. Imagine stadium-wide toga parties. It will be unlike anything anyone's ever done."

"There's a reason no one's ever done it, Chuck. No. And

don't waste any more company time on this thing. I should have known whatever was keeping you busy these last couple of weeks wouldn't be anything worthwhile."

Chuck gave a sideways smile and offered, "Oh, that's not the only thing I've been working on."

Kurt was about to ask what he meant when the doorbell rang. Deciding that whatever conversation he was about to have with Chuck was better unhad, he opted to get the door. Bernie was standing on his porch with a case of Budweiser and an anxious expression. "Hey, Kurt. Can you hold this?"

Kurt took the case of beer cans without a word as Bernie rushed past him and into the house. He took quick mincing steps through the living room and into the kitchen. Kurt followed him, hearing the slam of the bathroom door as he entered the kitchen. Putting the case on the counter, he shook his head, thinking that it must have been a long drive for Bernie. "You really had to take a leak there, Bernie?"

Bernie answered Kurt's question with a thunderous fart that seemed to shake the bathroom door. From the basement he could hear a momentary hush fall over everyone. It even seemed as if the leaves on the kitchen plants actually swayed just a little.

Kurt picked up the beer and was ready to take it down into the man cave, when a second fart ripped through the room. The stench from the first outburst was finally hitting Kurt's nostrils, so that he had to grip the case of beer one-handed, while his other hand went up to his face. "Christ! Are you eating too many of those fiber bars again?"

"Just for the next three weeks. If I can just lose ten pounds in Oh—" Bernie interrupted himself with still another fart.

Kurt descended back into the man cave, trusting that Bernie would have the good manners to open the windows and turn on the bathroom fan before joining him. Placing the case of beer on the floor of his cave, he announced rather simply, "Bernie's here."

Chuck was already grinning. "Yeah, we heard. He really knows how to make his presence known. I figured he must be dropping a deuce right now."

Kurt shrugged. "He's trying to get in shape for Shannon; he's eating way too many fiber bars again."

Darci shook her head. "Doesn't he remember the last crash diet he went on? He ended up gaining back more weight than he lost."

Brian added, "And he smelled so awful that no woman would come near him, no matter how skinny he got."

Chuck was about to make another joke, when the stairs began to creak.

Without looking Kurt yelled, "You better have opened the windows!"

The response was a halting, "I come through the door, not the window. The door was open, so I made myself welcome."

Victor was standing on the bottom step, a bottle of wine in each hand.

Kurt waved him down. "You are welcome, Victor. Sorry. I thought you were Bernie."

Victor shook his head. "I did not see Bernie, but I think you should know that I think your dog is not feeling well and should see a veteran."

Darci answered, "We don't have a dog."

"Then your cat."

Again Kurt and Darci both shook their heads.

"Well, then, there is some very sick animal in this house. I did not see it, but it smells as if it is dying or maybe it is dead."

Kurt shouted toward the stairway, "Bernie! Windows! Open! Now!"

The response that thundered back down couldn't be considered a positive or a negative. Turning back to Victor, Kurt explained, "It's Bernie. He's on his fiber bar kick again."

Victor nodded. "Ah, trying to look better for his belle amour?"

"Something like that."

The party went on for another hour before the pizzas arrived. Chuck made several more attempts to pitch his Olympians idea, all of which were quickly shot down by Brian and Kurt. Darci and Alice had their own stories to tell about shooting the video in New York. Victor had seemed especially interested in hearing about the various models the two women had met. And the subject of the impending NFL meeting kept coming up, only to be shrugged aside. It was just too big to consider at the moment.

Eventually it was Chuck who excused himself to use the bathroom. "If I'm not back in ten minutes, bill the funeral to Bernie." Plugging his nose, he made his way up the stairs.

Brian asked Bernie, "Why do you keep doing this to yourself? Going on these crazy diets, ripping your insides out with those fiber bars. For what? A girlfriend you'll see maybe three or four times a year."

"Hey, Shannon and I have something special. She's already talking about maybe relocating to Chicago."

Brian sputtered, "Fat chance, no pun intended. Look, Bernie, we're not trying to make you feel bad. Well, except for Chuck. Chuck's an idiot; he's probably trying to make you feel bad. But the rest of us, we just don't want to see you hurt yourself."

Darci joined in. "He's right, Bernie. If Shannon isn't happy with you being a bit overweight, then maybe she's just not the right woman for you."

Alice began coughing, then muttered, "A bit overweight?"

"Stuff it, Alice," Kurt snapped.

Brian ignored both of them, keeping focused on Bernie. "We just don't want to see you get hurt."

Before Bernie could say anything in response, Brian's cell phone went off. Checking it, Kurt could see his friend start to blush as he answered, "Hello?"

Brian began walking toward the stairs as he listened to whoever was on the other end of the call. As he walked up, Kurt could hear, "I've just been really busy. We got an appointment with the NFL today. No, it's more of a preliminary thing. We present our proposal and—"

The conversation faded away as Brian made the top of the stairs and turned a corner.

Darci looked at Kurt. "Who's that?"

Kurt shook his head. "This woman who's been stalking Brian. He told me he was going to stop taking her calls, but apparently he hasn't."

"Stalking? What do you mean?"

Kurt offered Darci a soft smile. "Don't worry. It's just someone who saw Brian at the auction and decided to make contact with him afterwards."

"That doesn't sound too stalkerish."

"Well, it turns out she was also accused of killing three of her previous boyfriends."

"What!"

"Don't worry. It's just phone calls right now. I don't think Brian's stupid enough to actually see her in person."

Everyone went quiet in the room. The silence was finally broken by Victor's hesitant "um, I do not wish to speak ill of my friend Brian, but he may be—"

"You're right," Kurt said without having to hear the rest of it. "When it comes to women, Brian is that stupid."

Alice nodded. "Especially if this is who I think it is. Are you talking about Claire Winters?"

"Yeah. You've heard of her?" Kurt's skin began to feel cold as some great realization began bubbling to the surface of his thoughts.

"Well, she has been in the news. Chuck and I watched a special on her just a couple of weeks ago. She's pretty screwed up, no matter what her lawyers said. No woman can lose three boyfriends to extreme blood loss just by coincidence."

Victor asked, "Blood loss? Excuse me, but do they think she is an umpire?"

Before Alice could say a word, Kurt answered, "No, Victor, no one thinks she's a vampire. They lost their blood after having a part of their bodies, um, amputated."

"What part?"

"A part only boys have."

"Oh." Victor seemed to consider the matter for several seconds, then added, "I am thinking I would prefer death by umpire. They are always so beautiful in the movies."

Kurt nodded dismissively. "I'll try setting him up with a nice Goth chick. But right now I think I need to use the bathroom, too."

Kurt left the man cave without saying a word to anyone else. Alice and Chuck had seen a news special about Claire Winters a few weeks ago, just before Brian had started getting the phone calls and e-mails from her. And now Brian had just gotten another call from her…while Chuck was using the bathroom. Something about the whole situation stank.

The situation probably didn't stink as much as Kurt's kitchen. "Christ, Bernie, what did you eat today? Skunk?" The fan was buzzing inside the bathroom, but Kurt pushed the door open to find that it was unoccupied. At least the window was propped open.

Walking next to the garage door, Kurt cracked it open just far enough to see that Brian was in the garage, still on the phone. "No, it's not like that. I just got…nervous. You know. Of course I don't think you killed those guys."

Kurt shut the door again, shaking his head and making his way upstairs. There was another bathroom on the upper level, and it was likely that, if Chuck had needed to use one, that's the one he would have picked. Halfway up the stairs, he could hear a woman's voice coming from his bedroom. He saw the upstairs bathroom door was open and the bathroom empty as he made his way to the bedroom.

The bedroom door was shut. The woman's voice was practically purring on the other side of it. Pushing it open, Kurt saw Chuck sitting on his bed. He was speaking on a cell phone in a deep, breathy voice. "Oh, you don't know how hard it's been, Brian. All those horrible things they said about me on the news. No man wants to come near me. I guess I just wanted to pretend for a while that someone could still find me…desirable. You do? Oh, that's—"

Chuck stopped when he looked up to see Kurt staring at him. He offered no shock or regret, only a shrug. He was about to press the disconnect button on the phone when Kurt raised a hand and shook his head. Then he spun a finger as if to say, *Carry on.*

Chuck smiled as he went back to the call. "Nothing. I just...I was overcome for a moment. You actually still want me, even after all those things the reporters say I did?"

Kurt shook his head and walked into the room. He sat on the bed, next to Chuck, close enough that he could hear what Brian was saying in response. Chuck had been catfishing Brian. It was a dirty trick, of course, and if things had gone a different way, the police might have gotten involved. But as it stood it might serve as a lesson to Brian. He'd been far too careless in the past. Whatever had happened on his auction date had apparently not been traumatic enough to make him change his ways. Maybe finding out that the latest woman of his dreams was actually Chuck would do the trick.

From the other end of the conversation, Kurt could hear. "Reporters are always making up shit, Claire. You shouldn't worry about what other people say."

"Oh, Brian, you've made me so happy. I can't wait to see you. I'll make you happy, too."

Kurt stood back up, waving to Chuck to do the same. Both men made their way into the hallway. It was a good joke, but Chuck had never been a good judge of when a joke had gone too far. As they made their way down the stairs, he continued. "Well, you seemed to like that picture of me in my panties, so maybe I will give a very...special show. And then, oh who knows? Have you ever played with handcuffs?"

When they reached the main floor, Chuck held back a laugh before continuing. "Really? You have? What else? Oh, I don't know. I've never let anyone take me...that way, but if it's something you really—oh! I had no idea."

They walked through the stench in the kitchen to the garage door. Kurt slowly pushed it open. Brian was sitting in the passenger seat of Kurt's car, the door still open. "I swear to you,

Claire, you'll love it." He looked at Kurt, pointing at the phone to say that he was on a call and didn't want to be bothered.

Chuck stepped in front of Kurt, phone still to his ear, and cooed, "Well, if that's what you really want, Brian."

Both Kurt and Chuck started laughing as Brian sat there, no doubt working out what had just happened. It took several seconds for him to figure out that the last three weeks had been one long setup. When he finally did realize it...

"You son of a bitch!" He dropped his cell phone in Kurt's car as he ran toward the garage door.

Chuck was already gone as Brian passed Kurt. From inside the house, Kurt could hear the pounding of feet on stairs. Still laughing he made his way back into the house.

By the time he reached the stairway, he could hear the frantic pounding of a fist on a door. "You bastard! You think this is funny!"

Kurt made his way upstairs, shouting, "Hey, don't break my door down!"

"Screw you, Kurt! You were in on this whole thing."

As he reached the top of the stairs, he saw Brian, both hands pressed against his bedroom door, face red with rage. He decided it best to keep just a little distance for the moment. "I didn't know until two minutes ago, when I walked in on Chuck. I thought it best that he tell you now, rather than let this thing go on any longer."

Brian stared at him in silence for several seconds, then nodded. "Yeah, okay. But I'm still beating the shit out of this little weasel."

Kurt shook his head. "Chuck's just being an asshole, same as Chuck's always been."

From inside the bedroom, Chuck added, "Yeah. I'm just being myself. Now back off, or I will tell everybody all the weird kinky stuff that you were willing to do."

"And I'm sure that if Chuck realizes—should he ever breathe a word of anything you said to him to anyone—not only will you give him the beating of his life, but I'll help you cover it up."

Brian said nothing, but Kurt could tell he was considering it.

From inside Kurt's bedroom, however, Chuck was showing once again that he had absolutely no survival instincts. "Oh, come on, Kurt. You wouldn't believe the twisted stuff Brian's into. He just needs the right kind of woman to bring it out of him."

Another slam of Brian's hand on the door.

Kurt shook his head. He knew the door wouldn't be able to take much more abuse. "Brian, forget it. Chuck played a stupid joke on you. That's all. Look, how about this? We get him back. You and me. Like when we worked for Frank. Whenever he screwed with us, we'd do something twice as awful to him."

Brian's complexion began to lighten as a smile crept to his lips. "Yeah. How?"

Kurt nodded to the door. "We don't want him to hear it. Come on. We'll get together tomorrow and think of something really awful to do to Chuck."

Brian began to nod slowly. "Yeah. Yeah, okay. That sounds good. Chuck really got me; I think I was falling in love with her."

From inside Kurt's bedroom, Chuck offered, "Hey, it was just a joke."

Kurt was about to shout a reply when Darci's voice echoed through the entire house. "Kurt, get down here!"

Kurt and Brian both ran down the stairs. Kurt could hear his bedroom door opening and Chuck's footsteps catching up with them. Soon all three of them were back down in the man cave.

No one was hurt. That was the first thing Kurt registered. There was no blood. No one was lying on the floor. So what could have been so bad that—

Darci's face was white as she pointed to the television. "It's the news. Kurt? We just saw a preview of the news."

Kurt turned to watch. The news had just begun.

"Our top story takes us to the Masonic Health Care Center, where sources tell us…"

Kurt shook his head. It simply wasn't possible. After all this time…

EPILOGUE

Victory Belongs to the Most Persevering

The battlefield is a scene of constant chaos. The winner will be the one who controls that chaos, both his own and the enemies.
—Napoleon Bonaparte

Frank was still alive. And, as usual, he had no one to thank for his good fortune but himself. He must have been, at most, ten minutes late for takeoff, but Pierre had flown off without him anyway, leaving Frank to drive through the hazardous weather. And the fact was that Frank had made pretty good time, probably due to the fact that hardly anyone had been on the road that night. He remembered passing a Welcome to Wisconsin sign about an hour before his car had skidded off the road and into a tree. A stupid man would have sat in his car, waiting for help that would never arrive and freezing to death in the meantime. Frank had been smart enough to get out of his car right away, smart enough to go looking for a house, and smart enough to let himself in when no one answered the door of the first cabin he found.

It had been a weird setup for a house. No television. No telephones. A basement filled with canned food. But he knew better than to dwell on it for too long. He was always surprised by the way some people chose to live (his nephew Meathead being an excellent case in point).

He'd fallen asleep under a half-dozen blankets and awakened the next day to take in his surroundings. There were several

333

gasoline-driven generators, a room filled with gasoline canisters, and half a dozen space heaters. He'd made do with what was at his disposal. The cabin was a dead zone for cellular service and the road was no longer even visible beneath the snowfall. So he'd just wait it out, heating whatever room he was in with a generator-driven space heater, tapping into the canned foods, heating what he wanted on the space heater, and melting snow into clean drinking water. There was a library of survivalist magazines in the cabin and a private stash of alcohol in the trunk of his wrecked car.

The more he'd thought about it, a few days of isolation with whiskey and magazines for company might just be the vacation he needed.

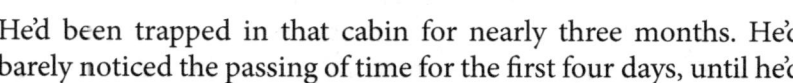

He'd been trapped in that cabin for nearly three months. He'd barely noticed the passing of time for the first four days, until he'd finished off the last of the alcohol.

After a month of withdrawal, the hallucinations had pretty much subsided, except for the occasional visit from Linda Davis and Napoleon. Frank had figured out early on that talking to hallucinations would only make him crazier, and he was too smart to give in to that temptation.

The only one he'd come to trust was dear old Jack. Jack Daniel's was the last bottle of whiskey he'd drunk, and it seemed only right that he should keep Frank company until he could return to civilization and booze. Over the weeks that followed, he'd told Jack his plans for the future, brainstormed ideas for how to get out of the cabin and read him the letters from *Soldier of Fortune* at night to put himself to sleep. Jack never complained, never contradicted him, never brought up his own bullshit. He was a damn sight better company than any man Frank had known in his life.

And so it was Jack that Frank had clutched protectively when he'd been awakened to the sound of intruders. He'd begun sleeping in the lower level of the cabin, where it was warmer. He heard the intruders first as they pushed open the door. He'd placed several pieces of furniture in front of the door. With the locks broken, the furniture was the only thing holding the door shut against the cold. Holding Jack close to him, Frank put a finger to his lips, cautioning silence.

Of course he knew putting a finger to his lips was a foolish thing to do. Jack couldn't see him after all. It was too dark.

After the door was pushed open, he heard voices. A man's voice. "What the hell happened?"

A woman's voice. "It looks like someone broke in and trashed the place."

A girl's voice. "We saw that crashed car up the road. Maybe whoever was in it—"

Man's voice. "Well, whoever did this is gone now. Let's clean up."

More scraping around for several minutes. Frank remained huddled under a pile of blankets, Jack clutched in one hand, a kitchen knife clutched in the other. They sounded like a decent family, but he knew these survivalists could be sneaky. He'd seen *Deliverance* More than once. And no family of backwoods inbreeds was going to make him squeal like a pig.

He heard the girl's voice, much closer, probably right at the basement door. "Ew, Dad, something stinks down here."

All movement stopped for a second, then the man's voice snapped, "Get away from there!"

More footsteps, then a heavy tread descending the stairs. The woman's voice asking, "What is it?"

The man answered, "Think about it. The state of this place. Nothing human would have done this."

"But what else could have broken open the door?"

"My guess? Bear. And if he's still here, get ready to run."

Frank shook his head. Did they really think he was stupid enough to fall for this trick? Of course they knew he was down here. The two women were probably already going through their redneck cookbooks, looking for the best recipe for slow-roasted city slicker. Frank had heard stories.

All he had going for him at this point was the element of surprise. If he tried reasoning with this hick, chances are he'd shoot first and ask questions later, probably cannibalize his corpse to remove the evidence. And who would ever know?

No. If Frank was going to get out of this thing alive, he'd have to make the first move. Dropping the knife, which would be useless if the man had a gun, Frank instead wrapped a hand around one of the blankets. The footsteps began to slow down as he drew closer. Frank guessed he was less than five feet away.

"What the hell—" was all the man managed before Frank sprung up, knocking away his blanket mound and swinging the one blanket in his hand forward like a flail, whipping his attacker in the face before he could make a move.

A second whip of the blanket knocked the weapon out of the man's hand. It looked like a small cudgel. No doubt he'd planned to brain Frank so as not to bruise any of the tender meat. Pushing the redneck out of the way, Frank made for the stairs.

At the top of the stairs was the woman redneck, dressed in a red blouse and blue jeans. "Who—?" was all she managed before Frank had knocked her aside. He had to get to the door. If he could get outside… They'd come in a car. He could break through a window, hot-wire it.

Frank wasn't sure how to hot-wire a car, but he'd seen it done in movies quite a few times. Probably just experiment connecting different wires until the engine started. He'd hot-wire the car then drive back to civilization.

The girl slammed into him, hitting him with both fists while kicking at his legs until he fell over. Jack flew from his hand. "Jack!"

The bottle spun away from him as the girl continued to punch his face and chest. "What did you do?" she screamed.

Frank kneed her in the groin (which didn't hurt as much as when he'd done it to men, but still hurt quite a lot) then reached for Jack. But then the woman was on his back. She was screaming at the girl, "Check your father!"

Frank cursed not having punched the man in the throat while he'd been momentarily disoriented. He'd been so intent on escape that he hadn't considered the family regrouping. Straightening his back, he slammed himself backward into the wall over and over until the woman let him go. He turned to give her one good punch in the face to hopefully knock her unconscious, but then the room went white and filled with the sound of shattering glass.

—≡≡≡—

Frank woke to find himself tied to a chair. The redneck family was surrounding him, no doubt considering which part of him would be best to start one of their backwoods cannibal feasts. He'd been foolish to try overpowering the three of them. He could see that now. He'd have to try outwitting them.

The man looked to be in his midforties, gray hair and glasses, dressed in a red flannel shirt and jeans. "Do you know where you are?"

Frank nodded. "Cabin. My car crashed, and I came here."

"How long ago?"

Frank shrugged. "Three months."

The woman shook her head. "My God."

The man put a hand on her shoulder. "What's your name?"

"Frank."

The man nodded. "I'm Tim. This is my wife, Faye, and our daughter, Emily."

Emily nodded, fiddling with something plugged into her ears. Frank asked, "What is that?"

Pulling one earbud out, Emily answered, "It's called an iPod. How long did you say you were up here?"

Apparently these weren't run-of-the-mill rednecks. They were obviously scavengers, waylaying passersby and stealing whatever technology they could gather. Frank didn't want to think about the poor soul who'd died for Emily to get her iPod. "Look. I know I was trespassing on your…dwelling, but I can pay you for any damages."

Tim nodded. "That would be nice, Frank. I'm actually surprised you managed to break in. As you might guess, this cabin was built to be a sort of safe house. And it doesn't look too safe now."

Emily shook her head. "Dad, can I go out?"

Tim shook his head. "No. We all have to pitch in and clean up the place."

"But you're just talking with this hobo. Why should I clean while you and Mom are—"

"You stay here!" Tim shook his head. "Got any kids, Frank?"

Frank offered a reassuring grin. "No, but I've been looking after my sister's kid for a while."

Faye asked, "Oh, God, you mean there's someone else down there!"

She began running toward the basement door when Frank stopped her. "No! He's not. I left him in Chicago. He's…he's being taken care of, I'm sure." No need in telling them that his little boy was actually a twenty-three-year-old man. He was gaining sympathy, getting them to humanize him. "I'm sorry I freaked out when you came in. I guess, after a few months, I might have gotten a bit paranoid. But I'm all right now."

Tim and Faye looked at each other, and Frank breathed a sigh of relief when he saw them nod in unison. Tim stepped behind Frank and began undoing the knots. "You should probably get to a doctor to look at that bump on your head."

Frank nodded, only vaguely aware of the pain. His hands had gone a bit numb from the knots around his wrists, and he felt pins running across his fingers as the circulation returned. "I've been hit worse. Is there a way for me to call someone? I'd like to check on my, uh, nephew."

The ropes fell from his wrists, and Tim came around to start working at Frank's ankles. "We're too far out for cell phones to work. I'll drive you into town. You can make a call there. I'm just glad none of the glass got in your eyes."

"Glass?"

"From the bottle."

Frank looked around the room until he saw the spot where he'd been taken down. There was still shattered glass on the floor. One large shard still had the Jack Daniel's label stuck to it. "You hit me with a bottle," he whispered.

"Actually Emily did. You understand, though, that we didn't know who you were."

"You hit me with Jack."

He felt circulation return to his left foot as the knot came away. "Yeah, she hit you with a bottle of Jack. Say, are you sure you're all right."

"You. Killed. Jack!"

Frank lunged for Tim, unleashing a torrent of profanity as he wrapped his hands around the redneck's surprisingly pale throat. "You killed him, you killed him, you killed him!"

He could feel the women punching him on his back, letting the pain fade away as he focused on revenge. Jack had been the only one who'd stayed by him. Jack had been the only one who had never questioned him, never talked back to him, never betrayed him. And these murderous hicks had killed him.

Eventually Faye and Emily managed to pull Frank off of Tim, who immediately began struggling for the ropes.

He'd continued screaming as they retied him, as they dragged him to their truck, and all during the two-hour drive to the nearest town. The "town," near as Frank could tell, was Madison. He didn't begin calming down until he realized they were taking him to a hospital.

It had worked. He'd shown those backwoods hicks that he wasn't the sort to be messed with, and they'd decided to do what he wanted by bringing him back to civilization. The fact that he'd never explicitly stated that this was what he wanted didn't seem to change the facts at all. Once Frank was admitted into the hospital, the nurses immediately untied him—

And then immediately cuffed him down to a hospital gurney. "That's not necessary. I'm safe now," he muttered as someone injected him. "What's that?"

"Something to keep you calm. Just relax and—oh shit!" The nurse looked away from Frank. He followed her line of sight and saw the most welcome sight he could have imagined.

Reporters. There were a dozen of them, cameras and microphones pointing toward him. The questions preceded them like thunder before the storm. "Frank, where have you been? Did you fake your death? Is Pierre La Fontelle alive, too? Who brought you here?" And on and on.

Frank was feeling a bit woozy from the injection, but answering questions from reporters was old hat for him. He'd done it while barely conscious in the past. "I was stranded in a cabin in the woods. My car got wrecked in the snow. I had to fight off a family of redneck cannibals before they agreed to bring me back to civilization. And what do you mean about Pierre?"

One of the reporters answered him. "He was supposed to have died in a plane crash—the same one you allegedly died in. What happened?"

"Pierre's dead?" He knew that should have bothered him more than it did, but Frank just couldn't muster much in the way of emotions just now. If Pierre was dead, then… "What happened to Franklin and Friends?"

"Dissolved," one of the reporters answered.

He shook his head. "I had millions, hundreds of millions invested in that venture. It couldn't just dissolve."

"Most of that money went to your nephew, Martin—"

"Meathead! Meathead got my money?" Frank began struggling at his bonds.

"So you're saying this wasn't just an elaborate publicity stunt to promote Surviving Family?"

"Meathead…what? Surviving Family? What's that?"

"The Reality Frenzy show being filmed in the cabin you were found in. You're saying this wasn't just a cross promotion?"

Reality Frenzy? That was Skip's reality show venture. The one that had gotten that stupid fitness program off the ground? The one where Kurt had bailed early to meet with Skip in New York to…?

"They did this," Frank whispered.

The reporters took a step back, clearly disturbed by his expression. "Set me up. Somehow…it all makes sense."

"Frank! Frank! Who set you up? What happened?"

"Kurt Weichert. Skip Bower. Set me up. Got me out of the way, long enough for Meathead to get my money! Holed up in a cabin where they knew no one would find me for months! Then they sent those rednecks out to kill me! But they couldn't do it! They couldn't kill me!"

"None of you sons of bitches could take me out! This isn't over! They tried getting rid of Napoleon at Elba, and he came back! And you're all going to pay! For Jack!"

―――――

Kurt didn't know what to make of the broadcast. At first he thought there was a mistake, but as he watched the footage of the rambling maniac being carted into the hospital, he knew it was Frank.

He'd survived. He hadn't been on the plane. He'd been hiding out in a cabin all these months. Kurt couldn't say if Frank's ranting was because of drinking too much or too little, but he was certain that alcohol was a key factor, one way or another.

And he knew he should be happy that Frank was alive. It wasn't as if he'd ever really wished Frank dead. Not really. Not for more than a second or two, here and there, over the years. No. This should be good news.

But the fact was that everything was working out for the *Sportsfan Chronicles*. Half the bullshit they'd had to clean up had been through Frank's drunken shenanigans (the other half being

Chuck's sober shenanigans). Even Frank's incompetent nephew Meathead had become Martin, easily one of their most important partners.

Looking at Martin, Kurt tried to understand what he must have been going through. True he'd grown so much once he'd come out from under Frank's shadow, but that kind of shadow could also be comforting. Now that his uncle was back, would he regress to the bullied slacker he'd been?

Any hints of Martin's intentions were unreadable through his glazed eyes. His mouth hung slightly open. Darci sat beside him, hand on his shoulder, trying to offer comfort for the strange tragedy of discovering his uncle was still alive.

And whatever Frank had been through, he blamed Kurt. And Skip. Kurt could appreciate the irony of someone suspecting Skip of conspiring with him, despite the circumstances. It actually wasn't terribly surprising. Frank had always shown a talent for casting blame on the unlikeliest of culprits, as long as not a drop ever spilled on him.

Frank blamed them, and Kurt knew that would translate into some stupid and ugly revenge plan down the road, probably something involving the Sportsfan Chronicles and their upcoming meeting with the National Football League. And probably involving Jack, whoever the hell Jack was.

Kurt couldn't help but smile when he realized that less than twenty-four hours ago he'd been bored. As if to mark the end of that boredom, everybody started yelling, with Chuck's voice being the loudest.

"I knew it! I bet Fredo was in on this! I knew we shouldn't have trusted him."

Brian didn't know whether to laugh or cry. He did know there were ramifications to this turn of events, and Chuck going off the deep end by hurling accusations every which way was not going to help anything. "No, Chuck, no! Martin wasn't in on this. What I know is that this is going to be one big mess, especially when Frank comes after Martin's investment. And what does that mean, exactly? Is Frank our partner again?"

Kurt answered immediately in an effort to preempt another tirade of hysteria by Chuck, although he was not quick enough to stop his usual histrionics as he jumped around. "Calm down, Chuck, for heaven's sake, calm down! First off Frank is going to go after Martin for investing in Sportsfan Chronicles. Then he's going to get really pissed off that his nephew did this for only fifteen percent."

"You think so, Kurt? No reason for him to be pissed. That was a fair deal because our company was worth almost five hundred fifty million dollars when Martin invested in it."

"It doesn't really matter. Frank will see that the investment brought no more than fifteen percent no matter what that fifteen percent amounts to. Frank is linear, has no peripheral vision at all. He'll be mad...so what! Martin is the one screwed. Not by us, but by his uncle when Uncle Frank dearest takes everything back from him."

"Ouch! Can't we stall Frank until we can meet with the NFL? Come on, Kurt, there must be something we can do."

"Brian, Frank will be coming after Martin's investment in our company. That means we have to be prepared to deal with him. He may not be able to take the investment back because he had been declared dead at the time. Everything was good faith, and since Martin was the trustee and sole beneficiary, he was entitled to that money...at that time. Frank is also going to go after the estate taxes levied by the IRS and paid by Martin. Since he didn't die, he didn't owe it."

"I hadn't given a thought to the IRS. How does the estate tax affect us? We have nothing to do with that."

"It doesn't affect us, but Frank's attorney, Mark the Shark, is going to go on a feeding frenzy. You remember what he was like when he was our attorney? That guy was ruthless, just like Frank, and I have no reason to think he has changed."

Brian was remembering and giving thought to everything Kurt had said. The ramifications were mind-boggling. "Well, Mark the Shark is really going to want to stick it to us now... especially since you got Martin to fire him last month."

Kurt recognized the truth of what Brian was saying, but he had never been one to act as if the blade might fall across his neck at any time. A man, especially an attorney, acting on emotion makes mistakes. "Yeah, he was pretty pissed off at us, especially since he thought he was going to get all our business again and instead lost Martin's. I guess I gave him more credit than was due. I thought he would have gotten over that by now."

"I don't think so. He blames you for losing the business. The Shark's last words were that one day he was going to tie your balls into a knot and twist...real hard."

"Thanks, Brian, I forgot he said that. It didn't help that Martin made me go with him when he fired the guy. I was convinced that the Shark was going to stab me in the neck with his pen that day."

"Hey, guys, it's simple, let's just give him the one hundred fifty million back."

"Sorry, Chuck, but no. His estate is in legal contract with us, and I expect him to honor it. It galls me to say, Frank is now a minority owner."

"I, for one, do not think for one minute he is going to accept those terms."

"Chuck..." Kurt's exasperation was showing in his tone of voice. "Chuck, I don't know either, but what I do know is that rotten son of a bitch came back from the dead to make our lives miserable. When snatched from the jaws of death, tooth marks are to be expected. We just need to do damage control until we meet with the NFL. This is going to get really interesting. We don't have a choice; we are going to have to link up with Frank, hold hands, and walk out of this hell together."

For more information please visit
www.sportsfanchonicles.com

Follow the author on Twitter: @kurtweichert

www.ingramcontent.com/pod-product-compliance
Lightning Source LLC
Chambersburg PA
CBHW070201260626
47160CB00002B/415